Also by Eloisa James

Potent Pleasures
Enchanting Pleasures

Eloisa James

❦

Midnight Pleasures

❦

DELL BOOKS

Published by
Dell Publishing
a division of
Random House, Inc.

Library of Congress Catalog Card Number: 99-087020
ISBN: 0-440-23457-3

Reprinted by arrangement with Delacorte Press
Manufactured in the United States of America
Published simultaneously in Canada

May 2001

OPM   10   9   8   7

Midnight Pleasures is dedicated to the talented, generous, and supremely knowledgeable women of the Regency Loop. When I burst onto the Loop, full of nervous questions, they responded with bibliographies, facts, kindness, and support. I would like to thank particularly those authors who took time away from their own work to read through one of my manuscripts: Mary Balogh, Karen E. Harbaugh, Emily Hendrickson, Nancy Mayer, and Eliza Shallcross.

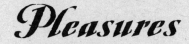

Midnight Pleasures

Chapter 1

❧

Lady Sophie York, the only daughter of the Marquis of Brandenburg, had refused to marry a baron who had asked on a balcony. She had refused two honorables, a handful of sirs, and a viscount, all of whom punctiliously requested that honor in her father's study. She had refused a marquess in the midst of a hunt, and plain Mr. Kissler at Ascot. Less fortunate young women could not fathom Sophie's motives. In two seasons, Sophie had rejected most of the *ton*'s eligible bachelors. But after tonight there would be no more proposals, hurried, paced, inarticulate, or otherwise. After tonight the uncharitable would unite in agreement: The girl had held out for a man of high rank. Lady Sophie was affianced to an earl, and she would be a countess by next season.

Sophie grimaced at her mirror, thinking of the avid faces and deep curtsies she would face at the Dewland ball that evening. Uncertainty quaked in her stomach, an unusual flutter of self-consciousness. Was this the correct gown in which to announce her engagement? It was constructed of pale silver, gossamer-thin silk. Perhaps the color would make her look washed-out in the ballroom, once she was surrounded by glittering plumage, the bare breasts and crimson cheeks of the female half of the beau monde. Silver was such a nunlike color. A glint of amusement lit Sophie's eyes. A nun would swoon at the very idea of wearing a bodice made in the French style, low-cut and caught just under the breasts with silver ribbons that wound around the bodice. And the skirt flowed narrowly past Sophie's curves, flirting with the roundness of her hips.

Just then the Marchioness of Brandenburg swept into the bedroom.

"Are you ready, Sophie?"

"Yes, *Maman*," Sophie said, throwing away the idea of changing her gown. They were already late to the Dewland ball.

The marchioness's eyes narrowed as she looked over Sophie's apparel. Eloise herself was wearing a gown of mouse-colored satin embroidered with flowers and fringed at the bottom. If it wasn't precisely hooped, it gave that impression. It resembled nothing so closely as the styles of twenty years ago, from the early years of Eloise's marriage.

"That dress," Eloise said with asperity, "is a disgrace."

"Yes, *Maman*." That was Sophie's usual response to her mother's sartorial comments. She gathered up her wrap and reticule, turning toward the door.

Eloise hesitated, uncertainty crossing her face. Sophie looked at her in surprise. Her mother was French and seemed to view life as a battleground in which she was the only general with a standing army. It was uncommon to see her pause.

"Tonight," said Eloise, "it will be announced that you have accepted the hand of the Earl of Slaslow in marriage."

"Yes, *Maman*," Sophie agreed.

There was a short pause. What could be the problem? Sophie wondered. Her mother was never short of words.

"He may desire some token of your affections."

"Yes, *Maman*." Sophie lowered her eyes so her mother wouldn't see her mischievous enjoyment.

Poor Mama! She had been raised in a French convent and likely had come to the marriage bed exceedingly ill prepared. Given that Eloise had married an English marquis so obsessed by France and things French that he preferred the French spelling *marquis* to the English *marquess,* her daughter had been raised in a house thronged with French émigrés. Her nanny was French, the servants were French, the cook (of course) was French. Eloise had no idea just how earthy discussions had become in the nursery, long before Sophie had even made her debut. The last thing Sophie needed was instruction on what men wanted from women.

"You may allow him one kiss, perhaps two, at most," Eloise said heavily. "I am sure you understand the importance of this limitation, Sophie. I am thinking of you. Your reputation . . ."

Now Sophie's eyes flashed and she looked directly at her mother, who was, however, gazing at a spot on the far wall.

"You have insisted on wearing gowns that are little more than scraps of tissue. Your neglect of a corset must be obvious to all, and sometimes I have wondered if you are wearing a chemise. I have many times been embarrassed by your behavior, your flirtatiousness, if one can call it that. You have the chance of an excellent marriage here and I *demand* that you not ruin your prospects by encouraging the Earl of Slaslow to take liberties."

Sophie could feel her heart beating angrily in her throat. "Are you implying that my behavior has been less than correct, *Maman*?"

"I certainly would say so," her mother responded. "When I was your age, I would no more have dreamed of spending time alone with a man than I would of going to America. No man kissed me before your father. I knew my place and what was proper to my position. You, on the other hand, have shown no respect for the position to which you were born. You have consistently embarrassed your father and myself with your fast behavior."

Despite herself, Sophie felt a curl of mortification in her stomach. "I have never done anything out of the proper, *Maman*," she protested. "Everyone wears these clothes, and manners are more liberal than they were when you were my age."

"I take part of the responsibility; I have allowed your extravagant escapades to continue, and I have overlooked many of your lapses. But now you are to be a countess, and what may possibly be overlooked as youthful spirits in a girl can never be done so in a countess."

"What lapses? I have *never* allowed a man to take liberties with my person!"

"I know that chastity is an outmoded word, but it is not an outmoded concept," her mother rejoined sharply. "Your constant joking and flirting makes you seem more accomplished than you are. In fact, Sophie, you have precisely the manners of a top-flight courtesan!"

For a moment Sophie stared at her mother in outrage, then consciously took a deep breath. "I have never done anything out of the proper, *Maman*," she repeated firmly.

"How can you say that when Lady Prestlefield found you in the arms of Patrick Foakes, alone in a reception room?" her mother retorted. "When you chose to be indiscreet, *improper,* you were discovered by one of the most talkative women in all London.

"It would have been one thing if you became engaged to Foakes. But to be found kissing in a corner! You embarrassed me profoundly, Sophie. So I will tell you again—I forbid you to allow the Earl of Slaslow more than the most token gesture of affection. Any more of these heated embraces and your reputation will be ruined forever. Moreover, Slaslow will be justified in calling it off if he suspects your rackety nature."

"*Maman!*"

"Your *rackety* nature," Eloise repeated. "Which," she added, "you inherited from your father. And he has encouraged you. From the moment he supported your study of all those languages, he fostered your unladylike nature. There is little behavior more unmaidenly than learning Latin."

She raised her hand as Sophie began to reply. "Fortunately, *that* is over. When you are a countess you will be too busy running a large household to indulge yourself in such fruitless pursuits."

Suddenly Eloise remembered her primary grievance. "Had you married Foakes, the gossip would have died, but naturally your reputation has suffered since you turned down his offer." She continued without pause. "No one believes he was able to bring himself to scratch!" The marchioness's tone was biting, and an ominous red flush had mounted up her neck.

"I could not accept Patrick Foakes's proposal," Sophie objected. "He asked me only because Lady Prestlefield walked into the room. He is a rake whose kisses mean nothing."

"I know little about meaningless kisses," Eloise commented magisterially. "It would be nice if my daughter had the same delicacy of person that I have maintained. And what does it matter if Foakes is a rake? A rake can make as good a husband as any other man. He has extensive holdings—what more do you want?"

Sophie looked at the tips of her delicate slippers. It was hard to explain her aversion to rakes without making reference to her beloved papa, who made a practice of chasing every Frenchwoman who arrived in London. And given the turbulent situation in France, he had been very busy in the last seven years or so.

"I would like to marry someone who will respect me," she said.

"Respect you! You certainly don't try to achieve that goal in a very intelligent fashion," her mother said, with a sharp twist of her lips. "I'll warrant there's no gentleman in London who doesn't think of you as an approachable minx, if not worse. When I debuted, poetry was written in praise of my modesty, but I venture to say those verses would not apply to you. In fact," Eloise concluded bitterly, "sometimes I think that you are entirely your father's child—both of you destined to make me the laughingstock of London."

Sophie took another deep breath, and this time tears began to prick the back of her eyelids.

Eloise's expression softened. "I do not wish to be snappish, but I worry for you, Sophie. You will have an excellent husband in the Earl of Slaslow. Please do not place your engagement at risk."

Sophie's anger drained away, followed by a wash of guilty sympathy. Her mother endured a great deal of mortification due to her husband's flagrantly public love of Frenchwomen, and now Sophie had thoughtlessly added to the gossip. "I never meant to cause you embarrassment, *Maman,*" she said quietly. "I was caught by surprise when Lady Prestlefield found me with Patrick Foakes."

"Had you not been alone with a man, no one could have surprised you," her mother pointed out, with irrefutable logic. "A reputation is not a trifling thing. I never thought to hear *my* daughter called a light-skirt—but that, Sophie, is what is being said about you."

With that, Eloise turned and walked from the room, closing the door behind her.

Tears welled in Sophie's eyes. It was not unusual for her mother to descend on a member of the household like an avenging Fury out of a Greek play, although generally Sophie was able to ignore her embittered comments.

But tonight Eloise had struck a nerve. Sophie knew that she skirted the edge of propriety: Her gowns were the most daring in London and her manner was seductive.

Sophie had heard those dreary odes composed for her mother many times: "Thus from a thousand virgins, heav'nly fair,/One sees the Diana of the sex, whose hair—" Eloise's hair was the same reddish-gold color as hers, but Eloise's lay sleekly along her head, the line of her chignon never disturbed by a curl or a streamer. Sophie's hair curled, and it rebelliously escaped from ribbons and pins. What's more, Sophie had cut off all her hair before any other woman in London had thought of imitating the French fashion, and now that every young miss cropped her curls, she had chosen to grow hers again.

What her mother didn't understand was how impossibly difficult it had been to turn down Patrick Foakes's offer of marriage. She stared at herself blindly in the mirror for a moment, then sank onto the bed as she remembered the Cumberland ball last month. The glory of it when Patrick made it clear that he was stalking her. The twisting excitement in her stomach when she glanced up from the intricacies of a cotillion, and caught his glance.

Even thinking of the lazy greeting in those eyes, the way his right eyebrow flew up in silent acknowledgment, the utterly masculine arrogance of his glance made her stomach jump. Her heart beat fast the entire evening, and excitement tingled in her limbs and weakened her knees. By ten o'clock Patrick Foakes had exerted such a pull over her that she was living for those moments when he would suddenly appear at her elbow or when she would turn in the swirl of a dance and catch a glimpse of silver-streaked black hair on the other side of the room. At supper, in the midst of a chattering crowd huddled around a small round table, her heart leaped every time his leg or arm accidentally brushed hers, sending a drugging velvet excitement down her legs.

They danced together once; they danced together twice. To dance together a third time would be akin to announcing an engagement.

Sophie didn't dare speak during their second dance, a Maltese Bransle that kept parting them and then suddenly jolting them back together. She was afraid that Patrick would guess the spinning tenderness that shivered down her body every time the figure brought them back together.

When he silently took her arm and led her out of the ballroom as if to fetch a glass of syllabub, but instead turned into a quiet room full of spindly tables and frothy chairs, she followed with no objection. Patrick propped himself against a biscuit-colored wall and looked down at her teasingly, and Sophie's only excuse was that the emotional stimulation of the last hours had gone to her head. She impishly grinned back, behaving precisely like the wanton her mama believed her to be.

And when Patrick pulled her into his arms, the moment had the rightness of inevitability. But the purely carnal, fevered urgency of that kiss was a shock. Sophie had been kissed before, so many times that her mother would faint if she even suspected, but this kiss was not the adoring, gentle compliment that she was used to.

This kiss began as an exploration and flared into summer lightning, began as a simple meeting of lips and ended with burning touches and whispered moans. Patrick broke off the kiss with a surprised curse and then instantly bent his head again, his hands walking a fiery line down her back to the curve of her bottom.

It was unfair to say they were kissing when Lady Sarah Prestlefield walked, or rather tiptoed, into the salon, Sophie thought bitterly. They had kissed, and kissed, but at that moment they were merely standing very close together, and Patrick was rubbing his finger across the curve of her lower lip. She was looking at his face in a rather bewildered way, conscious that her cultivated urbanity, her sophisticated manner of dalliance, had entirely deserted her and that in fact she couldn't think of anything clever to say.

"Merde!" Sophie whispered, shaking off the memory. She could hear her father's distant bellowing from the antechamber of the Brandenburg house, undoubtedly shouting for her to hurry. She knew exactly why he was in such a rush. Her father had started a new flirtation with a young French widow, Mrs. Dalinda Beaumaris, and probably had an assignation at the ball.

The thought steeled her resolve. It didn't matter that she had been sobbing every night for a month since rejecting Patrick Foakes's hand. The important thing was that she was right to reject him. Remember the shadow of relief that crossed his eyes when she disengaged her hands in the library the next morning and politely said no, she told herself fiercely. Remember that.

She was not going to have her heart broken by a libertine, the way her mama had. She was not going to turn into a bitter old woman, watching her husband circle the floor with Dalindas and Lucindas. She might not be able to stop her future husband from chasing other women, but she could certainly control the extent to which she cared about the matter.

"I am not a fool," Sophie said to herself, not for the first time.

Hearing a scratch on her door, she stood up.

"Enter!"

"His lordship would be very pleased to greet you in the antechamber," said Philippe, one of the footmen.

Sophie had no illusions about the wording of the actual message. Her father had bawled to Carroll, "Get that chit down here!" and Philippe had been dispatched by a nod of the butler's head. Carroll's portly demeanor and his French sense of dignity precluded delivering messages of this sort.

She smiled. "Please inform my father that I will join him directly."

As Philippe backed out the door, Sophie picked up her fan from the dressing table. She paused again in front of the mirror. What looked back at her was an image that had set fire to gentlemen's hearts all over London, had inspired some twenty-two proposals of marriage and numerous intoxicated compliments.

She was small in size, only coming up to Patrick's shoulder, Sophie thought absently. And her wispy silver dress emphasized every curve, especially those of her breasts. The fabric stiffened above its high waist, making it look as if she might fall out of the inch of material.

Sophie shivered. Lately she couldn't even look at herself in the mirror without thinking about the melting softness of her breasts pressing against Patrick's muscled chest. It was time to go. She grabbed her wrap and left the room.

Chapter 2

I n the afternoon before the Dewland ball, there was an unprecedented gathering of young gentlemen in the Ministry for Foreign Affairs, presided over by the minister himself, Lord Breksby. Breksby was growing old, but at the same time he was growing more and more comfortable with the power he wielded. Thus, although he welcomed his visitors from a somewhat bent-over posture, and his white hair flew eccentrically off to the right, rather than staying neatly tied back as it ought to have, there was nothing humorous about him.

Lord Breksby had been England's Secretary for Foreign Affairs for some seven years. He saw the civilized world as a puppet theater in which he controlled many strings (never mind Pitt, as he had often told his wife, the man can't make up his mind). One of Breksby's greatest assets, to William Pitt and the English government in general, was his skill at creative manipulation.

"One must make use of the tools at hand," he rather pompously told his wife over a dessert of orange jelly.

Lady Breksby sighed in agreement and thought longingly of a small cottage in the country, next to her sister, where she could grow roses.

"England has underutilized its nobility," he told her yet again. "Of course, it is true that aristocratic rakes tend toward dissipation—look at the degenerate nobles who thronged around Charles II."

Lady Breksby thought about the new kind of rose that had been named after Princess Charlotte. Could it be trained to climb a wall? she wondered. She quite fancied a southern wall, covered with climbing roses.

Lord Breksby thought about the libertine rakes of the old days. Rochester was probably the worst, writing all that naughty poetry about prostitutes. Must have been getting up to Lord knows what. A regular hellion, he was. Boredom, that was Rochester's problem.

"Still, that was the past," Breksby said meditatively, spooning up the last of the orange jelly. "Our rakes now are useful chaps, if you approach 'em the right way. They've got money. They're not elected. And they've got *class*, m'dear. Invaluable when dealing with foreigners." Even though his own title was only honorary, he found it served him well. Lord Breksby privately thought that the day might come when England would have to rely on class more heavily than on its navy.

"Take this Selim III, for example."

Lady Breksby looked up politely and nodded.

"He's ruling the Ottoman Empire at the moment, m'dear."

Now that she thought about it, the Princess Charlotte rose probably had too heavy a head to be a good climber. The best climbing roses had smaller heads . . . like that lovely pink specimen that Mrs. Barnett had growing up her front gate, back in the old village. But how could she find out what that rose was called?

"The man is dazzled by Napoleon, even though Napoleon invaded Egypt a mere six years ago. Thinks Napoleon is God, so I hear. Recognized him as emperor. *And* now Selim is planning to exchange the title of sultan for emperor! His father must be turning in his grave." Breksby considered whether to have more orange jelly. Better not. His waistcoats were already a trifle strained.

He returned to the subject at hand. "It's up to us to dazzle old Selim in return. Otherwise he'll go hand in hand with Napoleon, the silly turnip, and declare war on England, no doubt about it. And how are we going to dazzle Selim?"

He looked triumphantly at Lady Breksby, but after thirty years of marriage she knew a rhetorical question as well as the next person, and simply looked past him, trying to picture Mrs. Barnett's roses more precisely. Did they have just a tinge of crimson inside?

"We send over a prime piece of nobility. We dazzle 'em with some of our homegrown near-royalty, that's what."

Lady Breksby nodded dutifully. "That sounds wonderful, my dear," she said.

The result of this conversation, the fruit of the orange jelly, so to speak, was twofold. Lord Breksby sent out a series of beautifully inscribed notes that were carried around London by one of the king's messengers, and Lady Breksby wrote a long letter to her sister, who still lived in the small village of Hogglesdon where they had grown up, asking her to please walk by Mrs. Barnett's house and request the name of her roses.

As it happened, Lord Breksby enjoyed the fruit of his idea rather more quickly than did Lady Breksby. Mrs. Barnett turned out (disappointingly) to have died, and her daughter couldn't say what the roses were named. But the king's messenger returned to the Ministry for Foreign Affairs triumphant, having found all five noblemen residing in their London town houses and available to meet Lord Breksby at his convenience.

Alexander Foakes, the Earl of Sheffield and Downes, was the first to arrive at the ministry. Breksby looked up quickly as the elder Foakes twin was announced. Then he got up, holding his hand out affably. Sheffield was a prime exemplar of his, Breksby's genius, to his mind. He'd sent Sheffield off to Italy a year or so ago on an entirely successful, and very delicate, mission.

"Good afternoon, my lord," he said. "How are your lovely wife and daughters?"

"My family is very well," Alex replied, sitting down. "Why did you summon me, Lord Breksby?" He fixed his black eyes on the foreign secretary.

Breksby smiled genially. He was too old to be overset by an impetuous young man. Instead he sat back and templed his fingers. "I would rather wait until my small party is assembled," he remarked. "But I hasten to tell you, my lord, that I did not ask you here to request that you undertake an assignment on behalf of the English government. No indeed. We hesitate to interfere in a man's private life, once that man has children."

Alex rose a sardonic eyebrow. "Except when the government decides to press its citizens into the army." He was referring to the practice of sweeping up men and shipping them off to war, willy-nilly.

"Ah," Breksby responded gently, "but we never *press* our nobility into service. We rely on the goodness of their hearts and their wish to aid their country."

Alex almost snorted, but restrained himself. Breksby was a wily old Machiavel whom it wouldn't be prudent to antagonize.

"Your presence here is not exactly superfluous,

however," Breksby continued. "I have a proposition for your brother."

"He may be interested," Alex said, knowing well that Patrick would jump at the chance to travel. He had been back in England for only a year or so, and in Alex's opinion, Patrick was nearly mad with boredom. Not to mention irritable as a cat ever since Sophie York had rejected his marriage proposal.

"So I thought, so I thought," Breksby murmured.

"Where do you plan to send him?"

"I was hoping that he would agree to travel to the Ottoman Empire during the coming summer. We hear that Selim III intends to crown himself emperor, à la Monsieur Napoleon, and we would like an English presence at the so-called coronation. Given the inadvisability of sending any of the royal dukes"—with a mere waggle of the eyebrows, Breksby expressed his opinion of the fondly foolish and often drunk sons of King George—"I fancy that your brother would make a magnificent ambassador from England."

Alex nodded. Patrick would undoubtedly return with a valuable cargo of exports in his ship. It seemed a reasonable exchange.

"Now, the reason I asked you to attend this little meeting," Breksby said, "is due to the question of nobility."

"Nobility?" Alex looked at him blankly.

"Precisely, precisely. Granted, your brother will represent England in a resplendent fashion. His personal finances allow him to dress appropriately, and the English government will, of course, send a costly gift along with our ambassador. We are contemplating a scepter ringed with rubies—very similar to the scepter used by King Edward II. I believe we shall have to add more rubies to this version, as Selim is very vulgar indeed, and he particularly values that gem.

"But the real question is: What will Selim think of

Patrick Foakes? Given the delicate relations between our two countries, that is an important point."

"Patrick appears to have met with the approval of the leaders of Albania and India," Alex observed. "In fact, I believe that Ali Pasha begged him to take a place in his cabinet, and you know Albania is overrun with Turks. I shouldn't think that Selim will present a problem."

"You miss my point, dear sir. Selim is fascinated by titles: *Emperor Selim!*" Breksby snorted.

Alex, who had been staring meditatively at Breksby's oak desk, raised his head and looked the foreign secretary straight in the face.

"You mean to give Patrick a title." It was a statement, not a question. Then a smile spread across his face. "How splendid."

"There will, of course, be difficulties." Lord Breksby implied that these were a matter of little consequence to him. "I think they can be overcome."

Alex smiled. "He can have half of my estates and that half of my title." Alexander Foakes was the Earl of Sheffield *and* Downes, meaning that he ruled (nominally speaking) over two portions of English land.

"My dear sir!" Breksby was shocked by that suggestion. "We could never do such a thing. Breaking up a hereditary title: oh no, no, no. However . . ." A cunning look passed over his face. "We could petition to liberate one of your other titles."

Alex nodded thoughtfully. He was in fact not only the Earl of Sheffield and Downes. He was also Viscount Spencer.

"I was thinking of the Scottish title," Breksby said.

For a moment Alex was at sea. "Scottish title?"

"When your great-grandmother married your great-grandfather, her father's title—Duke of Gisle—lapsed, since she was an only child."

"Oh, of course." Alex knew of his Scottish great-grandmother but had never given a second thought to her father's lapsed title.

"I'd like to petition to have that title resurrected," Breksby said briskly. "I think I can present a reasonable case, given the importance of winning Selim III over to the English cause. If Selim is not sufficiently impressed by our ambassador, I would guess that the Turkish empires will declare war on England in the near future, following the lead of our dear Napoleon, naturally. I expect that the fact that you and your brother are twins will also please the Parliament. Patrick Foakes is, after all, only the *lesser* brother with regard to a moment or two."

Alex nodded. Given that Breksby never presented an idea until he was convinced it would be successful, Alex thought that Patrick would be declared the Duke of Gisle within a few months.

"I'm not sure—" he said, but the door opened.

Lord Breksby's servant announced, "Mr. Patrick Foakes; the Earl of Slaslow; Lord Reginald Petersham; Mr. Peter Dewland."

Lord Breksby immediately took charge. "Gentlemen, I asked you to visit me today because you each own a clipper ship."

"Goodness me," Braddon Chatwin, the Earl of Slaslow, said confusedly. "I don't think so, sir. Unless my man of business has bought one behind my back."

Lord Breksby gave him a hard look. Apparently the reports he had received about Slaslow's mental capabilities were not exaggerated. "You won this clipper while playing écarté with—" He paused for a moment and raised his glasses to read a piece of a paper on his desk. "Oh yes, while playing écarté with a Mr. Sheridan Jameson. A merchant, I believe."

"Oh, right you are," Braddon replied, considerably relieved. "It was that night you and I stopped at an inn, on our way to Ascot, Petersham. Do you remember that?"

Petersham nodded. "Remember you were throwin' the dice long after I went to bed," he confirmed.

"And I won a boat," Braddon said cheerfully. "I remember it all now."

"Is the government requisitioning our clippers?" Patrick Foakes asked, a trifle sharply. He was the owner of three clippers, none of which he cared to give up.

"Oh no, no, no," Lord Breksby protested. "A man's home is his castle, as they say. We were wondering whether one of you might like to sail down the shore and around the coast of Wales in the next few months. We have ordered the building of fortifications on the Welsh coast, but the West Countries are very difficult to manage." Breksby frowned. "They simply won't follow orders over there."

All five gentlemen looked at him expectantly.

"That's all there is to it, gentlemen," he said. "Sources inform us that there is a small chance that Napoleon may attempt to invade England from the rear, as it were, probably sailing from Boulogne around the coast, and landing on the coast of Wales."

Braddon frowned. "Why would he do that? It's much faster to just sail across the channel from France. Why, I've done it in six hours."

What his mother must have endured when he was a child! Why, the chucklehead doesn't even know the channel is blocked, Breksby thought. Then he said, with utmost courtesy, "I'm afraid that Napoleon has raised a blockade in the channel at the moment, my lord. In point of fact, that is precisely why I am asking one of you gentlemen to take on the task. Naturally, I could order our navy to inspect the Welsh fortifications, but it would pull a boat away just at the time when we are forced to deal with Monsieur Napoleon's attempt to block the channel. In short, we would be very grateful if one of you would take on the task."

"Well, I can't do it until the season is over," Braddon said promptly. "I got myself engaged this morning, and now my mother tells me that I shall have to attend any number of events." There was a pause. "And then, of course, I have to get married," Braddon added.

Lord Breksby looked interested. He liked to know exactly what alliances were being formed within the aristocracy.

"May I enquire whether Lady Sophie York accepted your hand?"

"She did." Braddon beamed.

Alex met Patrick's eyes as they both stood up and offered their congratulations to the future bridegroom. Only his twin saw the spark of derision in Patrick's black eyes, the mocking twist to his lips.

Patrick turned abruptly to Lord Breksby. "I'll do it." His voice was clipped, cool.

Lord Breksby beamed. He too had stood up, and was leaning slightly forward, balancing his outstretched fingertips against the desk.

"Splendid, splendid. In that case, if you could spare me a few minutes of your valuable time, I will show you where the fortifications are *supposed* to be." Breksby's voice was suffused with irony. The Welsh were a trying and tenacious people who showed no sign of becoming accustomed to English rule. He had very little hope that the fortifications existed.

Patrick nodded. As the others made quick, relieved farewells, Patrick sat back down. His brother also remained in the room.

When the three of them were alone, Breksby succinctly explained the situation in the Ottoman Empire.

"I won't need the title," Patrick stated, his tone admitting no argument.

Alex grinned to himself. He had been about to tell Breksby that persuading Parliament to grant Patrick a dukedom wouldn't make his brother accept the title.

But Breksby did little without extensive research. He knew that Patrick Foakes had more money than almost any other gentleman in London, as much if not more than his brother had. He knew very well that Foakes literally had no interest in or reason to want a title. To the best of his investigators' knowledge, Foakes had never showed any resentment of his brother's rank, for example.

But Foakes was also a brilliant tactician, a man who had found himself in many a tight spot while traveling all over the East. If anyone, he would understand Selim III's passionate lust for Western fripperies—including titles.

"You don't have to use it," Breksby said with calculated indifference. "You can even repudiate the title after you return from Turkey. We certainly don't care. We would, however, prefer that you not jeopardize this ambassadorship by refusing to accept the title in the first place."

Patrick sat, utterly relaxed in his chair, thinking it through.

Breksby templed his hands and watched the two brothers. They made an arresting picture, the Foakes twins, two long-legged men whose faces were uncanny images of each other's, both sporting unruly black hair gleaming with streaked silver and eyebrows with a devil's arch. Carelessly dropped into chairs, their hard muscles relaxed for a moment, they resembled tiger-striped cats caught napping in the shining of a sudden light. And yet, had Breksby the imagination to amend that image, it would have been more accurate to see male tigers: identical, dangerous, exhibiting an ease as picturesque as it was momentary.

When Patrick shrugged, signifying that Breksby could petition for the title, the foreign secretary felt a surge of warm complacency.

"It will take around six months to have your title confirmed. If you would like to travel in late summer or

autumn of next year," he said chattily, "you should arrive
in Constantinople in plenty of time to attend the coronation. Our artisans will have finished the king's gift, a ruby
scepter, by April. I do not foresee any difficulties there."

"I don't want this made public," Patrick said shortly.
But they both knew that once Patrick Foakes became the
Duke of Gisle, London society would talk of little else for
months.

Breksby prudently ignored the request. He rose and
circled the desk. Alex and Patrick rose as well. At the door,
Breksby paused, a plump smile on his lips.

"May I be the first? Your Grace . . ." He swept a bow,
his absurd hair flying wildly off to the right.

Patrick didn't explode until they were out of the building. "That pompous little ass! He was enjoying that masquerade. Let him send one of the royal dukes to Turkey."

Alex grinned. "Don't try to gammon me, Patrick.
You're longing to go to that coronation. You'd never -
turn down the opportunity to travel to the Ottoman
Empire."

"You're right, of course." Now Patrick grinned, the
smile lighting up the stern lines of his cheekbones. "I
heard quite a lot about Selim when I was in Lhasa."
Patrick had spent four years traveling in Tibet, India, and
Persia.

"Oh? What's he like?"

Patrick grinned again. "A proper little poseur, Selim is. At
that time he was making a tour of European capitals. He
drove his father mad by importing all kinds of European
customs, clothing, *and* women back to Constantinople."

"Do you think that he really might throw his army behind Napoleon?"

"I think it's likely," Patrick replied, his mouth tight-
ening.

They had reached their waiting carriages.

"You know, little brother," Alex said mockingly, "you now outrank me."

Patrick looked startled for a moment. Then his eyes lit up. "Damned if you're not right! You're a mere earl and I'm a duke!"

Alex laughed. Between the brothers there had always been mutual agreement that Alex's title was a useless encumbrance.

Patrick's eyes narrowed. "If I'd been a duke last month, she would have accepted me," he said, voice dagger sharp.

Alex knew exactly whom he was talking about. He shook his head. "Lady Sophie is not that kind of woman, Patrick." Sophie York was his wife's closest friend; Alex didn't know why she had refused to marry his brother, but he doubted that her refusal stemmed from Patrick's lack of a title.

"Then why did she accept Braddon? Braddon!" Patrick's tone was savage.

"I didn't think you were quite so interested in Lady Sophie's future." Alex watched his brother's face intently.

Patrick didn't pay any attention. "Braddon is fat, foolish, and has approximately one-third the money I have. But he's an earl, Alex. He's one of our honored nobility."

"You're not being fair," Alex pointed out. "She may love him."

Patrick snorted derisively. "Love! There isn't a woman in the *ton* who believes in such a foolish notion!" Then he added, rather hastily, "except Charlotte, of course."

Alex smiled at the mention of his wife but he said again, "I didn't think you were so interested in Lady Sophie, Patrick."

"I'm not." Patrick shrugged. "She can do as she likes." He met his brother's eyes ruefully. "But I'm a sore loser, Alex. No one knows that better than you. It galls me to have lost out because Braddon has a title and I do not."

Alex was silent for a second. He didn't see any point in

insisting that Sophie York had chosen Braddon for some other reason. Who knows? Maybe she did want to be a countess.

"Are you going to the Dewland ball tonight?"

"I hadn't thought of it," Patrick replied. "But I'm having supper with Braddon tonight and he'll want to go on to the ball afterwards." He met Alex's eyes again. "I expect he's going to ask me to be his best man," Patrick said, an ironic twist to his lips.

"I'll try to attend," Alex said, throwing an arm around his brother's shoulders. "Wait till the matchmaking mamas get hold of this news," he said mischievously. "You are going to be a sensation."

Patrick shuddered. "All the more reason to leave for Wales immediately."

Chapter 3

❧

When Sophie York was announced in the Dewland ballroom, there was a rustle of fluting voices. Sophie was a wild, reckless girl—the very worst of the new generation, muttered spinsters in the corners of the room.

The most beautiful woman in England, noted the male arbiters of London fashion. She was diminutive, but gorgeous; she was a coquette, but she was also the daughter of the most starched aristocrat in London, the Marchioness of Brandenburg. Eloise's cold French admonishments had dented the reputation of many a young miss whose behavior walked a fine line between immodesty and rank wantonness. Quite naturally, the biting aspect of Eloise's judgments on the propriety of young women made the impudence of her daughter's behavior all the more delicious, all the more noteworthy.

Sophie paused at the top of the ballroom steps as her papa plunged down into the milling crowd, searching (no doubt) for the delectable Dalinda. Her mama proceeded sternly after him, her poker-straight back expressing an outrage that had hardly blunted with the years. Sophie scanned the assembly, looking, she told herself, for the Earl of Slaslow.

But Sophie knew inside that such a pretense merely stressed her weakness and lack of moral fiber, as her mother might put it. Her eyes were actually looking for a tall man with shoulders so broad that he looked only marginally comfortable in fine broadcloth. She was looking for tousled black hair shot with silver. She hadn't seen Patrick since she'd turned down his proposal of marriage, and she didn't see him now.

Her mother turned about in irritation at the bottom of the stairs.

"Sophie!" she hissed.

When Sophie obediently traipsed down the remaining steps, Eloise grasped her wrist in a steely hand.

"Stop making an exhibition of yourself!"

The gentlemen were on them now, flocking around Sophie, begging her for dances, handing her dance-cards, looking at her imploringly. Eloise contented herself with giving Sophie an admonishing look before heading off to the chaperones' corner, where only those women whose titles equaled their ferocity were allowed to sit.

Laughingly, Sophie divided her time among the beseeching gentlemen, but the exercise was hollow. Tomorrow, or at most in two days, *The Times* would carry a discreet announcement:

The Earl of Slaslow announces that he will marry Lady Sophie York, the daughter of the Marquis of Brandenburg. The ceremony will be held at St. George's Church and the formal presentation will occur at a Chapter of the Garter held in St. James's Palace.

Then the chattering flocks would fall to the side and all of London would know that the great heiress, Sophie York, had finally settled on a husband. By February she would be married to Braddon Chatwin, the "Amiable Earl," she'd heard him called. Braddon *was* amiable. He would be a pleasant husband. He probably liked his horses more than any human being, but he didn't gamble to excess at the races.

And he looked capable of mild affection, which was exactly the same emotion that Sophie felt she would bring to the match. They would have beautiful children (an important point), and Braddon would keep his mistresses unobtrusively in the background. It was too slighting to call him dependable, Sophie thought, as she swung into the first dance of the evening. Braddon was kind and without great sins, as far as she could tell. They would likely be happy together.

The evening wound on, and neither her betrothed nor anyone else important appeared at her side. Sophie danced with elegance and exquisite grace; only the most perceptive noticed that her contagious sense of humor was blunted, if not missing, tonight. A young beau found that his chattering pronouncement of love was greeted with a rather cool rebuff, rather than her usual kind response.

Sophie felt as if she were walking a tightrope, suspended over a dizzying audience of young men whose silly comments and sweaty palms made her task harder. She stopped looking for silver-shot hair. What was the point? She was to be a countess, not Patrick Foakes's wife, she thought drearily.

She went to supper on the arm of the hostess's son, Peter Dewland. Peter was a sweet-eyed, elegant gentleman whom Sophie had known for years. He was a restful companion, given that he showed no sign of expecting London's reigning beauty to fall into his arms. In fact, Sophie thought approvingly, Peter had never courted her in any fashion.

"How is your brother?" Sophie asked. Peter's elder brother had been cruelly injured in a riding accident and more or less confined to his bed for the past three years.

"He's doing much better." Peter beamed. "He's been taking a course of treatment from the German doctor who has been at court in the last few months. Have you heard of him? The doctor's name is Trankelstein. I thought it was all a bag of moonshine, myself, but Trankelstein's massages actually seem to be working. Quill—that's what we call Erskine within the family—is able to leave his bedchamber now, and the pain is diminished. In fact, he spends almost every day in the garden, says he doesn't want to be inside ever again."

Sophie truly smiled for the first time that evening, her face lighting up. "Oh, Peter," she said, not even noticing that she was using his first name, "how perfectly marvelous!"

"If you would like," Peter continued a bit shyly, "you could meet Quill, Lady Sophie. He's sitting up in the library tonight and I know that he would like to thank you for the fireworks you helped to arrange."

"I can't accept any thanks," Sophie protested. "The fireworks were entirely the work of the Earl and Countess of Sheffield. I simply happened to be in the party that attended Vauxhall." The trip to Vauxhall, and the resulting fireworks display in the Dewland back garden, had happened well over a year ago. Sophie had stood, surrounded by beaux, in the deep heat of a London summer evening watching twisting, magnificent fireworks light up the sky. In actual fact, her beaux watched the fireworks. Sophie watched her dearest friend, Charlotte, standing beside the Earl of Sheffield and Downes—Patrick Foakes's twin brother. She'd seen the secret blush warming Charlotte's cheeks as she leaned back against Alex's chest, protected from the eyes of gossips by the velvety night and the sparkling lights in the sky.

Sophie had teased Charlotte the next day, laughing at her for standing so close to Alex, for allowing his arm to circle her waist, for looking up at him so intently. Now, Sophie understood Charlotte's surprising quiescence.

Her own body had become foreign to her. She was irritable because the other Foakes twin wasn't in the ballroom. She missed a heady closeness that she hardly knew. Her mind had become a traitor, unable to fix on the prospect of her future husband, Braddon, and constantly straying off to think about wicked black eyes and a laughing mouth.

It was nauseating, paltry, humiliating—she broke off the strain of self-reproach and rose. "Shall we greet your brother now?"

Peter politely discarded his plate of savory pheasant without a backward glance. "It would be my pleasure," he replied. "I shall ask my mother to accompany us."

Sophie nodded, startled by her own forgetfulness. The last thing her reputation could bear was for her to disappear with yet another man.

Viscountess Dewland smiled on the young pair approvingly and left her cozy circle of gossips to stroll to the library. You would never catch her indulging in rusty complaints about Sophie York, she thought. The girl has a kind heart.

Kitty Dewland had noted with a mother's watchful eye that her beloved Peter was not genuinely attracted to Lady Sophie, and that unless she missed her mark (and she rarely did, Kitty thought to herself), Lady Sophie showed every sign of being in love with the Earl of Slaslow. The rumors she had heard of an engagement to be announced confirmed her impression.

Kitty sighed romantically. What a wonderful evening she had had when her own engagement to dear Thurlow was announced. The quiver of ignoble but delightful

triumph she had felt as she circled the room before a cluster of young misses, her future assured! Kitty mentally
shook herself and bustled into the library to introduce
Quill to Lady Sophie.

Quill—or Erskine—wasn't at all what Sophie expected. She had vague memories of a thin white face at
the window during the fireworks display in the Dewland
gardens. But the face that turned about from an armchair
was tanned chestnut, much darker than were the complex-
ions of most London fops, used to indoor amusements
and placid rides in covered carriages. Quill's face was lean
and stamped with lines of pain, but it was arrestingly intelligent and very good looking.

Now he was standing before her, cool lips brushing the
back of her hand. He seemed to stand without problem,
and it was only when he sank back into the chair that she
realized the effort it took for him to stand upright.
Quickly she sat down on the first thing she saw, a small
padded stool placed before the fireplace. She didn't want
Quill to feel awkward, given his inability to remain standing in the presence of a lady.

Peter pulled over one of the heavy leather chairs, and
his mother drifted over to speak to the Honorable
Sylvester Bredbeck, who had retreated to the library to
rest his gout-ridden left ankle.

Quill regarded Sophie through heavy-lidded eyes, his
face impassively registering no embarrassment, if indeed
he felt any.

"Are you enjoying the ball, Lady Sophie?" he drawled.

Sophie flushed slightly. She sensed mockery, and she
wasn't feeling nimble-witted that evening. In fact, the
practiced repartee that characterized most interactions between men and women in the *ton* seemed to have leaked
from her tired brain.

"Not particularly," she answered truthfully.

"Hmm," Quill murmured, his eyes noting the drooping edges of her mouth. "Perhaps you would like to take a break from ceaseless gaiety? We could play a game of backgammon, if you wish."

Sophie thought quickly. Ladies did *not* retreat into libraries to play board games during balls. On the other hand, she was chaperoned by none other than her hostess, and it would be very pleasant to let her jangled nerves settle. Neither Braddon nor Patrick was likely to walk into the library, so she would have a period of calm before returning to the ballroom.

She raised her eyes to Quill's green ones. "I would be very pleased to join you."

At a nod from his brother, Peter jumped up and fetched a small table whose top was an inlaid backgammon board. Sophie and Quill silently placed the pieces on the board, firelight leaping off the walnut paneled walls and flicking lightly on the white and black pieces, on Sophie's slender fingers, on the wine-colored glints in Quill's hair.

The game proceeded quietly until Sophie threw her second pair of doubles.

Quill raised his eyes and cast a gleaming look at his brother. "Just whom did you bring in here to enliven my solitude, Peter? An ivory turner?" His eyes laughed at Sophie. "Isn't it a good thing that I was too gentlemanly to suggest a wager?"

Sophie smiled back demurely. Throwing doubles encompassed her only skill at board games, and it used to drive her grandfather to distraction when she was a child. She sipped at the wine at her elbow, feeling much more cheerful. The library was like a shimmery refuge, a calm, firelight-flecked oasis from the rioting hunger that seemed to have taken over her body.

When she threw the next set of doubles, she smiled

gleefully in response to Quill's muttered complaints, and she looked up with a grin of utter delight when she managed to throw a final set—double sixes!—at the very end of the game.

Which was the very moment at which both men whom she had looked for that evening, Braddon Chatwin, the Earl of Slaslow, and his good friend Patrick Foakes, walked into the library. Braddon forged straight ahead, heading toward the woman of whom he was so proud, about whom he had just been boasting to his old school friend.

But Patrick stopped just inside the library. Sophie's hair was shining in the light of the fire behind her with a color like ripened peaches, or like apricot wine laid up in glass bottles. She had bound her hair up on top of her head but the curls meant to fall down her back had tumbled forward. The curls were spun in fifty colors, melting from red to gold to the purest sunlit yellow. . . . And ringlets had fallen into smaller ringlets, tiny sprays of curls, giving her head the slightly fuzzy softness of a peach, a swimming, sunny color that promised that her hair would be as soft to the touch as the ripest summer fruit was to one's lip.

He almost turned on his heel to leave. Sophie was laughing, her eyes brilliant. Until she caught sight of him. Her smile entirely disappeared for an instant, and then just as quickly the corners of her mouth turned up again, although this smile didn't touch her eyes. Probably afraid he would let on to Braddon just how proficient she was at the art of kissing, Patrick thought sourly.

Braddon had lurched over to the group like an overeager puppy, given his hellos, and now stood beaming down at his intended bride. Patrick strolled toward the fire. He'd be damned if he'd let his composure be shaken by an alluring wench who'd had the gall to turn him down for a bigger title. She had what she wanted. Now she was engaged to the only earl on the marriage mart this year, and given that there was only one unmarried duke, old Siskind with his eight children, she had snagged the best of the bunch—at least until he himself became a duke. Patrick's eyes glowed with a blighting fury.

Sophie cast one look at his face and instantly looked away, a flush as delicate as the pink champagne she held in her hand creeping up her cheeks. Braddon had cast himself down on the rug and was eagerly rearranging the backgammon pieces, enchanted to learn that his future wife knew how to play the game. Sophie forced herself to smile at him.

From the shadowed high back of the armchair Quill had watched the charming Lady Sophie freeze and then break into frail gaiety; he twisted about to see who had caused her to transform from an engaging damsel to a glassy society woman.

So a lean brown hand emerged from the armchair and a sardonic voice drawled, "Patrick, my man, come and greet me."

"Quill!"

In an instant Patrick's long legs had brought him in front of the armchair, his black eyes alight with pleasure. "My God, man, I thought you were bedridden!"

"Well, so I was, until a few months ago."

"You look splendid."

"I'm alive," Quill said simply.

Patrick squatted before the chair. "I thought of you when I was in India and a maharajah threatened to have me decapitated if I didn't kneel before his little idol. It reminded me of your tyranny at school."

Sophie could hardly bear it. Sitting back on his heels, Patrick was at her level as she sat on the stool. He was just at her shoulder. Her eyes instinctively drifted down his body and saw tight pantaloons stretched over hard-muscled thighs. She jerked her head away, nervous as a rabbit in high grass, but it was too late. Sophie swallowed hard and pulled slightly to the other side of the tufted stool.

Patrick, who had discovered that the ambitious little chit still had the capacity to wake his body, was beginning to feel uncomfortable. A soft fragrance came drifting to his nostrils from just beyond his right shoulder, a sweet, innocent odor like that of cherry blossoms. It inflamed his senses. He wanted to throw Sophie over his shoulder and take her to a bedchamber.

Patrick jerked upright, his expression suddenly forbidding. When he glanced down at the stool, his eyes were bright, sardonic.

"Lady Sophie, your servant." He bowed politely. "I must apologize; I didn't see you earlier."

Sophie flushed again. Of course he had seen her. His glance had reduced her to an immobile lump. She inclined her chin just as courteously, not trusting her voice.

He was just as beautiful as he had been a month ago, although his eyes had turned from entrancement to mockery. His hair was unruly, even when shaken into the careless elegance favored by London gentlemen. But Patrick's hair spoke eloquently not of pomades and hair oils but of windswept rides and fresh air. It was as black as ebony, as jet, except for the wild silver streaks that made it look moonlight-tipped.

Sophie took a firm grasp on herself. She was wilting like a Bath miss under the mocking gaze of an accomplished rake. And Viscountess Dewland was looking distinctly restless, still chatting to Sylvester Bredbeck.

Sophie straightened, coming gracefully to her feet. She smiled at Quill, a real smile that lighted her eyes and trembled on her mouth. Quill rose to his feet with a small lurch, bracing himself on the armrest of his chair.

Sophie dropped a deep curtsy. "Please, be seated."

Quill's mouth was twisted with pain but shatteringly sympathetic. "Lady Sophie, I would be most honored to meet you again. Perhaps we could have a rematch of our game when I am feeling more lucky."

"I should enjoy that," Sophie said.

She turned to Quill's brother, Peter, and gave him a twinkling smile. Her eyes slid coolly past Patrick and toward her betrothed, towering above her. She moved toward Braddon.

"My lord."

Braddon held out his arm and she took it, walking across the Persian carpet, the silver tips of her slippers pressing down on glowing ruby and crimson flowers. She was very conscious of the two men who watched her go—Quill, still on his feet, smiling a sympathetic half-smile that made her feel weepy, and Patrick with his mocking half-smile that made her want to throw a vase at him. I will not look back at that—that unreliable seducer, she thought. And she didn't.

For his part, Patrick watched Sophie walk toward the announcement of her engagement to Braddon Chatwin with a surge of wrath that sent a gathering wave of heat over his body. He had a horrifying urge to lunge across the room and bend her over his arms, to destroy the self-assured sway of her hips when she walked away with Braddon.

He knew, *knew,* it would take only one instant to return Sophie to the flushed and trembling woman he'd held in his arms, the woman whose confusion looked so touchingly real that if he hadn't known that she was a sophisticated wanton, a minx who had shared her kisses far and wide among the London beau monde, he might have . . . He might have what?

As Peter made his apologies and trotted back toward the ballroom, Patrick made no move to follow.

He plumped down on the stool Sophie had deserted, his large brown hands tidily sorting the backgammon pieces. Patrick finally looked up to find Quill's cool gaze on him.

Quill had always been blessed with iron restraint, even when they were all boys at school, suffering the indignities of communal life. Patrick would erupt into feverish anger, jumping on his twin brother, Alex, and trying desperately to pound his head into the floor; Quill expressed himself by spare words.

Now he leaned his head back against the deep brown leather and closed his eyes. When he spoke his voice lacked all innuendo.

"Don't I remember Braddon taking another of your women—a redhaired actress?"

"Arabella Calhoun. He still has her. She's been his mistress since last summer." Patrick's hard eyes skimmed the calm surface of Quill's impenetrable face. "Lady Sophie," he added savagely, "was never 'one of my women.' She turned me down flat."

At that, Quill's eyes opened. "*You* did the pretty?"

In the face of Quill's amused gaze, Patrick's mouth finally relaxed, quirked up.

"Quite a shock," he admitted.

"Yes, after all those women chasing you in the past year . . ." Quill waved a lazy hand. "Peter keeps me abreast of the London gossip. Since your brother married, what, a year or two ago, you've become something of a society darling, wouldn't you say?"

"No."

"Fleeing from the attentions of marriageable mamas, having made yourself too vulgarly rich for words over in India," Quill added wickedly.

"Shall we play?"

"Dished up by the lovely Sophie York! I must ask Mother to invite her to tea."

"She'll be busy in the near future," Patrick said, his voice indifferent. "I expect they're out there now, accepting congratulations."

Quill paused. "Gone that far, has it?"

"Quite. She's no fool, Quill," said Patrick, inadvertently quoting Sophie's own self-assessment. "She's gone for the title."

"Unfortunately, Braddon is a muttonhead. He'll drive her insane within a month." Quill's deep-set eyes watched his childhood friend with seeming carelessness.

"Shall we play?" Patrick repeated, his voice roughly impatient.

"Right."

Through thick walnut doors, the faint ebb and roar of a *ton* party continued. But the library quieted to the pinking sting of dice hitting a highly polished surface. A marble bust of Shakespeare looked down silently on the men's bent heads.

After the third game, Patrick suddenly broke the web cast by Quill's calm presence and the flicking firelight.

He looked at Quill, his face lit with self-mockery. "Should I go congratulate the happy couple?"

Quill's hooded eyes betrayed nothing. Finally he drawled, "I shall go to bed. You've worn me out with your emotions." He pulled himself to his feet and then paused, leaning on the high back of the leather armchair.

"I'm glad you made it back from the Orient, Patrick."

"I'm sorry about that damned horse."

Quill chuckled. "It was my riding that did it. I shall see you soon, I hope."

They left the library together, one man's body a fluid symphony of muscled grace, masked only slightly by the skin-tight pantaloons of a London gentleman. The other man's body was equally muscled, but the muscles knotted and pulled, refusing to obey their master's commands. Iron self-control moved Quill across the

Persian carpet toward the welcome shaded recesses of a curtained bed; controlled passion moved Patrick in the other direction, toward the sun-shot wanton curls of a woman whom he desired with a ferocity that disgusted him.

Chapter 4

〜

ootmen, liveried in a dismal shade of puce, were still
standing stiffly in the marble entry as Patrick walked
down the stairs from the library. But the Dewland
mansion was emptying. Patrick could hear the end of the
ball in the ringing tones of his boots hitting marble. The
walls sent the noise back to him now, whereas when he had
climbed the stairs an hour or so ago the air had been plump
and warm with the clatter of feet, voices, and stringed in-
struments.

He turned into the ballroom. Candles still burned
brightly in sconces around the room. But the candles in
the huge central candelabra were guttering and faltering,
having been lit hours ago. The center of the huge ballroom had taken on a cavernous feel, long shadows finger-
ing out toward the lighted walls. Here and there little
groups of brightly gowned ladies and dimly grayish gentlemen still flocked, obstinate lovers of the dawn, those

who counted the evening a failure if they arrived home before six in the morning.

She was gone, of course. Lady Sophie York would never find herself among the dregs of a party. It wouldn't be fashionable. Better to leave before anyone yawns, better to leave before one's beaux grow unbecomingly intoxicated. But Braddon . . . Braddon never knew when to leave, poor duffer.

Patrick found him easily. Braddon was plumped into a chair in the corner, talking to someone Patrick couldn't see, his view blocked by Braddon's waving hands. He was talking nineteen to the dozen. Discussing horses, Patrick thought with an unwilling pang of affection. Good old Braddon. It was a pity that life in England was so small that women had to be parceled out among men who'd known one another since they were six or seven, when they were thrown together in the cold hallways of Eton.

But his stride quickened as he realized to whom Braddon was talking. "Alex!" The word echoed leadenly in the growing emptiness of the room.

His twin looked up, a smile lighting his black eyes. "I've been waiting for you, quite a chore. Braddon's in one of his starts."

Patrick sat down next to his brother, feeling tension drain out of him.

Braddon leaned forward, his eyes shining, his wide chin trembling with excitement.

"Not a start, Patrick—this is the real thing! My life is settled, complete, bound up." He smiled, lacing his hands together over his embroidered waistcoat.

"Congratulations," Patrick said softly.

Braddon seemed not to have heard the controlled menace in Patrick's tone and rushed on. "My God, she's gorgeous. The most beautiful curved little bottom I've ever seen, and her breasts—they're like—like . . ." Braddon's imagination failed, not for the first time in his life. "Well, they're big, beautiful, *big* for a small girl like her-self."

Ice crept down Patrick's backbone and his hands trem-bled. He was going to have to hit the son of a bitch. The blood was pulsing in his head.

"I caught her against the stable door," Braddon contin-ued, blissfully unaware of Patrick's expression. "I kind of caught up against her and grabbed her from behind and just gave her a little tweak, and my God I have never felt—"

His voice broke off as a hand lunged from the chair opposite and grabbed his neck cloth, twisting violently. The cloth cut off his windpipe. Braddon froze, his mouth agape, making no effort to free himself.

Actually they both froze for an instant as Patrick real-ized he had no right, no right at all, to admonish a man for pinching his future wife. He threw Braddon back into the chair, which creaked ominously as some two hundred fifty pounds crashed back into its velvet arms.

Alex's cool tones fell into the silence, a silence that had drifted through the whole room. The few people left at the ball were galvanized by the protesting chair, alerted like hounds at the whiff of a deer. Something was hap-pening, something more interesting than the stale frag-ments of gossip being served up at that late hour.

"Braddon," Alex remarked, "has found himself a new mistress, Patrick."

Braddon gaped at Patrick, his puppy eyes confused. "I thought you didn't give a damn about Arabella," he said, his voice aggrieved. "You could have told me earlier if you were affronted when I took on Arabella."

Patrick sat back in his chair, deliberately making his body relax. "Next time, ask me before you poach," he drawled.

The little group on the other side of the ballroom turned back into a circle, their voices purring with interest.

Everyone knew about Foakes's ex-mistress, the actress Arabella Calhoun, and her move to the protection of the Earl of Slaslow. Fascinating, though. No one thought that Foakes gave a damn.

Why, the story had been that Foakes extended her lease for six months and then sent a copy of the bill over to Slaslow with a scrawled note of compliment. Fascinating. When curious glances cast toward Slaslow and the Foakes brothers promised no further excitement that night, the last little band of fashionable folk began to inch toward the door. Best to go on to a club and have a last brandy before heading home.

Braddon felt unpleasantly shaken, sitting with Patrick's disturbing eyes narrowed on him.

"Damme it, man, Arabella came under my protection ages ago! You can't have expected that I'd keep the woman forever." He worked up a wisp of indignation. "I paid her lease for the next six months, *and* I sent over a rope of emeralds. What did you expect me to do, Patrick? Marry her, for God's sake?"

Patrick opened his mouth and clapped it shut again.

Alex's dispassionate voice broke in. "I'd like to hear about your Madeleine. Where did you find her?"

Braddon's eyes shifted uneasily to Alex. Then back to Patrick, and a flash of true anger straightened his backbone. "You don't know Madeleine, do you? She's mine, Foakes, *mine!*"

At that, Patrick's mouth unwillingly quirked up. "Lord, Braddon, we've shared enough, don't you think?"

"Well, Arabella was one thing." Braddon's eyes were burning now. "But Madeleine is different. She's going to be mine and mine alone, forever."

"An unusual arrangement," Alex observed.

Braddon swung belligerently over to Alex, for all the world like a bulldog trying to answer two masters. "Not at all. My own father kept one mistress for thirty-six years. Lord knows I'm still paying her bills. Not that I mind. She's a good old thing, and kind. She was beautiful too, not like m'mother. I go and have tea with her sometimes, talk about m'father."

Alex stated the obvious: "Your wife . . . your future wife . . . is a very beautiful woman."

"It's not the same." Braddon was deadly serious now, trying to explain something that he had painstakingly worked out in the years since his father had first introduced him to Mrs. Burns. The former Earl of Slaslow had demanded complete respect from his heir and had sent him a look that shook Braddon to his bones when he didn't immediately bow. And so Braddon had bowed, as deeply as if Mrs. Burns were King George himself.

And then they had sat down to tea, he and his father and Mrs. Burns, and he'd looked with fascination at the beautifully furnished house, the elegant gardens visible through wide Venetian windows. Finally at the picture of a child on the piano—his brother! Only to find out from Mrs. Burns that the brother had died, dead at age seven. His father had moved a bit creakily over to Mrs. Burns and held her shoulders tightly after she said that.

And Braddon understood, without rancor, that his father had loved that boy more than he loved Braddon himself, or his sisters. And that he loved Mrs. Burns, and not his wife.

It had taken hard thinking, something Braddon wasn't good at. But he knew that *that*, what his father had with Mrs. Burns, that was something he wanted for himself too. So when his father was dying, a huge mound of flesh in the master bedchamber, he bribed his father's valet to keep everyone out of the room for an hour. And then he smuggled in Mrs. Burns.

Before he left the room he saw her sit on the bed and lean over, and his father, who hadn't spoken for two days, whispered "beloved." When the old Earl of Slaslow died that night, without saying another word, Braddon's mind was made up.

Ay, he'd get married as his witch of a mother kept demanding. And he would have the children required, as many as necessary till a boy sprouted from the pile. So far he'd asked three gentlewomen to marry him; the third had finally taken the lure. So that part of his life was taken care of. But he wanted to have a Mrs. Burns too, a Mrs. Burns of his own.

The miracle of it was that suddenly he had found a Mrs. Burns.

"Her name is Madeleine, Miss Madeleine Garnier," he said, his jaw stiff in case Patrick tried to make some prior claim. "Do you know her?"

Patrick's eyes were twinkling now and Braddon relaxed.

"Never heard of her in my life. No poaching, word of honor." If Patrick added hastily to himself, "at least, not on Madeleine," there was no need to say it out loud. But his brother looked at him keenly. Alex sensed the ellipse, the unspoken words. One of the disadvantages of having a twin was invariable detection of silent lies.

Patrick cleared his throat. "Have you known Madeleine long?"

Braddon's mouth tightened again. " 'Miss Garnier' to you." Then he blinked, hearing how foolish he sounded.

"I met her a few weeks ago. That's what I was telling Alex when you showed up. It's providence; has to be. I finally got myself a proper wife—my mother's up in the clouds about it—*and* I met Madeleine, all in the same week.

"And you know what else?" Braddon continued with a burst of confidence. "I quite like the idea of marrying Sophie York. She's got backbone. Perhaps she can even hold my mother off. Perhaps they'll have an argument and my mother will refuse to visit the house."

He beamed like a man granted a view of heaven.

"You'd still have to contend with *her* mother," Patrick

drawled. He himself quite liked the old martinet, the Marchioness of Brandenburg, but she would terrorize Braddon.

Braddon shuddered visibly. "I won't be around much. I think I'll buy Madeleine a house in Mayfair. What do you think?"

Patrick felt uneasiness stirring again. "You can't do that," he snapped. "*Your* house is in Mayfair. Buy Miss Garnier a house in Shoreditch."

"No." Braddon's long jaw set.

Patrick's heart sank. He'd seen that look before, whenever Braddon had decided on a plan of the utmost idiocy.

"I want Madeleine near me. I'm not ashamed of her."

"It's not a question of your shame," Alex put in. "One would hate to offend the feelings of your future wife. When Lady Sophie becomes your countess, she might meet your mistress face to face every week."

"That's why I picked Sophie York," Braddon said triumphantly. "She's up to snuff. It won't bother her at all. In fact, I have a mind to introduce them, after a bit of time has passed."

Patrick stared at him, nonplussed. His old friend had finally lost his mind. That was the only explanation. Who would want a mistress when he could have Sophie?

And Sophie! What would happen to her when her mutton-brained husband started flaunting his mistress all over the street? Patrick's chest tightened to think of it. He cast a wild glance at his brother.

"I've seen quite a bit of Sophie York in the last year," Alex said rather slowly. "She is my wife's closest friend, you know. I wouldn't describe her as worldly. If anything, she is remarkably naive for a woman who has been out for two years."

"She may be naive," Braddon replied with some impatience, "although I don't believe it myself. You must have heard the tales about her—my God, you'd think she'd kissed every man in London. Not that I care. Anyway, she may be naive, but she's certainly knowing when it comes to marriage. Look at her own father! She can't have missed his activities.

"And I do not intend to be anything like her father. Madeleine wouldn't want to go to society affairs. She's not that sort of woman. So I won't be waltzing around the ballroom in front of my wife with my mistress. In fact, I foresee a very peaceful home life. I will be careful not to embarrass Sophie or demand too much. I'll go my own way, after the heir, and we will stay friends. After all, ladies don't like to have children, ruins their figures. Maybe we'll be lucky, have a set of twins like you on the first go-around, and then we wouldn't have to bother anymore.

"Doesn't that sound like a good plan, Patrick?" Braddon looked at him appealingly.

Patrick's eyes glowered at him with an unmistakable threat. He said nothing.

After a second Braddon's lips quivered into an unmistakable pout. "You're a dog in the manger! A dog in the bloody manger! You didn't want Arabella anymore—bloody hell, you went right off and left her at a house party without even saying good-bye. And you didn't come back for six days. Six bloody days! What'd you expect? You didn't care at the time, so why do you care when I leave her?"

"Why the devil would I care whether you left Arabella?" Patrick shouted back. "This has nothing to do with Arabella!" His words rolled around the empty ballroom. He was blazing with rage.

Braddon jumped to his feet, taking a few agitated steps. "Then why are you so angry at me? What do you care whether I set up a mistress, if you've never even seen Madeleine before?"

Patrick blinked. He was conscious of his brother's interested gaze from his right. What a mess.

"I care," he said, picking his words carefully, "how you treat Sophie York."

"You *are* a dog in the manger!" Braddon burst out, his eyes bulging a little with anger. "I know you didn't offer for her! I heard all about you groping Sophie in an empty room, and then you didn't think she was good enough for you! Well, I don't have your standards, Patrick Foakes. Sophie's good enough for me."

Even Braddon's foolish long face could gain a bit of dignity in a pinch, Alex thought cheerfully, crossing his legs.

Patrick came to his feet in an instant. "You blithering idiot!" he shouted back. "I offered for her, you ass. I offered for her!"

There was a moment of silence. Braddon blinked at him, biting his lower lip. Which only increased his likeness to a bulldog, in Alex's uncharitable opinion.

"You offered for her? *You?* And she wouldn't have you?"

Patrick grinned suddenly. Who could stay angry with a dunderhead like Braddon? He sat down again.

"That's right. I marched up to the front door the next morning at ten o'clock, only slightly fortified with brandy. Got the question out pat with her father. But it didn't fly with her."

Patrick felt a curious rush of protectiveness, remembering Sophie's large uncertain eyes. She hadn't expected him to come, that was clear. Which didn't say much for his reputation. But there he was declaring his intentions. And she'd said no. He didn't really want to discuss why she refused him.

"I can't believe it," Braddon said in a numbed voice. "I—I, Braddon Chatwin, took a woman from one of the Foakeses? I mean, I don't count Arabella. Remember!" he said, rounding on Alex, who was grinning away in his arm-chair. "Remember when you came back from Italy and I told you about the most beautiful woman in London, the one I wanted to marry, and damned if two weeks later you weren't engaged to her?"

Alex laughed. "My wife," he said, bowing his head ironically. "I owe it all to you, Braddon."

"Sophie York turned you down and accepted me?" Braddon asked Patrick.

Patrick rolled his eyes. For a minute he thought his friend was going to cut a caper.

Alex came to his feet. "Gentlemen, I regret to say that, fascinating though this conversation is, I must go home."

Patrick looked up at him. "Henpecked?" he asked.

His twin smiled at him unashamedly. "Charlotte worries if I'm out too late. Sarah is still occasionally waking up to nurse at night—"

"Ugh!" Braddon broke in. "I can't fathom why you have allowed your wife to nurse the child herself, Alex. It's disgusting." His lower lip jutted out, a sure sign of deep thought. "I shan't allow Madeleine to do anything of the sort, I warrant you. A good wet nurse, that's the ticket. I won't have Madeleine turn herself into a milk cow."

"I shall ignore the implication that my wife is a cow," Alex murmured. His eyes met Patrick's. "Will I see you at dinner tomorrow?"

"Of course he's coming," Braddon broke in. "He's my best man, isn't he? He has to come to the engagement dinner!"

Patrick rolled his shoulder. "Why wouldn't I? I want to see those little calves of yours, brother."

"Ugh," Braddon repeated, with emphasis. Then he looked alarmed. "You don't suppose that Sophie will pick up this nursing business from your wife, do you, Alex? Because I won't have it. Not in my house. It's disgusting."

Alex looked at his twin warningly.

Anger was burning a hole in Patrick's backbone. But he took silent note of Alex's unspoken opinion. Sophie York, and the way Braddon talked about Sophie York, was not his business.

"Well." Braddon pulled down his embroidered waist-coat cheerfully. "Would you like to go around and say hello to Arabella, Patrick? You know she's appearing at the Duke's Theater in Dorset Garden these days, and I'm sure she'd like to see you. She's playing Juliet, a pretty good role for her, eh? Although Bella's no Juliet to die for love. Do you know that when I broke off our attachment she wrote me a note, as cool as you please, saying that I was her life and joy, or some such nonsense, and since my passion for her had decayed, she felt the need for security—and the upshot of it all is that she wants me to give her a house. Vixen."

Patrick was striding ahead of him, out of the ballroom. "And are you?" he tossed over his shoulder.

There was a pause. Patrick threw Braddon an amused glance. "You're an easy target, aren't you?" He fell back a pace and walked next to his friend. "You tell me when she's found a house and I'll plunk down the blunt for half," he said as their boots clattered through the empty marble halls. Viscount and Viscountess Dewland had long ago retired to bed and only a weary-eyed butler bade them good night.

"I can sport the blunt," Braddon said, his tone defensive.

"Well, I can buy and sell you," Patrick drawled, "and I'd like to contribute to Arabella's house."

Braddon looked at him, his light blue eyes unenvious but curious. "So did you really come back from India as rich as a nabob, then?"

Patrick shrugged, tossing his hair back from his eyes. "M'father sent me out East by myself, you know. Not much fun raising hell without Alex. It seemed to come naturally."

And it had. His mercurial, mocking nature took infinite pleasure in the delicate rhythms of Indian negotiation and export.

Designing trade routes, finding rare spices, loading the holds of ships with delicate gold bird cages, rippling silk so delicate that it tore at the touch of a fingernail, and casks of peacock feathers, pleased him. He took great risks and received greater rewards. At the moment, his fortune was to be rivaled in England only, perhaps, by those of his brother and a few others. Those London gentlemen like Braddon who limited their financial ambition to training a horse for the next Ascot were a dying breed.

Alex stepped into his carriage with a wave. Patrick shrugged off Braddon's plan to visit the back door of the Duke's Theater and then, in a sudden decision, waved off his own coachman as well. He stood in the deserted street, watching his well-slung carriage disappear around a corner.

A light rain had begun to fall. London was ripe with the smell of settling dust and horse manure. Patrick settled his cloak and started down the street, his legs eating up the pavement. As he walked, tension uncurled from his leg muscles and his stomach lost a knot he hadn't been aware of. His scalp eased.

Patrick had walked the hot breathless alleys of Whampao Reach, Canton, strolled under the delicate arches of Baghdad, tramped the byways of mountain villages in Tibet. It was when he was ambling along a small back street in Lhasa that he'd heard a chorus of avadavats singing: the small black and red songbirds that he had later exported to England, and that had become the rage in London.

He wasn't much of a sleeper at the best of times. It was while walking that ideas floated into his mind, unbeckoned. But now Patrick brooded rather than thought. Even the memory of the sweet curves of Sophie York's breasts—exposed to the whole world in that ridiculous gown she was wearing!—made his loins tighten. And so he strode on, telling himself to cut Sophie from his mind.

For God's sake, he had had a mistress in Arabia, what was her name? Perliss. Until a pasha took a liking to Perliss, and she to him, and within a few hours his mistress became an honored wife, the twenty-fourth, or was it twenty-fifth? He hadn't turned a hair, although he missed Perliss's undoubted skills and graceful long legs for a few days.

But now! He'd kissed the chit only a few times, for God's sake. Held Sophie in his arms once before kissing her, but that was when his sister-in-law was almost dying in the next room. Even then he'd been conscious of what he held, although he knew that Sophie had no awareness of him whatsoever. She was grieving for Charlotte's death. Except that Charlotte, of course, hadn't died.

Patrick had bided his time. Sophie returned to her family the day after Charlotte's child was safely born. Patrick was no stranger to the hunt. He deliberately didn't follow her. Instead, he waited until the gentry began returning to London, in late November.

But then, when he had awakened her, turned a sleeping beauty into a flushed, silently begging woman who had pressed herself into his arms, she had turned him down. Not that he really wanted to marry, of course, but given the circumstances . . .

Weeks had passed since his proposal of marriage. He'd hadn't been with a woman since and he hadn't stopped thinking about Sophie's body. Obviously it was frustration. Simple sexual frustration, and if he had any brains he'd walk himself over to the Duke's Theater and see if Arabella would take him to her bed for old times' sake.

But his feet didn't listen. They headed home, ignoring

the tigerish frustration that pulsed up and down his muscled limbs. He'd be damned if he'd let Sophie marry Braddon. Patrick's eyes narrowed as an image flashed across his mind, unbidden: Braddon punctiliously removing his embroidered waistcoat and preparing to do his duty—but only until he got an heir.

What was Sophie supposed to do after Braddon had his heir? Become one of those shallow, bored society matrons who took on lovers from the *ton* or, worse, slept with their gardeners?

Patrick found himself in front of his house. The walk hadn't done its magic tonight. His heart was pounding and his hands were clenched.

The engagement party. He slowly climbed the stairs, his grateful butler almost running toward the servants' quarters and his own bed. Patrick walked into his bedroom unseeingly, dismissing his sleepy-eyed valet with a wave.

The dinner that Charlotte was giving for Sophie.

I'll talk to her, Patrick thought. Talk, my ass! His thumbs itched to rub themselves over the tender arch of her nipples. He longed to pull Sophie against his hard body, an intoxicating encounter of muscle and yielding softness, bumps and curves that were made to be linked together.

I'll talk to her, Patrick decided. I'll talk to her, that's all.

❧

Lord Breksby went to his bed that night in a glow of self-satisfaction. He lay back, hands tucked behind his head, which was trimly covered in a nightcap.

"I tell you, m'dear," he told his sleepy wife, "sometimes I fancy myself a genius. I really do."

Lady Breksby had no complaints with that assessment—in fact, she merely grunted—so after a moment Lord Breksby composed himself for sleep.

He dreamed of ruby scepters; she dreamed of roses.

Patrick dreamed that he was dancing with Sophie York while wearing a huge insignia proclaiming that he was a Duke of the Realm. Lady Sophie dreamed that she was kissing her future husband, Braddon Chatwin, when he suddenly turned into a lop-eared rabbit and hopped away, somewhat to her relief.

Only Alex had no dreams that night. Baby Sarah was teething and cried half the night. "We should be glad that she has sound lungs," his wife observed sleepily at three in the morning. Alex merely sighed and turned to walk back to the nursery. If the Earl of Sheffield and Downes day-dreamed of sailing to the Ottoman Empire with his brother, far from the damp and wailing child in his arms, who would blame him?

Chapter 5

B y the time Sophie had been bathed, gowned, coiffured, and placed in a carriage tooling its way to her engagement dinner, she was feeling a burst of happiness. She was alone. The carriage would drop her at Sheffield House an hour early so that she could visit with Charlotte. She leaned back comfortably on the salmonpink velvet.

Her mother, the marchioness, invariably sat forward, her back stiffened as if by a steel rod, her gloved hand clenched on a wall strap. Whereas, Sophie decided, my back naturally curves into seats.

She felt recklessly sensual, the prickling call of nerve points making her heart dance, reminding her that the source of this giddy happiness was the slim, paltry, ridiculous fact that Patrick Foakes would be at the dinner party. She would see him and perhaps, if there was informal dancing afterward. . . . She rather fancied there would be.

Then he might, would, hold her in his arms. After all, Charlotte loved to dance. And Charlotte was more than a little interested in Sophie and Patrick's future. *Not that I have a future with Patrick Foakes,* Sophie quickly reminded herself.

The carriage rattled on. It clattered over rounded paving stones and swung around a corner altogether too fast. Sophie had to make a quick grab for the strap, and even so she was thrown against the padded wall. It was the pity of being so small. She couldn't brace herself against the corner the way men could. André was driving too fast again. He thought of himself as a cross between a coachman and a courtier, and he had even adapted the trick of a Corinthian: He caught his whip as it coiled back through the air.

The horses trotted on and the carriage resumed its normal creaking rattle and sway. Sophie stuck out a foot in front of her, thoughtfully regarding her slipper. She was wearing a gown the color of bronzed gold—which was the closest she ever came to white. She *never* wore white. White was her mother's preference. White was the preference of virtually every other unmarried girl in London. White, for innocence, engagements, and virginity. Sophie dropped her foot in exasperation.

Gold was not innocent. What was the name of the play she'd seen last week? *Eros Undoubted*? That didn't sound right. *Cupid Defeated*? No, it wasn't Cupid, it was Eros. Cupid was the god of love, but Eros was the god of desire. At any rate, Eros had been wearing a little toga of pale gold as he trotted around the stage shooting people with his gilt arrows. The play itself was terrible, one of those tragedies in which a pious young woman fell in love with a scoundrel (thanks to Eros). In the end she threw herself—in a remarkably unconvincing manner, to Sophie's mind—off a bridge.

That's what I need, Sophie thought. One little god in a toga to match my gown, and could he please plant a big fat arrow in Patrick Foakes's back? Although now that she thought of it, Eros had done just that to the scoundrel in the play—and then the man had blithely left the heroine with a small child.

A secret smile tipped the corners of Sophie's red lips. She had little fear that Patrick lacked *desire* for her. She could read it in the way his eyes darkened when he saw her. So what she needed was not Eros but Cupid. . . . That's right. Cupid, wearing a pure white virginal night-shirt, to shoot Patrick Foakes with one of *his* arrows. Because if there was one certainty in life, it was that rakes never fall in love, especially with their wives, and if they do, it isn't for long.

The thought calmed Sophie. She took a deep breath. The dream that Patrick Foakes might fall in love with her was just that, a dream. Whatever he wanted from her, it wasn't marriage. Yes, she would see him tonight. But it was a dinner celebrating her engagement to another man.

Still . . . her heart danced. Even the hair falling down her back, spilling in precisely ordered curls, felt airy, silky, about to be touched.

The carriage jolted sharply as André drew up the horses before Sheffield House. The team reared into the air in tandem, settling back to earth with an irritable jangle of their harnesses and a petulant stamping of feet.

"Best not let his lordship see that trick with the hoasses, Andy," one of the footmen called saucily. He hopped down from his perch and nipped around to open the door. Everyone knew that the young lady wouldn't never complain about the rough ride, but Lord a'mercy, the markessa, or whatever her title was, she could give a rare trimming when she put her mind to it.

If the truth be told, Sophie was feeling slightly battered.

First her shoulder had crashed into the corner of the coach, and then when the coach finally stopped she had been propelled sharply forward and landed on her knees in the center well between the seats.

"Philippe," she said, accepting her footman's assistance stepping out of the coach, "would you tell André that I feel like a tub of cream which Cook is determined to churn into butter?"

Philippe ducked his head to hide a grin. "Yes, my lady, I will convey the message," he said, his voice half muffled by his high cravat.

Sophie ran lightly up the marble steps to Sheffield House and paused to smile at the portly butler who stood with the door opened.

"How are you, McDougal?"

"Ach, Lady Sophie, it's beautiful that you look tonight," McDougal said, pushing the door backward as he spoke. Sophie handed him her velvet pelisse.

When she crooked an eyebrow at him inquiringly, McDougal winked. "You'll find the countess in her rooms."

As Sophie disappeared around the curve of the great marble staircase that led to the upper regions of Sheffield House, McDougal smiled to himself. That was a bonny lass, Lady Sophie. Small as a bonnet bee, she was, and light as a fairy, but her smile—it could warm the moon, it could.

When Sophie entered the master suite, Charlotte swung about from a stool before her dressing table, her face lighting up.

"Sophie! How lovely to see you early."

"No, don't stand up, sweetheart." Sophie nimbly bent to kiss Charlotte's cheek. "I see that Marie is planning something very complicated." Charlotte's maid was combing her mistress's hair, preparatory to fashioning an elaborate nest of braids, satin ribbons, and flowers.

"*Bonsoir,* Marie."

"*Mon dieu!*" Marie squeaked in response. "Look at that gown!"

Sophie looked down obediently. Sure enough, the front of her dress was creased where she had fallen on the carriage floor.

Marie darted across the room and yanked on the bellpull. "I'll have someone come up immediately, Lady Sophie, and attend to it. Please, slip out of the gown. Here"—she snatched up a flowing peignoir— "you might wear this until your dress is pressed."

Sophie obediently bent down as Marie eased the delicate silk over her head. Then she sat on the bed.

"Don't forget that I dampen my chemise, Marie," she said mischievously.

"*Mais oui,* my lady, *naturellement,*" Marie breathed, gently handing Sophie's gown to the curtsying maid who had appeared at the door. Sophie wrapped the peignoir around herself, pushing up the sleeves.

"How are the girls, Charlotte?"

"They're very well, except that Pippa has taken to ordering everyone to do her bidding. She's a tiny despot."

"She always had that potential." Sophie laughed. "Remember how she used to drive nannies out of the house, one after another—and then she was only a year old! Now she's what? Two or three? Wait until she's sixteen!"

"True enough," Charlotte admitted ruefully.

"Look at this, Charlotte. You're a veritable giant compared to me!" The slippery lace of the peignoir's arms wouldn't stay up and cascaded past Sophie's hands.

Charlotte grimaced at Sophie, looking at her in the mirror. "In truth, I feel like a giant when I walk next to you."

"Pooh! You look like a princess and I look like your page," Sophie said impudently. Her smoky blue eyes were shining with amusement.

"Hurrah!" Charlotte exclaimed. "You're back!"

Sophie knit her brows. "What on earth do you mean?"

"You look happy again," Charlotte said. "You've had a fragile look the past few weeks. . . ."

"Like a moth singed by the candle?"

"That's not the analogy I would have chosen," Charlotte replied. "Like a person who has made a difficult decision and wonders if she made the right one."

"You're blunt," said Sophie, meeting Charlotte's eyes again in the mirror.

Charlotte twisted about on the stool, heedless of Marie's muttered reproach as she dropped hairpins on the floor.

"Are you *sure*, Sophie? Absolutely sure?"

Sophie nodded, her eyes meeting Charlotte's without flinching.

"Because . . ." Charlotte's voice trailed off. "Well, Braddon is a nice person, of course, but he's not very—"

"Handsome? Interesting? Intelligent?" Sophie suggested, her mouth twisting wryly.

"How can you marry him!" Charlotte flashed back. "Can't you see how much better it is to marry someone handsome and intelligent?"

"I don't want to marry your brother-in-law, Charlotte," Sophie said patiently. "You have to allow me to know what's best for myself. I don't want to marry a rake."

"But Braddon *is* a rake," Charlotte insisted. "Why, I distinctly remember you telling me that Braddon had more mistresses depending on him than a lawyer has cases!"

A flash of amusement lighted Sophie's eyes. "The point is not that Braddon is or isn't a rake, it's that I *like* Braddon. He's trustworthy. He doesn't have deep emotions, and he will be very discreet with his mistresses. He assured me of it himself."

"You mean you have discussed his mistresses?" Charlotte was horrified and fascinated, both at once.

"He brought it up. I have to admit, I was a little surprised myself." Sophie tried hard to keep any doubt out of her voice. "That's the kind of marriage we're going to have, Charlotte: a calm, reasoned, and friendly alliance. I want a placid marriage. You did not want that particular kind of relationship, and so you and Alex are happy together. But I want the kind of marriage where neither person is blinded by passion. Remember how Alex behaved toward you?" Sophie hesitated and then plunged on. "When you had to travel to Scotland?"

"You don't have to be so delicate," Charlotte said wryly. "Alex behaved like a royal devil, that's true. But we worked it out, and now——" She looked at herself in the mirror. Half of her hair still spilled over her ears and the other half garlanded her head. Marie's hands were busy plaiting a crimson ribbon into her hair, preparing to tuck the braid in among the rest. Even the thought of her husband stained her cheeks a faint echo of the ribbon.

"I know what you mean." Sophie's voice was somewhere between dispassion and despair. "But the *grand amour* is not going to work for me, Charlotte. I know that you wish for me to find the same happiness that you have. But we all find happiness in different ways. For me, the anxiety of marrying a man whom I loved so passionately, the way you care for Alex, could never be worth it. *Your* parents are happy; mine are not."

Ignoring Charlotte's open mouth, she rushed on: "I certainly don't mean to pry into the circumstances of your parents' marriage. My point was only that the circumstances of *my* parents' marriage are known far and wide. It's a rare month when my father doesn't surface in *The Morning Post* under some pseudonym or other. My mother won't hire a Frenchwoman under the age of seventy; it means we've likely pensioned off more servants than your mother has hired in her entire married life!"

Charlotte sighed. Sophie's logic was impeccable. It was just that she was talking nonsense.

"I don't see what your parents have to do with whether you marry Braddon or Patrick."

"I like Braddon," Sophie insisted. "I will never fall passionately in love with him, and therefore I won't become bitter, as my mother has, if Braddon takes more notice of his mistresses than of me. With Patrick . . . it's different."

"You know that Patrick is coming tonight?"

Sophie's head swung up. She had been restlessly watching her pale gold slipper swing back and forth, hitting the tasseled edge of Charlotte's counterpane.

"Yes."

In the secret depths of Sophie's eyes Charlotte saw an aching confusion, a languorous question that made an answering smile curl the corners of her mouth. Perhaps all Sophie's rhetoric wouldn't matter—much. Perhaps, if she found some way to throw Sophie and Patrick together tonight . . .

There was a brisk knock at the door and a maid half ran into the room, carrying Sophie's gold dress draped across her outstretched arms as if it were an altar cloth being offered to a pagan deity.

"My lady," she stammered, curtsying while holding her arms stiffly outstretched.

"My goodness, Bess," Marie said, scolding her with the freedom of a valued member of the household—more than a valued member, one who ranked only just below the earl's own manservant, and he only just below the butler. "You will have to learn to be more graceful if you ever want to become a lady's maid. Go along downstairs, do."

Bess tripped on the way out but managed to close the door.

"Now, Lady Sophie."

As Marie approached, Sophie stood up. First Marie briskly dampened Sophie's all-but-invisible chemise, making the fine lawn cling to her legs. Then she threw the gown up over Sophie's head, carefully protecting her hair.

The dress rustled sweetly over Sophie's shoulders, smelling of orange blossoms and, faintly, a hot iron. As it fell down to her feet the silk twisted in the breeze of its own fall, barely glazing her limbs.

"There," Marie said with satisfaction, after hooking up the back of Sophie's gown. "If you would give me a minute while I pin up the last of my lady's braids, I will refurbish your curls."

"That is a lovely gown," Charlotte said to Sophie, as Marie nimbly pinned up a few stray curls.

"Thank you," Sophie replied. "I had it sent from Madame Carême."

Marie ruthlessly stuck a few extra pins in the coils of Charlotte's hair, and Charlotte rose, feeling awkwardly top-heavy. She crossed the room to stand before Marie, who had clambered onto a stool and was waiting to slip a crimson evening gown over her head. One of the disadvantages of being so tall was that her lady's maid had to stand on a stool to put on a dress, or to undo buttons for that matter.

There was a light knock on the door. Marie rushed over and then shut the door smartly in the speaker's face.

"That was Keating, my lady. The Heppleworths have arrived."

Charlotte held out her wrist as Marie fastened the clasp of a slim band of rubies. Sophie came over curiously.

"What a beautiful bracelet, Charlotte." The glowing burgundy of the rubies picked up the sheen of Charlotte's gown and set off her dark hair.

"A birthday gift from my doting husband," Charlotte said impishly. "To celebrate our placid life."

"More likely you threw a chamber pot at him and this was his ploy to reenter the bedroom," Sophie teased.

Charlotte wrinkled her nose. "Shall we go down and excite the assembled men . . . all of them?"

Sophie cast a look at herself in the mirror and then deliberately pulled down her tiny bodice, arranging the dress so that the silky gold material just barely skimmed her nipples.

Charlotte chuckled. "You couldn't possibly look more enticing, Sophie."

"Yes, well." Sophie's eyes were alight with deep excitement. "I see no reason not to make everyone at the dinner party a little interested, no? I am only an engaged woman; I'm not dead!"

"Oh, Sophie! Sometimes you are *so* French!"

"I like being French in the evening," Sophie retorted. "One can be English all day, especially when riding a horse, but then one can dress—and think—French after six o'clock."

Charlotte thought about this a bit doubtfully as they walked down the hallway together. "How French will you be once you're married?" Charlotte asked.

Sophie cast her friend a laughing look. "Are you trying to find out whether I will be faithful to my husband, Charlotte?"

"Yes."

"I shall be," Sophie replied. "Because it is too much trouble to become involved in liaisons and such. I shall flirt, naturally, and I shall take on a cicisbeo, of course. A married woman must have admirers. But no, I will not allow anyone into my bedroom. Why should I?" She gave a charming little shrug.

That shrug was purely French, Charlotte thought. But Sophie's lack of knowledge about the delights of the bedroom was purely English. Charlotte couldn't help smiling. If Patrick was anything like his twin, her husband, Alex, he would make sure that Sophie knew exactly what she was giving up by putting Braddon's ring on her finger.

They walked down the marble stairs together. Charlotte moved toward the Yellow Drawing Room, where the party was assembling.

"Splendid," Sophie whispered to Charlotte when she saw in which direction they were heading. "This room is a perfect accompaniment to my gown."

Charlotte rolled her eyes at Sophie. The Yellow Drawing Room had curtains and upholstery of a pale amber and an elaborate Axminster carpet of a slightly darker color. Sophie was right. As she drifted into the room, the saffron-brown tones made her dress glow with a pale gold sheen.

Patrick had not yet arrived. Sophie had developed a sixth sense about him. Without even looking about she knew whether he was in a room.

Braddon bustled toward her and she paused, sweeping him a curtsy. Braddon grinned and bowed. As he straightened he automatically yanked at the bottom of his waistcoat, hauling it back down over his bulging tummy. Sophie lowered her eyes politely.

Braddon bowed again, to Charlotte, before taking Sophie's arm importantly. This evening his future bride would be formally introduced to his family, and he had thought out the hierarchy of the whole occasion carefully.

"My mother first," he whispered, steering Sophie toward the far end of the drawing room, "and then my sisters, and finally my godmother because she can be such an infernal nuisance, and also she is a duchess, so . . ."

Braddon's family was known far and wide, and only the kindly referred to them as "difficult." The average gentleman was more likely to label the Countess of Slaslow a hell-born virago. But Sophie had survived nearly twenty years of her own mother's scathing comments. No amount of rudeness could shake her calm.

Braddon stopped in front of his mother, hovering slightly on the tips of his toes, as if poised to fly to the other side of the room. To Sophie's mind, Prudence Chatwin looked surprisingly young for one with so fierce a reputation. Her face was deceptively unlined, given that she must be (Sophie calculated swiftly) at least fifty.

Sophie sank into a deep curtsy, bowing her head submissively.

The countess rose to her feet. "Lady Sophie," she said, her voice as sweet as syrup and clear enough to carry straight across the long room. "How grateful we are to you for rescuing our poor son from the throes of bachelorhood." She turned a dragon's eye on Braddon, who was already quailing. "Why, do you know that more than three young ladies turned him down? What can they have been thinking of? But they were *very* young; it obviously took a more mature eye to see the shining light of dear Braddon's virtues."

Quite good, Sophie thought appreciatively. In one stroke she had made Braddon into a slacker and Sophie herself into an aging and desperate spinster.

"Just so," Sophie murmured. The last thing she wanted was to cross swords with Braddon's mother.

"And how is your dear, dear mother?" The question was accompanied by a poisonous smile.

"Mama is quite well, thank you. She will be here any moment, I am sure."

"Poor dear," the countess said kindly. "We all know

what a burden she struggles under. Your father . . . Well, well, mum for that!"

Sophie ducked her head again, biting her lip.

"Must introduce you to m'sisters," Braddon broke in. "Our excuses, ma'am." He tried to pull Sophie hastily to the other side of the room.

But Sophie walked slowly. She needed to collect herself before meeting Braddon's sisters.

"She can't help it," Braddon said dismally. "Mama just says whatever thing comes to her mind, and—"

"And everything that comes to mind is unpleasant," Sophie finished.

"Yes," Braddon admitted. He awkwardly patted Sophie's arm. "Doesn't mean she's not glad that you're marrying me, because she *is*. Must have told me a hundred times in the last week that she never thought I'd do half so well. It's just that she doesn't notice what she says, or she doesn't know what the effect is, or something like that.

"And I haven't been turned down by more than three ladies," he added with some indignation. "There were only two, before you, and you accepted me."

Sophie smiled at Braddon's tangled speech. "My own mother is not very tolerant." Although, she thought silently, Mama is not a patch on that old dragon!

It was when she was curtsying to the second of Braddon's sisters that Sophie sensed Patrick's arrival. There was a little flurry of giggles from a group of three young women standing close to the door. Sophie stiffened her back. She would not look around. She smiled pleasantly at the freckled woman before her. Margaret had obviously tried to smooth her hair into a semblance of a chignon, but it looked disheveled, wisps falling around her ears.

"Lady Sophie," Margaret almost hissed at her, "how many children do you intend to bear to the head of our family?"

Sophie drew back, slightly alarmed.

"Ah, I'm not sure," she said. Then she added, thinking fast, "We must leave it to God's will."

Margaret's eyes kindled with approval. "Children are God's greatest gift, Lady Sophie. And as the head of the family, the Earl of Slaslow *must* have at least five and possibly six children. One cannot be too certain." She stood back a little. "Of course, I have seen you dancing and such, but I never considered you in this light before." Her eyes scanned Sophie's middle section. Sophie turned her head, looking up at her betrothed questioningly. Braddon avoided her eyes.

"Your hips look ample," Margaret pronounced briskly. "Of course, you'll need to begin producing children as soon as possible. Do you have any idea whether your own mother had some impediment? She seems to have produced only one child, unless you have deceased siblings?" Margaret paused expectantly.

"Not that I am aware of."

Margaret pursed her lips. "We must hope for the best." A fleeting frown crossed her face. "Your father's title will become extinct when he dies, Lady Sophie. So I am sure you are aware of the importance of this question."

"In fact, the title will pass to my cousin," Sophie felt bound to answer.

Margaret curled her lip. "A cousin is not the same as a *son,* Lady Sophie. I am sure that your father considers his title dead."

To Sophie's mind, her father thought very little about his title. If he'd really wanted a son he would have visited her mother's bed after the first two months of their marriage, at least according to her mother's version of events.

"The important thing," Margaret continued, "is that you start as soon as possible. You are no longer a young girl, and childbearing is not easy for older women."

Sophie started to feel a slow burn in her spine. "I am

not yet twenty years old," she said a bit stiffly. "I feel sure that I can provide his lordship with eight or nine bundles of joy." She gave Braddon a cloying if slightly wild smile.

"That is an excellent attitude." Margaret unbent a trifle, seeing that her brother's future wife had a bit more substance to her than she had previously thought. "I myself granted my husband his first child a mere nine months after we married, and I pride myself on the fact that seven infants have followed, in almost as many years."

"Goodness," Sophie said faintly.

A voice broke in, a darkly amused voice. "Lady Sophie could hardly do better than to model herself on you, Mrs. Windcastle. I feel sure that Lady Sophie will be a most, ah, fertile partner for old Braddon here."

Braddon cast his old friend an accusing look.

"Forgive me, forgive me," Patrick murmured, a wicked gleam in his eyes. "Perhaps 'fertile' harks too much of the stable."

"Not at all." Margaret Windcastle was unwilling to drop the subject dearest to her heart. "I see no reason why the subject of children does not belong in every lady's drawing room. Far too many gentlewomen quail at the thought of children—and what happens? Their husbands' lines die. Their titles expire." Her voice dropped dramatically: *"Imagine if there were no more Earls of Slaslow!"*

Patrick replied in a honeyed voice, "Why, Lady Sophie might be quite opposed to the idea of having children! That would be a disaster for the future Earls of Slaslow."

Braddon tugged down his waistcoat again, glancing down at Sophie. She seemed to be trying not to giggle. "We'd better go meet m'godmother."

Margaret smiled brightly. "Actually, Lady Sophie has just announced her intention to have eight or nine children."

"Eight or nine?" The teasing note in Patrick's voice compelled Sophie to meet his eyes. "My goodness, and here I was in danger of thinking that Lady Sophie was nothing but a frippery society miss."

Despite herself, the corner of Sophie's mouth quirked up. "Not at all," she said, repeating Margaret's phrase. "While I have always had the ambition to have ten children—such a nice, well-rounded number—I realize that at my advanced age I may have to settle for a smaller sum."

"Excellent," Patrick exclaimed. "I do love a woman who has no fear of getting old, don't you, Braddon?"

Braddon was staring in fascinated horror at his future bride. Had she really said *ten* children? Had he inadvertently promised to marry a broodmare like his sister?

"I look forward to old age," Sophie rejoined sweetly. "Male attention can be so . . . tiresome, don't you think, Margaret? I may call you Margaret, mayn't I, since we are to be sisters?"

Margaret smiled. "Of course, dearest Sophie."

"Yes, men can be quite dreary," Sophie continued. "The way they plead and implore."

Patrick's raffish eyes glinted at her. "Plead and implore, hmm?"

"Exactly," Sophie assured him. "Plead *and* implore."

Braddon gulped. "Time to meet m'godmother," he blurted, drawing Sophie's hand into the crook of his arm. "Excuse us, please, Margaret. Your servant, Foakes."

Sophie couldn't resist. She smiled at the fruitful Mrs. Windcastle, and then she flicked a glance at Patrick . . . a teasing, flirtatious look from under her lashes.

Devil-bright eyes looked back at her with a glance that was more of a command than a request, and which certainly had naught a drop of imploring, pleading emotion in it. It shivered her bones, the promise in his eyes; his glance skated from her face to her breasts and down her body. Warmth trailed down her legs, warming and weakening the back of her knees.

As she and Braddon walked away, Sophie reflexively

looked down at her bodice. She had the sudden impression that her dress had fallen off, leaving her breasts tinglingly exposed to the air. But all was well. Madame Carême's cleverly constructed bodices were proof against the most rakish of rakish glances.

Chapter 6

‍

Sophie ate her dinner, laughing and talking to Braddon on her left, and Braddon's friend David Marlowe on her right, while resolutely ignoring Patrick Foakes. He was seated diagonally across from her, quite a way down the long table, and she could see him under her lashes if she peeked, but she did so only a few times. David was delightful, a boyish curate who had come up from the country to meet Braddon's intended wife.

"You're very brave to take on Braddon," he said.

"Why so?" Sophie took another sip of her champagne. She could feel the wine going to her head and she was letting it, letting the bubbles cloud her judgment and lend her a breathlessly intoxicated joy.

"Braddon was such a task at school." David chortled. "There was a group of us—myself, Alex and Patrick, Quill—we took it on ourselves to get Braddon through. But it wasn't easy. Someone had to hammer facts into his head the night before an exam. Not that it was such a chore," David added hastily, remembering that he shouldn't insult the brain of Sophie's soon-to-be husband. "The real problem was Braddon's schemes. He was almost thrown out several times."

"Schemes?" Sophie was only half listening. Down the table that French minx Daphne Boch was flirting madly with Patrick. Under the table the toe of Sophie's slipper started tapping as she saw Daphne lean toward Patrick, wantonly brushing his arm with her shoulder.

David was still talking and Sophie wrenched her attention back to him.

"Take, for example, the time that Braddon decided he could fool Master Woolton into thinking that he was his own uncle. You see, Braddon's uncle is a famous explorer. And Woolton had mentioned to Braddon how much he'd like to meet this uncle. So Braddon got the idea that if he rented an appropriate costume he could pretend to be his own uncle and tell Woolton how remarkably intelligent he thought Braddon was, and then Woolton would be nicer to Braddon."

Sophie was fascinated despite herself. "That's absurd. How old was he?"

"Around thirteen, perhaps fourteen." David chortled again. "Believe me, we did our best to talk him out of the idea, but Braddon was convinced it would work. Braddon has a great weakness for acting, you know, that's why—" He broke off suddenly. One did not tell a lady that her future husband's mistresses had mostly been actresses.

"That's why . . . ?" Sophie prompted.

"That's why so many of his schemes have a theatrical element," David replied lamely. "Braddon is happiest when he puts on a great cloak and a fake mustache."

"What happened with Mr. Woolton?"

David shuddered. "Braddon went down to High Street and bought an absurd cloak. I can't think whom it was originally designed for. It was black with a red satin stripe around the bottom—quite the most gaudy piece of clothing you can imagine. But Braddon said this was what an explorer would wear. And he stuck a quantity of fake hair all over his face."

"Yes?"

"It was a disaster, of course. Woolton undoubtedly saw through him from the first moment, although Braddon maintains that Woolton politely offered him some coffee and the scheme fell apart only when he asked where Braddon had bought that cloak, and Braddon said it was the gift of the Tringelloo tribe in the upper reaches of the Alps."

Sophie turned her head and gave Braddon a long, speculative look. He was chewing busily, waving his fork as he talked to Miss Barbara Lewnstown, who sat on his right.

"It's hard to believe," she said finally, turning back to David. "Frankly, I shouldn't have thought that Braddon had the imagination."

"Oh, he didn't think up the details," David admitted. "Those were all Patrick's, of course. He was the one with imagination. Patrick made up loads of tales about incredible events that had supposedly happened in the depths of Africa and in the Alps, and Braddon was supposed to tell them to Woolton . . . but it all came to naught, because it turned out that the master's sister had a shop in the High Street and she had actually sold Braddon the cloak! And Woolton had seen it there, probably hankered after it himself, the lobcock, and so he caught Braddon out. He didn't take it nicely, either. He put Braddon on notice for three weeks afterwards."

"My goodness," Sophie said. "Your schooling sounds much more exciting than mine."

"Not Eton." David thought about it for a moment. "School was tedious, but Braddon always had a scheme, and Patrick—Patrick is a regular devil, you know—he egged Braddon into the worst of 'em, and so between them they livened things up."

Sophie risked another peek down the table. To her horror, Patrick was looking at her, and his eyes met hers with such an air of warm amusement that she colored and turned her head sharply back to David.

"I can certainly see Patrick Foakes indulging himself in falsehoods," she said tartly. Why, oh why couldn't she remember that Patrick was the worst of all rakes and exactly what she had sworn to avoid?

"Not falsehoods," David explained. "He's actually quite a stickler when it comes to honesty, Patrick is. I remember he would endlessly wrangle with his brother over the ethics of social fibs. Patrick hates lies. He would get enraged if Alex told the smallest sort of fib, even to get out of a music lesson."

Just then Charlotte stood up, giving the signal for the ladies to leave the room, and Sophie gratefully filed out after her mother.

After the ladies were assembled in Charlotte's private drawing room, Charlotte clapped her hands for attention. "We ought to have some dancing, don't you think?"

The younger girls chattered and clamored for dancing. Even Sophie's mother allowed as how it would be proper to get up some couples for a country dance or two.

So when the men rose from the dinner table they were directed to the garden room. They trooped in, carrying with them a faint, rich smell of cognac and a lingering woodsy smell of cigars, only to find that the ladies were busily directing footmen hither and thither, and that those footmen were carrying chairs out of the room and pushing sofas back against the walls.

Charlotte judged the party too small to move into the Sheffield House ballroom, where they might feel quite dwarfed and thin with only ten couples. But the numbers were perfect for the garden drawing room. Moreover, since it was an unseasonably warm night, she had had all the French windows opened onto the terrace, and footmen were arranging large potted torches around the veranda. One by one, the torches flared into light, casting golden rays into the dusky warmth of the London sky.

The Earl of Sheffield and Downes himself, who had strolled into the room at the tail of the group of male guests, narrowed his eyes. Where the devil had those monstrous torches come from? And why didn't he know anything about the twelve-person group of musicians even now warming up at one end of the long room? And what was this bothersome wife of his saying?

"I'm sure you agree with me, Alexander dear," Charlotte said sweetly, curtsying before him. Alex made an elegant leg in reply, but as he straightened he picked up his wife, tucked her adroitly into his arms and carried her out of the room.

There was a faint shriek of surprise from those ladies who caught sight of Alex's maneuver, but Charlotte just giggled. Sophie's mother shuddered and turned back to a conversation with her future son-in-law.

Out in the hallway, Alex let Charlotte slide slowly down his front until her toes touched the floor, keeping his arms around her.

"And what do you think you're doing, Madam Wife?"

Charlotte could feel Alex's large hands on her back . . . they were inching downward as his breath grazed her ear.

"Alex!" she hissed. Footmen were still coming in and out of the garden room door.

"Are you by any chance planning to influence the lovely Sophie's choice of husband?" Alex's hands ran a bit lower. Despite herself, Charlotte swayed.

"No!"

Alex bit her ear softly.

"All right, yes! I thought I would give your brother a chance to . . ."

"I love it when your voice goes all husky like that," her husband informed her. "Why don't we go upstairs and check on the children?"

"No!"

"Yes?" Warm lips traced a path down her neck.

"No." Charlotte pulled herself from Alex's grasp, smiling up at him. "You are a wicked reprobate," she informed him. "Just think what Sophie's mama is thinking about us. You know how strict the marchioness is."

"She's thinking the same thing she always thought," Alex said, looking pensive. "That you're a wild rackety thing who led me astray, and then did the same to Sophie . . . and if she knew that you had plans to derail this fine marriage she's managed to talk your Sophie into, she'd flay you alive, m'dear!"

"Well, we aren't going to tell her." Charlotte looked pleadingly up at Alex. "I need you to help me, Alex. Don't you want your twin to be happy?"

"I'm not absolutely sure that Sophie will make Patrick happy," Alex said. "He hasn't shown strong inclination to get married."

"That's not the point. They are on the verge of falling in love. And if Sophie marries Braddon, and *then* falls in love with Patrick—"

"I see your point." Alex rubbed his chin.

"Or what if Patrick marries the wrong person, out of pique because Sophie rejected him?"

Alex knew all about the perils of marrying the wrong person. He tucked his countess's arm under his and turned back toward the door.

"What do you want me to do?" He cast her a conspiratorial grin.

"Get Braddon out of the way," Charlotte shot back quickly.

The earl and countess walked back into the drawing room as if nothing had happened, as if earls always carried their countesses from the room without a by-your-leave.

Patrick was leaning on the piano. Daphne Boch was looking up at him with melting eyes as she played a languorous air.

Charlotte pinched her husband. "You see?"

Alex looked at her, eyes warmly black under his lashes. "Your every wish is my command, Countess." Then he added wickedly, "As always."

A pink flush crept up Charlotte's cheeks as her husband strolled toward the group at the piano.

As Braddon bowed before Sophie, she noticed out of the corner of her eye that Patrick seemed—naturally!—to have engaged Miss Boch's hand for the first dance, a cotillion. Sophie and Braddon went through their paces primly, a more-than-appropriate space between their bodies. Sophie caught her mother's eye and easily read the gleam of approval there.

They were making their way, rather tediously if the truth be told, toward the bottom of the room, when Braddon executed a quick step, pulling Sophie sharply back and to the right.

"Sorry, Lady Sophie." He was puffing a bit from the unwonted exercise. "Foakes is a foul dancer, always was."

Sophie looked curiously over her shoulder. Patrick did seem to have a reckless disregard for the welfare of other dancers. He and Daphne were coming down the dance floor. He was holding Daphne's hands high in the air. Maybe that was making Daphne's cheeks rosy, or perhaps it was Patrick's dancing. Even as she watched he added an improvised series of swinging circles. Around and around they went, Daphne half protesting, until they came to a halt at the bottom of the room, Patrick laughing down at his partner.

"My lord, my head is reeling!" Daphne's voice sounded prissy to Sophie, and she wrinkled her nose as she and Braddon decorously slowed to a standstill.

Braddon stopped with a grateful sigh. "There you are," he said, wiping his forehead with a large silk handkerchief. "Trifle hot in here, isn't it? Would you like to wander outside? I am sure no one could object, given our status."

Sophie stared at him, not at all sure what he meant.

"Our status as an engaged couple," Braddon repeated patiently. He was quite used to not being understood and never took affront.

"Oh yes," Sophie murmured. She allowed him to lead her out to the terrace, where they were joined by the majority of the dancers. But when Patrick solicitously led Daphne Boch onto the terrace, Sophie turned away.

"Come along, Braddon," she said briskly.

Braddon looked at her in a rather startled fashion. His betrothed had never addressed him by his first name before. And there she was, picking her way around the large pots lining the terrace and heading down a garden path.

"Oh, I say—" Braddon plunged after her.

Sophie paused just outside the circle of light cast by the torches.

"You are quite right, my dear sir," Sophie said encouragingly, patting Braddon's arm. "There can be no negative attention given to us, considering our status." They walked a little way down one of the brick-lined paths.

"It's rather dark out here," Braddon said. He was feeling a bit nonplussed. What were they doing out in the garden? What *would* people think? It looked peculiar, to his mind.

Sophie stopped and leaned against a tree. In the soft dark, her dress had a faint golden gleam, a faint golden echo of the moon.

"Would you like to kiss me?"

Braddon looked down at her and opened his mouth before he thought. "No."

"No?"

"That is, of course, naturally," Braddon scrambled, well aware that the expression of shock on Sophie's face boded ill for marital peace. "I just don't think of you in those terms," he added rashly, digging himself in deeper.

"You don't think of me in those terms?"

To his relief, Sophie seemed not to be the hysterical type. In fact, she looked rather thoughtful, and really quite lovely. He much preferred a woman with some meat on her bones, but still, Sophie York would make a very pretty countess, to Braddon's mind.

"You're very beautiful." His tone was hopeful, a peace offering.

"Thank you, Braddon." Sophie sighed. "I think we had better rejoin the party now."

Her mind was racing with humiliation and confusion. She was marrying a man who didn't think of her in terms of kissing, and the man whom *she* thought of (in terms of kissing) was completely ignoring her.

Just then Alex appeared in the tall French door, smiling genially. "Lady Sophie, may I borrow your beloved for a minute?"

With a huffing bow and a tug at his waistcoat, Braddon happily followed Alex into the house, leaving Sophie stranded on the terrace. She drifted to the right—she couldn't drift left, as *he* was over there.

Lucien Boch greeted her smilingly. Lucien was one of her favorite beaux. Even so, Sophie looked at him with guarded coolness. After all, it was Lucien's sister who was making a peagoose of herself by hanging on Patrick's arm.

"Woe is me!" Lucien said, his black eyes snapping with charm. "Somehow I have fallen into the bad graces of my favorite Englishwoman. Tell me it is not due to your upcoming marriage, Lady Sophie! My heart will always be at your feet . . . marriage or no."

Despite herself, Sophie found she was smiling at his nonsense.

Lucien leaned closer, his French accent making his words whimsically seductive. "I must tell you, Lady Sophie, that a true Frenchman would never allow a paltry thing like marriage lines to prevent him from laying his heart at his true love's door. No indeed."

"I am sure you would not," Sophie replied with a laugh. "But we who are only half-French . . . alas, we find ourselves bound by convention."

"What a loss," Lucien said mournfully. "At the very least, my dear lady, you must promise that I may remain your chevalier after you become a countess. I shall—" Whatever extravagant gesture Lucien was about to promise was interrupted by Charlotte, who clapped her hands sharply.

"Hear ye, hear ye," she said gaily. "Let's have an old-fashioned game before we finish the evening, shall we? I suggest that we play one game of hide-and-seek, or shall we play blindman's buff?"

"Hide-and-seek!" cried the young ladies.

"Hide-and-seek it is," Charlotte said. She opened her hand to show a long scarf of silky purple. "Lady Sophie is 'it,' since this party is in her honor. Whoever finds Lady Sophie may take the scarf, and then that person becomes 'it.' The only rule is that you must answer honestly if someone asks you whether you have the scarf."

There were only a few objections and questions, and Charlotte had to reexplain the new twist in the rules—the addition of the scarf—but she could tell that eyes were brightening. The possibilities for dalliance during this game were endless, as anyone could tell. At Charlotte's quick instruction, footmen picked up the lighted torches and deposited them around the winding paths of the garden, making it look like a twinkling starry patch of night.

Before Sophie had time to think, Charlotte swooped down on her and wound the scarf around her neck. "Go to the summerhouse!" Charlotte whispered, and gave Sophie a push toward the edge of the terrace. Sophie ran mindlessly down a garden path.

She felt miserable, really miserable. What if Charlotte was right to insist that marrying Braddon was a bad idea? Sophie found the summerhouse and sank onto a white bench, grateful for the moment of silence. In the distance she could faintly hear Charlotte's high, clear voice counting to one hundred.

No, marrying Braddon was the right thing to do. Because if she was clear-headed about the evening, it was not Braddon's disinclination to kiss her—who really cared anyway?—but Patrick's flirtation with Daphne Boch that was making her stomach twist into miserable knots. And burning jealousy was precisely the emotion that she planned to avoid by marrying Braddon.

Sophie leaned her head back on the latticed frame of the summerhouse and closed her eyes. Her mind was clearing, the anguish draining out of her. What I should do is hasten my marriage to Braddon, she thought. Because once I really *am* Braddon's wife, I shall stop hankering after the greatest rake of them all, Patrick Foakes.

Her eyes snapped open as there was a light tug on the scarf around her neck.

"Oh! I didn't hear you come up the walk," she said lamely.

"Hmm." Patrick Foakes increased his tug on the scarf and Sophie obediently bent her neck as the silky band slipped from her neck. She felt suddenly shy, meeting Patrick's eyes.

"Thinking about the delights of marriage?" His tone was soft, unthreatening.

Sophie stood up. She had no illusions about where this conversation might lead her. She took a step forward, but Patrick was standing in the doorway of the summerhouse, one knee up and braced against the top step. He didn't move back as she approached.

A pulse of excitement started in Sophie's spine, a weakening tremor of electricity that drifted down her legs.

"The delights of marriage," she repeated meditatively—wickedly. A smile trembled at the corner of her mouth. "Are they very sweet?" She cocked her head to the side like an inquisitive robin.

"I believe so." Patrick's face was impassive. She was an unbelievable tease, Sophie York. Damned if he'd ever met anyone as alluring in his life. Where her hair had fallen to the side, the moonlight painted her neck as white as a lily.

He stepped up and into the summerhouse. His large hand captured the fall of her hair, tugging her head to the side.

"What are you doing?" Sophie wasn't very worried; if she was honest with herself, she'd waited for this moment all night. His large body was so close to her that she could feel its heat through the flimsy material of her gown.

"Do you know a poem with a line like this: 'Your lips are red, soft and sweet'?" Patrick's voice was husky. She felt his fingers running down the silken currents of her curls. "Do you know that poem, Sophie?"

"No," she said a little shakily. He tugged on her hair again, her head tilting once more, as his right hand swept her against his muscled body. Her tiny gasp lingered on the air as warm lips caressed the sweep of her exposed throat.

" 'Your cherry lip, red, soft and sweet, proclaims such

fruit for taste is meet,' " Patrick said lazily, punctuating his words with kisses.

"Is this one of the 'delights of marriage'?" Sophie was desperately trying to be rational in the face of a whirlwind of sensations.

"One of 'em," Patrick agreed. He was holding her against him with both hands, hands that were wandering all over her small body, now touching the arch of her bottom, the tender curve where her leg began (Sophie gasped), and finally the generous curve of her breast, so easily released from Madame Carême's tiny bodice.

"I don't know if . . ."

Sophie's voice trailed off as Patrick's mouth closed over hers, a commanding, silencing promise of unnamed delights. Unbidden, she opened her mouth and welcomed his invasion, her arms creeping up to tangle in the curls of his hair.

When Patrick pulled away and cocked his ear toward Sheffield House, her body naturally swayed back toward him, her mouth raised.

"You're a treasure." Patrick's voice had a husky help-lessness to it. "Sophie."

Sophie smiled, emboldened by the heady freedom of the shadowy summerhouse. "If I am a treasure, do you have the key?"

An answering smile lit Patrick's eyes as he pulled her against him, almost roughly.

"Odd." His voice was deep velvet. "They seem to be playing even though we have the scarf." Sure enough, Sophie dimly heard the excited calls of players in the distance.

The sound brought her back to her senses. "No! We might be seen!"

Patrick stopped immediately, lifting his lips from hers. "That's the only thing that bothers you, isn't it?" His mouth twisted. "If someone discovered us, you would have to marry me rather than your earl."

Sophie didn't grasp his meaning. Patrick's face was caught in a beam of moonlight that stroked down through the lattice roof of the summerhouse. It caught the planes and angles of his bones, emphasizing the rough beauty of his cheekbones and the dark shadow cast by his eyelashes.

Unthinkingly she raised her fingers to his cheek. "You're beautiful," she whispered.

But Patrick pulled back from her touch. "I'm very much afraid, Lady Sophie, that your betrothed will be missing your presence." His tone was courteous, but his jaw was set.

Sophie opened her mouth—and then stopped. He was right.

Patrick's expression hardened at the heartbeat of silence between them. Briskly he wound the purple scarf around his arm. "It was lovely to see you, Countess. As always."

Sophie shuddered, standing there in the warm darkness. Two tears snaked their way down her cheeks.

Oh God, she'd done it. Without getting married, she'd managed to ruin her life by falling in love with a rake. Two more tears followed the first ones.

Then Sophie straightened her back in an unconscious imitation of her mother's ramrod-straight spine. At least *he* would never know . . . and the world would never know. She would make certain, absolutely certain, from that moment forward, that all of London thought she was desperately in love with Braddon. If they even suspected what she felt for Patrick, the humiliation would be unending. Sophie shuddered again.

Walking from the garden, Sophie fell into the company of two young ladies who were chattering feverishly about scarves and stolen kisses. Together they flung themselves through the doors to the house, Sophie's giggle sounding hollow to her ears.

In its inimitable way, the English weather had suddenly decided to stop imitating a southern clime. Wispy rain hissed into the garden torches, and footmen promptly pulled the doors shut behind the girls.

Braddon was sitting next to his mother and looked up gratefully when Sophie approached. "My lord." She gave him a blinding smile.

Braddon bowed. "Lady Sophie, I believe that they are calling for a dance. Will you do me the honor?"

As they moved rather ponderously into a boulanger, Sophie had a moment's qualm. A lifetime of labored dancing lay ahead of her. Nothing in her experience of the world led her to believe that Braddon's waistline would lessen after marriage; in fact, he looked as if he might attain the girth of his deceased papa.

But when they reached the bottom of the room, she looked up to find Braddon's friendly blue eyes twinkling down at her. "Did you have a good time in the garden, Lady Sophie? Some infernal game Lady Sheffield thought up, what? I had the scarf myself for a bit," he confided, "but then Patrick Foakes wandered up, bold as brass, and he had another one, just like mine. So it looks as if she was playing a bit of ducks and drakes with us, don't you know."

Sophie thought about that and wondered. Ducks and drakes was right. Two scarves—and how *had* Patrick found her so quickly?

"Braddon," she said, "shall we sit comfortably for a moment or two? I should dearly love to discuss something with you."

Braddon looked slightly alarmed. Ladies who announced the wish to converse with a person normally didn't have a very pleasant topic in mind, in his experience.

Sure enough, a moment later he was shocked to the backbone.

"But—but—Lady Sophie!"

"I simply can't wait. My feelings for you are so strong." Sophie's eyes were sweetly anguished, looking up at Braddon's face.

She saw immediately that there was no point in insisting that she wished to elope due to love. The concept wasn't in Braddon's emotional vocabulary. She lowered her voice.

"It's my mother. She's driving me to the brink. You and I"—she put her hand on Braddon's arm—"are adults, for goodness' sake."

"Absolutely." Braddon was still uncertain, but he felt a sympathetic glow when Sophie mentioned her mama. Now there they really had something in common. "I know just what you mean," he confided. "My mama has . . . well, you know her."

"Then let's elope!" Sophie looked up into Braddon's face hopefully.

"Can't do it, m'dear." Braddon was shaking his head. "Wouldn't be proper. Plus, my mother would never forget it, and I would hear about it the rest of my life. Do you know, she's still talking about the time I disobeyed her and ran off to see a cockfight? I was all of twelve years old."

Sophie leaned in toward Braddon, consciously making her expression as beguiling as she could. She pouted slightly.

"Oh, Braddon, you aren't *afraid* of your mother, are you?"

"Naturally," Braddon retorted. "My mother's a terrifying old bird, you ask anyone. Besides"—and he looked suspicious—"isn't this all because of you being afraid of *your* mama?"

Sophie was just marshaling her arguments for a new

attack when a stern voice broke into their conversation. Sophie's mother, the marchioness, was standing before them, the jut of her bosom indicating the utmost distaste.

"This party," she said, her tone dripping with rancor, "is a disgrace."

Automatically Sophie looked about for her father. There he was, seated quite properly next to Sylvester Bredbeck. In fact, George had acted with propriety all evening, at least at those points at which she had glimpsed him.

Braddon hastily rose and offered the marchioness his chair.

Eloise sat down, although she was clearly longing to call for her coach. "Miss Daphne Boch cannot be located," she remarked in glacial tones, "and neither can our host's brother, Patrick Foakes." She leveled a basilisk stare at her daughter. "It appears that they were last seen heading into the garden. Miss Daphne's brother can't seem to find her."

Braddon gulped. "I'm sure they will reappear very quickly," he said, all too aware of the stories that had circulated about Sophie and Patrick.

Sophie stared down at her lap. Somehow her fingers had laced themselves so tightly around one another that they didn't look as if they'd ever undo.

"I doubt *that* young lady will be foolish enough to reject Foakes's hand." Eloise dealt her daughter another enraged look. It galled Eloise to the quick that her daughter had made a fool of herself with a man who clearly made a hobby of compromising young ladies. Foakes must be desperate for marriage or some such.

Sophie felt Braddon's shoulder press comfortingly against hers as he drew up a chair. His voice was soothing. "Patrick told me that Lady Sophie rejected his suit, and I can say only that I consider it a stroke of the greatest good fortune that she was still available to accept my hand."

Braddon picked up Sophie's knotted hands and gave them a brisk shake, pulling them apart. Then he romantically raised the limp hand he held, pressing a kiss on its back.

The marchioness looked at Braddon approvingly. Here was a young man with proper sentiment, and a pretty way of saying things too. In fact, he quite reminded Eloise of the bucks who used to court her in her youth.

Sophie's heart was racing. Patrick was going to be married, going to be married, married to that French tart Daphne.

"Maman," she said, raising her head for the first time. "I seem to have quite a headache coming on. May Lord Slaslow escort me back to our house?"

Eloise bent a stern eye on her daughter. Was she going to wreck her engagement by some rash, impudent behavior that would make the earl take a disgust for her? No. In fact, Sophie looked a bit pinched and rather pale. A motherly frown crossed Eloise's face.

"Of course," she responded. "I shall rouse your father and make our farewells as soon as possible. And I shall give your apologies and those of Lord Slaslow to our host and hostess, as soon as they can be located." She cast a sharp look around the garden room but neither Alex nor Charlotte was to be seen.

"Do go home immediately, Sophie, and ask Simone to have Cook make you a posset. There's nothing like one of Cook's possets for a nervous headache."

Sophie smiled at her mother and rose, clutching Braddon's velvet coat with bloodless fingers. Braddon was such an accommodating person, she thought gratefully, as he whisked her out of the room full of chattering couples. No one was talking about anything but the disappearance of Daphne Boch, Patrick Foakes, *and* Daphne's brother, Lucien. The general consensus was that Lucien had challenged Patrick and they were at this very moment exchanging the names of their seconds.

Meanwhile, Sophie had thought of a second line of attack. "You see, Braddon," she said, scooting about on the coach seat so that she was sitting just next to her soon-to-be husband, "what we need is a *scheme,* a way to escape all the endless formal parties and tedious engagements that will bore us silly for the next four months . . . unless we come up with a scheme."

"A scheme," Braddon repeated.

Surely there was a kindling of interest in his eyes?

"I thought you could acquire a large black cloak," Sophie said enticingly. "And perhaps, if you knew where to find such a thing, you could rent one of those false beards that actors wear."

"By Jove, I know just the thing!" Braddon was excited. "But whatever for?"

"For our elopement," Sophie cried. "After we are married, naturally, we will settle down to a life of domesticity. No theatricals. In fact, we will likely attend the theater only rarely. This would be a last dash of excitement—and all we need is a brilliant scheme to carry it off!"

"Ahh," Braddon breathed. Visions of a rented wig and a curled mustache danced before his eyes.

"Because," Sophie said earnestly, "if we let our mothers dominate this period in our life, they will try to run every aspect of our married life as well. Why, my mother has announced the intention of spending every waking moment with me once I am a married lady."

"Really." Braddon's tone was hollow.

"Yes, and I expect it will only get worse once we have children. Because *both* our mothers will be constantly at our house, expecting to be entertained by the children. We must take this move toward freedom."

Braddon was a bit confused. Where did freedom come into the whole thing? "I don't see why I have to obtain a cloak."

"You need the cloak so that no one will recognize you

when we elope," Sophie said. "People look only at clothes. In a cloak and false beard, you could be anyone!"

There was a moment's silence. "That may be true," Braddon said, "but I still don't see why—"

"If we don't elope," Sophie broke in a bit wildly, "we might as well not marry at all. In fact, if you don't come to my house tomorrow night, I *won't* marry you, Braddon Chatwin!" To Braddon's dismay, his betrothed seemed to have a hysterical streak, and the way she was clutching his arm, she was sure to crush his velvet coat.

Visions of his mother's face when he told her that Sophie had broken off the engagement raced through his mind. Yet perhaps more significant, growing in his heart was a fervent longing for greasepaint and for the sticky glue used to affix a false beard to one's face. There was such delight in swirling a large black cloak. No one looked at him condescendingly or called him "silly Slaslow," or even less complimentary nicknames, when he was dressed all in black.

"There's no need to be tetchy about it," he said finally. "All right. I'll do it."

Sophie knew she had to capitalize on her success before Braddon thought it through or, worse, discussed the plan with one of his more sensible friends.

"I shall expect you tomorrow," she replied firmly. "Tomorrow at midnight. Be *sure* not to tell anyone, Braddon. People are such spoilers."

Sophie dropped her voice to a thrilling whisper. "Midnight is the best time for schemes. . . . I shall arrange to have a ladder propped up to my window. When you arrive in your cloak, you can climb the ladder and carry me off!"

Braddon was fascinated at the idea of climbing a ladder with his cloak billowing behind him, and carrying a lovely maiden off into the night. And since he was marrying Sophie anyway, why not get it over with?

"All right," he agreed. "Midnight."

The coach jolted to a halt. As the footman opened the door, Braddon descended, feeling a good deal more dashing than he had when he'd entered the coach. He held out his hand and Sophie placed her small fingers trustingly in his. As he walked her up the marble steps to her door, she paused a step ahead of him, so that their faces were level.

"You are my champion," she whispered.

Almost mesmerized, Braddon bent forward and his lips brushed hers reverently. Then he bowed and departed.

Sophie walked into the house, tired but well satisfied. So what if Patrick Foakes was to marry a horrid French girl who had thrown herself at his head? She, Sophie, was going to be married well before Patrick even sorted out the settlements with Lucien Boch, and once she was married, she wouldn't think about Patrick, or Patrick's disturbing eyes, or his quicksilver touch, ever again.

Back at Sheffield House, there was a faint hiss of excitement when the Honorable Patrick Foakes strolled through the French doors of the garden room shoulder to shoulder with his brother, the earl. Miss Daphne Boch was nowhere to be seen!

Barbara Lewnstown counted herself a special friend of Daphne's and had been busily recounting Daphne's likely married bliss with Patrick.

"Oh la," she cried airily to Patrick, "where is my dearest Daphne?"

Patrick looked singularly indifferent. "As soon as we stepped outside a bee stung her just below her eye. It swelled up quite hideously," he added, in response to Barbara's dismayed shriek. "Charlotte took her off to pack some mud on it."

From romance to a swollen bee bite . . . Not even the most assiduous of scandalmongers could believe that Patrick Foakes would feel any necessity to propose to the poor girl the next morning. Probably that bite put him off her for good, they reasoned. His tone was far too dispassionate for one whose heart had been touched by the girl's cruel fate. Why, Daphne might not be able to attend social events for a week or more!

Chapter 7

~⟡~

Braddon Chatwin woke up the next morning with a pleasurable sense of anticipation. For a moment he stared sleepily at the blue chintz hangings that adorned his bedstead. Black cloaks and false mustaches had tangled together in his dreams.

Then memory seeped back. Lady Sophie York wanted to elope, and she wanted him to wear a cloak and mustache, and she threatened not to marry him if he didn't appear at midnight. Laboriously Braddon sorted out the mingled strains of Sophie's demand.

In the cold light of morning it seemed as mad as Bedlam, that was the only thing one could call it. If they ran off to Gretna Green, people would undoubtedly assume that they had anticipated the wedding night. Except she didn't think of that, Braddon thought complacently. Well-bred young ladies don't know the first thing about sex, so of course Sophie didn't know what people would say about a runaway marriage. But given that there was nothing to prevent Braddon and Sophie from sedately marrying in St. George's some four months from now, people would naturally draw conclusions about why they tied the knot so hastily. It wasn't as if it were a love match or anything.

As to the question of *why* Sophie wanted to elope, Braddon put it out of his mind. He had decided long ago that the ways of women were impossible to understand.

He rang the bell for hot chocolate and then put his arms behind his head. Now what he had to do was turn his talent for schemes to one which would fool his future wife. In other words, he needed a plan that would outscheme her scheme, because there was no way in heaven he was going to do anything as featherheaded as tearing off to Scotland to get married when he didn't even have to.

And what's more, the trip would take at least two or three days there *and* the same back. If it didn't take longer—traveling to Scotland in December! Granted, not a speck of snow had fallen this year. But he'd be damned if he'd leave Madeleine even for a week. Not now, when the very thought of her fired his heart and made him want to jump from his bed and go down to her father's stables to see if he could catch a glimpse of her.

Braddon's eyes darkened with annoyance. It wasn't as if Madeleine would leap up to greet him if he did go to the stables. She was proving to be annoyingly, persistently, chaste. In fact, she showed no sign of succumbing to his imploring letters, or his gifts (which she refused), or any of his efforts to turn her into a lifelong mistress. She just said stoutly that she didn't care for the position, and that was that. He had explained in vain that the daughter of the man who ran Vincent's Horse Emporium could not expect to make a good marriage, or perhaps any marriage at all. She didn't seem to care.

Braddon thoughtfully chewed on his lip as Kesgrave handed him his morning chocolate. Perhaps Madeleine was worried about her future. After all, the position of courtesan was a risky one, and she might not believe that he intended to act in such an unusual fashion. Perhaps he should summon his man of business and have a contract drawn up, right and tight, that would settle a good sum on Madeleine. Then she would understand that the relationship was forever, not for just a brief time.

Braddon absentmindedly drank some of his chocolate. The real problem was how to make Lady Sophie dance to his piping, while making it seem as if he were dancing to *her* tune. If he sent Sophie a message, she'd cry off the engagement for sure, in his judgment. Braddon had seen a quantity of hysterical women in his day, what with having three older sisters, and Sophie looked ready to fly off the handle at any moment. No, the trick was to appear at midnight—but not to end up in Gretna Green.

Braddon swung his feet out of bed. He shouldn't have thought about Madeleine. Because now he knew he wouldn't be able to do anything until he saw her and maybe even snatched a kiss, if her father wasn't looking.

Lord but her father could be as surly as a butcher's dog! You'd think his daughter *was* a lady, the way he carried on about Braddon compromising Madeleine's reputation and other rubbish. Braddon couldn't seem to make either one of them understand that women who live above horse stables don't *have* reputations—they just make 'em! Braddon chortled.

When his man Kesgrave came in to dress him, Braddon told him the joke about having versus making reputations, but Kesgrave just gave him his usual blank look and said, "Would you care to wear the blue cutaway today, my lord?"

Braddon sighed. It was a good thing he was an even-tempered type, what with all the slow-tops he was surrounded by.

"I'll wear that dust-colored one, Kesgrave. You know the one."

"Not dust, my lord." Kesgrave's tone was critical. "*Dun*-colored."

"That's the one. I'm going riding."

"Before breakfast?" Kesgrave's tone grew even more reproving.

Damned if he wasn't getting sick of having servants around who'd ruled over his nursery, Braddon thought.

"I'm going out." His tone was a bit defensive, despite himself. Dressed, Braddon trotted down the front steps as if he were a boy escaping to the park, swung up onto his horse, and clattered down the street heading for the Blackfriars, the location of Vincent's Horse Emporium.

The long, low stables were quiet. It was far too early for the little groups who would congregate under large oaks in the front yard later in the day, watching in a desultory sort of way as boys led out prancing Arabians and barrel-chested quarter horses.

Braddon dropped rather heavily off his horse and tossed the reins to a lad who was lingering around the place, hoping to earn a shilling.

He strode toward the stables. Madeleine was almost never seen around the stables during the afternoon because of her father's ridiculous sense of her "reputation," although Braddon actually thanked him for that, because it meant that he didn't have to compete with every shabby-genteel officer who strolled in looking for a broken-down mare.

Braddon walked quickly down the long corridor. The stables smelled dimly of a molasses-sticky poultice, and where there was a poultice, one could usually find Madeleine. It was she who was in charge of all minor ailments such as sprained hocks and forelegs.

Madeleine was in the very last stall on the right. She was kneeling on the ground with a horse's bent leg poised before her. She must have heard Braddon's boots clopping on the stone walkway, but she didn't look up, just kept crooning to a sweet brown-eyed mare while she applied the poultice to its front leg.

Braddon waited for a moment, shifting uneasily from foot to foot.

"My lord," Madeleine said without turning about, "if you are not too bored, you might help me by holding Gracie's head."

"How did you know it was me?" Braddon moved to the horse's head, keeping Gracie from blowing warm kisses down Madeleine's bent neck.

Madeleine threw him a glance over her shoulder. "You invariably appear around this hour every morning, my lord."

"Hmm." Braddon was a bit nonplussed by her matter-of-fact tone. Didn't Madeleine want him to come? He dropped the horse's bridle and crouched next to her, trying hard not to puff as he went down.

"What is the problem?"

"Strained right foreleg," Madeleine replied shortly.

Braddon cast the horse's leg a quick glance. Then he edged a little closer to Madeleine.

"My lord!"

She sounds cross, Braddon thought resignedly. No kisses today. Why, oh why, was he enamored of a French miss who was possessed of a demon temper and the morals of a nun? She wasn't nearly as beautiful as Arabella, the mistress he had stolen from Patrick last year. In fact, an objective person might label her short and plump.

But just looking at Madeleine made Braddon's heart beat faster. Bent over as she was, rubbing the foreleg hard and not meeting his eyes, he could just glimpse the ample curve of her bosom between her arms. His eyes kindled, and his hand itched to slip under her arm.

"Don't!"

Startled, Braddon swung up his head to meet his beloved's infuriated eyes.

"Why not?" he asked boldly.

Madeleine clambered to her feet, pulling her thick, stiff skirt out of the way. Her French accent thickened, as it always did when she was in a fret.

"Please do not try to balboozle me!"

"Balboozle?"

Braddon was confused and his lower lip opened a trifle. It was hard to keep his mind straight when Madeleine was standing right before him, her lovely chest heaving. She had such luscious hips. . . .

"Bamboozle! That's what you mean."

"That's what I said," Madeleine retorted impatiently. What was she to do with this muffin-brained lord? How could she do an honest day's work with him following her about the stables, gaping at her bosom and generally cutting up her peace?

Braddon's muffin-brain worked perfectly well in some situations. He yanked Madeleine into his arms so fast that she didn't have time to shout for her father before Braddon's mouth descended. And he kissed her while backing out of Gracie's stall, thereby proving that he could do two things at once, a skill which several of his friends might have disputed.

Despite herself, Madeleine relaxed. Life had been so hard the last years. It was heaven to stand in the circle of Braddon's arms. When he held her, it felt as if nothing evil would ever happen again.

She shook herself briskly, pushing hard at Braddon's chest. He was whispering something in her ear—one of his fancy promises, no doubt. She got the main idea. Her bacon-brained suitor wasn't a real suitor at all. He was what her mama, back in France, would have called a *libertin*. He wanted to ruin her and not marry her.

Braddon's arms went around her shoulders again.

"Don't look so sad, Madeleine." He whispered that, but she heard it loud and clear. "I hate it when you look so sad."

Perplexed, Madeleine paused for a moment, looking into Braddon's blue eyes.

"I am not sad," she said. "I only thought of my mother for a moment."

"You looked sad," Braddon persisted.

"I miss her," Madeleine said despite herself. She didn't want to share any emotional confidences with her immoral suitor.

Braddon kissed her ear. "Someday you will be a mother, Madeleine. You will have your own children, and then you will forget."

Madeleine took a deep breath.

"Not if you have your way," she pointed out. "You want to turn me into a courtesan, and those women never have children. They cannot afford them, given their way of life."

Braddon grinned. Trust Madeleine's hardheaded French common sense to point out that unusual disadvantage in the life of a courtesan.

"We're going to have children," he said confidently. "I knew we would as soon as I saw you. I never wanted little brats around, until I met you."

Madeleine's heart melted. He was just what she would like, this English lord, if only things were different. A bit light on top, perhaps, but with a truly sweet heart. And he was safe, trustworthy, and large. To Madeleine's mind, men should be large. She could keep him from making too much of a fool of himself, too. . . . But no. She was not going to be any man's courtesan, even if she stayed unmarried her entire life.

She pushed him away. "Go away, do!"

Braddon looked at Madeleine doubtfully. Her face had gone fierce again.

"I may have to leave for a few days." Did she look sorry? Braddon could not fool himself that she did.

"Good. I shall finally get some work done."

No, she definitely didn't look sorry. There was a little pause.

"Where will you be?"

"I have to elope," Braddon said. "That is, Lady Sophie wants to elope, but I don't, so I'm going to climb up a ladder and get her, but then I'm not actually going to take her to Gretna Green, because I don't want to elope. And besides, no one elopes in the middle of winter."

Madeleine's heart was thudding painfully. "Does Lady Sophie truly wish to elope?"

"Yes." Braddon's voice was a little doubtful. "I'm not sure that she is as suitable as I told you before. She had hysterics last night and told me that unless I climb a ladder to her room at midnight and elope with her, she won't marry me at all."

Madeleine almost laughed at Braddon's hangdog look, despite her own leaden unhappiness.

"I can't start over, Madeleine—Maddie!" Somehow he had managed to get those long arms around her again and he was talking into her hair. "I'd have to start over, going to Almack's and trying to find a girl who seems half reasonable. I've got to hold on to Lady Sophie. I simply have to figure out how to elope without eloping."

At least he doesn't seem genuinely attached to his future wife, Madeleine thought painfully.

"Why don't you want to elope?" It seemed like a reasonable alternative.

Braddon pulled back, looking indignantly into Madeleine's unsympathetic brown eyes.

"Won't you miss me? It will take a week to get to

Gretna Green and back, if we don't get delayed. Why, I could be gone a whole fortnight!"

"I will not miss you," she retorted. "And you will not be welcome in the stables after you are married."

"Well, I would miss you," Braddon said stoutly. "And I don't believe you. I think you would miss me too. Anyway, I don't want to get married so soon." He gave Madeleine a little squeeze and then sank down on a pile of straw, pulling her onto his lap.

She gave a little *pooh!* of indignation, but relaxed. Braddon pulled her against his chest, enjoying the way Madeleine's soft curves felt against his legs.

"You're going to ruin your garments."

"Practical Maddie," Braddon whispered into her hair.

Practical Maddie's heart felt as if it were being squeezed.

"Why don't you pretend to break your leg?" The minute she said it, she cursed herself. What was she doing, showing interest in his marital plans?

"Break my leg? What d'you mean?"

"If you had a broken leg, you couldn't climb up a ladder," she explained brusquely.

Braddon slowly thought it through.

"Damned if you're not right, Maddie m'girl! I'll write Lady Sophie a note and tell her I broke my leg, and that will give her time to get over this odd start of hers."

"Was she really hysterical?"

He frowned. "Close enough."

"Well, then she probably won't believe your note," Madeleine said. "I wouldn't. I would think that you were just trying to beg off, and that you were too stuffy to elope."

Appalled, she listened to her own voice. Was there a note of rancor in her tone? She had no right even to *think* about marrying an Earl of the Realm! For goodness' sake, it was clear enough that the idea of marrying her, Maddie, had never crossed Braddon's mind.

"You think Lady Sophie won't believe my note?"

"She might break off your engagement."

Madeleine ignored the small voice in her heart that rejoiced at the idea of a broken engagement.

"Break off my engagement?" Braddon was clearly appalled. He clutched Maddie a little closer, thinking of his mother's wrath. Then he sat up.

"I have it! I need to really break my leg! I'll fall off a horse. Then all I have to do is get someone to fetch Sophie off that damned ladder and bring her over to my house, and she'll see the plaster. She can't blame me once she sees the evidence."

Madeleine sighed. Truly, her English lord needed someone to take care of him.

"Don't be such a bumble-brain! You can't break your leg as easily as all that."

"Yes, I can," Braddon retorted. "I broke my left leg when I was a young nipper, and the doctor told me to go easy, because it would break again as easy as look at it. I reckon all I'd have to do is fall off a horse on the left, and keep that leg under me, and I'd be sure to break it again."

Madeleine's heart chilled. "It would probably not heal properly, and you'd be left with a permanent limp. Then Lady Sophie wouldn't want you anyway."

"You think so?"

"Ladies all like to dance," Madeleine said with the certainty of someone who had no recollection of ever meeting a true lady. "No lady would ever marry a man who had a limp and couldn't dance."

"Oh."

Madeleine found, to her disgust, that she couldn't resist the disconsolate note in Braddon's voice. "I could give you an adhesive plaster," she stated baldly.

"What on earth do you mean?" Braddon had given up thinking about elopements and was nuzzling Madeleine's delicate ear with his lips, for all the world like Gracie the horse.

"We have all the materials here . . . for when a horse needs an ankle splint. I could give you a plaster and everyone would believe that you *had* broken your leg."

Braddon whooped and gave her an exuberant squeeze. "That's my Maddie!"

When Madeleine turned her head to shush him into silence, Braddon captured her mouth, and it was quite a while before they got down to business. But forty minutes later Braddon had suffered the slicing of his best breeches up the side, protesting only a little about Kesgrave's inevitable reaction, and Madeleine had wound a quite reasonable-looking plaster around his lower left leg.

There was an embarrassing bit, to Maddie's mind, when Braddon refused to let her see his bare leg and insisted on winding the first layer himself. But then she got revenge by slapping on enough plaster of paris to brace the ankle of an elephant.

In fact, by the time Braddon hopped out of the stables, supporting himself on Madeleine's shoulder, he felt as if he truly had injured his leg.

"Do you think you used a bit too much plaster?" Braddon looked dubiously at the monstrous bulge of white which covered his leg from knee to ankle.

"Oh no," Madeleine assured him. "Your leg was *very* broken. If you were a horse, we'd have had to put you down."

Braddon tossed two shillings to the boy watching his horse. "You'd better tie it up in the stables and then get me a hackney."

The boy looked curious. "Got yourself an injury, milord?"

Braddon sighed and threw him another coin. "The hackney."

"Right you are, milord." The boy ran off toward the street, leaving the horse tied to a pole.

"I suppose he'll remember my horse later," Braddon said doubtfully. He started to hop toward the gate to Vincent's Horse Emporium, delicately carrying his spare boot in his fingers. Kesgrave would kill him if he got greasy fingerprints on a boot, broken leg or no.

"Don't worry," Madeleine said. "I'll rescue your horse."

Braddon looked down affectionately at her soft rumpled hair.

"I love you, you know that?"

Madeleine stopped and clutched his arm. "Don't talk like that! What if Papa heard you? You're not even whispering."

Braddon shrugged. "I'm a wounded man. What can he do? And it's true. I love you, Maddie."

"Pooh! You are a rake," Madeleine said rudely. "You love me only because I have not given in to your demands." They were at the edge of the street now, and the hackney was waiting, its door open.

Madeleine turned about and almost marched off without saying another word. Then suddenly she thought of something. "You'll have to come back when you want that plaster removed. Unless you tell your man that it's a fake."

"No!" Braddon was revolted by the idea. "Kesgrave is a knaggy old gaffer. He'd have no sense of the fun of the thing. I shan't tell anyone. Madeleine . . ."

She stopped and looked back at him, a rounded, curvy girl, her brown hair catching gold lights in the dusty sunlight of the horse yard.

"Thank you for helping me."

Madeleine gave a sudden, sparkling grin. "It behooves a courtesan to ensure that her master doesn't get married," she observed. Then she laughed outright at the look of disgust that crossed Braddon's face.

"You are not just a courtesan!" he protested.

"I'm not a courtesan *at all*," Madeleine pointed out, and turned about again, walking quickly into the shadow of the stables.

From there she watched Braddon hop his way into the hackney, swearing fulsomely when the plaster caught and banged loudly against the hackney door. Good thing he hadn't really broken his leg. That little maneuver would have hurt like the devil, in Madeleine's opinion.

It was hard not to feel wistful, watching Braddon cram his large frame into the hackney. Life as his mistress would be blissful.

Madeleine shook herself. Poor Gracie! She had quite deserted her in the middle of bandaging her foreleg.

Poor Gracie indeed! Gracie had just licked up the last of the poultice intended for her leg, and when Madeleine's father appeared he found his daughter scolding the greedy nag in bursts of irritable French.

Chapter 8

❧

Patrick stared at his old friend in utter disbelief and then laughed, a short brutal laugh that had nothing to do with humor.

"She's your bride—you fetch her."

Braddon looked at him appealingly. Patrick was the only friend he had who could be trusted to follow through on a scheme in a pinch. Then he gestured at his monstrous plaster propped on a tufted footstool before him.

"Damn it, man, I can't make my way up a ladder with my leg like this!"

Patrick shrugged. "Then you can't elope."

"That's just it," Braddon squealed. "I don't *want* to elope. If you go up that ladder and bring Lady Sophie over here, she can see the state of my leg. Then she'll understand that eloping is out of the question. I'm in a cursed hobble, Patrick; you've simply got to help me."

"Send her a note."

Braddon stuck out his bottom lip in a characteristic pout. "Sophie'll toss me over. She seems to be the hysterical sort. She told me last night that if I don't fetch her off that ladder, she won't marry me at all.

"Hey!" he said suddenly. "I know why you're acting like a bear with a sore head." He grinned and looked at Patrick assessingly. "You're getting married yourself, aren't you? Miss Boch. Been out sizing wedding rings, have you?"

He almost quailed under the furious glance leveled at him by Patrick.

"Don't be more of a dunce than I'm used to, Braddon."

Braddon pouted again. "I hate it when you get that icy tone," he observed. "You can be more knaggy than your brother, and that's saying quite a bit. What's caught you on the raw? The whole room was talking about you strolling out in the moonlight with Miss Boch last night."

Suddenly Patrick's eyes flashed to his. "Last night," he said slowly. "Last night before you left?"

"That's right," Braddon confirmed. "You thought m'mother wouldn't notice when you two wandered off for a bit of a cuddle and didn't come back?"

"The girl got stung by a bee and started yowling," Patrick replied almost absently. "When did you hear about my supposed marriage? Before or after Sophie proposed such a rapid conclusion to your engagement?"

"Oh no!" Braddon said. "You can't get away with that! Sophie proposed an elopement well before you made such a scandal." He preened a bit. "I told you, Patrick. This may have been the only time I've been able to take a woman off the Foakes brothers, but Sophie *adores* me."

He paused. "You know, perhaps you shouldn't be the one to take her down the ladder." Braddon pulled at his long lower lip meditatively. "Do you think she might take offense at it?"

Patrick looked at him in disgust. Sometimes, for all the bonds of boyhood, he wondered how Braddon managed to get through the day without being murdered.

"Undoubtedly she will," he said coolly. "So you better just send one of your footmen up the ladder, because I'm not your man." He tossed off the glass of brandy in his hand.

"I can't do that," Braddon protested. "How can I send a footman up the ladder into the bedchamber of a gently bred lady—more, my future wife? No, it has to be you, Patrick, because I sent a message over to Alex and he hasn't shown up, so he probably didn't receive it."

"Alex is in the country," Patrick said.

"Well, there you are," Braddon replied. "I'd rather it not be you, given that you have a past with Sophie, but you're all I've got. I can't ask David to go up the ladder, because he's a priest, and besides, he didn't answer my note either. Lord knows Quill is in a worse state than I am. He can't climb a ladder."

"Oh for God's sake," Patrick said moodily.

"I'll tell you what," Braddon said, with a brighter note in his voice. "You can wear my mustache and cape, and she'll never know who you are."

Patrick poured himself more brandy. "Why should I?"

"What do you mean, why should you? Because we're friends, that's why. Because you're practically my brother. Because you *know* what my mama's like, and what she's liable to do to me if Sophie gives me the bag!"

Patrick stifled a sigh. Braddon's soulful eyes were fastened on him like those of a retriever that knows you're holding a bone behind your back.

Well, what the hell. Sophie didn't want to marry him, so why not act as a procurer for the man she *did* want to marry?

Braddon was still babbling away. "Look, look right here, Patrick!" He held up a large sack and pulled out a black thing that looked like a stubbly hedgehog.

"What in God's name is that?"

"A beard," Braddon said happily. "I bought it from the very best, Henslowe, the man who supplies all the Drury Lane costumes. And there's a cape too. Look—"

Patrick grimaced and drank some more brandy. So what if Lady Sophie York was suddenly wishful to ruin her reputation by eloping? What was it to him? Nothing. Not a thing. Why shouldn't he fetch her from the bloody ladder?

Braddon had been looking at him inquiringly and saw the telltale signs. "You'll do it!" He whooped out loud. "I knew it, Patrick. I knew I could count on you. Damn it, man, but you're up to the rig on every suit!"

"Insane, more like it," Patrick said. He cast a nasty glance at Braddon's leg. "How long do you have to wear that thing anyway?"

"Oh, a couple of weeks," Braddon said airily.

Patrick leveled him a glance under inky brows. "I thought it took six weeks for a broken limb to heal."

"You're probably right," Braddon agreed. "But you'd better be off, Patrick. Sophie is expecting me up the ladder at midnight—cursed late hour for eloping, if you ask me—and it's twenty to the hour now."

Patrick fingered the black hedgehog Braddon threw to him. It fell into two parts, revealing itself to be a beard and a mustache. Braddon then tossed him a small bottle. "There, stick it on with this stuff. You can use the mirror over the fireplace."

Patrick took off the bottle top and sniffed it. "No." His voice admitted no argument.

"Well at least wear the cape," Braddon implored. "It has a hood, so she won't be able to see who you are, at least until you get her on the ground. I don't want her to start screeching and wake the whole household. Sophie probably won't be pleased to realize that you've come up the ladder instead of me."

In Patrick's estimation, that was a vast understatement of Sophie's likely feelings about the matter.

But Braddon continued blithely. "What's more, you need the cape to wrap around her once you're on the ground. You can't ruin the reputation of my future wife by being seen with her in the middle of the night!"

Patrick's eyes flashed with amusement. "You're asking me to go into your future wife's bedchamber and fetch her into a solitary carriage, in the middle of the night, without her parents' knowledge, and you're worrying about her reputation?" He threw on the cloak and pulled up the hood, catching a glimpse of himself in the fireplace mirror. "My God, I look like a caricature—one of those medieval figures of Death. All I need is a rope belt and a sickle!"

Braddon pulled on his lip. "Sophie's reputation will be compromised only if someone recognizes the two of you. So you should wrap her in the cloak on the way to the carriage so that no one can see her face. I mean, if someone happens to be walking down the street at that hour."

Patrick sighed. The situation was ridiculous. The best he could do would be to fetch the chit and dump her at Braddon's house.

"I suppose you've thought about what you're going to do with her once she's in your house?"

Braddon nodded. "I'm sending her over to my grandmama's. The house is just a few streets over, and I already warned the housekeeper. Grandmama is in the country, so in the morning the housekeeper will simply escort Sophie back to her own house with no one the wiser."

~≈~

The cloak had about twice the volume of his riding cloak and Patrick had no doubt that he looked absurd. But it wasn't until he was standing in the pitch-dark gardens of

Brandenburg House, looking through his deep hood at a ladder which innocently leaned against a window, that he realized forcefully how absurd the night had become. He almost turned about and headed out of the garden; but just as he started to turn on his heel a soft voice hailed him from above.

"Lord Slaslow!"

Patrick looked up. He could only indistinctly see Sophie's small head and shoulders peeping out the window through the ladder studs.

"Well, come on down then," he snarled. "If you want to elope." Some Romeo I make, he thought savagely.

"Lord Slaslow—Braddon—I can't!" Sophie's voice was almost a wail.

Patrick moved a bit closer. "Why not?"

Sophie stared down at the dark form below her. Braddon's voice sounded surprisingly rough; he usually affected a soft, gentlemanly lisp. He was undoubtedly cross at the unconventional way in which she had forced him to appear in her garden and elope with her.

"Lord Slaslow, will you please come up and talk for a minute before eloping? *Please?*"

Sophie heard what sounded like a growl escaping through clenched teeth. Then the man below her moved toward the house and she nervously gripped the ladder. What if the ladder swung backward while her betrothed was climbing and he fell to the ground? That would certainly awaken the servants. And what if Braddon hurt himself? He wasn't exactly a nimble man.

But he seemed to be negotiating the ladder with careless grace. Sophie giggled nervously to herself, wondering if he had practiced during the day. As Braddon neared the windowsill she backed up in a little rush and perched herself on the bed. She had snuffed the candles, so the only light in the room was a very dim glow from the window itself.

Sophie almost gasped as the large cloaked figure swung his leg over the windowsill. Then he seemed to catch sight of her sitting on the bed and stopped for a second. Sophie could almost feel Braddon's eyes moving slowly over her body, even though she couldn't see his face at all, since it was buried inside the hood of his cape.

Finally he swung the other leg over the sill and jumped lightly into the room. He said nothing but simply leaned back on the windowsill, his cloak giving a tiny billow behind him and then settling around his broad shoulders. Sophie gulped.

"I suppose you're wondering why I'm not ready to elope." She stopped for a moment. "The reason I asked you . . . well, I asked you to come up here, Lord Slaslow," she said in a rush, "is that I've decided that I've been a complete peagoose and I know you'll be as mad as fire over it, but I just can't go down the ladder with you, not tonight and not . . . not anytime." Sophie tried to see Braddon's face but only the silhouette of his body was visible in the window. His cloak was really quite annoying.

"Oh?"

She hurried on. "I've been miserable all day, and I've thought and thought; I know how excited you were to elope, so I didn't want to simply tell you in a note, but I can't elope—and I don't wish to get married, either!"

At that, her betrothed—whose large frame was really starting to intimidate her, Sophie thought—crossed his arms over his chest.

But all he said was, "Why?"

"I know how much this means to you, to get married, that is, because of your mother, and I am *so* sorry about it, but . . . it just wouldn't be right!" Sophie ground miserably to a halt.

Something about the menacing silence in the window forced her back into speech, and all the thoughts that had been revolving in her head during the day tumbled out willy-nilly.

"You see, I had thought that we could scrape along in a marriage famously because we don't ... we don't *feel* anything for each other. Well, that's not exactly correct," she added punctiliously, "because I like you very much, Braddon, er, Lord Slaslow. But we—I—don't have the kind of feelings that a wife should feel for a husband!"

There was a moment of silence. Then: "No?"

"No!"

"Ah."

There really was something odd about Braddon's voice, Sophie thought. Surely it was much deeper than normal. And it had a velvety resonance that made her stomach feel a bit quivery; perhaps it was because it was the first time they had been alone together, unless she counted the garden when he'd said he didn't want to kiss her. The memory recharged her determination.

"Do you remember when we were in the garden and you didn't want to kiss me, because you don't think of me 'that way'? Well, a husband *should* think about his wife that way!" Sophie finished defiantly.

Still no response from the window. Then he rose with a fluid movement and walked a few steps toward the bed. Sophie stared hard at his face, but the cloak had such a deep hood that she couldn't see a thing. Hard hands cradled the back of her head, and she felt, rather than saw, a dark form bend over her.

"Experiment," a husky voice murmured, and lips descended on hers ... hard, forceful lips that invaded and pleasured, caressed and conquered.

"Oh!" Sophie gasped. Now Braddon was bending her backward—or was she falling backward? Her lips parted naturally to his and his tongue raided her soft mouth, making liquid fire rush up her limbs. No one had kissed her like that except for Patrick ... so a part of her mind said defiantly, See? There's nothing special about Patrick Foakes! Then niggling little thoughts about voices were lost in a sea of sensation.

For his part, Patrick wasn't thinking at all. He'd finally got Sophie where he wanted her, on a bed, and the discovery that her soft lips were just as intoxicating as they had been earlier was not one to inspire rational thought. His mouth burned over her skin. With a warm tongue he traced the outline of her lips, descended into the depths, kissed her until her body trembled and arched instinctively toward him, her fingers clenched in his curls.

He leaned over her, weight propped on one arm, then pulled back slightly and feathered kisses over her lips, teasing her until she moaned, a tiny broken noise that drifted into the midnight stillness. Sophie turned her head and tried to capture his lips, tried to bring him back, make him take her mouth again. Patrick's lips burned on hers, but lightly, danced up her cheekbone, pressed kisses on her eyelids, returned to her lips. She gasped, the breath hot in her chest as he finally took her mouth again, his tongue stabbing in and out, his thumb roughly rubbing her nipple through her nightgown.

A strangled whimper burst from her throat, and yet ... and yet ... Somewhere in the depths of her, she didn't *want* to feel this with Braddon. Even if Braddon was— somewhat surprisingly—capable of arousing this passion, she still didn't want to be Braddon's wife.

So she turned her head, sharply, and half croaked, "No!" When his lips pursued hers, and his tongue swept liquid fire down into her belly, Sophie sobbed or panted, but still she whispered "No," and "No, no, no." Finally small hands pushed at Patrick's chest and she sat up, staring straight ahead. Her betrothed stayed where he was, balanced on his side, propped on one elbow. She could feel his thoughtful gaze on her, but she didn't look.

"It doesn't make any difference, Braddon," Sophie gasped, catching her breath. "I don't know why . . . why we're doing this, but I still don't want to marry you." She stared ahead rigidly, not moving as large hands moved delicately among the long curls hanging down her back. When there was no answer she finally, reluctantly, turned.

Her heart stopped.

The hood was gone, and in the faint moonlight . . . Well, her body had known it wasn't Braddon all along, but now her eyes saw the sweep of long eyelashes and silver-tipped hair, the devil-bent eyebrows and square jaw. . . . Her mind grasped slowly what her body had known long ago, if only from the touch of his hands, from the press of a hard-muscled thigh through her gown.

"Oh," she whispered, the word falling on the night like a baby breathing in his sleep.

Patrick smiled back at her lazily, one eyebrow raised, his right hand still caressing her hair. Then the hand wrapped itself in silken strands and tugged, gently, pulling Sophie's warm body back onto the bed.

"I promise," said a smoky voice just at her ear, "that I feel *that way* about you, Sophie." A wicked, seductive tongue toyed with the delicate curves of her ear, warm breath igniting the burning warmth between her thighs again and numbing the surprise in her brain. Despite herself, she relaxed as Patrick drew her face toward his, lips descending to inflame hers. Oh, *this* was right; this was so right. She abandoned the tangled thoughts of cloaks and elopements, marriages and engagements, which had so plagued her during the day.

The moment Sophie's small fingers lightly touched his cheeks, running down the angles of his chin, something in Patrick relaxed as well. Her lips opened to his with the eternal allure of the seduced who seduces the seducer.

He almost growled, rolling over and pinning her beneath his body. Sophie gasped as his muscled male weight settled on her. Instantly, he rolled back on his side, lifting his weight.

"I'm sorry, sweetheart." The words drifted to her ear through a cloud of disappointed sensation. "I forgot what a little bit of a thing you are."

Sophie didn't bother to answer. Something within her was longing, aching, for his body to lie back on hers again, to press her down into the bed with his intoxicating weight. She reached up and tugged fiercely on his shoulders, straining up to meet his lips, her mouth open and inviting. So Patrick half rolled on top of her, one leg pinning her to the bed, his mouth caressing her lips.

His hands started to migrate over her body, pulling aside the soft gathers of her bodice, exposing the perfect cream of her breasts to the night air.

"Oh God, Sophie, you're so beautiful, so beautiful," and then Patrick's voice trailed off as it was smothered against her soft flesh, and the next sound was Sophie's whimper as his mouth followed his hand. She was writhing against him now, uttering weak murmurs that set Patrick's blood on fire. He swept a hand under her gown and twirled his fingers in the soft curls there, loops that looped around his fingers with a softness that gave way to dewy promise.

Sophie's body went rigid.

"What are you doing?" Her voice was panicked, shaky with passion but afraid, and a small hand gripped his wrist like steel.

Patrick stilled instantly, but left his fingers where they were. The sensation sank into Sophie's bones like wildfire and her eyes blurred, looking at him through the pale, incandescent moonlight in the room.

"I won't do anything you don't like, sweetheart." His voice was a husky promise, his lips sweeping over her face, licking her lips apart, plunging into her mouth with a gesture that made her understand, suddenly, all those details that she'd heard tell of, things that happened between men and women. And his fingers moved, dipping restlessly, driving her into a frenzy of sensation.

"Oh Lord," Sophie whispered suddenly. "You're making love to me."

Patrick's mind was leaping from fact to fact, putting together Sophie's untutored caresses, the surprised leap of her flesh every time he touched her somewhere new, and the shocked amazement in her blue eyes. He'd made the mistake of thinking that she was as sophisticated in sexual matters as she was in dress and conversation. . . . He let his fingers drift to the soft flesh of her thighs.

"Sweetheart, I can hardly see you." He kissed her nose lightly. "May I light a candle?"

Sophie stared at him in fascination. "Simone, my maid, said that the moon was as thin as a mouse's whisker tonight," she finally replied.

"Hmm." Patrick gave her lips a brief kiss, as a reassurance and because he couldn't bear not to. Then he rolled to his feet and struck a match, sending a flame flickering around the room. He lit the candle on Sophie's bedside table and sat back down on the bed, his weight pulling down the mattress.

"How you look at me!" Sophie whispered, half shy, half cross. She sat up sharply, tugged up the bodice of her nightgown, and pushed the skirt back over her knees.

"I look at you the way a man looks at the woman he wants more than anything in the world," Patrick said, his tone light but his eyes fierce.

"Oh," Sophie whispered. Patrick had thrown off his cloak; underneath all she could see was a fine lawn shirt, the collar lying open against his chest.

"I've never seen a man's shirt without a cravat," she said irrelevantly.

A wisp of a smile crossed Patrick's face. Then in one swift movement he tugged the shirt from his breeches, pulled it over his head, and threw it down beside the bed. Sophie's eyes widened. The candle flame danced and bent in the sudden breeze as the shirt fell to the floor. Orange shadows played on bronzed skin, flickered over ridges of muscle.

Sophie opened her mouth, then closed it again. The only thing she could think of to say was "oh," and she was tired of sounding like such a nitwit. So she said nothing, but she took courage from Patrick's dark eyes and reached out to touch his chest as he had touched hers. They were sitting side by side on the edge of the bed now, almost primly, Sophie thought, except . . . except. She spread her hand flat on his chest and brought the other up to meet it. Her little finger rubbed across Patrick's nipple and he drew in his breath suddenly, his eyes dark with desire.

Sophie's eyes darted to his and a little smile turned up the corners of her mouth. She repeated the movement, slowly, with both hands, then slid her thumbs down to the same position. She felt Patrick's heart beating under her hand like that of a small mole she had found once in the garden at twilight.

Suddenly, just as she was relaxing into a sense of power, Patrick's hands dragged her from the bed and she found herself sitting on his lap, her hands crushed against his chest, her heart beating wildly. He smelled like a midsummer night, like the midsummer madness that was racing through her veins like potent canary wine; he smelled male and faintly like brandy. She held her breath and just . . . waited.

Patrick looked down into her trusting eyes and momentarily closed his own, resisting a wave of passion that threatened to turn him into a satyr who would thrust her back on the bed and leap on her. Instead he kissed her little nose.

"You're marrying me."

His voice was deep with unstrained conviction.

Sophie gave an assenting little sigh, a little, fuzzy, unargumentative puff of breath. And so, without a moment's further thought, she consigned a thousand childhood oaths to oblivion.

Patrick tipped up her chin with his knuckles.

"Sophie."

"All right," she said, not pettishly, not irritably. "All right, I will marry you." But the question didn't really interest Sophie at that moment. She was fidgetingly aware of the rosy glow in her cheeks and a matching glow of warmth low in her belly.

"Patrick?" Her eyes were caught on his.

He lowered his head so that his lips were a whisper from hers, his warm breath caressing her lips as he spoke.

"It wouldn't be proper, Sophie," he said, his voice husky with desire. "We must wait."

But wells and springs of joy were washing over Sophie's body. She was marrying a rake, yes. But she was marrying a rake whom she loved, so surely. . . . Daringly she reached up and ran her tongue along the chiseled outline of his mouth. He tightened his grip, but said nothing. Her hands slipped from around his neck, down to his chest, running again over the planes and angles, down to where a small feathered arrow of hair disappeared into his waistband.

She risked a glance at him. His face had taken on an erotic languor, and a sensual promise hung in the darkness of his eyes and the shadowed curves of his cheeks. Sophie smiled.

Reluctantly Patrick smiled back.

"You're a hell-born brat," he murmured.

"Oh dear." Sophie pursed her lips teasingly. "Are you an archbishop?"

Patrick's hand found its way back to the generous undercurve of Sophie's breast. She gasped and her head fell back; Patrick pulled her head toward his for an aching kiss, and another, and another. . . . Somehow they found themselves flat on the bed again, and this time when Patrick pulled up Sophie's gown she did naught but shiver with anticipation.

He rose for a moment and came back without clothes.

"Oh my," Sophie said, her eyes wide. "You're . . . you're without a stitch!"

Patrick's eyes lit with laughter. "So are you."

Sophie looked down at her body in confusion. It didn't feel like her own body anymore, and she hadn't really marked the disappearance of her garments. The pink creamy expanse of her skin had become a maze of sensations and hot aches, unlike anything she had known or dreamed of. As she watched, Patrick's hand lazed its way over her breast and down her belly, and then Sophie couldn't watch anymore.

She looked at him instead. Even as Patrick's hands wrought magic, and his lips made her shake and tremble, she looked at the parts of his body she could see.

A small voice broke the erotic haze in the bedroom. "This isn't going to work," Sophie said precisely. "I'm afraid that we are not appropriately, ah, sized."

Patrick desperately pushed back waves of lust. He was hanging on to control by a thread, by a glimmer of a thread. Somehow he found himself propped on his elbows above the rosy, yet frightened face of his own Sophie.

"You have to trust me, sweetheart." He brushed his lips back and forth against hers, persuading and cherishing, all at once.

Sophie gasped, but managed to reply, "In this instance, I think I am a better judge of my capabilities."

"Logic," Patrick murmured. "Logic is for widgeons. God made our bodies to go together, Sophie."

She felt his treacherous persuasion between her thighs; every inch of her was screaming for him to continue. Her mind raced. Patrick kissed her eyes, tenderly pressing them closed, letting his body continue its silent seduction, an urgent, infamous demand.

Breathless, Sophie opened her lips.

"It is true," Patrick murmured against her lips, "that it doesn't feel very good for women, the first time."

But Sophie was past caring.

Her arms clenched around his neck and her body arched up against his in an unconscious plea that broke through his last reserves like fire hitting a thatched roof. He took her mouth and her body in the same breath, catching Sophie's cry in his throat, staying absolutely still for a moment.

"I'm sorry . . . I'm sorry."

Patrick really did sound sorry, Sophie thought, her mind drawn away from the sharp pain that accompanied his entrance. So she concentrated on the rustling, tender words that he whispered into her hair, and her ears, and against her throat.

Then he started a slow, thrusting rhythm that at first stung and hurt. But slowly, slowly, the pain fell away, or at least became partnered with something else, and small whimpers started to fly from her mouth.

And when Patrick, still holding on grimly to his self-control, pulled back and slipped his hands under Sophie's bottom, she began to writhe under him, her body rising to meet his, her mind narrowed to a single point. Finally that elusive spark burst, shedding light that wrenched its burning way down Sophie's arms and legs, driving her body up against Patrick's like a tidal wave hitting the shore.

Patrick's restraint turned to a shout of thankfulness as he lunged forward, in the grip of an ecstasy of which he had never felt the like. He surrendered with a prayer, a half-strangled, "Sophie, Sophie, Sophie," smothered in the long, tangled curls spread over the bed.

And on the bedside table the candle dipped and swayed again, visited by the vague caress of a midnight breeze from the open window.

Chapter 9

D own the hallway, Sophie's mother sat bolt upright in the palatial splendor of her bed. Eloise had slept there alone since discovering her husband in the arms of a housemaid some two months after their wedding. Her harsh command never to visit her bed again had been met by the marquis's stiff agreement. Since then, the only noises that disturbed her at night were caused by her husband's late arrivals in his chamber and, very occasionally, by errant servants.

Without hesitation she hauled on the velvet cord that hung next to her bed. The marchioness was not one to disturb the servants unnecessarily in the middle of the night, but she also had the firmest belief in her ability to sleep soundly (the gift, she frequently announced with a sapient look at her husband, of a pure conscience). If she had awakened, then there was reason for it. She had heard a gasp, and a cry. She was sure of that. Perhaps a gentleman was being robbed on the street in front of the house; if so, it was their duty to go to the poor soul's aid. She rang the bell again.

Finally her maid appeared, dazed and disheveled looking. She curtsied in a remarkably slovenly fashion, to Eloise's mind, and said, "Yes, my lady?"

"I heard a noise," Eloise snapped. "Have Carroll check the front walk immediately."

Her maid curtsied again and disappeared. Eloise lay stiffly, staring at the blush-rose canopy that covered her old-fashioned tent bed. An awful thought had crept into her mind. What if her husband had taken to sneaking women into Brandenburg House? It sounded like a *woman's* voice, now that her mind was clear and wide awake. Yes, she had heard a woman gasp. In fact, it reminded her of the time when the second housemaid went into labor, right in the parlor, without a word of warning. No matter how much the housekeeper had wrung her hands later and assured Eloise that everyone simply thought the girl was a tad large for her age, Eloise still remembered the scene with a stab of pure rage. The Duchess of Beaumont had come to take tea, and the mortification! Eloise would remember it to her dying day.

Thinking of the Duchess of Beaumont reminded her of Braddon Chatwin, because weren't they related somehow? Eloise fancied that the duchess was dear Braddon's godmother. He was a nicely mannered young fellow, Eloise thought. A dunce, of course, but what man wasn't? And he came with a pretty set of relatives. It would be very pleasant to be related to the Duchess of Beaumont.

There was a sound of slippers running down the hallway, and Eloise's maid slipped back into the room.

"Oh, my lady, there's such a stir! Carroll has found a ladder in the back garden, and it's set up right against the house." She paused, native intuition telling her that the fact that the ladder was perched against Lady Sophie's bedroom window was information better conveyed by the butler than by herself.

Eloise clambered out of bed and firmly tied her bedrobe around her. Without a word she marched through the connecting door to her dressing room and from there to her husband's bedchamber. She had absolute confidence about the location of the ladder—directly to her husband's window, no doubt about it. Things had come to a pretty pass when her husband had to import women up a ladder, like a spendthrift sneaking into a brothel.

Thus it was with a profound sense of surprise that she flung open George's bedchamber door to find the marquis peacefully asleep and quite alone. What's more, his windows were shut tight, and from the way he was snoring, he'd probably drunk more than was good for him before going to bed and wasn't expecting visitors.

Eloise darted to her husband's bed and grabbed his upper arm, shaking it vigorously. "Robbers, George, robbers!" She didn't notice in her excitement that she was calling her husband by his Christian name, a courtesy she hadn't granted him in years.

"Eh? What is it? Robbers?" The marquis sat up, his hair falling ludicrously over one eye. Eloise almost gasped in surprise. Had George grown old then, behind her back, as it were? His dark hair was speckled with white. He looked like a tired old man, peering at her blurrily. But his legs were still strong and muscled as he swung them out of bed and grabbed a robe. It seemed that George still slept without a nightshirt.

Eloise followed him out the door almost wistfully. The memory of the first few months of their marriage was hardly dimmed by the intervening twenty years. How much fun it had been when the marquis—George—had twinkled at her from the doorway connecting their rooms and strode into bed, naked as the day he was born.

Nostalgia, however, was the last thing on George's mind as he charged down the front stairs. He was barreling toward the back garden when Carroll caught him by the elbow.

"My lord." Something in Carroll's tone chilled George's blood. "The ladder has addressed itself to the window of the young lady's chamber, my lord."

"The ladder has addressed itself," George repeated, puzzling over it. "Addressed itself? Why the hell can't you speak English like the rest of the human race, Carroll?"

Carroll restrained a retort along the lines of a reminder of his French nationality, and simply said, stolidly, "The top of the ladder is leaning into Lady Sophie's bedroom, my lord. And," he added with some satisfaction, "her window is open."

George gaped at him. "Her window is open," he repeated.

"Open." Carroll nodded, almost genially. "It appears that she has eloped, my lord."

"Eloped."

Carroll contented himself with nodding. He saw the marchioness walking swiftly down the hallway toward the marquis's back, and he wanted nothing to do with her once she knew this pretty piece of news.

"You might check her room for a note, my lord." With that advice, Carroll faded back through the servants' door.

He was just in time to quell a rising wave of hilarity in the servants' quarter. Eloise was starchy enough about personal matters that her employees were hysterical with laughter to hear that her daughter had run off to Gretna Green.

Carroll delivered a stern lecture about not talking of the family disgrace (little chance of that!) and sent them all off to bed, inconspicuously counting to make sure that every one of his seventeen footmen were in bed where they should be. Footmen, he knew well, were an eternal lure to young ladies, and he'd never get over the shame if Lady Sophie had set her eye on one of his lads.

Meanwhile, the Marquis of Brandenburg stayed exactly where he was, staring at the pieced Italian marble that adorned the front hallway.

His wife arrived silently, lighted taper in hand. She wasn't the kind of woman who wore fluttery negligees over her nightdress; she was swathed in a sturdy piece of blue linsey wool that covered her from neck to toe.

"Well?" Eloise asked rather belligerently. And then, much more urgently: "George, George, what is it?"

Her husband raised his head and looked at her. "She's gone. Carroll says that Sophie has eloped, our little Sophie."

Eloise's mouth fell inelegantly open, for perhaps the first and last time in her life.

"No!"

"The ladder's at her window and the window's open," George said miserably. "I suppose there's no way to hush this up, is there?"

Eloise snapped her jaws shut. "It's impossible," she whispered. "She would never do such a thing to me, to us. The shame . . . a daughter who eloped . . ."

"I don't think we were too lenient with her, do you?" George's face was pinched. "I thought a few times of saying something 'bout her gowns, but I thought it was just me getting old and outmoded in my notions."

"Nonsense," Eloise said uncertainly.

She turned about and started down the hall. Then she swiveled and looked back at her motionless husband. "Come *on*, George. We must see if she left a note. Perhaps she hasn't gone very far. If so, we must catch up with them tonight."

Obediently George fell in behind her as they climbed the stairs again. Husband and wife made their way down the hallway shoulder to shoulder, neither aware that it was the first time they had walked so closely in exactly twenty years.

Eloise paused, then pushed open the door to her daughter's bedchamber. To be sure, the window was open, and the delicate muslin curtains were billowing slightly in the night breeze. The room was dark, but Eloise could just barely see two black points poking above the windowsill—obviously the top of a ladder.

"Do you see a note?" George stood behind her, peering into the room.

Eloise held up the taper she carried in her hand and walked to the dressing table. There was nothing. No note perched on the marble fireplace either. She was just turning about to survey the room as a whole when George loomed up at her shoulder. Eloise stifled a scream. George huffed, and the candle burned out, leaving them in nearly pitch darkness. The only light was a flickering glow from the hallway sconces, which Eloise had lit on her way down the hallway.

"Eloise, we need to go after them as soon as possible!" George's voice had a queer, hurried tone to it. He grabbed her shoulders and hustled her toward the door. Eloise felt as if she were an awkward bundle of laundry, particularly when George knocked her against the door frame in his eagerness to get out.

In the hallway she pulled her arm out of his grip. "What on earth has possessed you, my lord?"

George sighed. That was it for "George." Clearly, the state of armed warfare had descended again.

"We must get dressed and into a carriage immediately, Eloise. If we leave now, we have a decent chance of catching them either tonight or tomorrow, before they reach the border. You know it takes at least two days to get to Scotland."

"But who is he?" Eloise asked, somewhat pitifully. "I never told Sophie she couldn't marry anyone she pleased.

Why would she need to elope? Why wouldn't she leave me a note? She *must* have left me a note!" Eloise started back to the door of Sophie's bedroom.

George grabbed her arm again, his grip like steel. "We don't have time for the note, Eloise. You need to get dressed. If we catch up with them in time, we can pretend that we are simply returning from a late ball." He half marched his wife to her bedroom and pushed her in the door before him.

"Here, put this on!" George pulled a dress at random from the wardrobe. Eloise looked wildly at the saffron-colored ball gown.

"I can't."

Although his wife was one of the most stiff-rumped ladies in London, George thought, one might almost think she was near tears.

"Yes you can." He caught the tie to her robe and pulled it off. Eloise instinctively clutched the front of her night-dress.

"You have five minutes," George said very slowly, but his tone left no room for interpretation. "I shall order up the carriage. I'll return in five minutes and I want you dressed and ready to go."

Eloise nodded numbly. When he appeared at her door again she was wearing a neat walking dress of blue serge, rather than the ball gown. It gaped at the back where Eloise had been unable to hook it herself.

"No! You have to wear a ball gown." And, in answer to her silent question: "It's only one-thirty in the morning, Eloise. We must look as if we were returning from a ball."

Eloise nodded. George briskly pulled the walking dress down over her shoulders, exposing the creamy white expanse of Eloise's chest. Eloise backed up.

"You leave and I'll get dressed," she said hoarsely.

Her husband stepped back, a sardonic smile lurking at the edge of his mouth. "Do you know, Eloise, I haven't been in this room since you gave birth to Sophie? I was invited in to see the new child—five minutes, I think—and never darkened the door again."

Their eyes met for a moment and George walked back to his room.

Eloise put on the ball gown and tumbled her hair into some sort of order. Then she ran through her dressing room to the adjoining bedroom. George fastened up the back of the dress without a word, and they made their way downstairs. Carroll emerged from the shadows of the back hallway.

"The marchioness and I are attending a late engagement," George announced. "You'll be glad to know, Carroll, that your suspicions were for naught. Lady Sophie is safely in her bed, with no thoughts of elopement."

Carroll bowed and murmured his delight at the news. He held the door open as the marquis and marchioness clambered with unseemly haste into their waiting carriage.

"And where are you off to in the middle of the night, if not the post road leading to Gretna Greene?" Carroll liked to ask himself the questions that he could never address to his master. "And what shall I do about that ladder? And are you *really* telling me that Lady Sophie will ring her bell for hot chocolate, without a hair out of place, at seven in the morning?"

Well, one question could be answered. Without further ado, Carroll ordered Philippe to remove the ladder in the back garden.

~∽~

Up in Sophie's bedroom, Patrick was leaning on one elbow, looking down at Braddon's—no, *his* future wife. As he watched, Sophie opened her eyes and looked up at him, eyes midnight blue in the dusky light.

Patrick ran a finger over her lower lip. "We're going to

have to find Braddon another wife, you know. We can't just leave him in the lurch. What a pity that you don't have a sister, my love!"

"Or you," Sophie said impishly. A telltale blush was rising up her neck. She was in bed, unclothed (at least she seemed to have a sheet over herself), talking to Patrick, whom she was going to marry, and with whom she had just—

"Your parents were in here just now," Patrick said. His grin widened. "You were sleeping like a baby."

"What?" It emerged from her mouth like a half-strangled shriek.

The finger which Patrick had been rubbing over her lip began to wander down her neck. "Your mother didn't see us. Your father did, though. He practically threw your mother back out into the hallway. Apparently she thinks you've eloped, because she was looking for a note." His finger wandered below the sheet.

Sophie fastened her eyes on Patrick's face, trying to ignore all nonverbal communications. "Are you saying that my father *saw* you and said nothing?"

Patrick nodded.

"But why?" Sophie's eyes were as round as robin's eggs. "Why on earth wouldn't he challenge you, or stop and call me a doxy, or do something?"

"A doxy?" Patrick looked at her quizzically. "Where did you get that outmoded term, my love?"

Sophie blushed. "It's . . . that's what my mother calls some women."

"Humph." Patrick rolled one of his legs over on top of Sophie's. She turned even pinker. "I think he was giving me a chance to get out of here," Patrick said.

"Oh!" Sophie gasped. The blood was rushing to her head.

Patrick shifted his weight and suddenly every nerve in her body was clamoring. He bent his head and brushed his lips across hers, but at that moment there was a scraping noise and the top of the ladder bobbed, fell back against the house once, then silently swung away into the air.

"Alas," Patrick murmured against Sophie's lips. "Discovery appears to be imminent."

Sophie didn't reply. Her hands were discovering the smooth planes of Patrick's back as his mouth plunged and took, sending a stroking heat down all her trembling limbs.

Reluctantly Patrick pulled away and sat up, running his hands through his hair. "My love, I had better be off." He looked down at Sophie, who lay quietly. Slowly he reached out and rubbed her cheek with the back of his hand.

"You're the most beautiful woman I've ever seen," he said huskily.

A smile flickered on Sophie's lips. "When I refused to marry you, last month, you looked profoundly relieved."

"Really?" Patrick laughed. "I felt rather piqued, if the truth be known."

"Oh." Sophie nodded. That explained why Patrick had come up the ladder instead of Braddon. She didn't quite like the idea of her future being decided due to a childish rivalry between two men, but she felt too happy at the moment to worry about it.

"So why did you reject me?" Patrick asked.

A shadow passed Sophie's eyes. "It wasn't *you,* my lord." A blush mounted in her cheeks. "I was quite— well," she shifted direction quickly, "I just wasn't thinking about the way the world is. I thought . . . I don't know what I thought." She started once again. "I was being very cowardly, I realize that."

Patrick was pulling on his breeches and shirt, but he turned and looked at Sophie in surprise. Cowardly? Just as he opened his mouth, she asked a question.

"How are you going to leave? I think the ladder is gone."

"Down the front stairs, naturally." Patrick's face took on a momentary hauteur lent to him by generations of aristocratic ancestors. "I should be very surprised if your butler questioned my presence in the house."

"Where do you suppose my parents went?"

"I expect your father will direct the coachman to drive out the post road for a time, then order the horses home again." Patrick's voice was muffled for a moment as he cast the great cloak over his head. "You should expect a good deal of conversation in the morning, sweetheart. I think your mother will be particularly annoyed with your father."

"She's frequently annoyed with him," Sophie observed.

Patrick cast her an inquiring glance.

"He sleeps with too many women," she obligingly explained.

Patrick sat down on the edge of the bed, fully swathed in Braddon's theatrical cloak once again.

Sophie looked up at him, her eyes heavy lidded. "My mama is very irritable about the whole subject of mistresses. But you needn't worry; I shall be accommodating."

Patrick smiled a bit tightly. "I hope you won't have anything to accommodate."

Sophie was clearly drifting off to sleep again. "It's quite all right, Patrick. I am not the sort of woman who will make a fuss. Now that I'm going to marry you, I won't whimper about it." Her eyes closed.

Patrick's eyes narrowed as he watched Sophie's face relax into dreams. It was not without a frisson of shock that he realized her complete lack of belief in his ability to stay away from other women. As he watched she turned a bit, nestling her face against her hand.

Patrick ran his hand down the silky mess of Sophie's curls, spread out against the sheets. She must have bled when he took her virginity, this future wife of his, but she hadn't said a word. Not a coward, then. But she had no faith in him. Why? What could she have heard about him? Stories, perhaps, about his behavior before his father sent him abroad. But Patrick couldn't think of anything remarkable, other than the normal pranks of lustful men in their twenties. And yet, since Sophie had agreed to marry Braddon, whose reputation was not the best, a truly egregious tale must be circulating about himself. No. He'd forgotten about Braddon's title. Sophie had wanted to be a countess. Well, now she would be a duchess.

Patrick's jaw tightened. Whatever reluctance she'd had to marry him before, Sophie York didn't have a choice anymore. She was *his*. He stood up, then leaned over her once more, almost compulsively running a hand down the lovely curves of her relaxed body. God, he'd better get out of here or he'd lose his head again.

Patrick stood, his cape swirling from his shoulders. With the silent stealth of a jungle animal he walked over to Sophie's dressing table and swiftly pocketed the strand of matched pearls she had worn earlier in the evening. Then he left the room, shutting the door silently behind him. He walked down the stairs slowly, making no effort to hide the firm sound of his feet striking the marble risers.

Carroll had left Philippe in the front hall with instructions to await the master and mistress's return from a ball. The footman looked up in confusion as a swell, dressed in a black cape, walked composedly down the stairs. His mouth fell open, but Carroll's excellent training snapped Philippe to attention. He sprang to the door and held it open, bowing his head.

Patrick threw him an amused glance as he strolled through the doorway. Then he paused.

"I wasn't here," he said gently.

Philippe nodded. Not for nothing was he born in France.

"It is possible that a thief has been in the house, however," Patrick added.

Philippe's eyes shifted desperately to the side. He wished Carroll were there.

"A thief, sir?"

"Unfortunately," Patrick murmured. "There is a thief in London who brings a ladder, climbs into open windows, and steals whatever jewels have been left out on a dressing table. It is entirely possible that the thief is on the prowl tonight."

Philippe felt a chill of alarm down his spine. What was he supposed to do next? The tall aristocrat's eyes were making his head whirl.

"Perhaps we should summon a runner," he said with a gulp.

He was rewarded by a cool smile. "That would undoubtedly be wise." Patrick jauntily walked down the outside stairs. Even as Philippe watched, he vaulted into a carriage waiting at the corner. Only then did Philippe dare look at the banknote in his hand.

"Gorm!" Philippe had been handed more money than he could make in three years . . . enough to get his little sister out of her position as a scullery maid, which she hated so much, and into an apprenticeship with a mantua maker. A flood of gratitude washed his soul.

Then he turned quickly, running back toward the servants' quarters. He'd just remembered hearing a rumor about a thief who entered houses by a ladder, stealing jewels so quietly that sleeping inhabitants heard not a whisper.

And thus it was that when an extremely disgruntled marchioness and her husband returned to their house, an hour or so later, they disembarked from their carriage to find all the lights burning, and a small circle of Bow Street runners standing about awkwardly.

Eloise stopped in utter confusion. There was her daughter, hastily dressed and with her hair tied back with a simple ribbon. Obviously Sophie was not belting down the post road toward Gretna Greene. Eloise was propelled into the room by her husband's strong hand in the middle of her back.

"What seems to be the problem here?" The marquis's voice was sharp and the little group swung about instantly.

The head runner's eyes brightened. Here was the man of the house to talk to.

"It's like this, milord," Grenable said importantly. "There's been a robbery here."

"A robbery?"

"Yes, sir. Your daughter's lost a valuable pearl necklace—"

"Pearls?"

Grenable cast a look at the mistress of the house. She seemed a bit dazed.

"Yes, milady, a string of pearls has been found to be missing." Grenable turned back to the marquis. "There's been a few thefts of this sort in the past, milord. We found ladder marks under the young lady's window, and the mess of quite a number of footprints. So my guess is that we're talking about a gang here. Likely they came along and set up a ladder, and one of 'em nipped up the ladder as silent as you please, and the young lady has admitted that her pearls were lying right on the dressing table in her room, just asking to be picked up, begging your pardon." He bobbed his head at Sophie, who nodded confusedly.

She was only beginning to understand the situation. The process wasn't helped by the jolting surprises of the past hour: waking to find herself alone in the bed, roused by Simone's hysterical comments. It seemed that her mama's maid had somehow figured out that the house had been robbed, or was it one of the footmen? No one seemed to be too clear. At any rate, the throbbing pain between her thighs kept stealing her attention away from the loss of her pearl necklace. And Patrick had left her without a word, without even saying good-bye, that she could remember.

Grenable's unwelcome voice intervened again. He was a rather squat, oily man with a scrawny beard. "I shall need to question the young lady quite closely," he was saying. "It is not yet clear to me exactly why Lady Sophie opened her window last night, given that her maid insists that she closed the window quite securely before going to her own room."

Sophie gulped and looked up. Her mama was frowning at her, and even her father was looking at her rather sharply. She felt as if she were acting in a play without having learned the lines.

"I simply wanted some night air," she said, her voice wavering. And then, when she spied a gleam of approval in her father's eyes, she burst into tears. She cried because Patrick hadn't said good-bye, and because she was bewildered by her thoughtless submission to his seduction.

And thus Grenable's underlings were treated to the sight of his discomfort, having driven a gently born young lady to tears.

Her father was beside her in an instant; Eloise was a little slower, given her surprise at the sight of Sophie's tears. In her recollection, she hadn't seen her daughter cry since she was six or seven. Yet there she was, choking back sobs—and over the loss of a pearl necklace!

"It's shock," George said soothingly, meeting his wife's bewildered eyes. "Very frightening, having a marauding criminal tiptoeing around one's room during the night."

Eloise turned and gave Grenable a fierce look. He involuntarily fell back a step. "I fail to see what information my daughter might give you that could possibly aid you in your attempt to apprehend the criminal who broke into our house tonight," she said bitingly. "I suggest you begin searching the streets without delay."

Grenable swallowed. Of course the marchioness was right. The open window had just seemed a bit havey-cavey to him. He would do better to go back to Bow Street and send a description of the pearl necklace out to the best-known fencers. He rubbed his hands together, bowing very low as the marchioness swept her daughter from the room.

"I agree, I agree," he said, turning to the marquis as the door closed behind Eloise and Sophie. "There is nothing more for me here. I must warn you, milord, that the possibility of recovering the young lady's necklace is very slim."

The marquis looked remarkably calm as he shook Grenable's hand. "Do your best, man, do your best. I'm not one of those who criticize the runners. From what I've seen, you're good men, the finest. Always chasing after malefactors."

"Yes," Grenable said a bit uncertainly. "We certainly do our best." Somehow he found himself out the front door and heading back to Bow Street before he thought twice.

Given that one of his operating rules was never to show indecision in front of his men, Grenable decided to dismiss the queerness of the marquis's behavior. After all, what was a string of pearls to such a man, anyway? Grenable should just bless his lucky stars that this particular peer wouldn't kick up a row if the bloody pearls couldn't be traced. The very thought cheered him up.

The family butler, Carroll, was even more cheerful when he found that the master seemed to have no intention of turning him off as a result of his slanderous suggestion that Lady Sophie had eloped.

"Don't think about it twice, Carroll," George said expansively. "It was a viable conclusion. I thought it m'self. But there, we told you Lady Sophie was safe in her bed, didn't we? Too bad we didn't know about the thief when her mother and I left for the ball. But the important thing is that Lady Sophie was right and snug in bed. Well, good night, Carroll." And off went the marquis, rubbing his hands together.

Funny behavior for a man who'd lost a mint of money to a thief, to Carroll's mind. But what was it to him?

Chapter 16

❧

P atrick Foakes climbed the stairs of Brandenburg House the next morning a trifle wearily. He'd been up half the night. Braddon had taken the news of his confiscated bride very badly indeed. In fact, the vehemence of his reaction stunned Patrick, given Braddon's easygoing attitude toward most things. He would never forget the moment when Braddon snatched up a port bottle and started smashing the plaster adhesive on his leg. For a second Patrick thought his friend had been driven mad by grief, but in truth Braddon was only royally peeved.

Braddon had always been fidgety when it came to his mother, Patrick thought as he waited to be announced. And Braddon's marriage was essentially a matter of Braddon's mother.

The Brandenburg butler returned, bowing magnificently. "The marquis will see you in the library," he intoned.

Nothing had changed in the library since Patrick's last visit, one month ago. Except, perhaps, the attitude of the Marquis of Brandenburg. Last time, Brandenburg had greeted him expansively, striding across the floor to meet him. Patrick remembered being faintly surprised that the marquis would be so happy to greet the man who had damaged his daughter's reputation the night before. But now Sophie's ruination lay between them, and George's eyes were as icy cold as a northern glacier.

As Patrick walked into the room, George dismissed Carroll with a brief nod. Neither of them said a word until Carroll had closed the two heavy oak doors of the library, bowing on his way out of the room.

Patrick met the furious eyes of his future father-in-law steadily as he walked over to stand before him. "I've come to request the hand of your daughter in marriage," he said mildly.

George simply raised one of his clenched fists and aimed it at Patrick's face, striking him with all the rage of a sleepless night. There was a substantial *thunk* as his fist met Patrick's hard jaw, bounced upward, and struck him again at the corner of the eye. Patrick lurched back, catching himself on the corner of George's desk. Then he straightened and looked at the marquis again.

George was panting with exertion. "I didn't think you'd let me do that," he observed.

Patrick's response was brief: "I deserved it."

George was beginning to feel foolish. He was too old for boxing gymnastics in the library. He made his way to a group of chairs by the fireplace and dropped into one, not even glancing at his guest to see whether he would follow. Patrick walked over and sat down.

"I went up that ladder last night to help your daughter elope with the Earl of Slaslow," Patrick said quietly.

He glanced at the marquis, whose face had grown even redder, if possible.

"What in God's name are you talking about?"

"The elopement," Patrick continued, leaning back and closing his eyes, "was Lady Sophie's idea and carried out on her plan. However, Slaslow himself was dead set against the idea of an elopement, and when he injured his leg yesterday, he persuaded me to bring your daughter to his grandmother's house. His plan was to convince Lady Sophie that an elopement was neither desirable nor possible, given his impairment."

There was silence from the other side of the fireplace.

"When I arrived in your daughter's room, she had already decided to break off her engagement to Slaslow."

"I *assume*," George said sardonically, "that she has now changed her mind about your proposal of marriage."

"I believe so."

"And what a scandal this is going to be." The marquis's voice sounded weary.

"Not as much of a scandal as if your daughter had eloped with the Earl of Slaslow," Patrick retorted.

George stared into the dying embers of the fire, his heart heavy. Not only was Sophie going to break her engagement to an earl, but unless he was greatly mistaken, she was going to have to marry another man with indecent haste.

"It will be a nine-days' wonder," Patrick said calmly. "I shall take my bride on a lengthy wedding trip, and by the time we return a more potent scandal will be amusing the *ton*."

"What am I to tell my wife? She'll be a mite curious about why you two have to get married so quickly, after Sophie's engagement to another man was just announced."

"Why don't you tell her the truth?"

"God, no." George frowned into the fire. "Eloise looks pretty stiff, but she's actually quite naive. It would be a terrible blow to her to learn that our daughter was seduced before her wedding."

Patrick felt a sharp pang of guilt. In the cold morning's light, he was shocked by his own behavior. What had got into him last night? What was it about Sophie that had driven him into such a frenzy of lust? He had broken every rule of civilized behavior that he'd been taught since a boy.

"Tell the marchioness that it's a case of true love."

"*True love!*" George scoffed. "My wife has never been one for rosy fantasies."

"Then why did you protect her from seeing me in Lady Sophie's bed last night?"

"I told you. It would be a huge blow to her. . . . She'd think that Sophie takes after her papa. And she doesn't," George said with a fierce glare.

Patrick met the marquis's eyes steadily, even given that his own eye was beginning to swell and appeared half closed. "I know," he said with a crooked half-smile.

George turned a trifle redder at the reminder that his daughter had anticipated her wedding night.

"I'll look after her," Patrick said quietly.

"I know, I know," George mumbled. "I always thought she'd be happy with you. Although I hoped she'd find a quieter sort of fellow. Braddon and you, you're cats of the same color, aren't you? Rakes, the both of you." He cast an apologetic glance at the young man before him, heaving himself to his feet. "I haven't always behaved as I should."

Patrick's lips twitched but he managed to stifle a grin. This, from the man whose name regularly adorned the gossip columns of every London rag published? Patrick could hardly hope to convince George that he had no plans to take a mistress after marrying Sophie. George's tempestuous extramarital history meant that rakes, from his point of view, never reformed.

George started again. "My wife has a powerful temper,

and sometimes Sophie was . . . saw more than she should have."

Patrick stood up, his relaxed demeanor not letting slip a clue to his keen interest in George's confession.

"She's a good girl, my Sophie is." George was walking toward the door now, going to ring the bell and summon his daughter to the library to entertain Foakes's proposal yet again. "She's a good girl. She's gotten me out of a curst hobble more than once, helped me out when her mama was acting like a termagant."

Patrick walked up behind him.

"How did Lady Sophie aid you with these entanglements?" His voice sounded mildly curious.

"Oh, she would smile, as sweet as new butter, and tell her mother that I'd taken her to the races, that sort of thing." George's round eyes were full of self-condemnation. "Do you think that Sophie came up with this infamous plan to elope because of my indiscretions? Did she let you stay in her bed last night because I've been such a—"

"I take full blame for what happened last night. Lady Sophie is a true innocent. She had no idea what might happen when I climbed the ladder to her room."

"Really?" For a moment the marquis's eyes widened with surprise. "She's—" What in the devil was he doing, trying to convince his daughter's future husband that she was some sort of female libertine? She wasn't, of course. It was just that Sophie had lied so convincingly in the past, protecting him from her mother's wrath. He'd somehow fallen into thinking of his own daughter as a sophisticated lady of the town, instead of an innocent maiden. For a moment George was swamped in self-reproach.

Then just as he opened his mouth, the doors opened and Carroll stood there.

"My lord?"

"Ask Lady Sophie to join us, Carroll."

Carroll cast a quick, speculative glance at Patrick Foakes. Of course, the entire household knew of Foakes's earlier proposal to Lady Sophie, the one she'd rejected. The whole household also knew that Lady Sophie's engagement to the Earl of Slaslow had just been celebrated. So what was Foakes doing in the house?

Sophie came down the staircase slowly, trailing her hand on the railing. She was wearing a remarkably demure morning gown with a high neckline trimmed with two rows of fabric roses. In fact, she had worn the dress only once before and then discarded it as too dowdy for words. But this morning, visited by tidal waves of embarrassment, her aim was to show Patrick—and her father!—that she was *not* one of the muslin company, even though she had acted like one the night before.

For the fortieth time that morning, a wash of rosy color swirled in Sophie's cheeks. Could she even enter the library? What must her father think of her? Her stomach roiled with nerves. But there was no stopping time, no matter how slowly she descended the stairs. Carroll again opened the library doors. There stood her father.

Reluctantly she met his eyes, and what she saw gave her some courage. George didn't look as if he was about to throw her out of the house.

"Sophie," he said gruffly. "It seems you are going to marry Patrick Foakes rather than the Earl of Slaslow."

She lowered her eyes, her cheeks stained raspberry. "Yes, Papa," she whispered.

"We'll have to figure out something to tell your mama." George sighed. "I won't have her know the truth, as I've just been telling Foakes. She'd vex herself to death over it."

"Yes, Papa." Sophie's throat felt tight.

"Well, I'll leave you," George mumbled. "Not for long, mind!" His voice erupted into something of a roar as he met his future son-in-law's amused eyes. Did nothing overset that fellow? Here he had one eye practically swollen shut, and a distinct bruise forming along his jaw as well, and still Patrick Foakes looked like a buck of the first cut. It was dashed annoying. George got himself out of the room, practically choking with irritation.

Sophie took a deep breath but was too embarrassed to raise her eyes. She heard Patrick walking toward her. When he stopped she could see his boots just before her.

"You look quite lovely this morning, Sophie. A new Sophie, in fact, a modest, bashful . . ." Patrick let the words trail off suggestively.

Sure enough, Sophie lifted her head and her eyes flashed dangerously. "Don't make fun of me!"

Patrick's large hand cupped her chin. "Why not? We won't be able to survive marriage without making fun of each other, love."

Just then Sophie realized what she was looking at. "What happened, Patrick?" She reached out and delicately touched the dark swelling around his eye.

"My just desserts," Patrick replied. "Nothing to worry about." He reached up and captured her hand, bringing it to his mouth. Then he turned it over and brought her palm to his lips with exquisite gentleness.

"I have formally asked your father for your hand in marriage," he remarked, his eyes twinkling at her.

"You have?" Sophie's mind seemed to have become rather dizzy again.

Patrick didn't want her to know the cold truth, which was that she had no choice in the matter of marriage since the moment she had succumbed to his kisses. He had been struggling with his conscience all morning—in fact, ever since he left Brandenburg House last night.

"Will you marry me, Lady Sophie?"

Sophie wasn't paying much attention. Patrick's lips were caressing the center of her palm, and for some reason that simple touch was making her knees weak. "Yes," she said rather faintly.

Patrick frowned. "I am genuinely sorry that our actions last night curtailed your choice of marriage partners," he said formally. "However, I feel sure that you and I will rub along just as comfortably as you might have with Braddon."

Sophie's eyes wandered over Patrick's wanton black curls and deep-set eyes. What was he talking about? She would never be "just comfortable" living with him. In fact, the whole idea of sleeping in the same house with Patrick—in the same bed—sent a thrill of anticipation from the very top of her head to her toes.

What she really wanted was for him to wrap her in his arms again, the way he had last night. As if he read her mind, Patrick pulled her gently forward.

"Sophie." His voice was insistent. "I truly want to apologize for preventing your marriage to Braddon. I know you were excited about being a countess."

She looked up at Patrick in disbelief. Did he really think she was so shallow that it mattered what title her future husband had?

Before she could say anything, Patrick bent his head and captured her lips, drawing her up against his body. He'd been aroused ever since she'd walked into the room, even given that sacklike morning gown she was wearing.

As Patrick's hands danced among her curls, pulling out the carefully arranged loops and ribbons that Simone had spent so much time on earlier in the morning, Sophie didn't say a word. She melted against him, trembling as her breasts crushed against his chest and his mouth dipped languorously into hers again and again. Somehow her arms entwined themselves around his neck. When Sophie's tongue timidly met his, Patrick let out an oath and pulled her arms from his neck, moving back a step.

He stood there staring at the beautiful woman before him. Sophie's father would have been amused to see his future son-in-law now. Every vestige of the modish buck about town was gone. Patrick's eyes had gone black as midnight, and he was breathing quickly, the only thought in his head a fierce desire to pull Sophie down onto the hearth rug and make love to her then and there.

"Bloody hell," he finally said through clenched teeth, running his hand through his tousled hair.

Then he met Sophie's bewildered eyes. Involuntarily his eyes dropped to her swollen crimson mouth and he reached out again, pulling her soft body against the rock-hard mound in his breeches.

"We have to be married immediately, Sophie," he muttered into her neck. "I think I'll die if I don't get you into my bed soon."

Sophie smiled a bit, into the curve of his shoulder. Then she raised her head, winding one slender white arm around his neck.

"I don't see why we shouldn't wait a few months before getting married," she said saucily. With her free hand she touched his lips with her fingertips, giving a little gasp when her index finger was suddenly engulfed by moistly demanding lips.

"You've forgotten one thing, love," Patrick said in a voice as smooth as French velvet. "We have to be married immediately."

A smile trembled at the corners of Sophie's mouth. "Because of this?" With a heady sense of daring she leaned forward, just slightly, so that her body suddenly came into full contact with Patrick's breeches.

Patrick groaned. "No!"

But he took the invitation, and suddenly Sophie was the one unable to think clearly as Patrick's large hands meandered around her bottom, fitting her body to his as if they were a pair of nestling spoons.

Yet she managed to gasp, "If not because . . . then why?"

Patrick pulled away from her. "Get thee to a safe distance, wench! Because of last night, of course." He turned back to catch Sophie's mystified look. "You might be carrying a babe, Sophie."

"Carrying a babe!" She colored. Of course she knew that. She certainly had heard enough tirades from her mother about her father's absence from the marital bed and her resulting lack of children. Not to mention the more pungent comments of maids who seemed endlessly to discuss various ways to prevent conception.

"Actually, we should be more careful in the future." Patrick frowned. "You aren't truly one of those women like Braddon's sister who are obsessed with having children, are you?"

Sophie hesitated. She wasn't obsessed, but . . . what did he mean? Of course she wanted children. And didn't every man want a son? Even Braddon had said flat out that he needed an heir.

"Are you uninterested in children, sir?"

"For God's sake, Sophie, call me Patrick. After last night—"

Sophie blushed again at the mocking look in his eyes.

"And no," he continued, "I am not very interested in the idea of children. In fact, I'd just as soon not have any."

Sophie stumbled into speech. "But . . . but, no heir?"

Patrick gave her a flippant smile. "I don't have a title for a boy to inherit, so why should I worry about it? And my brother has two children, with more, I'm sure, on the way. So there will be plenty of family members to inherit my millions," he said with a distinctly ironic cut in his voice.

Sophie was bewildered. "You don't want to have *any* children?"

Patrick caught the tone in her voice and looked at her. Then he took her hand and drew her over to a low sofa.

"Are you very attached to the idea of becoming a mother? If so, I am even more sorry about what happened last night. I assumed that you shared Braddon's rather matter-of-fact attitude toward children. In my experience, very few well-bred ladies are interested in offspring."

Sophie swallowed. She didn't know what to say. Should she reveal the belly-deep, longing ache that she felt when she saw Charlotte with her babies? Patrick seemed to have such a dislike for the idea, and she found that the idea of *not* marrying him was more than she could bear.

"I always thought I would have children," she said, her voice faint.

Patrick clasped Sophie's hand, trying to see into her eyes, but she fixed them resolutely on the rose pattern of her gown.

"Perhaps we could have one child," he said after a silence. "I don't want to act as a tyrant in our marriage, Sophie. If you want a child, then we'll have one."

One? As an only child, Sophie had always planned to have many children, so that they could be playmates to one another. Oh, she didn't want ten children, as she had frivolously told Braddon's sister, but she definitely wanted more than one. She had spent her childhood sitting about her nursery, with no other children to play with.

But then, look at all the childish plans she had put to the side in the last twenty-four hours. She had thought never to marry a rake, and she was marrying one of the most notorious rakes in London. So she would marry the rake, and have only one child.

Sophie raised her blue eyes and met Patrick's black ones, and what she saw there warmed her resolve. It was better to marry Patrick and share him with other women than not to have him at all. And if they only had one child, so be it. She would cherish that child so much that he or she would never be lonely.

Patrick looked a bit anxious, so Sophie smiled at him reassuringly. "One child would be fine, Patrick."

He felt a wash of relief. He didn't know why his mother's death in childbirth had affected him so much—it appeared not to have affected his brother, Alex, at all. But Patrick was terrified by the idea of watching a wife go through childbirth. Even after nearly losing Charlotte when she gave birth to Sarah last year, Alex was still happily counting on having a boy the next time. But Patrick didn't ever want to put a woman at risk of death simply to produce babies. Children weren't worth it—not by any measure that he could think of.

Patrick gathered up Sophie's hands and trapped them just under his chin. "Would you like to take a trip in my clipper for our wedding trip, Sophie? I fear that Napoleon has precluded our making a civilized journey to the Continent."

Suddenly Sophie remembered something and snatched back her hands.

"Aren't you going to marry Daphne Boch?"

One of Patrick's eyebrows flew up. "The French girl? Well, I compromised her, but I compromised you *more,* don't you think?"

Sophie stared at him in shock.

"Oh for God's sake," Patrick half shouted. "Of course I didn't compromise Daphne Boch! The girl was stung by a bee and had to be taken off to get a mudpack. If I were affianced to Daphne, I certainly wouldn't have stayed in your room last night, Sophie."

She quirked an uncertain smile. She was glad to hear that Patrick wasn't supposed to marry Daphne. But she discounted his other reason almost entirely. Of course he would have stayed in her room. She had practically thrown herself at him, hadn't she? The details of last night were beginning to filter through her mind. What on earth was she thinking, welcoming a gentleman into her bedchamber? She must have been deranged!

Although, to be fair, she was expecting Braddon to

climb the ladder, and Braddon hadn't even wanted to kiss her. Braddon wasn't a likely candidate for the event that had happened last night.

Patrick stared at his wife-to-be in frustration. Sophie obviously saw him as unhesitatingly eager to compromise two young ladies in a single week.

"Sophie, you are the *only* young lady whom I have ever compromised in my life, either with a kiss or a longer encounter."

Sophie smiled at him reassuringly, but Patrick was no fool. Her eyes revealed a complete lack of trust. Well, she could learn to trust him after they were married.

"How does Thursday fortnight sound to you as a wedding day?" he asked.

"So soon?"

Patrick was a little startled himself at the suggestion. There would be no harm in waiting a month or even six weeks. But he found a deep impatience inside him at the idea of nights spent without Sophie.

"There will be a scandal anyway," he offered. "Why not be married and on our wedding trip before the *ton* grasps that you have broken your engagement to Braddon?"

Sophie thought this over. "I shall have to send a message to the Earl of Slaslow."

Patrick grinned. "It's generally considered de rigueur to inform your betrothed when you are planning to marry another man. But in this case you needn't if you don't want to. I told him myself last night."

"Last night!" Sophie's eyes flew to Patrick's. "Did you tell him everything?"

Patrick's eyes had a cutting edge. "No, I did not tell him everything. I simply explained that you had decided to marry me instead."

Sophie was unpleasantly shaken by the sudden chill in the air. "I'm sorry," she said humbly. "I didn't mean to imply that you boasted. What did he say?"

Patrick met her strained look and his eyes grew even colder. Could it be that Sophie *was* sorry not to be marrying Braddon? Could Braddon be right in his ranting and raving about how Sophie adored him?

"He was naturally dismayed that you no longer chose to marry him," Patrick said carefully.

"The devil of it is, Sophie, that we can't do a thing about it now." Suddenly he swung about and picked her up effortlessly from the sofa. "You're mine, Sophie. I can't give you back to Braddon. Things will never be the same as they were."

Sophie's eyes filled with tears. She was exhausted from lack of sleep and confused by the turn in the conversation. When Patrick swore softly and pulled her into his arms again she raised her mouth for consolation, trying to pretend that the whole conversation had never happened.

"Kiss me, Patrick, please," she breathed against his lips.

With a small moan, Patrick complied. He managed to back her up against a chair and her body was responding to his rhythmical touch in a way that suggested mindless pleasure. For a moment Patrick took objective stock of the small whimpers coming from Sophie's lips, the way in which her arms were holding him close with all her strength. Whatever unrequited love she might feel for Braddon didn't really matter. Patrick had been on the receiving end of quite a few whispered vows of love, and in his view it was only a matter of time before Sophie felt the same thing for him, given the passion that flared between them now. Women seemed to feel it necessary to explain physical pleasure by babbling about love—and Sophie and he were likely to share that pleasure in abundance.

So when they drew apart, following the marquis's discreet knock on the library door, Patrick looked keenly at Sophie's flushed face, her trembling fingers, and her swollen lips. She looked like a woman who had been thoroughly kissed and had enjoyed every minute of it. He'd woo her, that's all. In no time Sophie would be in love with him rather than with Braddon, resolving this uneasy feeling of guilt he felt about having taken her virginity.

Yet even after Sophie went upstairs to talk with her mother, and Patrick sat down with the marquis to draw up plans for the marriage settlement, he still felt curling pulses of guilt in his stomach. Finally he shrugged it off, naming a settlement figure that made the Marquis of Brandenburg's eyes bulge.

"My God, man, are you some sort of a nabob?" he finally asked.

"Something like it," Patrick answered laconically.

George had no particular desire for his only daughter to marry a man of money. Far more important was that Sophie find someone of birth, and someone she might love. But there's no parent in the world who doesn't feel a small thrill of satisfaction to find that his daughter has fallen into the way of marriage with an extremely wealthy man.

"I'll have my lawyer draw these up," George said as they shook hands. Then he glanced at Patrick's eye and the bruise on his jaw. "I apologize again for striking you."

Patrick said nothing but smiled with more than a hint of irony. "I deserved it," he repeated. "Luckily one of my uncles is a bishop. I shall arrange for a special license this afternoon."

"A special license?" The marquis was startled. He had thought the marriage might be held in haste, but this was paramount to an elopement.

"I have decided," Patrick said, "that the best way to survive the scandal with a minimum of unpleasantness for Lady Sophie is to get married in the very near future and leave London on an extended wedding trip."

"Oh, I see," George said, not really seeing at all.

"It will be accepted among the *ton* as a love match," Patrick said patiently.

"Oh, I see," George said again.

Patrick hesitated for a moment. Should he tell his future father-in-law about the title that Parliament might grant him? Better not, until it was official.

He bowed his farewell. "Shall I return tomorrow, my lord?"

"Oh right, yes indeed," George replied. "Join us for dinner, and we'll have the contracts all sewn up. Then you can marry my girl whenever you please."

"Thank you, my lord." Patrick bowed again and departed.

George stared after him, somewhat stunned by the events of the morning. Damned if he wouldn't have thought that it *was* a love match, if he didn't know better. Something about the way Patrick's eyes glowed when he said he wanted to marry Sophie immediately.

George pulled down his vest thoughtfully. He remembered very well the burning desire he had had to marry Eloise out of hand. The hours he had spent trying to persuade her to elope with him! But no, Eloise was always a stickler for convention, he thought. An unwilling smile lit his eyes as he remembered his younger self almost sobbing with lust over Eloise's white bosom. Ah well, things change.

Chapter 11

⟨⟨⟩⟩

S ophie pushed open the door to the nursery and found Charlotte, the Countess of Sheffield and Downes, sitting on a stool next to the fireplace while a small, very round girl seriously pulled a comb through Charlotte's curly black locks.

"Pippa! Ouch! Sweetheart"—Charlotte twisted about slightly so that she could look into her daughter's eyes—"you must be *very* gentle if you wish to become a lady's maid someday."

Sophie laughed. "Charlotte, aren't you afraid that Pippa is looking above herself?"

Charlotte looked up and beamed. "Look who's come to visit us, Pippa!"

The intent hairdresser dropped her comb and threw herself violently against Sophie's knees.

"Lady Sophie! Lady Sophie!"

Sophie leaned down, laughing, and swept Charlotte's

stepdaughter, Pippa, into the air. "My goodness, Pippa. If you grow any larger, I won't be able to pick you up like this!"

Pippa clung tightly to Sophie's side. "Did you know that I'm going to be three soon, Lady Sophie?"

"Is that true?" Sophie dropped a kiss on Pippa's nose. "And here I thought your birthday wasn't for a long time . . . until the summer had come and gone."

"Summer's happening soon," Pippa replied in a serious voice. "Why, Christmas is almost here, and then it'll be summer again before you know it!"

Sophie laughed again. "When did you become so wise, Pippa?"

Pippa's little chest swelled with pride. "Sometimes I'd rather have been born a bird, 'specially a swallow, but Mama says she likes the way I was born, like this." She pulled disparagingly at her rosy lawn dress.

Sophie gave Pippa a tight squeeze and put her down. Her eyes met Charlotte's, brimming with laughter.

"So, Charlotte, you'd rather have a daughter who wears a gown than one who wears feathers, hmm?"

Pippa plumped herself down on the floor next to her mama's knee.

"Mamas are like that, Lady Sophie," she announced. "They like their babies to wear dresses and stay clean. Someday you'll have your own baby, and then you'll know!"

"What if I have a little boy?"

"Little boy?" Pippa's brow wrinkled. There wasn't much thought about little boys in the nursery. "Mama and Sarah are girls," she said reprovingly. "And so is Katie." Sarah was the baby, and Katie was the girls' nanny.

"I know that, Pippa." Sophie's eyes were dancing. "But what if I have a baby and it's a little boy? He may not wish to wear dresses forever."

"You won't." Pippa was absolutely positive. "You'll

have a little girl, just like us. Do you think you'll have one soon, Lady Sophie?"

Charlotte giggled.

"No!" Sophie said hastily. "No, I'm not planning to have any babies, girls or boys, in the near future."

"Why not? Katie said that the party Mama gave was for your 'gagement 'cause you're going to move into your own house, and then you'll have lots of room for a baby. Who are you marrying? Is he nice?"

Sophie sat down in a chair, her eyes twinkling at the little girl leaning on her mama's knee.

"I was planning to marry a very nice man named Braddon."

From the corner of her eye Sophie saw Charlotte's head swing up, her eyes narrowed.

"Well, won't nice man Braddon want to have a little girl right away?"

Charlotte laughed, breaking in. "Pippa will persist all night once she's got hold of an idea, Sophie." And then: "Did you say *was* planning?"

"The truth is, Pippa," Sophie said, carefully not looking at Charlotte, "I've changed my mind about marrying Braddon, so he'll have to find a baby somewhere else."

Charlotte grinned exuberantly, and Pippa stopped her line of questioning and clambered over, on her knees, to pat Sophie's hand.

"You know, Lady Sophie, since you're not going to have your own little girl soon, perhaps Mama would let you take Sarah home. Since she's got two girls, she could give you one."

"Pippa, I told you to stop offering to give Sarah away!" Charlotte wrinkled her nose at Sophie, her eyes twinkling. "I'm afraid you aren't the first recipient of Pippa's generosity. So far she's offered Sarah to Katie's sister, to most of the servants, and, several times, to my mother."

Sophie tried hard not to laugh at the unrepentant child

before her. "If I do have a little girl someday, I'll borrow you occasionally. You could visit us and teach her how to keep her dresses clean."

Pippa scrambled to her feet, revealing the creased and messy front of her dress. "I can do that, Lady Sophie! When you *do* decide to get married, I'm going to wear my best dress and be very good."

The nursery door opened and Katie's plump face appeared. "Here's the little lamb now, my lady," she crooned, cradling a sleepy bundle. "Just woke up."

Charlotte stood up and lovingly took Sarah. "Time to feed you, sugarplum. And"—she swung around and leveled a mock glare at her best friend—"I would like to speak to you, Sophie York. So why don't we take tea in my sitting room?"

"Me, me, I want to go too," Pippa shouted enthusiastically.

"But, sweetheart, I think Katie needs her hair attended to," Charlotte said to Pippa, who scooted over and picked up her comb, torn between the idea of tea downstairs with Lady Sophie and practicing the beloved art of hair design.

"Now do look at that gown, Lady Pippa!" said the girls' nanny.

Pippa looked down inquiringly and carefully straightened out a few of the creases. "Well, I was careful, at first, Katie. Then I forgot."

"Oh my goodness," Katie exclaimed. "There's me with my hair all a mess, and I didn't even know it! Thank goodness Lady Pippa is here to help." She sat down and plucked off her cap, and Pippa began carefully pulling pins from the smooth coil of Katie's hair.

Sophie stooped and rubbed noses with the little sprite. "May I borrow you for an afternoon soon? We'll have ices; and you can tell me how a lady goes along. It will be good practice for when Sarah needs your help."

"All right, Lady Sophie," Pippa said happily. "Papa says ices are my vice. Do you know what that means?"

"It means that you like ices very, very much."

"What's your vice, Aunt Sophie?" Pippa's black eyes looked at Sophie inquiringly, her beautifully arched eyebrows the picture of her father's—and her uncle's.

The wish for a little girl who looks just like you, Sophie thought, unbidden. And everything that might lead to that wish.

"She shares your vices, Pippa." Charlotte's voice came from the door. "Sophie wishes for ices, and that's enough of vices!"

"Vice . . . ice . . . mice!" little Pippa shouted, waving her silver comb.

With a final wave Sophie slipped from the room, following Charlotte's slim figure down the stairs to the countess's sitting room on the first floor.

The minute Charlotte was inside the door she dropped into a rocking chair by the fireplace and arranged her loose morning gown so that she could nurse Sarah. Sophie wandered restlessly around the sitting room, a room entirely without the manicured formality of the majority of ladies' sitting rooms. Of course, this wasn't where Charlotte did her real work—she had a painting studio on the third floor—but the rose sitting room was the center of their family life. It was a warm room that tolerated a certain tumbling of books on the shelves and an occasional litter of papers by the fireside. It also tolerated the unprecedented affront of a mistress, a countess, who nursed her own child *and* without retiring to the darkest recesses of her bedchamber to do it.

Finally Charlotte looked up, bright eyes expectant.

"Well?"

Sophie had been watching wistfully as Sarah snuggled against her mother's breast, one small fist clutching a stray piece of bodice lace.

"Well . . ." Sophie repeated teasingly. "I jilted Braddon."

"Oh, Sophie, that is *so* wonderful!" Charlotte crowed. "Braddon wasn't intelligent enough for you. He would never have understood you, and in his own way he is quite strict in his notions, you know. You would have scandalized and terrified him at once. He is a very nice man, of course, but *not* the right one for you."

"And who is the right one?" Sophie's eyes were full of mischief.

Charlotte was prudently silent. If Sophie didn't want to marry her brother-in-law, that was all there was to it. Never mind that they were perfectly suited to each other, at least to Charlotte's mind.

"Oh dear," Sophie said with mock lamentation. "I'm afraid you won't approve of my new betrothed."

"Your *new* betrothed!"

"You couldn't possibly think that the most talked-about woman in all of London—at least since you've become so domestic and stopped making scandals—would settle for being *unengaged* for a whole twenty-four hours!" Sophie giggled as she danced tiny pirouettes around the sitting room. "Naturally I discarded Braddon only when I had a new applicant in hand."

Charlotte wrinkled her nose. "Don't, *don't* be so cynical, Sophie! It isn't like you at all, and I hate it when you put on the airs of a matron twice your age."

Sophie stopped pirouetting and smiled, acknowledging Charlotte's rebuke. "I don't mean to be flippant," she said, then stopped. It was so embarrassing to admit that she had agreed to marry Patrick after all her protests to the contrary.

So she flew over to Charlotte's armchair and bent over Sarah. "Oh, look at Sarah's little ear!"

There was a moment of silence as they both looked at Sarah's fuzzy round head and Sophie traced a delicate caress with one finger.

But Charlotte looked up, frowning in mock admonishment. "Don't try to change the subject, Sophie York! You tell me whom you have promised to marry." Then she looked dismayed. "You didn't accept Reginald Petersham, did you?"

Sophie laughed. "No. He's an agreeable man, but the oddest creature! Any other suggestions?"

Charlotte pressed her lips together. She was not, *not,* going to bring up Patrick's name again, given that Sophie had so firmly dismissed him as a possible candidate only a few nights before.

"What do you think of the Duke of Siskind?" Sophie asked impudently.

Charlotte looked aghast. "Oh, Sophie, you didn't! Why, he's ancient, and he has eight children!"

Sophie stroked Sarah's head again. "But I love children, Charlotte," she crooned, hiding her eyes so that Charlotte couldn't see her merriment.

"No, no," Charlotte moaned. "He must be sixty-five if he's a day!"

"I didn't accept him," Sophie admitted. "I'd like to have my own children." Child, she silently corrected herself. "Actually, I decided to take Patrick," she said carelessly. "He seemed quite insistent."

For a moment Charlotte didn't understand her. Then she half shrieked with delight. Startled, Sarah began to wail, so Charlotte had to stop talking and jiggle her babe until she settled back at the breast.

Finally, Charlotte was able to look at Sophie. She threw her arm around Sophie's shoulders, drawing her close.

"Now you're my sister," she said, her face alive with joy.

As an only child, Sophie had longed and longed for a sister . . . and now she had one. "Sister," Sophie agreed softly.

Questions were bubbling up inside Charlotte like a wishing

well hit by an early spring storm. "But how? And when? Where will you go on your wedding trip? Oh, and did you tell him about your languages? And what *does* your mother say about it?"

"Mother," Sophie said wryly, "had approximately three fits of hysterics over my ingratitude yesterday, but today the affront has shifted to my future husband's stubborn nature, given that Patrick thought to hold the ceremony one fortnight from today. Mama refused to contemplate a ceremony earlier than three months. In the end, it appears we will be married in six weeks. We are being married by his uncle, the Bishop of Winchester." Sophie looked confused for a second. "Actually, I suppose you know that your uncle-in-law is a bishop."

As Charlotte smiled, Sophie held her breath. Was Charlotte going to delve into the reason for their scandalously brief engagement? Was there ever such a thing?

She rushed back into speech. "Mama is frantically planning a grand wedding. My father did his best to dissuade her, but she is convinced that flamboyant display is the only way to save me from certain social ruin. All the maids are making horse blankets from pink taffeta. Mama wants the invitations delivered in proper style."

Charlotte was drawing her own conclusions about Patrick's demand for a hasty marriage. "My goodness, Sophie." A smile lurked at the corners of her mouth. "When Henrietta Hindermaster broke her engagement to Baron Siskind, even *she* allowed three months to go by before she married her parents' butler!"

Sophie felt an uncomfortable pink rise in her cheeks. She had adapted an exterior sheen of sophistication for so long that it was surprising to find how very much she minded making a scandal. Lord, her scanty dresses had been scandalous ever since she attended her first ball.

Charlotte smiled sympathetically. "Poor Sophie. I shouldn't tease you. The only wonder is that Patrick didn't climb up the balcony to your room and sweep you off to Gretna Green!"

As the color in Sophie's cheeks deepened, Charlotte's dark eyes widened. "Sophie! He *didn't*!"

Crazily, Sophie was caught between an impulse to laugh and one to blush even harder. So she quickly rose and took a few steps back from Charlotte, brushing her curls behind her shoulders.

At her silence, Charlotte caught and forcefully held her gaze. "Sophie York," she demanded, "I want to know *everything*!"

At that very moment Patrick was looking anywhere rather than at his brother's face, as he tried to figure out how much to tell him. Damn! Why hadn't he asked Sophie what she planned to tell Charlotte? He had the hazy sense that women told each other everything. Did that mean that Sophie would regale Charlotte with all the details behind their hasty marriage?

Alex and Patrick were sitting in the changing room of Jackson's Boxing Salon, relaxing after a punishing bout of sparring practice with Cribb himself. They had washed, and an attendant now stood alertly at each of their sides, waiting to aid them with their attire. Gentlemen who padded their garments, for example, invariably needed a final twitch here or there to make sure that their calf pads were lying evenly.

Granted, little Billy Lumley had figured out with one glance that these two particular men had no need of padding anywhere, but there was still the possibility of a tip, so he waited patiently, holding one of their coats. Damned if he knew which one the coat belonged to, since their lordships looked as much alike as those heathen Indians he'd seen, the ones imported from America. In fact, they didn't look so different from the Indians, given that their skin was an odd golden color, not pasty white like most of the men they had in there.

But Patrick stretched out his long legs, drew in a long breath, and waved Billy and his fellow attendant off to a safe distance. Alex looked at him inquiringly as he pulled a fresh shirt over his head.

"I'm getting married in six weeks," Patrick said, a smile biting at the corner of his mouth. "I thought you might like to be there."

There was a moment of silence. "Daphne Boch?" Alex finally offered, his tone noncommittal.

"No. Your wife's choice, in fact. Sophie York."

Alex's mouth curled in a smile uncannily like his twin brother's. "I like Sophie, not that it matters. Mother would have liked her too."

"She would, wouldn't she?" For a moment both men thought of their effervescent mother, and the way she would run laughing into the nursery, gathering them up in a hug that smelled like bluebells. Until she died giving birth to a stillborn brother, and they were left with a taciturn, gouty father who promptly sent them away to school, and shipped them to whomever would agree to take two small boys during school vacations.

Alex was the first to stand up. "Why so soon?" he asked mildly.

"I have a fancy," Patrick drawled.

"A fancy?" Alex's tone was meditative.

He waved Billy over and took the coat from his hand, slipping into it without a bit of trouble, to Billy's sorrow.

"Well, you're a fine one to talk," Patrick retorted. He put on his own coat, absentmindedly giving both attendants a healthy tip.

A smile lightened Alex's eyes. "And then?"

"We'll take a trip down the coast on the *Lark*."

Alex looked at him sharply. "Down the coast?"

Patrick nodded. "From the *Lark* I can discreetly check

Breksby's fortifications in Wales. This seems as good a time as any."

Alex grimaced. "The whole notion that Napoleon might invade Wales is absurd. Napoleon—if he got the boats together to do it—is sure to head for Kent or Sussex. For God's sake, he only has flat-bottomed boats! He'll go straight from Boulogne to Kent."

Patrick shrugged. "It's a good excuse for a wedding trip."

"One doesn't need an excuse, Patrick." Alex hesitated. He had destroyed his own wedding trip by falling into a desperate fit of jealousy. "Don't repeat my mistakes," he added lightly.

Patrick grinned. "I'm not such a lobcock as that. I'm looking forward to it. Besides, I'm not planning to have the same kind of marriage that you have, Alex. Oh, I'm not saying it won't be a good marriage—but remember, Sophie wanted to marry Braddon Chatwin. I shouldn't think we'll share the paroxysms of emotion that you and Charlotte indulge in."

Alex looked at him silently, one eyebrow raised.

"I told you. She wanted Braddon's title."

"What did she say about your becoming a duke?"

"I haven't told her." Patrick's calm answer admitted no questions.

But twin brothers are not known for reticence. "What do you mean, you haven't told her? Are you waiting until you're married?"

Patrick's shoulder lifted in a tight shrug. "Not particularly. The subject never came up. I will travel to Turkey by myself. I can't imagine that Sophie would be very interested in an event almost a year in the future."

Alex slanted his brother a glance under black lashes. "Are you certain you wish to be married, Patrick?"

"If I have to get leg-shackled, why not to Sophie? I like her, and she's—"

"Unbelievably beautiful," his brother broke in.

"There is that." Patrick smiled as a vision of Sophie's sun-dusted curls drifted through his mind.

"And remarkably intelligent," his brother prompted.

Patrick shrugged again, looking back over his shoulder. "Yes, in a flirtatious sort of way. She'll be good company."

"Flirtatious?" Alex seemed to be choking on a private joke. "Sometime, little brother . . . sometime you must ask her about languages."

"I must go." Patrick was so edgy that he was barely listening. It was nearing time for dinner with his bride-to-be and her parents. He wasn't looking forward to an evening with offended parents, but it would be nice to find Sophie clinging to him, her lips cherry-sweet, her breath caught in her throat. He wanted to remind himself why he was committing the heinous act of getting married. He had always sworn never to go near the parson's mousetrap.

"So you picture your marriage along the lines of a calm affair that just happens to last sixty years or so," Alex said with a twinkle as they strolled out the door of Jackson's and onto Piccadilly. "In fact, this marriage is going to be so civilized that Sophie won't even notice if you wander off to Turkey for a few months. And you will wave good-bye as happily as if you were off to a hunting lodge for a week."

"Hearts and beauty have nothing to do with each other," Patrick replied. "Believe me, I've been dealing with beauties for years, and my heart has never been in danger."

"Well, aren't you a knowing one," his brother said mockingly. "We'll see, shall we? Care to make a small wager?"

"A wager on what?"

"Your heart, naturally. I'll bet you five hundred crowns that a year from tomorrow you'll admit to being desperately in love with your wife."

"I'd hate to take money from a washed-up jack-pudding like yourself," Patrick said with a dry chuckle. "Having fallen into a sloppy state, you're eager to persuade your own brother that he will share your affliction."

"Then you'll have no qualms accepting my wager," Alex retorted.

"I'll hand the five hundred crowns to charity, in your name," Patrick replied in a devilishly sweet tone. "Because, by God, you're as likely to find me sleeping in a nightshirt as to see me hand over a tuppence."

Alex's eyes brimmed with laughter. "You forget, dear brother, that I have seen you around Sophie. You want her so much that you pant when she walks within a fingertip of you. If—no, *when*—you give me five hundred crowns, I'll buy you a nightshirt trimmed with the finest Brussels lace."

Patrick took the reins of his low-slung phaeton and swung up on the step. "May I give you a lift back to Grosvenor Square?"

"No, thanks. I think I'll drop in at White's and see what the betting books are saying about Lady Sophie's new betrothal."

Patrick cast him a keen glance. "Dress it up with frills and bows, won't you?"

"Of course." The Earl of Sheffield and Downes set off down the road, swinging his mahogany cane with a jaunty air. His demeanor indicated that he was far from indifferent about the fact that his dearest relation had consigned himself to the ignominious fate of leg-shackling, to take place at three o'clock in St. George's chapel, precisely—and scandalously—six weeks from today.

Chapter 12

❧

Six weeks later, Sophie still felt the wedding was due to arrive too soon. Her bridal gown had just been fitted for the umpteenth time. Five seamstresses had scurried off to the upper regions of the house, bearing the gown as if it were an altar cloth embroidered by the pope himself. Sophie sighed. If this were an ordinary afternoon, she would sit down and work for an hour or two. She drifted over to her desk and stared down at the book of Turkish grammar that waited invitingly.

But just as she picked up the book, which sat precisely where her billets and bills would have reposed had the desk belonged to another lady, the door opened and her mother entered the bedchamber.

"Sophie, I think—" Eloise stopped. "Sophie, are you holding one of those language books?"

Sophie looked down at the small brown book in her hand. "Yes, *Maman.*"

"How did I raise such a featherheaded daughter?" Eloise ignored her own question. "Don't you yet understand that childish things are put aside once a woman is married? Languages are the—the flummery of your childhood, and must be left behind, like all subjects of the schoolroom."

Sophie hesitated. "Perhaps Patrick would not mind if he knew I spoke a few languages. He seems to be most amiable."

"Don't be a twit, Sophie. Men naturally find fault with bluestockings, and rightly so; overeducated women are the most boring creatures alive!"

Sophie bit back the obvious rejoinder. Eloise's daughter probably ranked among the foremost bluestockings in London and yet not one gentleman had called her boring.

"Lord, I wish I had never let you continue in this silly vein of behavior," Eloise said pettishly. "There's something so dreadfully commonplace about studying languages."

Sophie watched Eloise rustle about the bedroom, pushing small ornaments into straight lines. Her mother didn't really care one way or the other about Sophie's unexpected brilliance at languages. Other than decreeing that Sophie was never to be tutored by a male, Eloise had allowed Sophie a free hand at French, Italian, Welsh, Gaelic, and then German and Turkish in tandem, given that Sophie had had the good luck to hear about a Turkish immigrant's wife from the German woman who visited the house every morning.

"I'm not a complete widgeon," her mother said curtly, as she pulled open Sophie's wardrobe and frowned at the gowns. "Your father is trying to pull wool over my eyes, but I have as good an idea as the next person about why this marriage is happening so hastily. So we can dispense with an explanation of wedding nights."

Sophie's heart began pounding in her throat with pure shame and embarrassment.

But her mother continued, with more difficulty. "That isn't truly important anyway, Sophie. I would like to give you advice that would make your marriage different from mine. But I don't know what to say."

Tears pressed at the back of Sophie's eyes. "It's all right, *Maman*."

Eloise swung about and sat down in a high-backed chair by the fireplace. "It is *not* all right, Sophie. I ruined my marriage somehow. After all the years of finding fault with your father, I am beginning to wonder if there was something I could have done differently. Perhaps I was too bitter."

Sophie sank into the chair opposite. Her mother had reached the same conclusion that Sophie had: that if only her mother had overlooked her father's mistresses, they would have had a happier life together. Certainly Sophie would have had siblings.

"I couldn't do it," Eloise said in a harsh whisper. "I wasn't made that way, and I was barely eighteen when I married. You are almost twenty years old, and lighter of heart, Sophie. Please, please, I beg you, turn your eyes away when your husband courts other women. Welcome him back into your bed without a word. Don't do anything that will give him a dislike of you, such as flaunting your ability to speak languages."

Sophie took a deep breath. "I will try, *Maman*." She strove to make her tone reassuring. "I won't allow Patrick to know I can speak anything but English. And I won't be angry when he sleeps with other women. I know that I am marrying a rake."

"Turn the other way," Eloise said. She was leaning forward now, looking earnestly into her daughter's eyes. "Ignore it. The real pleasure—the delight—in marriage comes from children."

Sophie gave her a crooked little smile.

"I longed to give you the siblings you wanted so much, Sophie!" her mother cried passionately. "Do you remember? You used to beg and beg for a sister. But what could I do? Your father and I had stopped speaking to each other, and I didn't know how to mend it. The only thing we have in common now is you, Sophie. We both love you. Believe me, children can be a link between you and Patrick, if pride does not sour the marriage."

Sophie swallowed again and then blurted, "Patrick wants to have only one child, *Maman*."

Eloise was silent for a second. "I am very sorry to learn that. I know how much you love children. Guard your one child then. Did you ever wonder why I was so stern with regard to your playmates?"

Sophie nodded. She was never permitted to visit other children, and her nanny was strictly instructed to chase off anyone who approached them on their brief, supervised walks.

"I had to protect you, Sophie. You are my only child." Eloise visibly regained her composure. "But what is important is not the number of children you have, but the pleasure you are able to take in your marriage. A marriage like mine—of bitterness on one side and disinterest on the other—is worse than having no children at all."

Eloise looked faintly embarrassed. "To be blunt, never refuse your husband in bed. I have thought for years that perhaps I shouldn't have rashly ordered your father from the bedroom. I was a capricious little fool. Now that I'm almost forty, I would give anything to take back those words. Don't do it, Sophie. No matter how angry you are, never let Patrick know. *Never* banish him from the room. Unless you're with child," she added.

Sophie nodded silently.

"I won't, *Maman*," she whispered.

Just then Sophie's maid, Simone, entered the bedchamber followed by a small phalanx of maids. Simone's arms were full of crackling tissue paper.

"Begging your pardon, my lady," Simone said, curtsying in the marchioness's direction, "but we are ready to start packing Lady Sophie's trunks now."

Eloise nodded and stood up, then paused, looking at

her daughter. She ran her hand over Sophie's hair. "He cannot help but fall in love with you, *mignonne*. I am sure all my advice is for naught."

Sophie smiled at that, but after Eloise left the room she sat for a moment, hands clutched around the small leather book she held. Her mother was right. Eloise's blunder as a wife had been to deplore behavior over which she had no control. In other words, Sophie thought, if Patrick's eye wanders, I must appear never to notice.

~∼~

Lord Breksby drummed his fingers on his desk in an unusual display of agitation. "This is infamous!"

A little man, dressed in a thoroughly insignificant fashion, flashed Breksby an amused look. "Napoleon always has been an inconvenient sort of chap," he agreed.

"He's beyond the pale," Breksby said, almost choking with annoyance. "How on earth does he think to get away with it?"

"Pure luck that we found out," his guest pointed out.

Breksby sighed. "I suppose I'd better tell Patrick Foakes."

"M'understanding is that Foakes is setting off on his wedding trip . . . down the coast." With a mere twitch of his eyebrows, the small man conveyed that he was perfectly aware of the reason why Patrick was sailing toward Wales.

"Yes, well. Damnation." Breksby drummed his fingers again.

"Why tell him?" The small man's eyelids drooped.

Breksby eyed him. His guest knew more about the inner workings of several governments than he himself did. It galled him, but it was the truth.

"How can I not tell Foakes? He may be walking into danger. What if we slip up and the scepter does explode?"

"The scepter will not explode unless we allow a substitution of the original scepter," the small man pointed out. "The scepter is the key and Foakes doesn't have it—we do."

He drifted to the door, indicating that his brief visit was over. "Better not to risk Foakes dropping a hint to his wife," he murmured as he left. "Men in love are dangerous."

Breksby stared at the closed door. The man had shown himself out, and Breksby had let him go. Lord only knew what secret documents he would be riffling through in the next hour or so. Breksby shrugged. There was no stopping him anyway.

Breksby sat down and pulled out a sheet of paper. But a moment later he tore up the elegantly written note, addressed to Right Honorable Patrick Foakes.

He was right, the little man. It was damnable that he was always right, but . . . Perhaps the best idea would be to send the scepter out incognito, as it were. If the scepter wasn't delivered to Foakes until a mere hour before it was due to be presented to Selim, the risk would be minimized nicely. An exploding scepter! What an absurd notion. But—and Breksby sobered, thinking of it—if Foakes did bring such a device to Selim's coronation, and it did blow up, the resulting imbroglio would be a disaster for England. Selim's delicate sensibilities would be insulted, if indeed his royal person survived the explosion. He would undoubtedly side with Napoleon on the spot, and declare war against England.

"Damn and blast," Breksby muttered to himself. He summoned his attendant and clapped a hat on his head. The Treasury would have to know about Napoleon's little scheme.

❧

That evening the Marquis and Marchioness of Brandenburg found themselves alone in the drawing room, awaiting the arrival of their daughter. They were having a family dinner. The last family dinner, Eloise thought, with a lump in her throat. Tomorrow her child would leave the house for St. George's chapel and never return, except as a visitor.

She took the glass of sherry Carroll handed her and walked to the large window looking over the gardens. Something about the conversation with Sophie . . . Eloise had never, ever said out loud the things she had told Sophie. It made her feel subtly embarrassed even to be in the same room with her husband.

But if George noticed the faint feeling of constraint in the room, he said naught. He cheerfully strolled to the window as well and stood at her shoulder.

"I think it'll be a pretty match, don't you, my dear?"

Eloise felt unwontedly short of breath. Now that she'd seen George naked again, the image of his chest and legs superimposed itself onto his ordinary presence. He stood there, fully clothed, at her shoulder, and she shivered as images from early in their marriage drifted through her mind.

A sudden memory came, unbidden: how George used to kiss the back of her neck again and again. Eloise turned and looked up at her husband. He was gazing out over the garden and apparently hadn't even noticed her lack of an answer.

"George," Eloise said. She felt herself flushing.

George looked down at her. His gray eyes sobered. Then he reached out and curled his hand around the nape of her neck, precisely the spot she had just thought of. He hadn't touched her so intimately in years.

Eloise stood with all the stillness of a terrified rabbit. It was a moment for courage. But the courage to overcome years of estrangement is hard to come by. Her breath burned in her chest. Words clogged in her throat. She bent her neck, helplessly ashamed.

But George merely spread his hand a bit wider and rubbed his thumb in a small circle, dropping his hand only when Carroll opened the drawing room doors to usher Sophie into the room.

Chapter 13

～❦～

Sophie woke up so early that it was barely light outside, clambering out of her bed to see the first gray streaks of dawn. What does one do on the morning of one's marriage? Sleep, her mother would say. Sleep so that you look your best. But Sophie couldn't sleep.

Her heart was pounding with excitement. She leaned on the windowpane where Patrick had come into her room, and told herself for the sixtieth time that she was doing the right thing. If she looked closely, Sophie could see faint white scratches on the windowsill: the marks where Patrick's ladder had rested.

Two men trundled by, driving a large open wagon. The night-soil men were heading out of London with their loads of fertilizer. The city was waking up; down in Covent Garden the fruit merchants would be arriving, and in Spitalfields the bird sellers would be opening their shops. When she was a girl Sophie used to love to look at the rows of goldfinches and woodlarks, linnets and green-finches. Today the thought of small birdcages caught at the back of her throat and made her want to cry.

"Stupid, don't be stupid!" she whispered to herself furiously. Some marriages work; some don't. What right did she have to dramatize her upcoming nuptials, as if she were Juliet being forced to marry Paris?

Sophie wrapped her arms around herself, hugging her breasts through the thin chambray of her nightdress. Ah, but she wanted him, she did. She wanted Patrick Foakes as much as Juliet ever wanted Romeo. Probably more, given that she had already experienced a night of leisured bliss before marrying Patrick.

So really, what was she worrying about? Sophie leaned forward, planting her forehead against the chilly glass, her eyes fixed on the street below. Two sturdy delivery carts rounded the corner and steered their way carefully into the alley running alongside Brandenburg House. The first phaeton of the morning clattered its way along the street.

If it had been an ordinary morning, Sophie would have rung for hot chocolate and then worked at her desk for two hours before ringing for a bath. For a moment she let her mind laze over the idea of returning to her study of Turkish verbs. But her mother's scornful words echoed in her head. Childhood play doesn't belong in marriage. As she watched, the housekeeper sailed out of the house to finger vegetables in a cart stopped before the door.

Mama was as embarrassed as I was, Sophie thought, her forehead still pressed against the cool glass. But she gave me good advice. If knowing about my languages will give Patrick a dislike of me, then he must never know. It was very hard to imagine not welcoming Patrick to her bed, and Sophie quickly dismissed that part of her mother's advice as warmth crept up her cheeks.

The key was never, never to let Patrick know that she had developed a foolish *tendresse* for him. If Patrick didn't know the truth, then she could play the role of the sophisticated woman who watched her husband come and go with ease. But the humiliation she would feel if he ever found out that she loved him—it chilled her blood.

"I shall never tell," Sophie whispered, her breath momentarily fogging the glass window. Somehow comforted, she realized that her toes were cold, curled against the chilly wood under her feet. She ran back over the warm carpet beside her bed and tucked herself under the blanket.

When Sophie next woke, great golden swashes of sunlight lay across the tangled roses that bordered her carpet. Sophie turned over and blinked sleepily at the canopy. She had been dreaming in Italian, something she hadn't done since she'd learned the language some four years ago. It was an odd little dream, and it slipped away even as she tried to bring it to mind. Something about a masquerade ball in which she was to be dressed as a gypsy, with a straw hat tied under the chin. Sophie grimaced. Today was the beginning of a masquerade, in a way. She reached out and pulled the rope next to her bed, swinging her legs out of bed yet again.

◦≈◦

Eloise York felt a warm glow of satisfaction in the pit of her stomach as she looked discreetly over the mass of gentlefolk occupying St. George's chapel at three o'clock on a Wednesday afternoon. She had rummaged up every single relation she and George could lay claim to, and had, in essence, done the same with Patrick Foakes's family, given that it consisted of one brother (Alex), an uncle, and an aunt. However few in number, they were all prominently in view. Patrick's uncle would conduct the ceremony, and his aunt, Henrietta Collumber, had been given a place of honor next to the bride's mother.

"Stop peering, Eloise," Henrietta said, with the freedom

of a rather crotchety woman on the far side of seventy. "They're all here, no need to worry. Thinking it's the love match of the century, no doubt!" She positively cackled.

Eloise looked at Henrietta with a pang of extreme dislike. Could she risk giving the old harridan a sharp setdown? No. Instead, Eloise turned her head back toward the altar. She had been very pleased to learn that the Earl of Slaslow was standing up for Patrick. That should put a sock in the gossips' chatter! Slaslow looked a bit peevish, but then he was the peevish sort anyway. In fact, the more she'd thought about it, the more it seemed clear that Sophie would be better off with Patrick Foakes.

Patrick looked imperturbable, standing in front of the church with his twin brother. Unlike Braddon, who was nervously shifting from foot to foot and yanking at his vest, the two Foakes brothers stood like rocks.

Just then the brief hush and hum that always precedes the entrance of a bride fell over the chapel. Sophie appeared in the recessed columns at the side of the chapel, her hand resting lightly on her father's sleeve.

Eloise had persuaded her to wear white, and as Sophie walked quietly beside her father, her gown gleaming palely in the late afternoon light, she looked innocent, fragile, otherworldly. No one would think that she was a young woman who drew scandalous attention like a magnet to the true north. Even the most vicious imagination must hesitate to speculate why this marriage had happened with such speed. Sophie's hair spilled down her back in a glowing flood, adorned only by creamy rosebuds tucked among the amber curls. She was the snow princess from a Russian folk tale, the guileless fairy queen from an Irish love story.

Her dress was made of pearly ivory satin, caught up under the bodice, and laid over with a shimmering overdress that extended into a train at the back. The sleeves were short, the bodice modest, and Sophie was wearing high satin gloves. When Madame Carême produced the gown, Sophie had wailed that she would look a veritable dowager.

In truth, it was probably the most conservative dress Eloise had seen Sophie wear since her daughter's debut. But Madame Carême's seamstresses had sewn frantically to add the one touch that turned the dress from conventional to enchanting. Madame added golden Brussels lace to the bodice, to the line of the overskirt as it fell from Sophie's bosom, to the border of the shorter gown, and to the longer flow of the train. The lace caressed Sophie's creamy skin and emphasized the curve of her breasts and the length of her slim legs.

And, Lord, but Madame Carême *did* know how to make a woman look enthralling. The gold lace echoed Sophie's hair, making her look like an enchanting ivory and gold icon. A blasphemous icon, of course. No man in the chapel looked at her with reverence; the pure wanton lust rising in their loins fought so pallid an emotion. Against ivory silk and ivory skin, the blood beat in Sophie's cheeks in a way that spoke of life, pagan life, life in the meadow, not the church, life in the bed, not the tomb.

Patrick's breath caught in his throat as Sophie moved toward him without meeting his gaze. She raised her eyes only after she and the marquis reached the altar.

Then, for a brief instant, Sophie's eyes met Patrick's and she colored, looking down at the roses in her hand. A smile trembled on Patrick's lips but the intent, languorous heat rising from his body stifled any impulse to laugh.

At least he knew why he was getting married. He had never experienced, nor would he ever experience again, a desire as profound as that which he consistently felt for Sophie York. Unbidden by the priest, he reached out and drew her small hand into his.

Bishop Foakes cast his nephew an admonishing look

from under bushy eyebrows. He'd agreed to lead the service out of respect for Patrick's dead father, his own brother. Lord knows the boys had caused Sheffie grief. But Sheffie would have been happy to be here today, Richard judged. Get 'em both married and they'll calm down, that had always been his advice. Not that Sheffie had paid any attention, packing the twins off to the Continent and the Far East rather than sewing them up in a couple of solid marriage contracts. He was lucky that the boys had returned safe and sound. Although his brother hadn't managed to see either of 'em before he died, now that Richard came to think of it.

Well, time to get on with the ceremony. Richard surreptitiously adjusted his high bishop's hat. It had a tendency to ride backward and look like a ship listing in a storm.

"Dearly beloved," Richard intoned, "we are gathered here together in the sight of God . . ."

Sophie began to tremble like a leaf as the bishop's deep voice jerked her out of a dreamlike state. Her hand was engulfed in Patrick's large one, which made her feel a longing wave of desire for him. And *that* feeling made her want to run from the chapel. Her life seemed to stretch ahead of her, gray and fruitless, marked by anguish and embarrassment as her husband dallied with other women.

As Richard wound through the familiar words of the marriage service he noted that the groom was still holding the bride's hand. Ah well. It would probably be taken as a romantic gesture by the guests, and Lord knows they needed to emphasize romance in order to get through this particular wedding without scandal.

The bishop turned his attention to his nephew. My goodness, Patrick has sarcastic-seeming eyebrows, floating half up his forehead as they do, Richard thought. It makes the boy seem satirical even as he stands in a holy place.

Finally he turned to Sophie with the command, "Wilt

thou have this man to thy wedded husband, to live to-gether . . ." But Sophie's head was thronged with images of her mother crying. Suddenly all the lies her father had asked her to tell about his whereabouts reverberated in her mind, ugly specters of a marriage in shreds and tatters, run—and ruined—by falsehoods. She looked up at Patrick, her eyes asking an agonized, unspoken question.

Patrick's hand tightened, almost as if he knew what she was thinking. And his eyes smiled at her: those lovely black, black eyes with small crinkles at the corners from the sun. Sophie straightened her backbone and said, clearly, "I will."

Well, at least Patrick seemed to be marrying into a good family, Richard thought. He, for one, approved of Sophie's white face and trembling fingers as she swore on the prayer book. Brides should be meek and small. Yes, small and meek, that was the best sort of bride. Richard clapped the prayer book shut, suddenly realizing that he'd droned his way through the whole service.

"I pronounce that they be Man and Wife together," he said, deftly adjusting his hat.

Sophie's lips moved, but no noise came out.

Richard frowned. Could it be that the blushing, trembling bride muttered *"Merde"*? No, surely not. She looked a wee, refined creature, not capable of swearing in any language. Richard smiled at the pair before him in a jovial fashion. "You may kiss the bride," he told Patrick.

Patrick turned Sophie to face him. He felt very pleased with himself. The whole transaction felt *right*. He had had the same feeling when he purchased a Baltimore clipper from that new American company. Sure enough, the ship had weathered a hurricane off the shore of Trinidad and was on her fifth voyage now.

Sophie looked up at him, her blue eyes so dark as to look almost black. For a moment Patrick was startled by the enormous reserve he glimpsed in them. He drew her to him and lowered his head. Sophie rested passively against his chest, her lips cool and unresponsive.

Oh hell, Patrick thought to himself. He needed to coax a romantic kiss from Sophie's lips in order to emphasize the idea that true love had dictated their brief engagement. He slid his large hands up her back and drew her more sharply to him, his lips demanding. Then suddenly Sophie's lips softened and she melted against him, her breath a caress that set his blood on fire. Patrick's head swam and his body turned to flame as a surge of heat rushed up the back of his neck.

As they drew apart, husband and wife looked at each other for a moment. Patrick was shocked, his breath coming fast, his body urgently aware of every facet of Sophie's body. Sophie was aware only of the wanton way she had pressed against Patrick. Had anyone been able to see her knees buckle?

There was a little rustle in the chapel. Members of the *ton* were used to couples who turned briskly and trotted down the aisle together to the sound of trumpets, couples who wasted little time looking at each other.

"Oh my, I could almost think that it *was* a love match," Lady Penelope Luster said to her best friend. "Just look at the way he's looking at her! It's enough to make me swoon, I do declare."

"Oh, don't be such a widgeon, Penelope," her companion replied, in a whistling half-shriek. "That's the same look he was giving her when I found them together at my ball a month or so ago, and let me tell you, that look has nothing to do with love! *You* wouldn't know, since you were never married."

Penelope shot her friend a look of near hatred. What did Sarah Prestlefield know of "looks"? She was a stout dowager of fifty-some and Penelope would eat her hat if Lord Prestlefield had ever looked at Sarah the way in which Patrick Foakes had just looked at his new wife. "I don't care what you say, Sarah," Penelope stated. "They appear the most romantic couple in the world to me."

Lady Prestlefield turned up her nose in a gesture of patent disbelief.

"I'll tell you something, Sarah," Penelope persisted. "Only a slow-top would think that any woman in her right mind would choose Slaslow over Patrick Foakes."

Sarah cast her another long-suffering look. "You're a fool, Penelope," she said shortly. "Slaslow is an *earl*. No woman in her right mind would turn him down for a younger brother, no matter how rich Foakes is."

The newly married couple was nearing their pew, and the way in which Patrick Foakes had folded his wife's arm into his, making her walk very close to him down the aisle, only strengthened Penelope's belief in the love match.

Besides, the Earl of Slaslow was walking directly behind his former betrothed, and his mild resemblance to a bulldog made her shudder. To Penelope's mind, Patrick's sooty eyes had distinct precedence over Braddon's plump amiability. Wealth and titles had nothing to do with this . . . this air of sensuality that breathed from Patrick Foakes.

"Look at that," Lady Prestlefield said. "Erskine Dewland is walking again. I thought the doctors said he would never walk."

Penelope watched Erskine—Quill, as he was known to his friends—make his way down the aisle with disinterest. Then she twisted about to watch the newlyweds leave. The great doors stood open and the Foakeses were standing at the top of the marble steps with their backs to the chapel. A ray of lazy sunshine caught them there, turning Sophie into a slim golden flame and Patrick into a dusky winter god next to her summer glow. As Penelope watched, Patrick bent over to kiss his bride again.

"You can say what you like," Penelope Luster said fiercely to her closest friend. "But I shall always maintain that this is a love match! And I don't intend to entertain anyone else's opinions on the subject."

Sarah cast a sideways glance at Penelope's tightly closed lips. Penelope was a mild woman most of the time, but when she took a notion, she clung to it like a cur.

"All right, Penelope, all right," she whispered. Sarah patted Penelope's hand. "I'll agree with you, of course. And you know that Maria loves a romance. Look at her— she's sniffing into a handkerchief." The Countess Maria Sefton was one of the most influential ladies of the London *ton*.

And so it was that Patrick Foakes was able to sweep away the reigning beauty of London, steal her from his own best friend, marry her out of hand, and escape with impunity. Rather than turning up their noses or whispering cruel commentary out of the corners of their mouths, the London *ton* glowed with consciousness of their own generosity. Such sweet, beautiful children, Patrick and Sophie! Lovers will be lovers, people reminded themselves.

Braddon manfully did his best, swallowing his resentment at losing yet another perfectly good woman to the Foakes brothers.

"It was like Romeo and Juliet," he said carelessly, as Lord Winkle sidled his way over to him at the ball following the wedding and asked how it felt, having his closest friend steal his betrothed. "Couldn't stand in their way, could I? Like Tristan and . . ." He felt a bit uncertain. What were the names of all those confounded lovers they had to learn about in school?

"Tristan and Isolde?" Miss Cecilia Commonweal, commonly known as Sissy, said helpfully.

"Yes, exactly." Braddon smiled at her in a grateful sort of way.

"Although," Sissy added punctiliously, "Tristan was Isolde's uncle, so that example is not quite as romantic as

Romeo and Juliet. Abelard and Eloise were another famous pair of lovers you might consider, except I believe
that something quite *unfortunate* happened to Abelard, so
that wouldn't be a proper example either."

Braddon's eyes glazed over. Sissy wasn't a bad girl, except that she was getting a little long in the tooth, and
spoke in the oddest, breathless fashion. A week ago he
might have considered her for a bride. But all that searching was over.

When Braddon didn't respond, Sissy continued. "As a
matter of fact, Romeo and Juliet make a rather melancholy exemplar, wouldn't you think, Lord Slaslow? Given
the fact that he poisoned himself?"

Braddon smiled at Sissy again and cast a haunted look
about the room. Where was his mother? Or rather, was
she in this room, in which case he had better flee?

His mother had taken the news of his broken engagement badly, fainting onto a couch and calling for
restoratives. But when Braddon tried to steal away, leaving
her to the ministrations of his sisters, she had bounded to
her feet and unleashed a flood of speech designed to im-
press upon him his duty to marry immediately.

Well, he was going to marry. Just not the kind of girl
his mother had in mind. Thank goodness he'd never invited any of his friends to meet Madeleine! Now he
needed to have a quick talk with Sophie before he could
gracefully bow out of the ball. He'd done everything possible to convince all of London that Sophie and Patrick
had married for love. Trouble was that the town was very
empty of news lately, and with nearly a dozen gossip
columns published every day, they all needed something
to talk about.

Suddenly Braddon stiffened like a hound on the scent.
He had caught sight of something alarming.

"Miss Commonweal." Braddon bowed deeply. He had
been trained by an expert (his mama), and his bows were

so low as to be positively alarming. Sissy watched with some interest as the bald spot on his head fell and rose.

She laid a gloved hand on his arm, cutting off his excuses. "Will you escort me to my mother, my lord?" Sissy had no more wish to marry Braddon than he did her, but she loathed being deserted in the middle of a ballroom.

Braddon involuntarily bit the inside of his lip. "I can't do that, Miss Commonweal," he finally said, realizing that she was staring at him in surprise. "Your mama's talkin' to my mama, and . . ."

Sissy gave him a wry smile. She knew all about irate mothers. In fact, she doubted that the mother of a late-marrying son was half as angry as the mother of a late-marrying daughter.

Braddon's eyes brightened. "Would you like to speak with the bride and groom for a moment? They just entered the room."

"I would be very pleased to do so, my lord," Sissy said, relieved.

Braddon wound his way through the crowd and before she knew it Sissy had been planted in front of Patrick Foakes, a man she scarcely knew.

"Excuse us for a moment, won't you, Patrick?" Braddon whisked Lady Sophie around to the far side of a large pillar.

Sissy felt consumed with embarrassment. What on earth was Braddon speaking to the bride about? And what would Sophie's husband think about it?

Patrick Foakes had the trick of turning his face coldly expressionless when he wished to, but Sissy felt that she wouldn't like to get on the wrong side of this particular man. She peered up at him anxiously.

"I understand that you are taking a wedding trip? I trust you are not going to the Continent, given the inclement political situation."

Patrick smiled at the girl before him. What was her

name? Sissy, wasn't it? Why on earth was she wearing those ridiculous plumes on her head, long after every woman in London had discarded them?

"We are merely sailing down the coast—leaving tonight," he replied.

Sissy frowned. "Tonight? I was under the impression that boats could leave only on the turning of the tide. And surely the tide has already turned, given that *The Times* . . ."

Patrick let her voice fade out of his consciousness. Why on earth is Braddon ranting at my new wife? he wondered.

My *wife,* Patrick thought with a sense of giddy ferocity. It had a nice, plummy sound, *wife.* His eyes lazily drifted over Sophie's slim white arm, which was all he could see around the pillar. Sissy Commonweal went on and on about tides.

Patrick felt ripe with self-congratulation. He'd done the whole rigmarole just right. Taken his wife's virginity before the wedding night, so that they could both look forward to uninterrupted pleasure tonight. First thing, he'd draw that gown off one shoulder and then kiss her all the way down her arm, to the inside of her elbow. . . .

But Patrick's plans were interrupted by two things: Miss Cecilia Commonweal's voice had droned its way into silence, and he was growing increasingly irritated by Braddon's monopoly of Sophie. This wasn't the way to convince the London *ton* that Braddon didn't give a fig about Sophie jilting him! And what were they talking about, anyway?

Sissy gazed at her pink slippers in an agony of perplexed embarrassment. The whole room could probably hear the Earl of Slaslow's sharp voice. Why, he was almost shouting at Lady Sophie. She had distinctly heard him say, "You owe me that, at least!"

Then she realized that Patrick Foakes had come out of his daydream and was looking at her again, with a charming smile. Surely he had heard Slaslow's comment, but he didn't look as if he cared a bit.

"Would you like to dance?" Patrick slid his hand under Sissy's arm and turned her toward the ballroom floor.

"Well . . ." Sissy glanced uneasily toward Braddon and Sophie. They seemed to be deep in argument. "Shouldn't you dance with your wife? I'm sure that you must wish to be dancing with her."

Patrick's smile grew a trifle cooler. "Not at all. Given that I wish to dance with you." And without another word he swept the annoying girl into a line of couples waiting to make their way down the floor in a reel.

Sissy colored. It was shocking to find herself on the dance floor with Patrick Foakes, and with everyone watching, of that she was sure.

"Oh goodness," she whispered. "Am I turning crimson?"

Patrick grinned at that. "No. Should you be?"

"Yes!" Sissy had utterly lost her composure. "I'm dancing with the groom, and your reputation, you know, and your wife . . ."

"Miss Cecilia—or is it Sissy?" At her shy nod, Patrick continued. "Well, Sissy, in a year we can twirl all about this ballroom and no one will give us a second glance."

Sissy considered this suggestion and didn't find it comforting. She had just caught her mama's eye, and she looked to be in a high rage.

"Why in a year?" she asked. Her mama was always telling her that it was a lady's duty to keep a conversation going.

"In a year we'll both be old married people, and Lord knows, no one pays attention to married people dancing together."

"They will to you," Sissy blurted, then hastily added, "And anyway I shan't be married."

Patrick smiled at her. The girl's miserable face had awakened a glimmer of sympathy in him. "Yes, you will."

"Oh no, I never *took,* you see." Sissy was so beside herself that she found herself laying bare her most agonized thoughts. "I kept falling in love with the wrong people, and they never came up to scratch, as my mother says." She tacked on that last phrase, belatedly realizing how excruciatingly vulgar she sounded.

But Patrick just laughed. His eyes were looking at her so warmly that Sissy felt her toes curl.

"I'll give you some advice," he said. "Pick out the young man you want. Then, every time you talk to him, look at him right in the eye. No matter what he says, and especially, no matter how idiotic it is, tell him that he just had a *tremendously interesting* idea. Young men are nervous, and they don't like to be corrected."

Sissy was looking up at Patrick as if he were an oracle. "Do you think so? Because my mother has always said that I should keep up my end of the conversation, and so often I find myself doing all the talking!"

"Let them do all the talking," Patrick said cynically. "Men like the sound of their own voices, you know. And don't tell 'em how much you know. Once you're married, you can lecture all day long on ocean currents, if you wish."

Having reached the head of the line, Patrick and Sissy started their progress down the floor: around, around again, up, back, step left, twirl right—and Patrick swept Sissy to a gentle stop in front of her mother.

He bowed, with a flourish. "Miss Commonweal, this dance has been a pleasure."

She curtsied. "Thank you, sir."

Patrick bent close and whispered in her ear, "And get rid of those plumes, Sissy."

With a final wink he was gone. Sissy stared after him,

repeating his words in her mind. When she turned, her mother was smiling, a thin smile that boded ill for the future but signaled the need for a show of warmth between mother and daughter.

"Dearest," she was saying. "I would like to introduce you to Fergus Morgan. Mr. Morgan is the son of Squire Morgan, over in the next county. He has just returned from an extended trip abroad."

Cecilia looked over the young man quickly as he bowed before her. Pleasant blue eyes, a little bald, but he looked nice.

"I understand that you're quite a literary expert," Fergus said a trifle nervously.

"She certainly is," her mother interjected. "Cecilia knows everything about literary matters!"

"I'm afraid my mama is exaggerating," Sissy said in a dulcet tone, looking straight into Fergus's eyes.

"That's a pity," Fergus replied, a tiny frown appearing on his forehead. "Because I was hoping to start a poetry club. I just returned from Germany, and poetry clubs are the rage over there among younger people."

"Oh, what a *tremendously interesting* idea!" Sissy said, her eyes glowing. It was nice that she actually believed it.

Fergus visibly perked up. "May I accompany you to dinner, Miss Commonweal? After this dance, I mean?"

Sissy smiled and barely restrained herself from declaring dinner to be a tremendously interesting idea. "I'd love to. Perhaps you could tell me more about your idea for a poetry club."

❧

Back at the pillar, on the other side of the room, Braddon and Sophie were, in fact, having an argument, just as Sissy had surmised.

Braddon had initiated the conversation with all his usual grace. "Sophie," he stated, "you must listen closely to what I have to say."

Sophie looked at Braddon in surprise. For one thing, he had addressed her formally during their brief engagement, at least when in public. Now she was "Sophie"?

There was a brief pause. "I need your help," he said, rather less confidently.

Sophie smiled at her ex-betrothed. She felt expansively happy and willing to help anyone. "I'd be delighted to help you," she assured him.

Braddon relaxed and lost a bit of his anxious bulldog look. "Here's the thing, Sophie. You know I have to get married right away."

She nodded, her eyes full of sympathy.

"Well, I've found the woman I want to marry." He gulped. This was the stickler. "The problem is that Maddie—Madeleine—isn't a lady."

Sophie looked perplexed for a moment. Then her eyes widened.

"No!" Braddon half shouted. "She's not one of the muslin company either, Sophie. For goodness' sake!"

Sophie almost laughed at Braddon's scandalized expression.

"She's a lady *inside*, Sophie. And I'm not going to marry anyone but her." His tone was fierce. "I could have got up to the sticking point with you, Sophie, you know that. But I'm not going to do it again. I want to marry Madeleine."

Sophie blinked at the matter-of-fact way in which Braddon characterized their engagement. At least she needn't worry about having hurt his feelings by jilting him. "Who . . . who is she?"

"Her father's name is Vincent Garnier," Braddon replied. His eyes pleaded for understanding. "Garnier has protected Madeleine's reputation just as if she were a lady," he said. "No one in London knows her, Sophie. No one except me, I mean. They came over from France after the troubles, and Madeleine doesn't even speak perfect English yet." He took a deep breath. "Her father is a horse trainer."

Sophie's heart sank. "You can't marry the daughter of a horse trainer, Braddon."

But Braddon smiled. "I'm not going to. I'm going to marry the daughter of a French aristocrat, guillotined back in '93."

Sophie stared at him a moment. "Oh, no! Braddon, you can't!"

"Yes, I can," he replied, unyielding. "And what's more, Sophie, you are going to help me."

She shook her head.

"You owe me that, at least! You broke off our engagement without so much as a by-your-leave, *and* the very day after you convinced me to elope to Gretna Green. Do you know how that makes me look?" Braddon's tone conveyed a strong sense of ill usage.

Sophie felt an embarrassed flush rising in her cheeks. "I am sorry, Braddon," she said humbly. "But I can't— what on earth could I do to help you marry this, this horse trainer's daughter?"

"You're going to teach her," he replied. "You're going to turn her into a lady, Sophie. You know all the odd bits of etiquette and such. You teach 'em to Madeleine, and she'll go to a ball and pretend to be a French aristo. Then I'll meet her and marry her right away, before people think about it too much."

"You're cracked, Braddon," Sophie said, staring at him in fascination. "This scheme will never work. It is impossible to transform a horse trainer's daughter into a member of the French aristocracy."

"I don't see why not." Braddon's face took on the bulldoggish look his family dreaded. "I don't see anything so difficult about being a lady. After all, Madeleine *is* French, so no one will expect her to act exactly like an English girl. There's swarms of French aristos over here, and I bet half of 'em are fakers."

Sophie had heard her father complain of the same

thing. "It still doesn't solve the problem of making your friend—Madeleine is it?—into a lady."

"She's a natural lady," Braddon said positively. "It'll be easy, Sophie. Tell her a few things about fans, and dresses, and the like. You can do it," he urged. "And you do owe me the help. You've thrown me back to the wolves. I can't go through that whole charade again, proposing marriage to a woman I don't give a toss about."

"I wasn't the one who broke my leg," Sophie retorted, casting a dubious eye at Braddon's obviously sound limbs.

He shot her a nervous glance. "Least said about that whole night, the better."

They finally parted with Braddon's pleas hanging in Sophie's ears. "I'll get Madeleine started, Sophie," Braddon said, his long eyes beseeching. "I'll teach her what I know, but I can only tell her what I've heard m'mother nagging at my sisters about over the years. You simply must help me."

Patrick had adroitly made his way about the ballroom, winding back toward the pillar where he had left his wife and Braddon Chatwin. He was stopped every few feet and offered congratulations. He had almost reached Sophie when Lord Breksby popped up like a jack-in-the-box.

"I must offer my congratulations, my lord," Breksby said. "And my gratitude. I understand that you will be making a small voyage down the coast. I assume you will cast an eye at the shore now and again."

Patrick bowed. "My pleasure," he murmured.

"I shall look forward to hearing about the fortifications, on your return," Breksby said genially. "I trust your marriage has not altered your intention to travel abroad in the coming year?"

Patrick stiffened at the implication that he might be henpecked before he was wed a full day. "Certainly not," he replied in his most top-lofty manner.

Breksby lowered his voice. "Then I must speak to you, when you return from your wedding voyage, about the gift we discussed."

Patrick stared at him for a moment. Oh yes, the scepter. Patrick bowed again. "I am at your disposal, naturally."

Breksby rubbed his hands together. "Good, good. We've had just a spot of bother over it. Just a nuisance, really. But I thought I should drop a hint in your ear."

What on earth was the old gaffer talking about? If they couldn't make enough rubies stick to the confounded scepter, what was it to him? Patrick bowed again. "I will attend you as soon as I return," he promised.

By the time Patrick finally made it back to the pillar, Sophie and Braddon had disappeared. Patrick stood for a moment, scanning the crowd while avoiding the curious eyes of gossips. Sophie was nowhere to be seen. Just then his sister-in-law appeared at his side.

"Sophie has gone to tidy herself," Charlotte said pertly, smiling up at Patrick.

He felt a surge of irritation. Was he so obvious? "I thought she'd run off with my groomsman," he said, his tone sarcastic.

Charlotte's smile deepened. "Ah, the zeal of the newly-wed husband." She laughed. "I expect I could disappear from a ballroom for an hour or so and Alex wouldn't even note my absence!"

"I wouldn't bet on it," her husband growled with mock ferociousness, appearing beside her and wrapping one arm around her waist.

"Oh Lord," Patrick said with a groan. "Uncle Richard has arrived."

Sure enough, their uncle had thrown off his bishop's robes and emerged in all splendor to honor his nephew's wedding. In the ceremonial glory of ecclesiastic garb, Richard Foakes took on the dignity of office, but in evening clothes he appeared a most awkward fop in white and gold, wearing a cherry and silver waistcoat and facings.

"Is he wearing a cravat string?" Charlotte whispered in awed tones.

"He wants only a sword knot to be a perfect dandy of some fifty years ago," her husband said, chortling.

Patrick began making his way toward the door, Alex and Charlotte behind him. Before they could reach the ballroom doors, however, Sophie appeared in the doorway behind Bishop Foakes. To Patrick's secret pleasure, she greeted his uncle with a charming and unaffected smile. By the time Patrick reached her, the bishop was smiling like a cat in the cream and chuckling gently to himself.

"Yes indeed, m'dear. Why, when I was young I was always meant to go into the church, being the third son. But I remember when strangers would fancy me to be a Member of Parliament at the least, and once I was mistaken for a Venetian Count." The bishop patted Sophie's hand with a good deal more enthusiasm than he had shown toward her in the chapel. "You're a charming gel, a charming gel, m'dear. I don't doubt but that you and young Patrick will be prodigiously happy together."

The little group of scandalmongers and gossips standing to the left took note of the readiness of the Foakes family to countenance the match. Of course, Lady Sophie was a great heiress, and it would be a baffling family indeed who wouldn't welcome her into their ranks. Still, if there were anything tawdry about the match, one would think the Bishop of Winchester wouldn't look quite so cheerful.

"Because it will reflect on the bishop if a child appears in seven months, won't it?" Lady Skiffing was born to intrigue and was never happier than when she was taking apart the reputation of someone she had just greeted with utmost civility.

Sarah Prestlefield was conscious of her decision to support Penelope's conviction that the hasty nuptials were romantic rather than scandalous. "Only those with an excess of spleen would imply such an ill-tempered thing," she pronounced grandly. "Lady Sophie has made a true love match, and although one doesn't see the like very often among the quality" (if ever, she added to herself), "none of *us* would like to imply that the dear children are marrying for less than the most virtuous reasons."

Though dubious of the matter, Lady Skiffing was outranked by Lady Prestlefield and knew it. She changed the subject. "Did you hear that Mrs. Yarlblossom, that redhaired widow who lives in Chiswick, is boasting of having an Indian prince as her suitor?"

Sarah Prestlefield was fascinated. "Do you mean the red-haired hussy who keeps sixteen lapdogs?"

Sophie looked up to find her husband looming at her shoulder. His eyes met hers with such a heady promise that she couldn't help glancing nervously at the bishop to see whether he had caught the message in Patrick's eyes.

"Don't worry about Uncle Richard," Patrick drawled, stepping so close to her that his breath stirred her hair.

Sophie turned an enchanting shade of pink. Patrick's hand slid up her hip to her waist. Would he always be able to make her tremble? Even the touch of his hand made her limbs feel strangely liquid.

Something in Sophie's eyes made Patrick's groin tighten.

"Time to go, sweetheart," he said, his voice husky.

Sophie jumped. "Go?" Her eyes were wide. She'd known, of course, that she and Patrick would leave the ball together. For heaven's sake, her trunks had been hauled out that very morning, and if her maid had overcome her fear of the water, she was already tucked onboard the *Lark*. Because, as Patrick had explained with a wicked grin, the boat was likely to sail at a very early hour, before they would want to be out of bed.

But somehow Sophie hadn't pictured actually leaving the ball. Getting into a carriage, alone with Patrick. Getting into a bed!

"Oh, we can't go yet," she said hastily. "I've barely spoken a word to your uncle." She twitched her hip away from her grinning husband and moved over to the bishop. He was talking busily to Charlotte.

"Since being on this new regimen, I have looked extremely well, and I think you'll agree that I have a most agreeable color in my face. Doctor Read allows me only one cup of chocolate a day, plain water gruel three times a day, and a roasted apple, to be eaten one hour before dinner."

Sophie's mind was filled with electrifying pictures of what Patrick planned to do once they were alone.

The bishop smiled graciously at her. "Please do inform me if you have any questions about my diet, my dear," he said. "I must tell you that Doctor Read is becoming quite famous for the ingenuity of his prescriptions!"

"Ah . . ." Sophie couldn't think of anything to ask. She was all too aware of Patrick's warm body behind hers. "What sort of apple do you eat, sir?" A hand seemed to be playing with the curls at the nape of her neck.

"A very good question, my dear! I prefer the apple to be a golden runnet. I have instructed my man to roast the apple on a clean brick, washed with spring water."

Patrick's deep voice intervened. "Uncle Richard, I fancy you will have to excuse my bride and myself. It is time for us to board."

"Board? Board *ship*?" Richard looked nauseated. "Don't tell me that you are taking that poor child onto the high seas?"

"We're taking a short trip down the coast, Uncle Richard."

"Close to land, I trust. Very nice. Still, any lady at sea must feel like a duck out of water. I expect you will be as sick as a horse the whole way there. Try the apple, m'dear," he said comfortingly to Sophie. "Send out for some golden runnets, tonight, before you leave. Patrick! You must obtain some golden runnets first thing in the morning. Don't forget to send someone out."

Patrick met his brother's laughing eyes over the head of his portly uncle.

"I will, Uncle Richard," he replied gravely. "I am sure that Sophie's stomach will be much soothed by a roasted apple."

The bishop was still thinking. "And there may not be an appropriate brick onboard, Patrick. You'll have to send someone out to get a brick tonight. Yes indeed. You'd better be on your way, since you need to make all these arrangements before daybreak tomorrow."

Despite her nervousness, Sophie almost found herself smiling. Uncle Richard was as preoccupied as she was, simply with a different appetite.

"My mother!" She looked about a little wildly.

Patrick drew her arm into his. "She's standing by the door, Sophie. Waiting to say good-bye."

Sophie took a deep breath and met Charlotte's merry eyes. Charlotte drew her into a warm hug, then whispered something in her ear.

Sophie pulled back. "I couldn't hear what you said, Charlotte."

Charlotte bent closer and whispered again. Sophie turned a fiery red but managed to nod.

"What on earth did you tell Sophie?" Alex asked Charlotte as they watched the newly wedded pair walk toward the door.

Charlotte turned and looked up at her husband, a flare of desire in her eyes.

"Oh," Alex said, his voice deepening. "Perhaps you should whisper it in my ear as well?"

Charlotte nodded, her eyes dancing.

There was a minuet beginning, so Alex drew his wife to him and they melted into the slow, graceful swing of the dance. After a second Charlotte put her lips next to her husband's ear and whispered.

"What!" His voice came out louder than he had intended.

"Do you think I was too indiscreet?"

Alex bit back a laugh. "Of course not, darling. I'm sure that's advice that every new bride should receive." Then he paused. "If you'll excuse me, I'm going to make a frenzy among the gossips by kissing my wife on the dance floor." Charlotte said nothing; only the slight uptilt of her chin and her sparkling eyes answered him.

When Sophie and Patrick reached the ballroom door, her mother and father were waiting for them.

Sophie curtsied gravely before her parents. Eloise looked at the golden head bowed before her, and her eyes swam with tears.

"Ma fille," she said, pulling Sophie into her arms and lapsing into French. *"Sois heureuse, ma chère! Je te souhaite tout le mieux pour ta vie mariée. . . ."*

"I will be happy, *Maman,*" Sophie promised.

Her father gave her a warm hug and then shook hands briskly with Patrick. "Take care of our little Sophie," he said. George looked a little strained about the eyes, but otherwise he was as jovial as if Sophie were setting off for a picnic in Hyde Park.

Sophie kissed him on the forehead. "Don't worry, Papa. I will be fine."

As she and Patrick walked out the door, Eloise caught her breath in a sob. Startled, George reflexively put an arm around his weeping wife.

"She'll be just fine, Eloise," he said uncomfortably. "No need to worry. Foakes is a solid man, a good man."

Eloise pushed him away, blindly heading to the anteroom outside the ballroom. George followed her as she walked into a salon off the hallway. Tears were streaming down her face. George's heart twisted; he'd never seen his wife cry like this.

He took her hands. "What is it, dear heart?"

Eloise sobbed again. "You don't understand. . . . She's all I've got!"

George stilled, and for a heartbeat there was no sound in the room but that of his wife's weeping. Then he pulled her slim body into his arms, tucking her head against his chest.

"You've got me, Eloise."

When his wife, still weeping, simply shook her head, he said it again. "You have me, Eloise. You always had me."

But it wasn't until Eloise raised her head and looked at him, eyes drenched with tears, that she understood what he was saying.

When she opened her mouth to reply, George's mouth closed on hers, stopping any protest. He kissed her into silence, and then said, his voice husky with passionate longing, "Take me back, Eloise. Please, take me back."

Chapter 14

❦

S ophie awoke in a daze. She had been sleeping, deep
in bottomless exhaustion, when something gently
threw her against—against what? Her bed was rocking slightly, accompanied by the roll and slap of waves.
Her nose was buried in fine sheets that smelled of lemon,
but the perfume was overlaid with the keen scent of salt-
laden air.

She turned over and opened her eyes. High above her
were the arched carvings of Patrick's bed. The bed was set
into one end of the most luxurious sea cabin she had ever
seen, or rather ever imagined, given that she'd never been
inside a boat before the preceding evening. Patrick had
bought the bed in India. From the outside, it looked like a
box, with a curved top and one open side marked by pillars ringed with carved flowers. The innumerable small
carved flowers had been painted crimson; they spiraled up
the pillars and rioted exuberantly on the curved roof of

the bed. For a moment or two Sophie traced their intricate byways. A marriage bed, she remembered drowsily.

Then she forgot all about the flowers. There, next to her, was a muscled brown arm. Because in a marriage bed one consummates a marriage, and to consummate a marriage, one needs a husband, and . . . there he was. Sophie choked back a giggle. Patrick was lying on his stomach, his face turned away from her. All she could see of his head was a silky mop of silver-streaked black curls. He didn't seem to be wearing any clothing. Sophie colored, suddenly finding that she wasn't wearing a nightdress either.

Images of the night before poured from the recesses of her memory, bringing with them a strange glowing heat that settled in her stomach and the backs of her knees.

The sheet had slipped down to Patrick's waist, leaving only the broad expanse of his shoulders visible. Sophie bit her lip. A fragmented memory of herself clutching those shoulders, arching up against Patrick's chest, pleading, gasping, panting, flew into her mind.

Cautiously she sat up, tweaking the sheet a bit so that it reached above her waist. Patrick had beautiful shoulders. In the morning light his skin was a dusky golden color that stretched smoothly over bumps and curves of muscle.

Suddenly he gave a little grunt and rolled over, twisting so that the sheet rode even lower on his hips. Sophie gasped and reflexively grabbed at her part of sheet, managing to pull up enough material to cover her breasts. Patrick stayed asleep, his breath coming deep and even, and finally the hasty beating of her heart calmed.

Oh Lord, but her husband was beautiful. Sophie stared in fascination. Midnight-black eyelashes lay curled against his cheeks, echoing the high arches of his eyebrows. Boldly, she lowered her eyes to Patrick's chest. After all, he *was* her husband, wasn't he? She had pressed herself against that chest last night—intimately.

The flare of rosy color in her cheeks heightened as she thought of Patrick's rough groans. He wouldn't seek out another woman immediately. Something in her relaxed, a spring wound so tightly in the area of her heart that she hadn't even noticed its presence.

Cautiously, cautiously, Sophie hooked one finger under the edge of the sheet where it lay low on the ridge of Patrick's hips. She could see the rise in the sheet that marked the particular *thing* that she would like to see in the daylight, and when Patrick wasn't watching. How odd it must be to have a part of oneself always bobbing straight out in front, Sophie thought.

She managed to ease the sheet up a few inches, and she was just leaning forward to peer under it when a choked laugh and a fluid motion erupted from the sleeping man. Before she had time to think, she was smoothly flipped onto her back—like a grounded turtle, Sophie thought indignantly. The very body part about which she had shown curiosity was even now, ah, nudging her. Color streamed up her cheeks as she met her husband's dark, laughing eyes.

"How long were you awake?"

"Long enough," Patrick answered with a hint of purely erotic elation in his voice. He bent down and brushed his lips against hers, making Sophie shiver with delight. "Long enough to know that my new wife was awake. Long enough to see you clutching that wretched sheet to your beautiful breasts. God, Sophie, do you know what glorious breasts you have?"

Sophie looked down at her breasts. There they lay, pinkish in the pearly light, heavy for her small body. "They look well in the French style of gown," she said uncertainly. What was she supposed to say? She'd never really given her breasts a second thought.

But then Patrick's mouth descended and closed on her

nipple, and without willful volition her body arched against his. A tattered moan tore from her throat. He thrust a knee between her legs and murmured something against her breast without stopping what he was doing.

It was only much later, after the sheet had finally given up the fight and lay twisted on the floor and the bed had settled back to the gentle rock of the ocean water, that Sophie thought to ask what Patrick had said. She was lying on her side, idly tracing a sweaty line down her husband's chest.

"What did you say about my breasts?" she asked.

Patrick's eyes were heavy lidded. He was trying to figure out why having sex with his wife would make him feel almost as if he would cry. It must be something about the ritual of marriage, he finally decided. Knowing that you're going to be with one woman the rest of your life, and never with another. There must be something about it that tipped sex from good to wonderful.

"Hmm?" he said lazily, pulling Sophie up against his side.

She repeated her question, rather shyly.

Patrick opened one eye. "Didn't I say they were glorious?"

Sophie nodded. "After that."

Patrick opened both eyes. "I can't remember." His voice was honey thick. "Perhaps I'd better take a look and see whether it comes to mind." Nudging Sophie back, Patrick slid down in the bed until his eyes were parallel with that exquisite part of her anatomy.

Irresistibly he reached out to touch her breasts, shaping their heavy, creamy perfection in both his hands. A slight relaxing of Sophie's spine was her only response.

"Did I say that they are larger than wild apples?"

"No," Sophie whispered.

"They're not the same color as apples, of course," he said conversationally. "Apples are red, as everyone knows, and your breasts are white as milk, with just a hint of rosiness under the skin." His thumbs were dancing over her nipples, making Sophie's breath press hot against the inside of his chest.

"Did I tell you that they taste sweeter than wine?" Patrick's tongue was tracing an errant path around the circumference of one breast.

"No."

"They taste of honey, as if I were eating peonies or poppies." He was tracing small circles now, coming closer and closer to her nipple.

"I don't think you said that," said Sophie, her voice an aching wisp of sound.

"Did I say that your skin is softer than . . ." Patrick couldn't think what he was going to say. He'd reached a nipple of the palest, sweetest pink. With a silent groan he bent over and pulled it into his mouth.

When he raised his head, his wife was looking at him, her eyes slightly wild, small pants coming from her lips.

"Now," Patrick said, his voice deep with desire. "Now we have to anatomize the other breast, don't you think?"

Sophie's response was fierce and immediate. She reached out and dragged his shoulders up until he was kneeling on the bed, ignoring his laughing protests.

"Wait, wait, O impetuous wife! I just remembered precisely what I said." His eyes had a wicked twinkle as he pushed her back down on the bed. "You seemed to be curious about *my* anatomy when I woke up this morning. I simply offered you the chance to satisfy your quest for knowledge."

Sophie blushed—but she obediently lowered her eyes, looking down her husband's chest to the planed lines of his stomach and even farther. A mischievous gleam lit her eyes. She trailed a finger over Patrick's muscled skin, tracing the path her eyes had taken.

"Hmm," she said, her voice husky.

Patrick's eyes narrowed. His voice emerged half strangled. "What does that mean? Hmm?" His skin was marked with fire where her finger had lingered, let alone what she was doing now with that innocent expression on her face.

Sophie found that her breath was coming quickly and she'd lost the thread of the discussion.

"In order for me to finish my investigation," she whispered, "I need to do some research." A trail of kisses retraced the path of her finger.

Patrick gasped and then groaned. His heart raced to a brutal drumming in his chest.

"No research." Patrick didn't sound like himself. His muscled arms braced as he provocatively drove Sophie toward the same flaming passion that had conquered him.

"We'll discuss it later," she managed, and then the time for talking was over.

∽

When Patrick and Sophie Foakes finally emerged onto the deck of the *Lark,* the sun was high in the sky.

Sophie blinked at the chilly, bright quality of the air. As far as she could see there was nothing but foam-tossed waves and swooping gulls.

"How far are we out to sea?"

"Not far," Patrick replied. "As long as these seagulls stay with us, we haven't gone far out. And we won't ever leave the shore far behind on this trip. We'll round the tip of Cornwall and then pull into the coast of Wales whenever we please."

Patrick thought of telling Sophie about the fortifications he was to inspect, and then dismissed it. He could tell her about it later. It wasn't exactly romantic talk.

"It's a shame we can't go to Italy, as my parents did for their wedding trip," he said idly. Then his eyes lit up. "If you weren't aboard, I might give it a try. Shoot across the channel, tiptoe around France, and dock at Leghorn."

"Leghorn," Sophie said with fascination. "Do you mean *Livorno*?"

"Exactly." Patrick leaned back against the rail, grinning at her as he tossed orange peels over his shoulder to the screaming gulls. "Did you study geography in school, then?"

"Oh no," Sophie said. "I was sent to Cheltham Ladies' School, and the best young ladies have no need for geography, since they never travel outside the boundaries of England."

"Why do you know the Italian name for Leghorn, then?" Patrick's eyes were automatically ranging over his vessel, checking the gaff rigging, the square sail on the foremost mast, the easy, orderly movements of his crew.

Sophie looked at him and said, "Oh, just a bit of knowledge one acquires."

But Patrick merely appeared to be distracted. "Do you speak Italian?"

Sophie froze inside. "No," she blurted. "I don't know very much . . ." What an idiot she was! Had she just said that she didn't know very much about languages? Or that she didn't speak very much Italian? And, oh dear, what about the book on Turkish grammar currently residing amidst her undergarments? Perhaps she could throw it overboard when Patrick wasn't looking.

"No one expects young ladies to actually speak foreign languages," Patrick said comfortingly. "I swear that most of the ladies I've met in Almack's barely know their native tongue. You must be fluent in French, given your mother's nationality."

Sophie nodded, afraid to open her mouth.

"I'm a dunce when it comes to languages." Patrick popped a sweet section of orange into her mouth. "I speak French poorly, and after that I know only odd phrases in other languages. Do you know what the most important sentence in any language is?"

Sophie shook her head, fascinated despite herself.

"Hazard a guess."

She thought for a moment. Her knowledge of languages was so academic that it was difficult to visualize herself in a different country. " 'Where can I find a constable?' "

Patrick rolled his eyes. "Believe me, constables are more trouble than they're worth."

" 'Will you direct me to an inn?' "

"No." Patrick moved closer to her and tipped up the rim of her bonnet. Then he tore off a section of orange and held it before her face. " 'Please, will you accept this unworthy gift, an offering from me and my country, O honored lady?' "

Sophie laughed as he sensuously rubbed the dripping orange across her lips until she opened them.

"I can say it in fourteen languages," he said, laughter lurking in his eyes. "Unfortunately, it is the *only* thing I can say in Welsh, so we will have to encounter the country in English."

Sophie swallowed. It was too late for her to admit to a fluent knowledge of Welsh.

But Patrick mistook her fleeting expression of alarm. "It's quite all right, sweetheart. The whole country speaks English. And anyone who doesn't had better learn.

"And they might want to start boning up on their French as well," Patrick added. "Some people think that Napoleon will launch a force from Brest and swing right around Cornwall, land in Wales, and attack England from the back side."

"Oh, Bonaparte." Sophie was having trouble concentrating on foreign affairs, given that Patrick had cut another orange slice in half and was tempting her lips with it. The sharp smell tickled the inside of her nose.

"Not to worry about him. The *Lark* is one of the fastest ships on the ocean. We can outrun whatever fleet

Napoleon has in the channel. All he really has are flat-bottomed boats, anyway."

"Is the *Lark* a Baltimore clipper?"

Patrick gave her a surprised, encouraging look. "Yes. It has a V-shaped hull, sharp-built to cut the waves."

Sophie grimaced at him, irritation cutting through the sensual haze he was weaving with his orange slices. "Don't you think I can read?" She said it mildly enough. "*The Times* has been talking of the shipyards in Fells Point for five or more years!"

Patrick absentmindedly ate the orange slice he had intended to give her. "I don't know much about proper English ladies. My mother died before I grew up, and since then—" He shrugged. "I haven't spent much time in England."

"I know," Sophie broke in, "and since you have been here, you haven't spent time with ladies!"

Patrick chortled. "Actually," he said teasingly, "it's not that they weren't ladies, just that they weren't the 'proper' sort of ladies."

He grinned. He liked this whipper-sharp bride of his, with her tart tongue and longing eyes. Patrick moved over and pushed Sophie back against the railing, fitting the front of his body against hers like a jigsaw puzzle.

Sophie looked up at him, a sweet wistfulness in her eyes. "Have you been to fourteen countries, then?"

"At least," Patrick replied.

"How I would love to travel," Sophie said longingly. "I would go to the Orient."

"What *do* proper ladies do all day long?"

Sophie's mind was clouding again. "They . . . they go on calls and leave cards."

"That sounds remarkably tedious. What else?"

"They shop."

"Why?"

Sophie gasped. Patrick was unmistakably moving his hips against hers, just slightly.

"Patrick! What if someone sees you?" She couldn't see anything around his body.

"There's nothing to see," her husband replied comfortably. He had braced both his hands on the rail on either side of her. "What do proper ladies buy when they shop?"

"Oh, bonnets and gowns," Sophie said vaguely. She was really at a disadvantage in this conversation, given that she generally summoned Madame Carême to her own house. It was hard enough finding time to work.

Patrick had stopped teasing her and was looking down with a bit of puzzlement in his eyes. "Are you saying that you go shopping *every day*?"

"I don't," Sophie said guardedly. Then she remembered that Patrick was a rake. No matter how much he was pretending to be ignorant, he knew everything about ladies and their pursuits—after all, he spent all his time chasing them, didn't he?

"What else is there to do?" Her eyes glinted provocatively at him. "As you well know, a lady's greatest devotion is reserved for a new suit of clothing."

"Is that so?" Patrick drawled. He pushed forward with his hips again, causing a melting warmth to flood Sophie's stomach.

Work! Suddenly she had a deep pang in her heart for what she had given up for this marriage. Somewhere deep inside, she was not reconciled to the idea of becoming the sort of matron whose idea of work was a visit to Bond Street. Not that apparel was to be ignored, naturally, but there was such a thrill in assembling fragments of language until a sentence unfolded before your eyes.

Patrick looked down at her, a bit puzzled. What was there in the description of a lady's day to make Sophie's eyes turn so bleak?

"Would my very proper wife wish to retire below and take a bath?" He brushed a butterfly kiss on Sophie's brow. "Because her very proper husband should have a talk with his captain."

Sophie's eyes lit up. "That would be marvelous," she said with utmost sincerity.

With some reluctance, Patrick backed away from her body. "Off you go, then."

Once inside the master cabin, Sophie dispatched a greenish-looking Simone to fetch a tub of hot water, then paused, her back against the heavy walnut door.

The room was spare but luxurious. Every piece of furniture was bolted either to the wall or to the floor, except for the dining-room chairs, which could be hooked over a rail attached to the wall when the weather became stormy.

And she was alone. She hadn't been alone since the morning before she married Patrick. With a sigh, Sophie drank in the silence.

Then she moved quickly away from the door as Simone entered, directing two young crew members who were hoisting large buckets of steaming water. Without further ado, the brass bathtub (nailed down in a corner of the room) was filled with water, scented with cherry blossoms, and her maid was sent back to bed, whimpering and clutching her stomach.

Sophie lay back as water lapped deliciously at the sore parts of her body. She stayed there for a long time, thinking over the night before. There'd been no time to think . . . and she had so much to think about.

For instance, what on earth was she to do about Braddon? His scheme was impossible. More than unlikely, it was inconceivable that a horse breeder's daughter could fool the *ton* into thinking that she was a member of the French aristocracy.

Sophie had seen her mama at work, picking into shreds the gentility of the daughter of a merchant. A young lady might be docile, beautiful, and have gone to the same school as Sophie. It wouldn't matter. Eloise and her friends were the most precise judges in the world. They would dissect the girl's conversation, the way she waved a fan, the bend of her eyelashes, and detect the bad blood coursing through her veins.

It's absolutely impossible, Sophie thought glumly. She'd simply have to persuade Braddon to discard the idea. Eloise would see through an impostor in a second. Let alone an impostor who was really a horse trainer's daughter. No, Braddon must give up hope of marrying his Madeleine.

Finally Sophie woke out of her half-daze, realizing that the bathwater had become a cool caress. She stood up and wrapped herself in a towel. Without allowing herself to think too much about it, she retrieved the book of Turkish grammar from where she had carefully hidden it.

With a sigh of pure happiness she sank into a study of Turkish verbs. They were remarkably interesting, the way they changed depending on who was speaking. *"Seni seviyorum,"* she whispered to herself. "I love you. *Seni seviyor.* He loves you." Sophie shook her head, shrugging off that dream. She turned to more mundane sentences.

She was consciously disobeying her mother—and it felt wonderful. No wonder Braddon thought she, Sophie, could train his Madeleine to be being a proper aristocrat, she thought drowsily. She had been drilled by the queen of aristocratic leaders, the Marchioness of Brandenburg. What Eloise didn't know about proper behavior wasn't worth knowing.

Guiltily, Sophie scooted her grammar book down beside her in case Patrick suddenly walked into the room. Depend upon it, her mother's voice said sternly in her memory, no prudent man will ever accept a wife who knows more than himself.

Sophie sighed and thought of Patrick's teasing confession that he was able to speak only poor French. Her mother was undoubtedly correct.

Poor Eloise! She had spent years trying to talk Sophie out of her passion for languages. Eloise had probably fought Latin the hardest. "Latin is as unfeminine a decoration for the inside of a woman's head as a beard is for the outside," she had protested, her lips white with fury. But George had stood up to his wife, and consequently Sophie's mornings had been filled with the conjugation of verbs.

Sophie's grin faded as she remembered what most of her mother's admonishments added up to. Eloise's favorite statement was "Young women need only study how to find husbands." Braddon's Madeleine would truly have to study if she had a hope of carrying off his scheme. Sophie dismissed the plight of Braddon and the horse trainer's daughter, pulling up her grammar book again. With luck she'd have time to get her mind around the complications of the past tense before Patrick returned.

When Patrick let himself into the stateroom, he expected to find an irritable wife waiting for him. Everything he knew of women had led him to believe that newly married wives were never to be left alone, particularly when one has rudely separated them from the pleasurable pursuits of taking tea and shopping. He had been absent three hours, discussing the sea currents around the tip of Cornwall and the crew's lack of a second mate.

He felt a mild surge of shame for his uncharitable thoughts when he found Sophie sitting in an armchair, looking sweetly peaceful, wrapped in a silky negligee. His surge of shame was followed by a surge of something else. Lord, but he'd married a beautiful woman! Sophie's hair fell in glistening honey-pale curls about her shoulders and down her back, still damp from her bath. Her eyes looked mulberry black in the candlelit room.

"Where's your maid?" Patrick's voice sounded rough even to his ears.

Sophie looked at him in surprise. "Simone is suffering mightily from mal de mer. I sent her off to her cabin for the night."

Patrick swallowed. He knew Sophie must be sore, far too sore to continue the kind of activity they had carried on that morning. He walked over and dropped to a crouching position next to her chair.

Sophie smiled. She was filled with overlapping pools of happiness. Marriage was possible, even wonderful, and she'd mastered the Turkish past tense. Buried in her memory was an unspoken sentence: "*Seni sevdi:* I loved him."

Deliberately she leaned forward, allowing the diaphanous silk to fall open at her neck. "Do you know, Patrick, that there's no English equivalent of *déshabillé?*"

Patrick's eyes darkened to an ink smudge below his eyebrows. "My French is getting worse by the moment." His breath warmed the skin on her neck as he pushed the negligee open with kisses. "What does *déshabillé* mean?"

Sophie gasped. "Undressed, or half undressed, although it can also be a *négligé.*"

Patrick's lips were trailing lower.

"Oh, woe is me . . ." His voice sounded half muffled. "My clever wife has thrown another foreign word at me. What is a *négligé?*"

Sophie giggled, her hands running up and down Patrick's muscled shoulders. "As if you haven't bought a thousand *négligés* in your lifetime!" she said saucily.

At that, Patrick's lips stilled and he raised his head, looking into her eyes. "Why is it that my own wife insists that I am an old *roué,* a *libertin?*"

Sophie gasped indignantly. "Your accent is perfect! You've been shamming it!"

"*Je ne suis pas un libertin, et je n'achèterai plus de négligé pour une femme qui m'est pas ma propre femme.* Translate *that,* O clever wife."

Sophie pouted. "You are claiming not to be a libertine,

and promising that you will never again buy a negligee for a lady other than your wife."

Patrick was about to insist on the point, but his eyes were drawn to Sophie's lips. "Lovely Sophie," he whispered huskily. *"Ma belle, ma mariée."*

Sophie closed her eyes. It was unbelievably erotic, hearing Patrick speak French. She had been raised speaking French and hadn't learned English until she was six years old. In many ways it was the language closest to her heart. But she never thought to be able to make love in it.

Suddenly her heart was beating thunderously. She opened her eyes, leaned down, and nipped her husband's lip. He responded with a growl, capturing her lips and pulling her forward so she half fell into his lap.

"Embrasse-moi, mon mari," Sophie breathed.

"Anything, *ma belle."* In one swift movement Patrick came to his feet, holding his wife in his arms, and moved over to the marriage bed. They fell under the twisting vines and cherry-red flowers as if they collapsed into a flowering grove in the depths of India.

Below deck, no bell rang, signaling dinner to be brought to the master cabin. In the kitchen of the *Lark,* Patrick's French chef, bribed at enormous expense to accompany him on this trip, became first surly and then hysterical.

"It's entirely ruined, my lovely dinner." Floret looked around tragically. The soup still waited in a silver tureen. The roast would be salvageable, but his masterpiece, the trout, was beyond recovery.

Patrick's sturdy first mate, John, shook his head. "It's a bit fancy, but all right," he said, with his mouth full of trout *au court bouillon.*

At that Floret broke into tears, to John's disgust.

Sophie's maid stayed gratefully in bed, suffering through one hazy attack of seasickness after another. To Simone, the fact that her mistress had no need of help to get undressed was a gift from God. Finally Simone took a dose of laudanum and became even groggier.

"She'll be sleeping in a state of nature," Simone muttered to herself with an unsteady giggle. "His lordship has that sort of look about him."

It wasn't until long after the *Lark* was dark and quiet, with no one awake but the first mate at the wheel, that Patrick and Sophie slipped out of the cabin and made their way to the kitchen.

They found asparagus soup waiting in its tureen; even better, they found champagne floating in a pool of melted ice. The dinner buns had gone hard, but that was all right. They sat side by side on the kitchen table (it was too bothersome to remove the chairs from their nighttime position strapped to the wall). They drank the soup and dunked the hard dinner rolls into champagne.

They sat so close that their legs pressed together and Sophie's hair, falling in unruly waves down her back, brushed Patrick's shoulder.

It was a feast fit for the gods.

Chapter 15

❧

"I won't do it, Braddon. I won't do it." Back in London, the Earl of Slaslow was employed in the task that had obsessed him since the *Lark* left its moorings, two weeks previously. He was pleading with Madeleine.

"What on earth will it hurt to try, sweetheart?"

Madeleine didn't even look up from where she was sweeping a curry brush over Gracie's round, hard sides. "It's not proper. You are asking me to lie." Her mouth was set in as firm and stubborn a line as Braddon's family had ever seen on his face.

He rolled his eyes, not for the first time. "Don't you see that it's a small lie in service of the greater good?"

"The greater what?" Madeleine's French accent became more marked when she couldn't understand something.

"The greater good," he repeated lamely. "It's a phrase

that means . . . well, that it's all right to do a small wrong in order to obtain a larger right."

"That's not what French philosophers say," she snapped. "Monsieur Rousseau says that *les bons sauvages,* those who are truly innocent, do only good."

Braddon dismissed the alarming signs of learning that Madeleine liked to throw at his head in moments of tension. He dared to reach out and stroke her cheek. Lately she had been like a tyrant and wouldn't even let him kiss her. At the moment, for instance, she had edged around the stall so that Gracie's bulk stood between them.

"Please, Maddie. Please. I want you to be my countess," Braddon whispered. "I want you to have my children. I don't want to leave your house at night and return to mine. I want you to live in my house. Don't you see, I want you to be my wife, not my mistress!"

"You can't have everything you want," Madeleine muttered, but her face was softening. Braddon could see it. And her hand wasn't moving as briskly over Gracie's side.

He looked at the neck of Madeleine's starched white fichu and gulped. He longed to plunder the sweet flesh that flirted modestly behind her lace scarf.

"Only for three weeks, Maddie. In three weeks I can meet you at a ball, be swept off my feet, and we can marry by special license, the way Sophie and Patrick did. After we're married, no one will think twice about your past. You will be the Countess of Slaslow, and no one questions a countess."

For the first time, Madeleine looked torn, rather than adamantly set against the idea.

"I wouldn't be able to do it," she muttered, leaning her forehead against Gracie's warm belly. "I am not an aristocrat, Braddon. I'm only a simple horse trainer's daughter."

He scoffed. He could smell victory. "Since when do simple horse trainers quote Rousseau and Diderot? Your father owns more books than he does saddles!"

Madeleine raised her head and looked straight into his eyes. "I am educated, Braddon; I can read. But that doesn't make me a lady. What do I know about dancing and, and all those other things ladies can do? I know how to splint a foreleg, but I don't even know how to embroider!"

Braddon scowled fiercely, ducking under Gracie's neck and forcing his large body into the space at the back of the stall, next to Madeleine. "Don't talk about yourself that way, Madeleine! You are more of a lady than most women I know. That embroidery business is all poppycock. My sisters couldn't do it worth a fig. My mother wailed about it endlessly. None of 'em learned to play the spinet or the harp, and Lord knows they're terrible singers. That's not what makes you a lady."

Madeleine looked at him imploringly. "You simply don't understand, Braddon. What about my clothing? I don't have the right gowns, and Lady Sophie is so elegant." She had read about Sophie in *The Morning Post,* which always carefully detailed where she had been, with whom, and, sometimes, what she was wearing. The very idea of meeting her was terrifying, let alone the idea of Lady Sophie teaching *her* how to be a lady.

"Sophie will take care of all that," Braddon said carelessly. "I'll give her some blunt so she can pick up a few dresses for you." He was deeply enjoying the fact that Gracie's huge bulk was pressing his body against Madeleine's.

"Oh, this is impossible!" Madeleine cried in a passion, pounding her fists against Gracie's back. Gracie snorted in surprise and turned her head to see what was happening. Then she backstepped a bit to get away from the annoying sensation. Braddon almost groaned as Gracie pushed his body even more firmly against Madeleine's.

"What are you doing?"

She sounds really furious now, Braddon thought muzzily.

"Get away from me! I can feel you . . . you . . . you reprobate!"

In response, Braddon wound his arms around her. "I love you, Maddie," he said, his voice husky. "I love you. I want you. Please, darling, do this for me so that we can be married."

"No," she said stubbornly, edging her hips away. Braddon was pressed against her in an utterly inappropriate fashion.

"Then I'll marry you anyway," he said with quiet determination. "It doesn't matter to me, Maddie. I'll marry you and we'll go live in Scotland—or in America. I don't care, as long as I'm with you."

Madeleine gasped. "You can't mean it. You're an earl. You would be cast out."

He tightened his arms around her. "I mean it," he said. He rubbed his cheek against her sweet-smelling hair. "I won't marry anyone but you, and if you don't wish to pretend to be a French aristocrat, then I shall marry you as you are."

"Your family will never speak to you again!" Madeleine was horrified.

"I never liked my family much," he said without hesitation.

"Your mother!"

Braddon sounded happy now. "I won't miss her."

"No, no, no," Madeleine cried, her French accent thickening. "I cannot allow you to make such a sacrifice."

"No sacrifice," he muttered. She seemed to not have noticed that he was holding her so tightly that he could feel every curve of her body. "Nothing to worry about, Maddie. Our son will still inherit the title."

"But . . . but he'll be an outcast!"

Braddon shrugged. "Perhaps by then the *ton* will have forgotten. Anyway, who cares? There's aeons of time between then and now."

Madeleine frowned. Her practical French soul was incapable of dismissing the future the way Braddon could. Go live in America? Was he crazed? Everyone knew that America was a vast wilderness, inhabited only by criminals and savage Indians. Rousseau was all very well in the pages of a book, but she doubted that American *sauvages* innocently longed to do nothing but good.

"No," she said. "If there is a chance that our son could be born with the approval of society, then we must try to do that. Even if it involves lies, and learning how to be a lady."

Braddon responded by capturing her mouth and muttering love words against her lips. But just when he was sinking mindlessly into the kiss, Madeleine erupted into speech again.

"Oh no! We forgot my papa! He will never agree to your wild scheme."

"Perhaps you're right." Braddon rubbed his hands up and down her back in a comforting manner, hoping that Madeleine wouldn't notice how his hands trailed over the delicious rise of her bottom. "Let's get married tonight, Madeleine. The scheme will never work. We'll go to the border."

Madeleine twitched herself away from his straying hands and frowned, an adorable line appearing between her brows. "You *are* a reprobate," she snapped. "Lord only knows why I want to marry you."

Braddon snatched her up the minute the words left her mouth. "You do? You will? You want to marry me? Oh Maddie . . ." He bent his head and ravaged her mouth.

Madeleine shivered as a wave of heat rose from her knees to her breast. He might not be the brightest in the world, her Braddon, but there was something about his kisses that turned her into a puddle of jelly.

❧

As the *Lark* headed to its first port of call on the Welsh coast, Sophie and Patrick were sitting on the deck, enjoying a bout of unusually temperate afternoon sunshine. Sophie was soundly beating her husband at backgammon.

"It's not fair," Patrick said moodily. "You've no strategy at all, other than throwing those bloody doubles every other turn."

Sophie smiled as she gleefully scooped up two of his pieces, sending them back to the beginning.

"My grandfather used to say it was my only skill at board games."

Patrick cast her an unwilling look of admiration. "I wouldn't say you're a peagoose at the chessboard, m'dear."

"Pooh! You've beaten me two out of three times."

"Yes, but normally I can't be beat *at all,*" Patrick pointed out. "And never before by a female," he added, with just a trifle of an edge in his voice.

"Dear Patrick. It quite wrings my heart to see how much you are suffering."

Patrick bared his teeth at her. "You're a witch, wife. A witchy wife."

Sophie delicately licked her lips. "Hmm . . . I wonder what spell I might cast on you?"

Despite himself Patrick leaned forward, a finger tracing the dainty outline of Sophie's lips. "You have the most kissable lips in the world, witch."

Her eyes glinting, Sophie touched his finger with her tongue and then drew the finger into the warm recesses of her mouth. "Perhaps you have cast a spell on me," she whispered.

Patrick was just rising from his chair when an awkward cough sounded at his left ear.

"Excuse me, sir." Captain Hibbert was standing, cap in hand, looking a bit worried. "I wonder if you'd cast your eye to the east and let me know what you think. Begging your pardon, madam."

Sophie smiled at him. She liked the tongue-shy captain, with his clumsy manners and bashful looks.

"Please, Captain Hibbert, don't let me interrupt your discussion," she said, rising from her chair. "I was about to retire to my cabin."

As Captain Hibbert bobbed an inept bow and turned back to his barometer, she cast Patrick a glance under her lashes. But Patrick was frowning off toward the east, where the sky had turned a streaky blue-green color.

"Is it a storm coming?"

"We call it a mackerel sky," Patrick said, throwing an arm around Sophie's shoulders and drawing her snug against his body. "See that dappling effect off to the right?"

"The rows of little clouds?"

"That's it. Hibbert was right to interrupt us before we retired down to the cabin." Patrick laughed as he saw Sophie's cheeks gain a slight flush. "My wife might not have let me out of bed for hours," he whispered.

Sophie didn't say anything, just leaned her head against Patrick's shoulder.

He gave her a reassuring squeeze. "There's no need to worry. This boat can outsail any storm. Hibbert and I have outrun hurricanes, on occasion." His blood raced with anticipation of the moment when the boat strained at every sinew, boards groaning and screaming, ropes flapping, the wind howling as they raced across the ocean. Fleeing in front of a gale was the only way to test a boat's mettle. No boat went faster than when it was in the arms of a storm wind.

Suddenly he looked down at the soft curls nestled against his shoulder and rethought the idea.

"Not that we're going to do anything of that nature today."

Sophie looked up, startled. "Why not?"

He bent down and kissed her, lingeringly, on the lips. "Because you're onboard." His deep voice allowed no argument.

Sophie stared after her husband as he followed Captain Hibbert. Then she turned and wandered off to the main cabin.

She realized more and more why gentlemen left their wives at home when they went about their activities. Patrick had been throwing his boat before a gale, while she prided herself on the remarkable freedom of being allowed to learn Turkish.

With a sigh, Sophie pushed the thought away. Her nurse had always said that there was no point in getting vexed to death over things that couldn't be changed.

Within an hour the *Lark* was nosing along the western coast of Wales, looking for a good place to draw in for the night.

"Aye, cap'n!" came a call from the lookout.

Patrick and Hibbert looked up from where they stood on the aft deck.

"I see a light!"

Patrick picked up a telescope and focused it on shore. There was a deep cove, so slender that it wasn't visible with the naked eye, at least from this distance. And the lights twinkling behind it looked like those of a large building.

"Could be an old monastery," he said to Hibbert.

Hibbert took a turn at the telescope. "It'll do," he said with characteristic brevity. He headed toward the wheel, trusting no one but himself with the tense job of bringing the *Lark* into a strange harbor.

A half-hour or so later, Patrick headed downstairs, whistling. He almost knocked but then stopped himself. With luck, he could surprise Sophie during her afternoon bath.

But as he swung open the door he saw his wife sitting in her favorite chair, reading. She didn't hear the door, so he paused for a moment, watching her.

She was reading so intently that her lips moved as she read. Poor sweetheart, Patrick thought. The education given to females was so trumpery that she was still mouthing words while reading. For some strange reason, the thought of Sophie as a schoolgirl made his heart twist tenderly.

As he stepped forward, Sophie caught the whisper of his boots on the floor and looked up, startled. In fact, to Patrick's dismay, she was so startled that she gave a little shriek and jumped up, only to sink back into her seat, frowning at him mightily.

"You gave me a proper fright!"

Patrick walked over and looked down at his petite wife, a smile lurking around his mouth. "I was hoping to catch you in *déshabillé*."

Sophie reluctantly smiled back.

"What have you been doing?"

"Waiting for you." Sophie's eyes were wide and innocent.

Patrick frowned. "You were reading, Sophie. Don't lie to me. At this moment, you are sitting on your book."

Sophie looked at him calmly. "So I am," she replied. The memory of something said by Patrick's school friend David raced through her mind. Patrick hated fibs, hated any kind of falsehood. Lord but he would be cross if he found out just *what* she was reading!

Patrick raised an eyebrow. Sophie must be indulging in a lurid French romance that she doesn't want me to know about, he thought. Politely he moved away and busied himself with pulling off his shirt. But he watched out of the corner of his eye as she tucked her book in a drawer with practiced ease.

Likely Eloise had never let Sophie read anything interesting, Patrick thought to himself with a grin. Stiff-rumped, the marchioness, that was for certain. She would have had an apoplexy if she caught her daughter with a popular novel. Hell, Eloise was probably the reason Sophie couldn't read very well. She likely had never let her daughter read anything but sermons! I'll have to speak to Sophie about it, Patrick thought, a bit complacently. I can't have a wife who's ashamed of reading, or thinks that novels are immoral.

"You should ring for Simone," he said, turning about as if he hadn't seen Sophie hide her book. "We'll be going ashore in a half-hour or so. John has been over in a rowboat and says there's an old monastery where we can stay the night. I hope to God they have a decent bed, because it'll be a little unsteady onboard the *Lark* tonight. I'd rather we weathered the storm in an eight-hundred-year-old building."

Sophie searched his face. For a minute, when Patrick pointed out that she was sitting on her book, he had *such* a look on his face—as if he knew about her Turkish grammar and was secretly laughing at her. No, it couldn't be. He looked perfectly normal now.

She rang the bell for Simone as Patrick pulled on his boots and left the cabin.

"Come above when you're ready, darling." With a kiss on her forehead, he left.

Sophie slowly pulled a warm gown from the built-in wardrobe along one wall. Patrick had taken to calling her "darling" the last few days. And there was something about the endearment, even though she knew it was casually given, that made her feel unsteady in the knees and near to tears.

Simone burst through the door. Her hair was blown out of its neat knot, and her cheeks were flushed.

"We must go, ma'am! There's a nasty wind blowing up, that's what John says. It's a mickle sky, he says."

"A mackerel sky," Sophie corrected her. She hadn't got any further than her second stocking.

"Whatever kind of sky," Simone replied tartly, "there's a nasty color to it, and John says we needs get off this boat right away!" Simone had struck up a flirtation with the first mate, and she was full of sealore and seamen's slang.

With a sigh Sophie stood up as Simone threw a gown over her head with reckless haste.

"No time to do anything much with your hair." Simone's fingers were trembling as she bundled her mistress's curls into a loose coil on top of her head. Simone had finally gotten over her seasickness, but she didn't want to be on the ship when a storm hit, no indeed. Likely the *Lark* would just break free and toss its way across the waves. Across the waves and right to the bottom, Simone thought, her fingers moving even faster.

Before Sophie had time to think, Simone had bundled her into a plum-colored pelisse, thrust a fur muff over her hand, and pushed her out the door.

Up on deck there wasn't nearly the frenzy there had been in the main cabin. Patrick was standing at the rail. The crew was pulling down the sails and lashing the masts in a calm and orderly fashion.

Sophie walked over to Patrick and stood for an instant, gazing at the sky. It looked like shot silk now; the coppery color was laced with darker, jaundiced-looking stripes. The fluffy little clouds had thinned into sullen streaks, like a banker's smile. And there was a wind starting. Strands of hair pulled loose from her velvet bonnet and whipped against her face.

Patrick's face was alive with excitement. "See how livid the air has become, Sophie? The wind is blowing, and yet in between gusts the air is heavy and still."

Sophie nodded. Now she was very glad that they had anchored the *Lark*.

There was a thud and a shout. The crewmen were ready to send a small boat over to the shore.

"Now's the trick." Patrick grinned at her. "We have to get you and your maid down a rope ladder. We couldn't sail all the way in, as the bottom is too shallow near the dock."

Sophie walked to the side of the *Lark* and peered over. It seemed a long way down, and the rope ladder was swaying in an alarming fashion. Moreover, the water had a gray tint that promised an icy bath to anyone who let go of the ladder.

"I shall carry you down." Patrick was standing at her shoulder.

"Nonsense," Sophie replied. "I shall climb down on my own. Simone!"

Simone edged over next to her mistress, clearly frightened out of her wits at the idea of scrambling down the ladder.

"If you climb down without screaming, fainting, falling off, or needing assistance, I will give you the ball dress with the fabric roses."

Simone was silent for a heartbeat. "The one with a train?"

Sophie nodded.

Simone's thin Gallic face lit with determination. Without a second's hesitation she moved over to the side and allowed a sailor to place her at the top of the ladder. Then she sturdily climbed down.

Sophie watched until Simone reached the skiff and was helped to a seat. But just as Sophie was about to move over to the ladder, two warm arms encircled her from behind and a voice whispered, "Don't you want a bribe?"

Sophie giggled. "Are you offering me one of your embroidered waistcoats?"

A deep chuckle tickled her ear. "The only one I own was embroidered by Aunt Henrietta with cornflowers and bluebells. It's a dreadfully garish piece, and besides it's too big for you."

"Oh dear," Sophie said sadly. "I'm afraid you're right. I simply haven't got the gumption to go down that ladder . . . especially now that I realize how pitiful your attempt at bribery is."

"Vixen."

Teeth nipped her ear, and she leaned back against Patrick's muscled chest. Her whole body was tingling warmly, despite the fact that a wintery sea spray had begun to blow across the deck.

"So clothing won't bribe my Sophie. You seem oddly unaddicted to fashion, given that you are considered the next best thing to a Frenchwoman by the London *ton*."

Sophie resented that. "I adore clothes!"

"Well, you don't spend hours getting dressed," her husband retorted. "And you don't talk endlessly about points of lace and such things. How about kisses as a ladder-bribe?"

"I seem to be getting those for free," Sophie pointed out saucily.

"That's true." Patrick's voice had deepened to liquid velvet. His lips were still caressing her ear. "Perhaps I shall bribe you with actions. They say that actions speak louder than words, or dresses. Ask me for something, Sophie, and I'll grant it."

Sophie didn't know whether she trusted herself to enquire exactly which actions he was referring to.

"All right," she said, ignoring the warm tongue caressing her ear. "I am very fond of . . ." But she couldn't think of anything that she *could* say aloud. Whenever Patrick touched her, her mind seemed to go hazy.

"The French miss is about to flash her hash, sir." The sailor who had been leaning over the railing was now pointing down to the skiff.

Sophie peered over the railing. Sure enough, Simone was wailing miserably and leaning over the side of the boat. Sophie moved toward the seaman, but again a strong arm caught her.

"Wait here, Sophie." Patrick swung his leg onto the ladder, hooked an arm around the rail, and held out his other arm.

"I can certainly climb down that ladder by myself," Sophie said with some annoyance.

He shook his head. "No."

She looked at her husband's unyielding expression, handed her muff to the seaman, and then hesitated again. In Patrick's eyes there was a command, not an entreaty.

"I don't see why I couldn't climb down the ladder," she grumbled as the seaman handed her into Patrick's waiting embrace. Patrick effortlessly held her small body against his chest as he made his way down the ladder.

"Sorry," he said. "You're *my* Sophie."

"Excuse me, ma'am," the sailor in the boat said as Patrick placed her in the skiff. Simone was retching over the side.

Sophie made her way over to her maid. "Shouldn't the crew be joining us?" she asked Patrick.

"Crew stays with the ship," Patrick replied. He didn't add that it was the first time he had deserted the *Lark* during a storm. "The rowboat will make one more trip and bring Floret over to the shore. He's threatening never to pick up a soup ladle again if we don't get him onto solid ground."

By the time the small boat made its way to the dock, the wind had picked up and icy nibblets of rain were beginning to lash against Sophie's face. Patrick jumped out of the boat and held out his arms for his wife.

As Patrick turned back to help Simone from the boat, Sophie smiled at the chubby young man who stood waiting for them. He had a round face and blond curls, with a rather impish expression. He was wearing what looked like a monk's long robe. But he couldn't be a monk; there were no monks left in the British Isles. Perhaps he just likes the robes, Sophie thought.

"How do you do?"

The man peered at her. "I do well, I do well," he said, after a pause. He had the rolling syllables of a Welshman born and bred.

Patrick came up behind Sophie and shook his hand. "I am Patrick Foakes, and this is my wife, Lady Sophie."

"Mine is John Hankford," said the Welshman, "just plain Mister John Hankford."

Hankford had a sweet look about him, Sophie thought, rather like a talkative cherub. Except that he seemed disinclined to say anything further.

"We are very grateful for your hospitality, Mr. Hankford," she said.

Hankford peeked rather nervously around the gentlefolk before him and saw that the rowboat had disappeared into the hanging gray sea spray. Then he pulled a long, rusty rifle from under his robes and leveled it at Patrick.

Sophie jumped but said nothing. Simone gave a faint scream. Patrick remained utterly silent, merely taking a quick glance at the rifle.

The Welshman erupted into speech. "There's no need to worry, no need to worry. I don't mean to scare the ladies, no indeed, no indeed. The fact of the matter is . . . well, the fact of the matter is that I've got to 'ave your promise of silence before I take you up the stairs to the house. Because there's something there that you might not like, or perhaps you will, I don't know, but you're all Lunnonfolk, I reckon, and so you'll 'ave to promise not to let out the secret."

Sophie looked up at Patrick questioningly. He was staring at Hankford, a small frown between his brows.

"Are you injuring anyone, or holding anyone against his will?"

"Oh no, oh no," the Welshman exclaimed, speech fairly rolling out of his mouth. "Quite to the contrary, as a matter of fact, quite to the contrary. We're healing people; it's just a matter of *who* we're healing. But I canna go any further, or rather you canna go any further, until I have your word of honor that you won't let out the secret to anyone in Lunnon."

Patrick glanced down at Sophie.

She met his eyes and then smiled. There weren't many gentlemen who would ask their wives' opinion at such a moment, even silently.

"I think we should accompany Mr. Hankford," she said to Patrick, ignoring Simone's moan.

Already Patrick had found that Sophie had an inexhaustible store of questions on any subject. He should have known that she would dash straight into danger if given the chance.

Patrick turned a steady eye on the Welshman, who visibly flinched. Whatever Hankford is up to, Patrick thought, he is not dangerous.

He nodded brusquely. "Right. As long as you are not injuring anyone, you have my word that we will not inform the London authorities of your activities."

Without a word, John Hankford turned about and started up the long, straggling stairs to the ancient monastery.

Sophie's eyes gleamed. "What on earth do you suppose he's doing up there?"

Patrick looked at the happy curiosity in her eyes and inwardly groaned. His wife was definitely addicted to French romances. Hell, she probably thought they were heading into a haunted monastery or some such nonsense.

"I expect he's smuggling." His tone was dismissive as

he turned to Simone. The girl was shivering, clearly about to have hysterics and refuse to climb the cliffs. "It's the monastery or the *Lark*," he said to the girl, not unkindly.

Simone looked uncertainly at the dark greenish storm clouds above them.

"The gun he's brandishing about is a little-used antique," Patrick pointed out. "And Hankford does not look handy with firearms."

Suddenly Simone realized that Sophie had started to climb the steps and was already a distance above them. "Don't you let the mistress go into that den of thieves by herself, sir!"

Before Patrick could open his mouth, she brushed indignantly past him and started after Sophie.

Patrick sighed and took after her. When the little group reached the top of the stairs, a great oak door stood open before them. Patrick stepped in. The room didn't seem to be the lair of a group of thieves. In fact, it was as empty as a tomb, and about as furnished. The pudgy Welshman had shucked off his monk's robe and was standing by the great stone fireplace.

Patrick strode over to him, irritation riding in his tone. "Well? Aren't you going to reveal your dark secret?"

John Hankford looked at him, a trifle uncertain. Foakes appeared to be a little black-hearted, he did. "There's nothing bad about the place. Nothing a'tall. This is naught but a 'ospital," John said.

Patrick sneered. "Now why would we have to promise not to tell about a hospital!"

But in a flash of an eye, he knew. "God forbid, we've found our way into a nest of Bony sympathizers!"

John glared at him defensively. "We're not for them French, we're not. But we're not for you English, neither. All we've been doing is mending a few of the boys who got torn up in their wars, and fled the place."

"Deserters." Patrick's entire body was stiff and still. "How did they get here?"

"They were left in a hospital with a drunken surgeon, and they were dying like flies. So the youngest of 'em put as many as he could in a boat and pushed off. They're naught but poor foot soldiers. Two of 'em are just fourteen years old. The French was letting 'em die."

"How terrible!" Sophie exclaimed. "And how good of you to take care of them." She smiled warmly at John Hankford.

"They're *deserters*, Sophie." Patrick's voice was strained. Perhaps the men were deserters—and perhaps they were able-bodied French soldiers pretending to be injured.

Sophie shrugged. "They are boys who are hurt. Who would possibly care that Mr. Hankford is taking care of their wounds?"

Off the top of his head, Patrick could think of a half-dozen gentlemen who would be remarkably interested in the existence of a Welsh group of Bonaparte sympathizers—and first in line would be Lord Breksby. In fact, this was precisely the kind of situation that had worried the English government enough that they had ordered fortifications built on the Welsh coast. But what was the good of fortifications if a group of crazy Welshmen simply invited French troops to land?

"You know, Sophie dearest," Patrick drawled with just a hint of condescension, "England did declare war on Napoleon last May."

"Well, of course we did," Sophie said, looking up at him with an adorable little frown between her brows. "We had no choice once Addington decided to hold on to Malta. That broke the peace treaty."

An ironic grin touched Patrick's lips. His wife was a constant surprise to him.

But Sophie had already turned back to John. "Would

you be so kind as to allow us to visit your hospital facilities? I have no knowledge of nursing," she added hastily, "but I do speak French."

John's eyes brightened. "You do? That's grand, missus. Mind you, I can make out a bit of French, and so can the parson, and so can my mother. And the boy who got them over here—his name's Henry—he speaks some English, but even so we haven't figured out what some of the lads are saying. No indeed."

Patrick snorted. The *parson*? A parson was involved in this unpatriotic mess. Still, if Hankford and his mother were tending a lot of French soldiers without speaking the language, likely they weren't true sympathizers with Bonaparte.

Sophie placed her hand on Mr. Hankford's arm as he turned toward a side door. "I would be very pleased to speak to your patients," she said.

John looked at her doubtfully. "I'm a bit worried as how I shouldn't let you in the nursing side, ma'am, begging your pardon. Because what if your gentleman takes it in his head to tell the great men in London, and then my boys have their heads cut off?"

"I gave my word, man." Patrick leveled a glare at the impertinent Welshman.

"That's as may be," John replied obscurely. But he seemed to have given in, for he opened the side door and held it as Patrick and Sophie walked through, Simone trailing behind.

They turned at an archway leading to a large room. Patrick pushed through the blanket hanging in the doorway and stopped at Sophie's shoulder. The room was lined with cots, and flung down on each one was a wounded man. Some had bandages wound around their heads and some had bandages around their legs; several seemed to be missing limbs. Most of the men didn't look over at the door when they entered. A plump woman did glance up, then went back to changing the bandage on a soldier's chest.

Patrick looked down at Sophie. Her face was utterly bloodless. He put a comforting arm around her shoulder.

"Oh God, Patrick, they *are* just boys, do you see?"

"They look younger because they are wounded," he said gently.

"No." Sophie drew in a shuddering breath. "That one can't be older than fourteen." Patrick looked where she was pointing. He'd seen head wounds like that in India, and he didn't think much of the boy's chance for survival.

Suddenly a small lad popped up in front of them. His arms were crossed over his chest, and he was wearing the remains of a ragged French uniform.

"Why are you here?" he demanded. His English was accented but clear—and his gray eyes were fierce. The boy was, in fact, more dangerous-looking than John Hankford had been, rifle and all. He slanted his eyes over to Hankford. "Why did you let them in?"

John cleared his throat apologetically. "Their clipper blew into the harbor and so they will stay the night here, Henry. I had to tell them."

Patrick looked at the Welshman in amusement, giving up the last remnants of his suspicion that Hankford was part of a Napoleonic plot. Clearly, this French guttersnipe had him over a barrel.

Sophie curtsied. "You must be the man who was brave enough to save your companions," she said, her soft voice full of admiration.

Henry looked at the beautiful lady before him assessingly. "I only put them in a boat," he said. "They were lying about dying, with flies all over them. I couldn't . . . I couldn't get them all in the boat, either."

Patrick looked about the room. "You saved ten men," he said.

Henry looked up at the tall Englishman.

And then Patrick bowed. "You are to be congratulated, Henry. You did a very brave thing."

For the first time since they had entered the room, Henry looked a bit confused. "My name is *Henri*," he said. Suddenly he swept a miniature, but exact, court bow.

Patrick's eyebrow raised and he involuntarily looked at his wife. There was more here than met the eye. Henri was no common French lad, that was certain.

"How old are you, Henri?" Patrick asked.

"I'm almost thirteen."

"Hell," Patrick exclaimed in disgust, "a twelve-year-old foot soldier?"

"No, I was . . . I don't know the word in English," Henri said. "I carried about the flag. I was going to be a soldier, just as soon as I turned fourteen."

Sophie swallowed and her grip on Patrick's arm tightened.

Henri, who was clearly ripe for a case of puppy love, looked rather shyly at Sophie. "Would you like to meet them?" He gestured toward the beds.

Sophie replied in French, and that broke the last of Henri's resistance. He beamed, and led her about the room, whispering the name of each of the injured boys.

Patrick watched Henri for a moment. The lad must have been three or four when the French began guillotining their nobility—and he hadn't learned that bow from a peasant.

"How did you end up in this monastery?" Patrick asked Hankford.

Hankford looked about the room, rather pitifully. "Mum here and I are members of the Family of Love. Have you heard of it?"

Patrick nodded. Who hadn't heard of the Family of Love? They were a Dutch religious group that had been variously accused of adultery and nudism, ever since the days of Queen Elizabeth. He looked at the plump nurse, who had finished changing the bandage and was now straightening the covers on a different cot. She certainly didn't look like the adulterous type.

"I didn't think the Family was still in operation," Patrick observed carefully. No point in getting Hankford riled up, at least not until after dinner.

"Oh yes, oh yes, they are, at least in Wales," Hankford said dispiritedly. "My grandfather became a member way back in 1731. He bought this monastery, thinking as he'd get a proper 'family' established here. But when he married my grandmother, she didn't cotton to the Family of Love, and so she threw all the members out. But later my mother became a member, and so did I. Well, my grandfather's dead now, but we're still part of the Family. We couldn't turn those French boys away when the boat washed up here."

Patrick was starting to piece together the story. "Henri put the lads in a boat and it came ashore here."

"Yup. They washed clear around the promontory and then came into the cove. As I said, we couldn't turn them away, because they'd just be shot by the government. And the Family of Love doesn't think much of government executions."

As well they might not, Patrick thought to himself. Quite a few members of the so-called Family had been executed by the British government over the last hundred years. Still, he could dismiss the danger of Napoleon spearheading an invasion through this particular monastery.

Dinner was served in the monastery kitchen, at a long, scrubbed table. Having been rescued from the boat, Floret was hunched condescendingly at one end of the table, seated across from Simone. Sophie slid onto the bench, followed by Henri, who appeared to have transformed into her shadow. He hadn't left her side since they met.

"Isn't this splendid?"

Patrick looked at his wife measuringly. If only London society could see its reigning beauty now! Sophie's hair was topsy-turvy, since she had pulled off her bonnet and tossed it somewhere. Her eyes were shining with excitement at the idea of sitting down to supper with her own servants in a thirteenth-century monastery.

"Yes," he answered, trampling down a sensation of warmth that threatened to make him dizzy. He deliberately put on the airs of a callous aristocrat. "Oh yes, this is an inimitable pleasure."

Sophie wrinkled her nose at him. "You are funning, sir," she said. "I can think of nowhere I would rather be than taking supper with Master Henri here."

Her husband, on the other hand, could think of many things he would rather be doing. But they were all too heady for the ears of a young boy, and so he kept them to himself.

Chapter 16

➜

The next morning Sophie woke early and crept out of bed. Patrick lay in a tangle of faintly musty sheets, only the tip of one ear showing in his mop of black curls. For a moment Sophie paused, curling her bare toes against the cool stone floor. Then she quietly pulled on the gown she'd worn yesterday and struggled to fasten the back without Simone's help. She slipped on her pelisse and her half-boots and crept out of the room.

As soon as she left, Patrick turned over and stared rather grimly at the cobwebby planks some twelve feet over his head. Something was happening that was beyond his personal experience. Seduce her no matter how expertly, his little wife had never succumbed. While he wasn't quite the libertine she presumed, it was true that his previous lovers had invariably vowed eternal love by this point in the relationship.

Patrick frowned. What an arrogant popinjay he was!

He had simply assumed that Sophie would forget all about Braddon, the man she was supposed to marry. The worst of it was that he had never wanted all those protestations of love so freely given by other women, but now ... things were different.

Patrick groaned out loud. He needed to hear those words from Sophie. Oh God, trapped in the parson's mousetrap. The words took on new meaning. He wasn't trapped by the archaic words of the marriage ceremony. No, he was trapped by his own distracting, ignominious need for his wife.

A glimmer of a smile appeared on Patrick's lips. After all, Sophie was his wife. If he was caught, so was she. So what if she didn't murmur sweet words? Maybe she didn't feel them. Perhaps those other women had simply told him what they thought he wanted.

Then a memory of Sophie, gasping as she frantically arched against his body, spilled into Patrick's mind. In fact, Sophie did tell him what she felt, if not in words. So what if those feelings didn't include frantic protestations of empty love? So much the better. They had an honest relationship. No empty bibble-babble between them.

Slowly Patrick sat up. A grim determination was growing in his heart. Somehow, some way, he was going to wrench those words from Sophie's lips. Because even if they were just empty embellishments, he wanted to hear them from her. No, he *needed* to hear them. Because ...

But he pulled on his clothes and left the room rather than face the answer to that "because." Why would he, who had never needed anything from anyone, need to hear words of love from a woman?

Patrick ate breakfast alone in the kitchen. Floret was holding court, surrounded by a bemused group of Welsh women who likely couldn't understand a word he said but looked fascinated by one of Floret's greatest accomplishments—breaking an egg with one hand.

The sky, visible behind a stained oilcloth that intermittently blew open over the kitchen window, was clear again. The storm had blown over. Patrick was anxious to get back to the *Lark* and see if she had suffered any damage.

He found Sophie in the sickroom. She was talking to Hankford's mother, over on the other side of the room. Patrick noticed immediately that Henri was still glued to her side.

"Young Henry has taken quite a shine to your wife," said a voice at Patrick's elbow. Hankford stood there, looking in the same direction. "He's been talking to her nineteen to the dozen, about his mum and such."

Patrick looked down at the cherubic young man beside him. "What will you do with Henri and the other boys when they are well?"

Hankford looked a bit anxious. "I don't rightly know. A few of 'em are good enough to leave now, but I don't know where to send 'em. There's precious few Frenchies in these parts, and they'll stand out, that's for sure and certain. And they can't go back, or they'll just become cannon fodder again."

Patrick sighed. "Send them to London," he said.

Hankford looked at him cautiously. "What do ye mean, sir?"

"Send them to London and we'll find them work somewhere. London is full of Frenchmen and they won't be conspicuous."

Blue eyes smiled up at Patrick as if he had suddenly turned into a gold statue. "It's right kind of you, sir, right kind indeed. Do you know, your lady suggested the same thing, but I told her no, because you might not agree. As the Good Book says, a man's the head of the household. That's right kind of you."

Patrick strolled across the large room, conscious of something odd. Hadn't John said that his mother spoke no English? And little French? So what language were she and Sophie speaking? But by the time he reached them, Mrs. Hankford had returned to her patient, and Sophie turned to him, smiling.

"Good morning, Patrick. I have been telling Henri that we would be very pleased if he could make us a visit—"

But Henri broke in. "Sir, I told her that you won't want me to make a visit, as if I were a true *personage*. I thought perhaps you might give me a position in your stables."

Patrick glanced down at Henri. His little face had fallen into anxious lines, and his body was hunched as if to ward off disappointment. But his gray eyes were fiercely proud.

"I was looking forward to making your acquaintance," Patrick said gravely. "As a guest, not a stableboy."

Henri shook his head. "I'm not a *cas de charité*. I must earn money to keep myself."

"Who was your father, Henri?"

Henri stood straighter. "That is unimportant, because he died when I was very young, and I was brought up by Monsieur Paire, who was a fisherman." Henri had clearly absorbed Republican principles as he grew.

"Who taught you to make a bow?" Sophie asked. "And to speak English?"

"Before, I had an English nanny," Henri said. "But she and *Maman* died too." He stopped there.

Henri was a gentleman's son, no question about it, Patrick thought. Perhaps they could locate some of his relatives, if any survived.

"Do you know your father's name, Henri?" Patrick asked gently, but there was an implicit command there too.

"Monsieur Leigh Latour," Henri said reluctantly. And then, after Patrick met his eyes, he added, "the Count of Savoyard."

Sophie knelt down and took Henri's hands. "I would like you to come to London as my guest," she said. "I become lonely sometimes, and you would be very good company."

Patrick suppressed a smile with difficulty. Sophie—lonely?

Henri glanced at her briefly from under a thick fringe of dark lashes, then stared back at the floor. "I think . . . I don't belong in a fine house," he said. His voice was perilously close to tears. "My parents cannot return the honor."

"You would be doing me a great favor," Patrick said. "I am away from the house a great deal of the time and, as my wife has explained, she grows lonely. You could be her—her aide-de-camp when I am gone."

Henri chewed on his lip.

"You cannot return to France," Sophie pointed out, "and you cannot stay here in this monastery forever."

The boy still looked unconvinced, so Patrick intervened. "Your father would have wished it," he stated firmly.

"I don't remember my father," Henri replied.

Damme, but the boy was as obstinate as a mule! "Then you will have to accept that I am right," Patrick announced, in the most stiff-rumped tone he could summon. "Your father would want you to live in a gentleman's house, not in a Welsh monastery, and certainly not in the stables."

Sophie stood up and shook out her skirts. "There, that's settled," she said briskly. "Henri, will you find Simone and Floret and inform them that we are ready to return to the *Lark*?"

As Henri trotted off to the kitchens, John Hankford stepped forward. He had been listening silently. "I was that sorry when your servant said you had to take shelter here," he said. "I thought as Lunnonfolk would certainly have black hearts. But I'm happy to say, and say I will, that it's not the case. All Lunnonfolk do na' have black hearts."

Sophie began to respond, but John broke in. "An' another thing . . . I never thought you'd be so well to speak, either, ma'am. Not in our tongue. I'm mov'd, that's what I am, mov'd. And so I'll tell m'friends at the pub tonight. Lunnoners who speak Welsh! It's enough to make one believe that the English aren't all bad."

Sophie cast Patrick a nervous glance. He was clearly lost by the turn in the conversation.

Oh well. The jig was up, so why not be polite? Ignoring Patrick, she smoothly switched into rolling Welsh and said a proper good-bye to John's mother. Then she turned to her husband, giving him a sweet smile.

"Shall we return to the *Lark*?" Her heart was pounding. Was Patrick angry? He didn't look angry. If anything he looked mildly bemused.

The minute they were out in the corridor, Patrick said, "Welsh? Welsh? Is your mother Welsh-French, if there is such a combination?"

"Oh no," Sophie replied. "It was the laundry woman who was Welsh."

"The laundry woman!" Her husband was clearly astounded. "What contact had you with the laundry or the person who washed it?"

"Her name was Mary. I used to spend a good deal of time with the maids," Sophie explained, "because my governesses kept leaving—or being dismissed. Finally, Mary taught me Welsh."

Patrick looked at her speculatively. "What were you doing to drive off governesses, hiding mice in their beds?"

Sophie choked back a giggle. "No! No, I was a most biddable child. It was my father, actually," she added uncomfortably.

"Oh." Patrick handed Sophie her muff. Henri—who was obviously taking his role as aide-de-camp very seriously—herded Simone and Floret down the winding cliff steps before them. The sun had risen on a clear, cold-hearted day. Far above, two hawks swooped and circled around the tumbling chimneys of the monastery.

"Look," Sophie cried, trying to change the subject. "My nanny used to say that hawks swept the cobwebs from the sky."

"Your nanny," Patrick repeated. "Where *was* your nanny while you were consorting with the laundry woman?"

"She was married to Mary's brother," Sophie explained. "That's how Mary found a position in our house. Normally my father didn't allow any servants in the house who weren't French."

Patrick was starting to get a very odd feeling about Sophie's childhood. "So all the servants were French, including the governesses—whom your father freely wooed?"

" 'Wooed' isn't precisely the word," Sophie said. "I wouldn't call it wooing, because he always pulled them into his arms just when Mama was going to pass by. He was quite obvious about it. Even as a child I realized that his behavior had more to do with vexing Mama than with the governesses themselves."

"Well, I'm sure they disliked that," Patrick observed.

"Yes," Sophie replied. "Perhaps they would have objected less had he expressed genuine admiration. However, I think even my father would have had trouble *wooing* some of my governesses. Mademoiselle Derrida, for example, had a bosom like the prow of a ship. She stayed with us for quite a long time."

"Then what happened?"

"Oh, Papa was discarded by his latest *amour,* which left him no way to provoke my mother in the ballroom. So he fell back on the household. But by this point Mama had replaced all the household servants with rather elderly and extremely unattractive women, so Papa was forced to resort to Mademoiselle Derrida."

Fascinated and revulsed, Patrick prompted, "What did he do?"

"Well, as I recall, he embraced Mademoiselle fervently in the Blue Parlor."

"And?"

"She struck him on the head with a brandy decanter."

Patrick winced involuntarily.

"It wasn't really her fault; it was the first thing that came to hand. But it was also the first time that my father rather than my mother dismissed a governess. He had a bump over his eye for days. I remember being quite happy because he stayed home every night for a week. After Mademoiselle Derrida left, I was sent to Cheltham Ladies' School. I think my mother despaired of finding another suitable governess."

Patrick gave Sophie a rather grim smile. No wonder she thought he'd be out buying negligees for other women the moment she turned her back. Life with the marquis sounded like Bedlam.

By this point they had reached the pier and the waiting skiff. Even Simone climbed the rope ladder back up to the *Lark* without complaint, eager to get out of the wind that was blowing the last of the storm clouds out to sea.

Patrick saw his wife off to her bedroom, placed Henri under the watchful eye of a dependable crew member, then went to find Captain Hibbert. The storm had caused no apparent damage to the *Lark,* and he preferred to round the point to Milford Haven without delay.

For some reason he didn't feel eager to bound down to the cabin and join Sophie, the way he usually did. In fact, he sent a message downstairs informing his wife that he would eat above, rather than join her for dinner, as was their habit.

It was only when he was standing at the wheel, rounding the point, that Patrick pinned down the source of his dissatisfaction. Damme it, would his wife ever fall in love with him when she was convinced that all men followed the pattern of her father? Sophie seemed to accept without question that he, Patrick, was a rake of the same cut. Patrick's heart sank. Who but a rake would seduce a maiden in her own bedroom? Who but a rake of the worst caliber would steal his school friend's betrothed?

Down in the cabin, Sophie was also wrestling with despair. Obviously, her mother was correct about male dislike of bluestockings. Patrick had never stayed above for a whole day before. He was disgusted with her. And it seemed that he was more top-lofty than she had thought—the very idea of her spending time with the laundry woman seemed to rattle him, let alone the question of her knowledge of Welsh.

Without a second thought, Sophie opened the porthole and tossed out her precious Turkish grammar. Patrick must never, never learn that she spoke seven languages.

By the time shadows began to steal across the polished wood floor of the master cabin, Sophie was utterly miserable. The worst thing was that she had secretly wanted Patrick to know about her fluency. If the truth be known, she had relished showing off her Welsh in front of him. Inside I was proud, Sophie thought. Well, pride goeth before a fall.

Ruthlessly she tamped down the seeds of disappointment. Patrick was her husband. The fact that he was a man just like any other was not significant. One lesson she could take from her parents' situation was that disappointment in one's spouse could not be allowed to fester.

One has to accept, and then forget, Sophie told herself. The lesson applies to little facts and large ones, to languages and mistresses.

Patrick finally appeared at the cabin door at supper time, feeling faintly ashamed of himself. The *Lark* was sweetly rocking at its moorings, ready for him to inspect a messy pile of half-built fortifications the next morning. But Sophie hadn't ventured from the cabin all day.

He had steered the ship, admired Henri's new skill at tying knots, reviewed the captain's log, and looked again and again at the staircase leading to the master cabin, hoping that Sophie would appear. But she hadn't. And he'd missed her.

None of the crewmen twitched an eyebrow when the master finally gave up and dashed down the stairs to the main cabin. They had become inured to such goings-on, especially after Captain Hibbert warned them to turn a blind eye to any irregular activity or it would be the worse for them.

But Sophie wasn't waiting for him. She was tucked into their marriage bed, fast asleep. With some surprise, Patrick saw traces of tears on her face. Somehow he'd thought she would simply appear if she wished to come above board. Now he really felt ashamed. Why hadn't he fetched her?

Sophie woke up as Patrick stroked her hair.

"What's this about?" Patrick's finger trailed over her cheeks, his voice slightly rough.

Sophie smiled. "I had a blue afternoon, that's all. You know, it's a woman's privilege to cry."

Patrick brushed her lips with his. "Were you crying because I didn't issue a formal invitation to join me on the deck for backgammon?"

"No," Sophie said.

"I missed you." His warm breath sent shivers down Sophie's spine. "I kept hoping you would appear, O wife of many languages."

Sophie looked at Patrick intently, but his dark eyes gave nothing away.

"Do you dislike it that I speak Welsh?"

"Lord, why on earth would I dislike it?"

His voice sounds genuinely surprised, Sophie thought.

"I was shocked," Patrick said, "not so much by your Welsh—that was a delightful surprise—but by what you said about your childhood. It cannot have been easy, growing up with your parents."

Sophie didn't see any point in discussing it further. "What about your parents? Did they argue?"

"I have no idea," Patrick replied, lying down on the bed beside her, propped up on one elbow. "I saw my father only on formal occasions. They must have dealt tolerably well together. I never heard anything to the contrary." He didn't need to add that Sophie's parents' incompatibility was known far and wide among the *ton*.

"What was your mother like?" Sophie asked, her eyes curious.

Patrick bent forward and traced a finger across her cheekbone. "She was rather like you," he said. "Small and delicate. I remember our nanny scolding because whenever mother came into the nursery, Alex and I would climb up on her lap and wrinkle her clothing. She was always very elegant, but she never minded it when we crushed her dresses. She used to wear hoops, I remember that. And she smelled like bluebells."

"How old were you when she died?" Sophie asked.

Patrick's hand dropped from his wife's face. "We were seven. She died giving birth to a boy who did not live either."

Sophie picked up Patrick's hand and cradled it against her cheek, wriggling over a trifle so that her body fit warmly against his.

"I'm sorry, Patrick. I'm so sorry."

Patrick turned his head in surprise. He had been staring at the wall, thinking back to those days. "It was a long time ago," he said, smiling down at her. One could become addicted to a wife who snuggled under one's chest like a chick going to nest, he thought.

"So, have you any other grand surprises for me, wife? Perhaps you speak Norwegian? Swedish?"

There was a heartbeat's worth of silence in the cabin.

"No, oh no," Sophie assured him, shaking her head vehemently. "No more surprises, Patrick."

He rolled over on his back, pulling her across his chest. "It's splendid to have such a knowledgeable wife," he said dreamily. "Tomorrow we'll dock the boat for a week or so. We will go to an inn and you can order all the food and argue with the innkeeper."

Sophie's cheek was resting against Patrick's linen shirt. "Did you miss your mother dreadfully when she was gone?" She was suspiciously close to tears again.

"Oh yes," Patrick said matter-of-factly. "I was rather a mama's boy, I think. Alex used to be summoned to sessions with my father, since he was the heir, and then I would have Mother all to myself. It was supposed to be a consolation, since I wasn't the heir, but in fact Alex would have given anything to be able to stay with Mother, and we both knew it."

A tear rolled down Sophie's cheek and disappeared into the creamy whiteness of Patrick's shirt. She couldn't bear thinking of a small Patrick missing his mother. She couldn't bear it.

"Did you cry?" Her voice was suspiciously high, but Patrick didn't notice. He was thrown back to the nightmarish week of his mother's death.

"Cry? I cried and cried. Unfortunately, I had misbehaved the day before she died. I told some fibs, actually, and she had, quite rightly, reprimanded me. But no one had any idea that the birth would be perilous since Mother had had no trouble with Alex and me. I waited for her that night. She always came to kiss us good night, and I knew she wouldn't be angry with me anymore. But she never came."

More of Sophie's tears soaked into Patrick's shirt. "Oh Patrick!" Her voice cracked, but Patrick was still deep in memories he had almost forgotten.

"So I got up. I got up and I crept through the halls, in my nightshirt, because she always came. But I hadn't got far when—"

"What happened, Patrick?"

His arm convulsively drew Sophie closer to his body. "I heard her screaming," he said. "I ran back to bed and hid my head under the covers. The next morning, I thought it had been a dream, but she had died."

"Oh, Patrick, that's so sad!"

He reared up on his elbow and looked at her in shock. His elegant wife was sobbing uncontrollably.

"What on earth? Sophie! Don't cry, sweetheart; it wasn't so terrible."

Sophie only wept harder, burying her head in his shirt. Patrick kissed the edge of her forehead, which was all he could see of her face. Finally she stopped, and allowed Patrick to dry her face with his handkerchief.

"I'm sorry," she said sheepishly. "I'm rather melancholic this afternoon." Then she blushed a little, thinking of all the fibs she was telling him. She knew exactly why she was melancholic.

Patrick looked at her blush and had a sudden thought. "Your fit of melancholy has nothing to do with my staying above board all day?"

"It has nothing to do with that," Sophie said, her voice wavering a bit as he traced a line of kisses down her neck. "I feel weepy, that's all." Her tone was just slightly defensive.

Aha, Patrick realized. Sophie is at that point of the month. Well, it was nice to know that his wife reacted with tears rather than by throwing things, as Arabella had done. Arabella was like clockwork. Every month she demolished a piece of crockery by tossing it at his head. What Sophie doesn't yet realize, Patrick thought, is that there is no disguising that particular event from one's husband.

"Are you regular?" he asked.

Sophie looked confused. "Regular at what?"

A small blush crept up Patrick's bronzed neck. "Regular . . . in the womanly way," he said, gesturing awkwardly with his hand.

Sophie noticed with fascination that Patrick seemed to be gesturing toward her waist. Finally she grasped his meaning, and then *she* blushed.

"Ah, yes, more or less . . . well, not particularly."

"Oh, irregular." Patrick's tone was smug. "That is likely because you were a maiden, and now that you're married, everything will steady down."

Sophie looked at him in horror. "How do you know such things?"

Patrick evaded the question. "We need to speak openly, Sophie, because regularity is the key to preventing the birth of a child."

Sophie gaped. "What are you talking about?"

"There are certain times of the month when a couple can make love without danger of conceiving children," he explained. "And then there are things one can do to prevent conception during the rest of the month. None of which I have been attending to," he added, a shadow of a frown crossing his face. "It must be you, Sophie."

"Me!"

"Your body," Patrick said, his mouth hovering just above hers. "I have been intoxicated for the last month or so. But we mustn't continue to act like feckless lovers, Sophie. As soon as your next monthly flux appears, tell me and we can determine a schedule."

"I have never shared this information with anyone," Sophie said, with just a bit of an edge in her voice. "Nor has anyone ever demanded schedules or information of any kind."

"You were never married before," Patrick pointed out. He was taking little nips around her chin. "We've been very lucky so far. Do you think it will start tomorrow?"

Sophie's voice was definitely stiff. "I have no idea."

Well, I do, Patrick thought to himself. But there was no point in throwing his intimate knowledge of women's moods in his wife's face. She already thought of him as kin to Don Juan.

"Let's have supper in bed," Patrick said, his tone persuasive. "I'll feed you."

Sophie's eyes widened. "You'll feed me?"

Patrick's smile was devilish, irresistible. "You'll like it. I promise."

In fact, Sophie was enthralled by the experience of eating in bed. She took to having lemon mousse nibbled from parts of her body with such entrancing eagerness that mundane thoughts of schedules, conception, and the like flew from both their minds.

Faced with the choice of losing his daughter to the great American wilderness or allowing her to pretend to be a French aristocrat for a few weeks, Madeleine's father did not hesitate.

"Do you love this galumph?" he asked Madeleine, in swift French, as Braddon stood politely by her side.

"Oui, Papa," Madeleine replied, with maidenly docility. "But he is not a galumph, Papa!"

"He is a galumph," her father said heavily. "However, he is also an earl, and you could make a worse match.

"Do you have a good estate?" Heavy gray eyebrows frowned at Braddon, who started, having lost track of the conversation once it shifted into French. He'd never been any good at languages.

"Yes," Braddon responded hastily, prodded by Madeleine's elbow. "I have twenty-five thousand pounds a year. My estate is in Leicestershire, and I have houses in Delbington and London. I have good stables in

Leicestershire," he added, "thirty-four horses at last count."

"Thirty-four! No great house has fewer than fifty horses," Vincent Garnier snapped. Then he looked keenly at his future son-in-law. Too much inbreeding among English aristocrats. That was Slaslow's problem. "And which earl are you?"

Braddon gaped. What on earth did the old fellow mean? "The Earl of Slaslow," he stammered.

"No! Which *number* are you?"

"Oh," Braddon replied. "I'm the second. M'father was made into an earl in the '60s."

He watched Vincent scowl. It seemed even horse trainers knew that second earls were new earls. "M'great-grandfather was a viscount," Braddon said defensively.

"Humph."

"I wish to marry this man," Madeleine said to her father, ignoring silly male fidgets over numbers of horses and numbers of earls.

"You may not marry him if he intends to take you to America," her father stated.

"Then we shall stay in London and pretend that I am a French aristocrat," Madeleine said practically. "Braddon's friend will help me learn how to be a great lady. I shall go to a ball, and Braddon will pretend to fall in love with me, and there we are!"

Garnier's mouth twisted. Clearly it went against the grain with him to countenance such a tricky scheme.

"And if someone finds out?" he growled at Braddon.

"I'll marry Madeleine immediately," Braddon said. "I'd just as soon get married now anyway. My family can't do anything about it, and I don't give a toss for my reputation among the *ton*."

Garnier looked approving at that.

"You could be the daughter of the Marquis de

Flammarion," he said grudgingly to Madeleine. "You are the same age."

"Oh, Papa," Madeleine cried, "what a splendid idea!" She turned to Braddon. "My papa worked for the marquis and his family. I was too young when we left France to be able to remember them, but Papa has told me all about their estate in the Limousin, and the house in Paris, on Rue de Vosgirard. The marquis was rather strange and rarely went about, but his wife was very beautiful and elegant."

"What about relatives, sir? London is crammed full of French émigrés, and they all seem to know one another."

"No one knew the family of the marquis," Garnier said. "He kept himself to himself. His wife, yes. She used to travel to Paris occasionally. But the marquis and his daughter were always at home."

"That's all right, then," Braddon said with relief. "You don't need to talk about it much, Madeleine. After all, if the marquis's daughter was around your age during all the troubles in France, she wouldn't remember much."

He turned to Garnier. "I presume the marquis didn't survive? He won't be turning up in London, will he?"

Garnier shook his head firmly, his lips pressed in a straight line.

But Madeleine didn't look entirely happy. "How can I pretend to be the daughter of the Marquise de Flammarion?" she said miserably, looking at her papa. "You have told me again and again how elegant, how perfect the marquise was. What of the people who knew her? They will take one look at me and know that I am nothing like the beautiful marquise!"

The two men who loved her most in the world looked at Madeleine blankly.

"You *are* beautiful," Braddon said, absolute faith in his voice. "Besides, daughters often don't look like their mothers. Look at my poor sister Margaret. M'mother used to swear that the girl had too many freckles to be her daughter, but Margaret made a perfectly reasonable marriage, for all that."

There was a moment of silence after this tangled speech.

Vincent Garnier's brows were drawn together in a terrible scowl. "You are a lovely girl," he told Madeleine presumptively. "Besides, people will assume that you take after the marquis."

"But they must have known what *he* looked like," Madeleine persisted. "I am sure he was slim and elegant too." She looked down at her curvaceous body. "I simply don't look like an aristocrat!"

"You look better than any of those frivolous muffin-brained women," her father bellowed. "I do not want to hear another word about it!"

Madeleine jumped in surprise. Her father was a taciturn man, not given to speaking overmuch. But he rarely shouted either.

"All right, Papa," she agreed.

Braddon took her arm and smiled down at her, his blue eyes clear and truthful. "I wouldn't want you to be slim and elegant, Madeleine. I want you just the way you are." Something about his tone made a flush rise in Madeleine's cheeks.

"Ne dîtes pas ça!" she protested. "Papa will hear you!"

But when Madeleine looked over at her father, he had turned back to his accounting books, and she couldn't tell by the little smile tugging at his mouth whether he had heard Braddon's comment or not.

"Go! Go!" Garnier barked. He looked sharply at Braddon. "You may ask Lady Sophie to visit us when she returns from her wedding trip. I should like to meet the woman who is supposed to teach my daughter to become a lady. From *The Morning Post,* she appears a mere fribble!"

Braddon bowed respectfully, hoping to God that

Sophie was not one of those women who would put up a fuss about visiting a public stable. And hoping that the *Lark* would return to London soon.

Lord Breksby fully shared Braddon's feelings about the return of the *Lark*. He was spending quite a bit of his time fretting over the unpleasant news that Napoleon hoped to sabotage England's gift to Selim.

Sophie's mother, caught up in a whirlwind of new, but not unpleasant, experiences, also wished fervently that her daughter would return to London. Eloise found the house strangely silent without Sophie, even populated as it was by some forty servants. On the other hand, she seemed to bump into George wherever she turned, whereas before her daughter married, she saw him only in the evening.

Somehow her husband wasn't as interested in ambling off to the club as he used to be. Now that he had breached the sacred portals of his wife's bedroom . . . well, it was a good bit of fun to lure his starchy marchioness into an afternoon indiscretion. But George missed his little Sophie, too. It hadn't occurred to him just how much he counted on her blithe acceptance and love to make him feel less—could it be lonely? Shaking off the thought, George went to find Eloise. Why not bother his wife, even if it was only ten in the morning?

All in all, there was quite a flock of Londoners thinking about the *Lark*'s return to port. Down in the district known as the Whitefriars, a sleek and sinuous gentleman was expressing that very wish.

"As soon as Foakes returns," he said, turning his eyes from the spiders dangling from the dark and lowly rafters above him, "I suggest that we approach him . . . gently."

His companion wrestled with his meaning. "Whether

we're gentle or not," he pointed out, "Foakes hasn't got the scepter. And now they won't give it to him till he's over there, I hear. It's a shame, that's what it is. A bloody shame."

Monsieur Foucault (for so he was known when in London) sighed. He did not know how the information had leaked to the English government about his delicious plan to substitute an exploding scepter for Selim's ruby scepter, but there was no point in weeping over it. "Clemper has been turned off, and we now have no way to obtain access to the scepter." His tone was a delicate reprimand. "We must, therefore, obtain our goal through other means. And our goal is to ensure that the English ambassador presents a serious danger to Selim's coronation."

"I still think it's a shame," said Mole (for so he was known among his intimates). "I had it all set up so beautiful. Clemper was going to substitute the scepter in the flash of an eye."

Monsieur Foucault sighed again. It pained him as well, since he intended to appropriate a few of the rubies with which the English government was so liberally adorning the scepter.

"Why don't I turn one of the new fellows working on the scepter?" Mole suggested.

"Impossible," Foucault replied. The odor in Mole's little house was truly distasteful. Foucault decided to breathe through his mouth, which gave his voice a curiously breathy tone. "The original jewelers have been dismissed, to the man, and I am quite certain that the new employees will be less amiable than our dear Clemper."

"Well, you may be right," Mole allowed. "So what do we say to Foakes when he returns?"

"I believe that we shall approach the gentleman as ambassadors from Selim's court," Foucault replied.

"Oh." There was a moment of silence.

"You *do* speak Turkish . . . I distinctly recollect that being a condition of my employment," Monsieur Foucault said gently, taking a lace handkerchief from his pocket and waving it before him. He did not look at Mole.

"I speak some," Mole said, just a trifle dubiously. "Learned it at my mother's knee, I did."

Monsieur Foucault did not express his belief that Mole's mother was an unlikely teacher. "*Bu masa mi?* Translate that, if you please, my dear Mole." Behind his dreamy tone was more than a hint of steel.

But Mole was up to the challenge. " 'Yes, this is a table,' " he ventured, rapping the sturdy wood before him.

Foucault smiled, and Mole relaxed. "You needn't say much," Foucault observed. "I shall present myself as a envoy from Selim's court. And *my* Turkish is excellent."

Mole nodded. He plucked at his worsted trousers.

"I shall send my tailor to you," Monsieur Foucault said, a glint of amusement in his eye. It suited his sense of humor to command the delicate François, his genius of a tailor, to enter the perilous darkness of the Whitefriars alleyways.

Mole nodded again.

"You, my dear Mole, might keep an eye on Patrick Foakes's town house in the next few days. I should like to approach him just as soon as he returns. And while you are there . . . perhaps you would be kind enough to enquire about his household, in the remote, *remote* possibility that our gentle approach does not prosper."

Mole's eyes brightened. This he could understand. "Right you are," he said cheerily.

Monsieur Foucault strolled back out to his waiting carriage, a smile hovering on his thin lips.

Chapter 17

⤥

The *Lark* docked late on a Tuesday evening in March, having been gone some six weeks. The Honorable Patrick Foakes and his party had to wait a good half-hour to disembark, to the delight of four stevedores lounging on the dock. They didn't notice the presence of a rapscallion French lad, but they certainly did notice Sophie, whose petite form and fair curls were the very emblem of a lovely Englishwoman. A demure, proper English lady.

Which she wasn't.

The *Lark* docked with a rebel onboard. Sophie had sailed to Wales with no thought of helping Braddon. Yet as the boat neared the dock, along with the realization that she had nothing to fill her time but the dreary round of shopping and taking tea, a sneaking, wicked ambition began to grow in her heart. Eloise prided herself on her social acumen, on her ability to spot a less-than-perfect lady at ten paces. Who better than her daughter to fool the entire *ton* and pass off a horse trainer's daughter as a French aristocrat?

Forget learning languages that she would never be able to speak. Sophie was going to become an artist, like her friend Charlotte. She would create the picture of a French lady. A living testament to Eloise's strong-minded training, if only Eloise knew. Which she never would, Sophie reminded herself. Her mother's moral sense was far too strong to countenance an intruder breaching the sacred walls of the *ton*.

One problem loomed large. What would Patrick think of the whole scheme? Sometimes Sophie imagined he would relish the drama and the hint of risk, and sometimes she thought he'd be disgusted by the attempt.

That evening, Patrick, Sophie, and Henri were just finishing a late supper when Sophie asked, "Didn't you and Braddon used to carry through a great many schemes when you were at school together?"

At the mention of Braddon's name, Patrick looked up. Oddly enough, he had just been wondering whether Sophie had yet forgotten about Braddon. It seemed not.

"Silly childhood stunts," he said brusquely, returning to his chicken. "Why do you ask?"

"Oh, no real reason," Sophie said airily. "I was just thinking about Braddon and you as children."

Worse and worse, from Patrick's point of view. Why on earth would his wife want to spend a moment contemplating Braddon, unless she was hoping to see him soon?

"What sort of stunts?" Henri's eyes were bright with interest.

"Braddon was always trying to gammon some teacher into thinking that he was someone other than himself."

Henri shrugged. That didn't sound very interesting. "May I be excused?" he asked. He was slowly returning to the normal pursuits of a healthy twelve-year-old, far from the rigors of war. He had spent the afternoon in Patrick's stables, and the stableboy had offered to show him a painting of a two-headed cow in the evening.

"Was Braddon successful in his disguises?" Sophie asked, after Henri had left the room.

Patrick rolled his eyes derisively. "Never."

"Oh, poor Braddon," Sophie said mechanically as her mind whirled. It seemed that Braddon was just carrying on a tradition by trying to pass off his future wife as a French aristocrat. And clearly, Patrick would not want to be party to Braddon's new "stunt." Perhaps more important, the idea sounded remarkably foolhardy, in light of Braddon's history of failed masquerades.

Patrick didn't like the pucker of worry that appeared between Sophie's brows. Why was his wife sparing any sympathy for that good-for-nothing lout? Braddon's honored place as an old and dear friend evaporated from Patrick's mind.

"Braddon lies," Patrick said, a blunt edge in his tone. Sophie's eyes flew to his, startled by the sudden disgust in his voice. In the back of her mind she could hear David Marlowe saying that Patrick was a stickler when it came to honesty.

"He lies? What do you mean?"

"He's precious close to a loose fish. He rarely distinguishes between truth and falsehood."

Sophie looked at her husband inquiringly, but Patrick didn't want to continue. In fact, what with one thing and another, he found himself in a pucker of a mood. The way to mend it, he thought, is a little intimacy with m'wife. So he nipped around the table and sat on the arm of Sophie's chair. Without another word, he began pulling the pins out of her hair and scattering them on the carpet. Slowly, slowly, curls the color of honey and sunlight fell down Sophie's back and over her shoulders. And by the time Patrick's long, clever fingers ran through her hair a final time and moved to the hooks on her dress, Sophie had long ago stopped thinking of Braddon and Braddon's problems.

≈

Thus, it was somewhat to Patrick's dismay that the very first billet to arrive the next morning was from the Earl of Slaslow.

"What the devil does he want?" he growled, the very picture of a jealous husband.

Sophie looked at Patrick in surprise. "I'm sure he is simply being polite. He invites me for a drive."

Patrick snorted. Since when was Braddon a punctilio? His manners were easy to a fault.

"You are not available," he stated presumptively.

"I'm not?" Sophie was really surprised now. Was Patrick the possessive sort of husband? It was a rather thrilling thought. Thrilling but impractical.

She folded her hands in her lap and looked up at her husband. "Is there some reason why you don't wish me to see Braddon?"

"It doesn't look right," Patrick replied.

"I'm a married woman," Sophie pointed out. "No one will think twice if I drive in the park with a bachelor."

"But you were engaged to this particular bachelor!"

"I'm married to you," Sophie remarked. "Surely you don't think that I would ever have an affair with Braddon."

Put in this cold, reasonable light, Patrick had to admit that no, he didn't think Sophie would ever break her wedding vows—with Braddon or anyone else. She had integrity, his little Sophie.

"Oh, all right," he said, feeling as if he had somehow lost a battle. "See him all you like! Set him up as your cicisbeo!"

"I don't think I shall do that," Sophie replied calmly. "A cicisbeo ought to be able to string more than two sentences together, don't you think?" There was a twinkle in her eye that made Patrick feel much better.

Sophie walked to the door of the morning room. "One always has one's husband," she teased, "if one wants to have a muddled conversation!"

Patrick gave a mock growl and reached out to catch his giggling wife, but she whisked through the door and was gone. Patrick caught up Braddon's letter, which she had left behind. It was a decidedly *un*-lover-like note: "I need to see you. I'll pick you up in the landolet tomorrow at four." "Landaulet" was misspelled.

He was being unreasonable, Patrick admitted. It was just ... it was just that Sophie had not uttered a word about being in love with him. In fact, she didn't seem even to be thinking of it. Here they had spent well nigh two months together, in the closest of quarters, and his wife had shown no sign of declaring herself.

Just then Sophie popped her head back into the room. "What's more, I shall expect all my cicisbei to speak excellent French!" she said saucily. As Patrick stood up he met her eyes, which were looking at him with wicked suggestiveness. It had been an enormously gratifying realization, the discovery that he could turn his wife into a melting, wild seductress simply by whispering a few throaty words in French.

Then her smile faded. "Are you reading my letter, Patrick?" Her voice was suddenly cool. Patrick looked down and realized that Braddon's note was still in his hand. He dropped it as if it had caught fire.

"Why does he *need* to see you?"

Sophie's backbone straightened. "Not because we are setting up an assignation. Given that, it is not your concern."

Patrick's mouth tightened to a thin line. The guilt he felt reading Sophie's correspondence made his tone much harsher than it might have been. "It damn well is my concern! You are my wife, and your reputation is my business."

"Are you implying that my reputation will be tarnished by driving with Braddon?"

"Well, your reputation is already not the best, is it?" Patrick said rashly. "Now that you're married, everyone will be expecting you to lead me a pretty dance!"

"A pretty dance," Sophie said, pausing on each word. Her heart was pounding in her throat. "You think that my reputation is so . . . tarnished as to make me notorious?"

"Your reputation isn't really a concern," Patrick said, reversing himself. "Braddon's intentions are the important thing. I fail to see what business a known rake could possibly have with a young married woman, besides the obvious."

"One rake would certainly know another," Sophie retorted, distaste clear in her tone. "However, as it happens, Braddon showed little interest in seducing me before I was married, and I am quite certain that his interest is now nil."

"Braddon is a loose screw," Patrick said, thrusting his hand through his hair in frustration. "I cannot like his stringing you along, for God only knows what purpose. What I mean is, I know his purpose! Pretty strong, fishing in his best friend's pond!"

"That is an indescribably vulgar thing to say," Sophie replied icily. "But since we are lowering ourselves, let me point out that *you* are the one who originally fished in Braddon's pond!"

"Why shouldn't I wonder what your business with Braddon is?" Patrick shouted back, his temper out of control now. "*He* may not have wanted to kiss you, but the same can't be said of you, can it?"

Sophie gasped. "What do you mean by that?"

"I mean," Patrick said furiously, "Braddon told me that you talked him into eloping because you were madly in love with him. It was just your bad luck that I came up that ladder when you were waiting for Braddon . . . in your bedchamber!"

Rage surged up Sophie's back. "You! You dare to imply that I seduced you? You! A man everyone knows is a lothario! The kind of man," she added scathingly, "who seduces his best friend's bride. You may *not* imply that I was planning to seduce Braddon. I had decided to cry off from my engagement—and you know it! You waited long enough before letting me know who you were."

"No lady invites a gentleman into her chamber unless she wants him to know of her availability. You sure as hell didn't fight me off when I came over to the bed!"

The back of Sophie's throat was burning. "I did," she said, caught between the urge to scream and the urge to cry. "I did push you away, until you took your hood off."

"Are you trying to tell me that you only succumbed because it was me in those robes? That's a bit of a tall order!"

"It's the truth."

"So you think I will believe that you married me for love?" Patrick sneered as he moved toward her, his feet silent on the wooden floor. "Let me see, you were so desperately in love with me that you turned down my proposal and begged another man to elope with you."

"I didn't say that!"

Patrick raised one mocking eyebrow. "Didn't say what?"

"I didn't say I married you for love," Sophie spat.

Patrick was within a handspan of his wife now, close enough to see the teary glimmer in her eyes. The sight made his anger abruptly disappear.

"So you married me for lust." His tone was milder now. "Well, we were caught in the same trap, weren't we?"

Sophie stared at him in dumb frustration. Then she steadied her voice. Not for nothing had she witnessed a hundred—or a thousand—marital quarrels.

"I am not having, nor am I planning to have, an affair with the Earl of Slaslow," she said slowly and clearly.

"Yes," Patrick said. He was beginning to wonder what it was they were fighting about.

"And I did not intend to seduce Braddon, had he appeared in my bedroom window rather than you," Sophie stated.

"I accept that."

"One more thing," Sophie said stonily. "I may have married you for lust, but I will never question what the current object of your lust is. It may be that in the future we shall both find other amusements, but I will not read your correspondence, nor will I countenance you reading mine."

"Fine. You don't question me and I won't question you. It's a lovely marriage you're planning for us, *my love*." Patrick emphasized the last phrase with bitter sarcasm.

Her face paper white, Sophie turned and walked out of the room. Rage touched Patrick's backbone again, like a whisper of fire. With a shock, he realized that he was unconsciously baring his teeth.

"Damn, damn, damn," he muttered with suppressed violence. One thing was very clear: He could not tolerate the idea of Sophie finding another "amusement." Not with Braddon or with any other man.

Patrick paused. Without thinking, he had started to follow Sophie up the stairs. Instead, he spun on his heel and headed out the front door. Grimly he started walking south toward the river.

A half-hour later, he was feeling much better. True, he still winced every time he thought of Sophie saying she married him for lust. But Sophie would never take a lover. Her personal integrity was one of his favorite things about her—that and the way she was so devilishly vulnerable at one moment and sophisticated at the next.

However, if he returned to the house now, he would

arrive around three o'clock, and Sophie would think he was watching for Braddon's arrival. Whereas he didn't give a toss whom she went riding with, Patrick reminded himself. What he should do is go to his offices on the West India docks. His man of business, Henry Foster, had left some fifteen notes for him, which had escalated in urgency as the *Lark* continued to meander around the coast of Wales.

Instead, Patrick jumped into a hackney and directed it to the Ministry for Foreign Affairs. He might as well see what was putting Breksby into such a twist that two notes had awaited his return from Wales.

But Patrick's temper was not mended by the interview with Lord Breksby. Breksby took the news of the haphazard fortifications stoically. He hadn't expected anything different.

"We're very grateful to you, my lord," the foreign secretary said punctiliously. "It is a pleasure to have my views so ably confirmed, and in such a timely manner."

Patrick inclined his head. "Will that be all?" he asked.

"No, no." For the first time in Patrick's recollection, Lord Breksby—the capable, pompous Breksby—looked somewhat discomfitted, almost anxious. "The other matter . . . the matter of the gift."

There was a pause as Breksby rethought his plan to keep Patrick Foakes in the dark about Napoleon's attempted sabotage. The man was so—so *formidable* in person.

"Yes?" Patrick asked impatiently. He ought to return to the house before Sophie went out with Braddon. Then he could be generous about the whole matter, perhaps inviting Braddon to join them for supper. That would show Sophie that he didn't care a fig whom she spent time with.

"There has been some unpleasantness surrounding the gift we are sending to Selim's coronation," Breksby said, making up his mind once again to avoid a discussion of

Napoleon's substitute scepter. "In fact, it appears that there may be a plan afoot to steal the scepter. That being the case, we naturally intend to guard it very carefully. We hesitate to put you at risk, given the scepter's vulnerability to thieves; therefore, we will transport it abroad through an alternate route. Our representative will bring the scepter to your dwelling in Constantinople a few hours before the coronation."

"You consider theft to be a serious possibility?"

Breksby nodded. "Exactly."

His tone did not invite questions, and Patrick asked none. "I plan to travel to Turkey in the beginning of September," Patrick noted. "I assume that your representatives will have no difficulty contacting me in Constantinople."

"I do not foresee any problem," Breksby replied.

Patrick stood up.

"Mr. Foakes," Breksby said gently. "There is still the matter of your dukedom."

Patrick sat down again, his stomach knotting with impatience. Damn it, Sophie would certainly have left with Braddon by now.

"I have set the process in motion," Breksby said. "I might add that, to this date, I have had nothing but favorable responses."

Patrick nodded.

Breksby stifled a sigh. It cut him to the quick to grant a dukedom to a man who clearly considered the honor to be a trifle. "The only question that has been raised is whether the future Dukedom of Gisle will be a hereditary title." He paused again.

Patrick simply waited.

By Jove, Breksby thought, the man's unnatural. Anyone would make a push to ensure that his son inherited the title! "I will do my best to confirm the title as hereditary," he said.

Patrick grinned. Breksby was a good-hearted sort, and Patrick knew well that he wasn't playing to the secretary's sense of proper gratitude. "I am indeed indebted to you for your efforts in this matter, Lord Breksby."

Like many before him, Breksby fell prey to the beguiling charm of Patrick's smile. "Ah, well," he said, "I always strive to do my duty."

Patrick's grin widened. "I am certain that my son, should I ever have one, will be even more grateful than I."

Breksby almost smirked. "*There* you are correct!"

Lord Breksby parted with the future Duke of Gisle well satisfied. He was right not to have informed Foakes that they were worried less about the theft of the scepter and more about its substitution. He himself found the whole possibility remote, anyway. Why would Napoleon bother to pack a scepter with explosives? The plan had a far-fetched ring that didn't appeal to Breksby's sensibilities. Likely nothing would happen at all—and saying naught about it would save his own reputation. What if Foakes spread it about that Breksby had got the wind up unnecessarily?

The sky was threatening rain as Patrick left the Ministry for Foreign Affairs. He had undoubtedly missed Sophie and Braddon. He walked down the great marble steps leading to the Thames and stood looking at its muddy depths for a moment. Then he turned and summoned a hackney. What on earth was he thinking, to neglect his work? Normally, after being out of town, he would have visited the warehouse immediately. He'd been married only six weeks and already he was overlooking his responsibilities.

When he reached the West India docks, his portly man of business trotted over to him with a look of acute relief. "By George, I'm glad to see you, sir!"

And Patrick was swept into the hurly-burly air of the warehouse. One of his ships had run aground off the

coast of Madras with the loss of a cargo of cotton; his
man in Ceylon had sent an urgent message about the availability of black tea; Foster had an inkling that the master
of the *Rosemary* was bilking them out of a cargo of sugar.
Patrick settled down with a will. There, in the dusty,
bustling offices that resounded with shouts and thuds
from the warehouses next door, there were no disturbing
wives, reproachful glances, or guilty consciences. He ate a
light supper at his desk and continued working far into the
evening.

⌖

Sophie looked suspiciously about the street before she
stepped into Braddon's landaulet, but there was no sign of
her husband. Tears still burned at the back of her throat,
but she was perfectly collected. Without hesitation, she
agreed to meet Madeleine's father the following day.

"Perhaps, if it is agreeable with Miss Garnier," she
said, "we could meet once or twice a week after that
point."

Braddon agreed eagerly.

"I have only one requirement," Sophie said.

Braddon squirmed. He'd seen that sort of look before,
coming from females, and he hated it. "Anything," he said
with a silent groan.

"My husband is to know nothing."

"Patrick? You mean Patrick?"

"Of course I mean Patrick," she snapped. "What other
husband do I have?"

"But, but—" Braddon was utterly nonplussed. "Why
on earth not? Patrick has always been in on m'schemes.
Not to say that he approves of 'em, but . . ."

"If he is to find out, then I will not be available to tutor
Miss Garnier," she stated, her tone allowing no room for
argument.

But obstinacy was second nature to Braddon. "Look here, Sophie. How are you going to explain where you are in the afternoon? What is Patrick going to think about the time you spend with Madeleine?"

Sophie shot him a stinging glance. "Husbands don't watch their wives as if they were lapdogs. My mama does precisely as she pleases."

There were a few seconds of silence as Braddon tried to decide how to point out that Sophie's parents were not an appropriate exemplar.

"My mama couldn't have gone somewhere every week without my father findin' out," he finally said lamely.

"I am quite certain that Patrick and I will have no disagreements over the matter," Sophie replied. "I doubt he will express any interest in my whereabouts during the afternoons, but if he does, I will inform him that I am visiting the children's section of Bridewell."

"Bridewell! Patrick would never let you go to Bridewell," Braddon exclaimed, thinking of the hospital for the poor, which was located in a highly disreputable area.

Sophie raised an eyebrow. "Are you planning to browbeat Madeleine like this?" she asked sweetly. "Because you might wish to know that ladies visit Bridewell regularly and play with the foundling orphans. We are welcomed by the hospital staff."

"Oh Lord," Braddon said, flustered. "Are you sure, Sophie? Why not simply tell Patrick, and then things will be so much easier?"

"I won't. And if you tell him, I won't lift a finger to help your Madeleine."

"Of all the stupid crotchets!"

Sophie's frayed temper mounted. "If it's a stupid crotchet, then you can find someone else to help you, can't you!"

Braddon cast her an appalled look. Trust a woman to start screeching just as a fellow had to transfer the reins to his whip hand.

"Don't give it another thought," Braddon said, once he had made the delicate maneuver and his horses were gently trotting through the archway and into St. James's Park. "I'm sure you're right. Now I think on it, Patrick wasn't at all nice about my last scheme."

In fact, the more Braddon thought about Patrick's reaction to his "broken leg," the gladder he was that Patrick would never know about his newest scheme. The expression on Patrick's face when Braddon started smashing his adhesive plaster was not to be forgotten, but neither was the lecture he read him afterward. Fairly made his ears peal, it did.

"Yes, you're right," Braddon said with sudden vigor. "The fewer people who know the truth, the better. You, Madeleine's father, and I are more than enough."

Just then Sophie leaned over, waving her gloved hand. "Oh, do stop, Braddon. Look, there's Charlotte and Alex!"

Braddon drew up and Sophie watched eagerly as Alex drew their two-wheeler parallel to Braddon's landaulet.

"Nice rig you have there," Braddon said to Alex. He was a friend of Patrick's, rather than of Alex's, and he remained a little in awe of Patrick's twin brother. Patrick had a ready temper an' all, but Alex had a steely glint in his eye that always made Braddon feel like squirming.

"Where's Patrick?" Charlotte called cheerfully from the far side of the two-wheeler.

Sophie squirmed. If only it weren't an egregious break in decorum for a woman to dash out of a carriage and run across the grass to another vehicle. She just shook her head, trusting that silence would tell Charlotte that something was wrong.

Her friend's response was immediate: "Will you join us for a light supper tonight, Sophie?"

Sophie leaned forward, trying to see around Braddon's considerable bulk. "I would be happy to do so, Charlotte. I'm not quite sure what Patrick's plans are, however. We arrived in London only yesterday."

"It's early days in the marriage," Alex said. "I'm sure Patrick will trail after you. At any rate, we must return to the house, Charlotte." He winked at Sophie. "Some people are henpecked by their wives, but we are henpecked by our nanny. It's time for Sarah and Pippa to pay a visit to the drawing room."

Charlotte wrinkled her nose. "Poor dears. Pippa appears all starched and miserable, and must act like a true lady for a brutal half-hour. Shall we see you at eight o'clock?"

Sophie nodded.

When Patrick had not returned by eight o'clock, Sophie left a neutrally worded note with the butler, Clemens, said good night to Henri, and directed the carriage to her brother-in-law's house.

When she arrived, Sophie surprised herself by not blurting out all the details of their quarrel. She had been longing to tell Charlotte . . . but did she really want Charlotte to know that her husband had forthrightly admitted to marrying her for lust? One had to maintain a corner of dignity, somewhere, somehow.

Dinner passed in chatter about baby Sarah's new tooth and the French soldiers rehabilitating in Wales. So it wasn't until Alex retreated to his study that Sophie met with a challenge.

Charlotte didn't bother with niceties. "Where on earth is he, Sophie? Have you quarreled?"

Sophie sat down on a low settee, constriction burning in her chest. "Oh, Charlotte," she said, trying not to sound pitiful, "I have the devil of a temper, you know that."

Charlotte's grave eyes looked straight past the light comment and into Sophie's eyes. "Sophie," she said ominously, her voice a command.

"I don't know where he is," Sophie said. Then she braced her shoulders. "I suppose he might be spending the evening with his mistress."

"Pooh!" Charlotte retorted. "He hasn't a mistress, and you're a nitwit if you think Patrick has eyes for anyone but you."

"We quarreled over Braddon," Sophie said.

"Braddon!" Whatever Charlotte had expected, it wasn't that. "What on earth is there to quarrel *about*?"

"Braddon invited me for a drive and Patrick refused to allow me to go."

"Goodness," Charlotte replied faintly. "He must be jealous. How very odd." She met Sophie's eyes and a smile irresistibly grew between them. "Jealous of Braddon! Goodness, how *absurd* men are! Well, it's not as if you have the inclination to spend much time with Braddon." She giggled. "Oh yes, Braddon the gay lothario, stealing Patrick's beautiful new wife!

"If jealousy is making Patrick quarrelsome," Charlotte added, "avoiding Braddon should do the trick."

Since Sophie had promised Braddon to tell no one about her plan to teach Madeleine the rigors of ladyhood, all she could do was nod in agreement to Charlotte's undoubtedly sage advice.

Back home, Clemens took Sophie's pelisse and asked whether she would like some refreshment. As she declined, he handed her the note she had left for Patrick. "Given that his lordship has not returned," Clemens intoned, bowing as his mistress climbed the stairs.

Sophie looked at the delicate clock in her chamber. It was eleven-thirty at night. She had stayed at Charlotte's house until the last possible moment, hoping against hope that Patrick would arrive home before she did.

Well, Sophie thought, unpinning her bonnet and tossing it onto a chair, Mama and Papa's marital bliss survived precisely two months, but we are rather less successful.

She counted on her fingers. My husband has vacated my bed in a mere seven weeks . . . obviously, my charms are eclipsed by my mama's. All those verses about the "heavenly fair" Eloise must have been true.

Or perhaps, Sophie thought bitterly, Papa thought he was in love when they got married and only found out later that he had married for lust. Whereas my clearheaded husband never considered love as a reason for marriage.

Sophie finally went to bed at one o'clock, but she didn't sleep. Neither did she cry. She lay, dry-eyed, staring at the ceiling above her bed and straining her ears to hear a noise in the adjoining chamber. But none came. At six o'clock she heard Patrick's man, Keating, enter the room and open the drapes. Perhaps Keating will think he slept in this room, Sophie thought drearily. It hardly matters.

At eight o'clock in the morning, Sophie finally heard brisk boots walking into the chamber next door and a jovial voice said, "Lord yes, man. Look at my face! I need a shave and a bath." She heard the rustle and thud of clothing being removed.

Sophie felt as if someone had placed a huge boulder on her chest. But still she didn't cry. At last the sounds of splashing next door quieted. When her own door opened again, Sophie waved out her maid and finally went to sleep.

Patrick wandered around the house all morning waiting for Sophie to rise, until he realized that she must be keeping to her room in order to avoid seeing him. He summoned Simone and cast a gimlet eye on her when she insisted that her mistress was, indeed, asleep. At three in the afternoon he finally lost patience when Braddon appeared on the doorstep.

"'Lo, Patrick," Braddon said cheerily. "Where's your wife? I'm here to take her for a drive."

"She isn't up yet," Patrick drawled.

Sophie had, in fact, just emerged from her room, but

she paused at the top of the stairs when she heard Patrick's voice.

"Didn't you go out for a drive with Sophie yesterday?"

"That's it," Braddon said. "Takin' her out again today, too. So, how is married life?" Braddon was in a mood akin to bliss. Madeleine was going to be his wife and all was right with the world.

Patrick glanced at him, and spoke with icy carelessness. "If I had to be leg-shackled, it's not bad."

"Leg-shackled!"

For a man who was trying to seduce his wife from under his own nose, Patrick thought, Braddon had no right to look so shocked.

"You're married to one of the most beautiful women in the *ton,* probably the most beautiful, and you call it leg-shackled?"

"Could be worse," Patrick said laconically. "Given her lack of siblings, likely I won't have a lot of brats underfoot."

Sophie felt as if each word were an arrow burning its way into her chest.

"That's a bit raw, isn't it, old fellow?" Braddon began patting his pockets, looking for his snuff case. "I say, Patrick, have you tried my new mixture? It has rose hips in it . . . somewhere here."

Patrick spoke through his clenched teeth. "I don't like essence of roses in snuff," he said.

Braddon comfortably helped himself. "Do you suppose Sophie will be much longer? My horses are standing in the street."

"I wouldn't know," Patrick replied.

Braddon cocked an eyebrow at him. "I must say, Patrick, you don't sound like a merry bridegroom."

"I'm merry. I'm merry." Patrick felt indescribably drained. He had worked in the warehouse half the night, and then had come home only to fall asleep in his own library, clutching a brandy.

"Are you still planning to set up your mistress in a house in Mayfair?" Patrick asked casually.

"No," Braddon replied. "As a matter of fact, we went our separate ways." He avoided looking at Patrick, who had a discomfitting way of knowing when Braddon was fibbing.

Patrick raised a sardonic eyebrow at Braddon's downcast face. Ashamed, was he? Damn well should be, given that he had apparently ditched his mistress in order to set up Sophie in her place.

Both men turned around as Sophie, exquisitely groomed and wearing a shimmering pale rose gown, walked down the stairs. Her eyes surveyed her husband with perfect friendliness.

"I hope you are having a good day."

Try as he might, Patrick could sense no bite in Sophie's mild words.

She took Braddon's outstretched arm and gave her husband a charming smile. "Perhaps I shall see you later?"

Patrick shook his head, not because he had plans to eat elsewhere, but just to see whether he could shake her calm. Apparently not.

"I'll wish you good night, in that case," Sophie said pleasantly. She and Braddon walked out the door.

"Damme," Patrick said. He turned and walked back into the library, where he had spent the night.

❧

Sophie swallowed hard as she climbed into Braddon's carriage, biting back the wish to retreat to her bedchamber. But, in fact, the afternoon turned out to be a delight. When Sophie considered whether or not to grant Braddon's request, she didn't give a second thought to the woman he had fallen in love with. A horse trainer's daughter? Impossible. But Madeleine was wonderful: French, practical, and very funny.

She and Sophie found themselves in gales of laughter, discussing the intricacies of proper behavior. Aspects of manners that Sophie had simply taken for granted, Madeleine found ridiculous.

"But *why* must I fib if someone spills his soup on me?"

"Because you must," Sophie said lamely. "Perhaps one day a drunken duchess will splatter meat juice all over your face. It happens; I've seen it. Even as you wipe your face, you must deny that the accident happened."

"Poppycock!" Madeleine had a laugh that burst out of her like small fireworks.

Teaching her to be a lady wasn't going to be as difficult as Charlotte had thought. Madeleine had an innate, natural grace that simplified their lessons. Sophie taught her a court curtsy, *la révérence en arrière*. By the end of the afternoon, Madeleine had it to perfection. She sank back with exquisite grace, her back foot sliding on the toes so that only her heels touched.

Sophie's mouth fell open. "It took me weeks of practice to achieve that, Madeleine!"

Madeleine grinned. "I shall curtsy to each horse in the morning." And they turned to the art of formal introduction.

Chapter 18

~~

I could do it," Mole urged. "Be the work of a moment, it would. The boy is around the stables at all hours." Monsieur Foucault said nothing, and Mole couldn't tell whether or not he appreciated this fine opportunity.

"I'm telling you, sir, the lad is in the palm of me hand. I told him I know of a horse that can count to five. I'll get him to meet me outside the house, and toss him in a carriage, and there we are!"

Monsieur Foucault raised his eyebrows. "*Where* are we?"

"Well, we'd have the young lad of the house," Mole blustered, with the uneasy feeling that sand was draining away under his feet.

"If by 'lad' you are implying that young Henri is Foakes's son," Foucault said languidly, "he is not. The boy is a French guttersnipe, picked up Lord knows where."

"But they like the boy, don't they? News is that he's

having a tutor next week, and he told me himself that he's being sent off to one of them fancy schools in the spring. We'd need to move fast, but I've got him in me palm," Mole repeated. "An' if they like him enough to hire him a tutor, then they'll pay a pretty ransom for him. I'm thinking he's a by-blow of Foakes's, that's what."

"But we don't need a ransom," Foucault said, the first signs of irritation appearing in his face. "Did you learn nothing of importance while you were entertaining all and sundry in the stables?"

"They're at the outs," Mole said promptly. "The honeymoon is over, they say. He's off every night, staying in his offices till all hours, never comes to her room at all, and she goes driving all the time with a great swell. They're telling, in the stables, how she wanted to marry this swell but then something happened and she gave him the mitten."

"Interesting but not useful," Foucault murmured. "Has François visited your humble abode, my dear Mole?" And, at his nod, "In that case, I shall request the pleasure of your company on Tuesday fortnight. We shall call on Patrick Foakes. You will be one Bayrak Mustafa, and I fancy that you speak no English. Will that be quite acceptable?"

And without waiting for a response, Monsieur Foucault rubbed a fleck of dust off his knee-high boots and strolled from the room.

Patrick stretched out his legs in the back of his box at Drury Lane and looked at his wife, who was sitting at the front of the box. If Lady Sophie York, the beautiful daughter of the Marquis of Brandenburg, had been a social success, Lady Sophie Foakes, the delectable wife of the Honorable Patrick Foakes, was clearly going to be a leader of the *ton*. At the moment Sophie was surrounded by gentlemen. Marriageable girls were all very well in their own way, but young matrons acquired a group of admirers who were afraid of being pushed into wedlock if they paid special attention to a young girl, and who delighted in witticisms considered too bold for the ears of maidens.

Patrick curled his lip as Sophie's chuckling laughter erupted again. Her admirers bent toward her like willow trees in a storm. Trying to see down her gown, he thought sourly. Sophie was wearing an opera dress of deep gold, dipping low over her breasts.

"Isn't that dress rather formal for the theater?" Patrick had asked when she appeared in the foyer of their house, smoothing elbow-high gloves.

Sophie had looked at him flirtatiously from under her lashes. "I like overdressing at times. It makes people think of undressing."

Patrick couldn't think of a response. Even glancing at the smooth, creamy expanse of her breasts, almost completely exposed in that gown, made his groin tighten. He had quickly swathed Sophie in a velvet wrap and whisked her outside, afraid that his wife might see the evidence of his lust.

What in the hell was he doing? She *was* his wife. Sophie showed no signs of being angry with him for their quarrel. But Patrick had spent the last few weeks walking the back streets of London, instead of ravishing his own wife, in his own bed, where he should be.

Patrick took a deep breath. He was sitting behind the cluster of gallants who formed Sophie's court, but even from where he sat he could see the way her breasts formed sweet, plump curves, thrust forward by her gown. He crossed his legs. It must be almost time for the damn play, *A Christian Turned Turk,* to start again. The Christian in question was lamentably slow at turning Turk, leaving Patrick far too much time to think about Sophie's body. At least the end of intermission would mean the clodpoles who were hanging about his wife would leave their box. Naturally Braddon was part of the group. Patrick was developing a positive hatred for his old school friend.

Sophie, in the front of the box, was aware of every restless move her husband made, although she studiously avoided looking at him. At the moment she was laughing and tapping Lucien Boch on the wrist with her fan. He was a particular favorite of hers, given that he excelled at the kind of light witticisms that didn't seem *too* pointed.

Lucien had captured her hand. He raised it to his lips. "I find myself a slave to your eyes, fair lady."

"God save you, then, because I won't," Sophie said impishly.

"No one but you can save me. . . . You are a goddess!"

"Then I order you to return to your own seat."

"Alack, I cannot." Lucien thumped his chest theatrically. "I am an apostle to your beauty, Lady Sophie. I fear for my life if I stray from the source of my bliss."

"Fustian!" Sophie giggled. "You lie!"

"I would you did, within my bedcurtains." Lucien laughed back.

Sophie involuntarily glanced at Patrick, who was frowning at his program. She was not yet accustomed to the level of suggestiveness common in conversation with married women. It was disconcerting to find herself embarrassed. Before she married Patrick, she had a reputation for racy language. But that was when she was a mere girl and didn't, she realized now, have any real idea what she was talking *about* most of the time.

And, to be honest, she wasn't concentrating on Lucien's flirtation. Every particle of her being was focused on her husband—although Patrick seemed not even to notice the way other men looked at her with desire.

Lucien gently took her wrist in his hand. "I spoke only in jest, Lady Sophie." His eyes met hers. "I flatter and flirt because it is the mode. But I do not wish to shock your sensibilities."

Sophie smiled. "You are saying that you would show this kindness to any lady, are you?"

"Precisely," Lucien confirmed. "I like you too much to offer you Spanish coin, my lady. And your blush reveals that you are still new to this kind of game."

Sophie's blush deepened.

Patrick happened to look up just then. He scowled. Knowing what he did about Sophie's predilection for being seduced in French, he didn't trust Lucien. Bloody hell, he groaned inside. If I don't watch it, I'm going to end up like Sophie's mother, allowing only elderly and decrepit Frenchmen in the house.

Sophie was whispering sweetly with Lucien. Just stay sensible, Patrick thought to himself. Everyone knows that Lucien is faithful to his dead wife, so he is only amusing Sophie with a flirtation.

Irritably Patrick got up and strode out of the box. Why should I sit around and watch other men make love to my wife? I am possessed, he thought, walking quickly down the theater corridor . . . possessed by irrationality and jealousy. For example, where did Sophie go yesterday afternoon? Braddon had picked her up at precisely two o'clock and hadn't returned her to the house until seven o'clock, barely in time to dress for the musicale they attended together. And the same thing had happened on Friday of the week before.

Striding down the dirty alley that ran beside the Drury Lane theater, Patrick's heart raced with anger. He felt unable to demand what his wife was doing all afternoon with her old beau.

Sophie, Patrick kept reminding himself, is like a drop of water: clear, honest, true. Her response to his lovemaking, for example, was unashamedly delighted. She had not erupted with false declarations of love, based on desire alone. Although Patrick had to admit that he didn't particularly care for that aspect of her truthful nature.

The worst of it was that Patrick had wound himself into such a tangled inner mess that he couldn't bring himself to enter his wife's bedroom, couldn't gather her into his arms . . . his own small, sweetly scented wife was lying alone at night.

If only Sophie showed some anger, or distress, or recognition of his absence from her bed, it would be easier to broach the subject. But she was ever pleasant, ever friendly.

"Doesn't give a damn whether I'm in her bed or not," Patrick mumbled to himself. He turned around to retrace his steps to the theater. It was bad enough that he was out roaming the streets of London at night or staying in his offices until the wee hours of the morning; Sophie shouldn't sit alone in the theater while her husband walked about, looking for a calm he never seemed to find.

Patrick emerged from the heavy velvet drapes lining the back of the box to find it empty but for Sophie and Braddon. The Christian must finally have turned Turk, since there was an enthusiastic swordplay going on, and the ex-Christian was using a scimitar.

Braddon and Sophie made a good-looking couple, Patrick had to admit. Sophie's curls were almost exactly the same color as Braddon's. They had a comfortable air of companionship, of old friendship, that Patrick did not like.

Patrick strode forward and sat down to the right of Sophie. Braddon looked up, saw him, and rose. For a moment he loomed behind Patrick's chair, giving him a friendly cuff on the shoulder.

"I'll be off, then, Patrick. M'mother is waiting for me."

Sure enough, Patrick saw the Countess of Slaslow, who

was sitting in a box directly across from theirs, give her son a piercing glance.

"She's as angry as a bear because I haven't found a wife," Braddon said glumly. Before Patrick remembered how much he disliked Braddon, he gave him a sympathetic grimace.

As the play continued, with much clanking of tin swords, yet another fragment of rational thought trickled into Patrick's consciousness. Braddon never was any good at keeping secrets. If nothing else, Braddon's utterly unself-conscious attitude suggested that his relationship with Sophie did not include improprieties. But that realization brought Patrick no closer to understanding Sophie's blithe attitude toward his desertion of her bed.

What the devil were Sophie and Braddon doing on their long drives, if they were not conducting an affair? Patrick's stomach twisted. No man and woman spent that quantity of time together without... And Sophie had such a *contented* air about her.

⚜

Later that week, Patrick looked up from his shipping accounts to see his twin standing before him.

"Alex!"

If Alex was a little surprised to have his normally undemonstrative brother almost knock over the table in order to give him a hug, he said nothing.

"I've been wanting to talk to you," Patrick said lamely.

Alex arched an eyebrow, a smile hovering around his mouth. "Let me guess ... you've bollixed up your marriage, in the style of a Foakes male, and now you would like me to help you sort it out."

"Not at all," Patrick said, meeting Alex's eyes without flinching.

"Nonsense," Alex retorted. "You don't think I dragged

Charlotte all the way to London in this weather just to have you shrug me off, do you?"

Patrick stared at him in frustration. "I didn't ask you to come up," he pointed out.

"You didn't have to," Alex reminded him, getting an edge in his voice. Oddly enough, although the twins were unable to sense each other's physical pain, one knew instantly if the other was emotionally wounded. When Alex's first marriage went gravely awry, Patrick suffered for months from an anxious stomach. "Cut rope, Patrick."

There was a moment of silence. "All right," Patrick finally said, turning his back to Alex and walking across the room to stare out the window. March snow was wearily drifting into puddles of rainwater. "I've bollixed up my marriage in proper Foakes style, but I don't think there is anything you can do about it, thank you."

Alex waited for him to continue.

"We're no longer sharing a bed," Patrick said, turning around, "and I don't know how to remedy the situation."

"Was it your choice or hers?"

"Mine, damn it! But that's just it. I didn't make a choice. I don't know how it happened. We had a fight over something absurd, and I didn't come home that evening—"

"A heinous error," his brother interrupted.

"I went to my warehouse, not to a brothel."

"My advice regarding marriage is never to leave the house until a quarrel is resolved," Alex remarked. "Women never forgive you for it. Charlotte would tear me limb from limb."

"That's just it," Patrick retorted. "Sophie didn't even seem to have noticed. So I stayed away the next night." He glanced at Alex, who was looking surprised and thoughtful. "It's absurd—but I was waiting for some recognition on her part that I had avoided her bed. But she's as cordial as a duchess at a damn party and, frankly, I don't think she gives a toss whether I ever come to her chambers again."

Alex frowned. "Did she enjoy being in your bed?"

Patrick looked bewildered. "That's just it. I thought she did. No, I know she did. And Lord knows, I did. But now . . . it's been over two weeks. She greets me as sweetly as if we were spending every night together. Sophie is perfectly *pleasant,* no matter what I do."

"You will have to broach the subject then," Alex observed.

Patrick threw him a disgusted look. "How does one ask a perfectly contented woman whether she has noticed that her husband has deserted her bed? She shows no signs of being inconvenienced!"

"You don't know that," Alex objected. "Find out. Go to her room. You don't need to discuss the matter necessarily. Simply go."

Silence puddled in the room for a moment. "I could try it," Patrick said slowly.

"You've nothing to lose."

Patrick grimaced. "I suppose you're right."

"Have you told her that you're in love with her?"

At that Patrick flashed him an irritated look. "Of course I haven't!"

"Well, you are," Alex assured him. "Otherwise, you wouldn't be in such a pother over the fact that Sophie doesn't seem as enthusiastic about marital pleasures as you are."

"Enthusiastic! You don't understand," Patrick snapped. "She's happy living the life of a damned nun. Hell, I don't know why she didn't enter a convent."

"You won't know until you enter her bedchamber again," Alex said. Then he grinned. "As for myself, I shall begin planning to spend my five hundred crowns. And you had better accustom yourself to the idea of sleeping in a frilly nightshirt."

Patrick frowned. "What the devil—"

"You didn't even make it a year," Alex said mockingly. "Remember? I bet you five hundred crowns and a lace nightshirt that you'd be desperately in love with your wife within the year. We're only a few months into the marriage, and here you are."

Then he sobered. "Why don't you tell Sophie? Tell her that you love her."

Patrick looked up from the carpet, his heart in his eyes. "The feeling is not mutual, Alex. She doesn't give a toss whether I'm around or not. She's perfectly happy spending most of her time with an assortment of men who hang around the house at all hours. Braddon practically lives with us."

It did sound bad. Alex wound an arm around his twin's shoulder. "We should be moving the household to London sometime in the next few weeks, but you can visit Downes anytime, you know."

Patrick gave him a wry smile. "Thank you."

"I have to fetch Charlotte," Alex said. "She wants to do some shopping before we return to the country. She will be visiting her parents tonight—will you join me for a game of billiards?" At Patrick's nod, Alex walked toward the door, then paused.

"Marriages aren't always successful, Patrick." Between them stood the knowledge that Alex's first marriage had been an unmitigated disaster from which he had barely escaped. "One cannot blame oneself."

As the door closed behind his brother, Patrick threw himself into an armchair. Consciously he relaxed his jaw. Alex was both right and wrong. The idea of discussing bedroom matters with Sophie was inconceivable. But he could simply walk into her chamber. Ay, that he could do. Tonight he was bound to have dinner with Petersham and then billiards with Alex—but tomorrow night he would enter that room. It was that or go slowly mad, Patrick realized. Whatever his cool little wife thought of the business, her bedlamite husband was burning to topple her beneath him on a bed—any bed.

Unknown to Patrick, up on the first floor that same cool little wife was shedding hot, inconvenient, and passionately angry tears.

Henri bounced through the door of Sophie's sitting room only to stop in dismay. "Lady Sophie! What is your concern?" Henri still spoke a queer, broken English, but Sophie insisted they avoid French so that Henri would be fluent enough to enter school in a few weeks.

Sophie brushed away the tears on her cheeks. "It's nothing, Henri. I'm turning into a watering pot, that's all."

"A watering pot?" Henri frowned.

"Someone who cries frequently," Sophie explained.

Henri hesitated. Even he knew that such a subject was delicate. "Do you weep because you are—you are . . . *séparée* from Monsieur Foakes?"

She might have known that the whole household would be discussing Patrick's desertion of her bed. Of course, the servants would know with whom Patrick was spending his nights—they always knew that kind of detail.

"Do they say, downstairs, who Patrick's friend is?" she asked baldly.

"What?" Henri was perplexed.

"Whom . . . Patrick spends his evenings with?"

Henri's face took on a knowing sympathy that was far older than his age. He shook his head negatively, not trying to hide the fact that the household believed in the existence of Patrick's mistress. But he did keep silent about the household's opinion of Sophie's frequent drives with the Earl of Slaslow.

Sophie's eyes prickled. She took a deep breath. This was a *most* improper conversation to have with Henri. For a moment she fought to keep her composure.

"I could discover," Henri offered eagerly. "This afternoon

I will follow Monsieur Foakes, as—as a Bow Street runner might do. And I will see where he spends his time."

"Absolutely not, Henri," Sophie replied, looking at the boy with affection. "I think we shall pretend that this conversation never happened. Weren't we planning to see the lion at the Exchange?"

And Henri agreed. But in the early evening he sidled into the drawing room in such a way that Sophie knew instantly that something was wrong.

"What happened, *chéri*? Are you all right?"

Henri walked over and stood next to her. Then he burst out, "I did follow him, Lady Sophie. Although you instructed me not to do so. He has . . . I thought I had lost him on Bond Street, and then he came out of a building. And oh, Lady Sophie, Monsieur Foakes does have a lady friend."

Sophie's stomach heaved. "Henri," she said, "that was not the correct thing to do. It was monstrous improper for you to have followed Patrick anywhere." Dimly, she listened with amazement to her unshaken voice.

In Henri's eyes was a confused sense of betrayal. He adored Sophie, and Patrick's behavior went against his sense of loyalty.

"It's not right!" he said furiously. "I shall tell him so! This . . . this black-haired woman . . . bah! She is a—a pig compared to you!"

Sophie almost smiled at that. But her heart was hurting too much. So Patrick had a black-haired charmer. Likely the woman was his mistress before they married, and he'd never broken off the relationship.

"Henri, it was not proper of you to follow Patrick anywhere, *especially* in order to observe him with . . . with his friend." Her eyes commanded Henri's attention.

He felt a prickle of shame. "But I didn't believe them," he burst out. "When they said, downstairs, that Monsieur Foakes was with a courtesan, I didn't believe them!"

Sophie's heart wrung. Henri's pointed little face looked so unhappy. " 'Tis the way of the world, Henri," she said gently, putting an arm around the boy. "It means naught for a marriage . . . it's just the way of things."

Henri went in to supper unconvinced. Sophie went in to supper miserable. She had never had a chance at Patrick's heart. A black-haired woman was there before her. And Patrick was likely sharing an intimate meal with his mistress, because he didn't appear at all.

That night Sophie lay in her bed awake until three in the morning, hoping, praying that tonight Patrick would come to her bed. But at last she heard him come in, dismiss his valet, and fall into his own bed.

Patrick slept so soundly that he hardly even turned over in the night. Sophie knew how well he slept, because she left the door between their rooms open, just a crack. He must be exhausting himself. But Sophie couldn't drum up any real anger over Patrick's activities.

Instead of anger, what she felt was a trickle of fear. While she hadn't wanted to discuss her monthly schedule with Patrick when they were onboard the *Lark,* even she couldn't help noticing that she hadn't bled once since Patrick climbed the ladder to her room. It seemed that she took after her mother in all things, Sophie thought bitterly: in immediate pregnancy, and in failed marriages.

The baby was already changing her body. Her breasts were larger and more tender; her stomach had a tiny, sweet curve that she cherished in private. She had begun to sleep longer and longer in the morning, but there was no one to notice except her maid.

Soon she would grow fat and unpleasing, and then Patrick, who was already amusing himself elsewhere, would never come back to her bed. So Sophie wept huge, wrenching sobs into her pillow, not precisely because Patrick was cavorting with other women, but because she was so shamefully lustful that she wasn't even happy about the babe she thought she had wanted. It didn't seem fair for it to come so soon. Patrick had already lost interest in her body, and he wanted only one child. Now he would have no reason to return to her bed, *ever*.

That meant years of marriage spent exactly like her mother's, meeting one's husband at dinner and parting immediately thereafter, going to house parties and having hostesses automatically separate your bedroom from your husband's bedroom, putting you at opposite ends of the corridor or, even worse, on separate floors.

Part of the problem was that whenever she saw Patrick, a prickling warmth blossomed in her stomach and spread down her legs, a dizzying, hungry heat that was all the more shaming for being so clearly unshared. That night Sophie lay in bed, the blood pulsing in her veins, and it was all she could do not to creep next door and throw herself on Patrick's sleeping body.

But pride came to her rescue. Would she go to a man who was exhausted from being with another woman? What if he flatly rejected her? What if he smelled of another's perfume? What if he said . . . The possibilities were endless, and equally terrible. Sophie stayed where she was, in her own bed.

Chapter 19

T he next morning, Sophie forced herself to think through the situation. Yes, her husband had deserted her bed for that of a courtesan. But the important thing was to stay on good terms, because otherwise the unborn babe would be doomed to the kind of childhood she had had. And it would be best if no one guessed that she cared a fig about Patrick's whereabouts. A show of jealousy on her part would start the kind of loathsome gossip that trailed after her parents.

"Dearest *Maman*," Sophie wrote on her best stationery. "I trust that you and Papa are enjoying a pleasant sojourn in the country. Your account of Mrs. Braddle's spring fête was very amusing. Patrick is remarkably busy these days, and so we cannot join you, but thank you so much for your invitation. London is still rather thin of company, but I have been spending a good deal of time with Madeleine Corneille, who is the daughter of the Marquis de Flammarion. You must meet Madeleine as soon as you return to London. I am persuaded that you will find her as delightful as I do. Henri is very well, and I thank you for asking about him. He is excited about beginning the term at Harrow. Patrick will drive him there next week. I will do my best to find the glassware that you desire and have it sent immediately." She signed the letter, "Your loving daughter, Sophie." It was not without a qualm that she sealed the letter and gave it to a footman. If her mother had any idea that she was carrying a babe, she would arrive in London by nightfall.

Eloise read the letter with a tiny frown. Sophie rarely mentioned her husband in her frequent missives, and Eloise couldn't decide whether she was simply getting a bee in her bonnet about it, or whether her daughter's marriage had somehow gone awry.

"George," she said that night at dinner, "what *do* you know about Patrick Foakes?"

George gaped at her. "Eh, my dear?"

"Does Foakes frequent the muslin company?"

Eloise always could be counted on to call a spade a spade, George thought to himself. He chose his words carefully. "Foakes got up to some shenanigans when he was young, m'dear."

"I'm not interested in his youth," Eloise replied impatiently. "Do you think that he has set up a mistress on the side?"

Given George's knowledge of the *ton,* it would be a very unusual thing indeed if Patrick was not supporting a mistress. His pause answered Eloise's question.

"Well, I knew it," she said, half to herself. "I advised Sophie to marry a rake, didn't I? What a fool I was!"

George jerked his head at the footman, and then appeared at Eloise's elbow, drawing her up. "Eloise, love, perhaps Sophie takes after her mother."

Eloise looked up at him, perplexed.

George bent his head, brushing his lips across hers. "Her mother has all those courtesans beat to flinders," he whispered.

Eloise's expression grew annoyed. "Now, George," she said reprovingly. "Don't you think that I can be lured off to the bedchamber in this harum-scarum manner. Your doxies might have missed their dinner in order to . . . to frolic with you, but I shall not." She lowered herself back into her chair, back straight as a marble pillar. "And ring the bell, if you please. Philippe appears to have deserted his post."

George grinned and circled the table back to his chair. Damme, but he was enjoying this endless fencing match with his marchioness. She was as obstinate as a mule.

"I don't think we should worry about young Sophie," he said comfortably, taking an apricot tart from the platter before him. "She's got her head screwed on right."

"You're a fool, George," Eloise replied. But her eyes were tender.

Chapter 26

M onsieur Foucault turned about and showed his pointed white teeth to Mole. "Remember, my dearest, you speak *only* Turkish."

Mole nodded. Given his grasp of the Turkish language, he figured on presenting himself as the silent type.

Monsieur Foucault disembarked from the carriage and drifted his way up to the open door of Patrick Foakes's town house. He was a vision of elegance in his striped waistcoat. His hair was cut *à la Titus,* and a lace handkerchief drooped from his fingers. Unfortunately, Mole did not achieve a matching elegance, although he too wore a striped waistcoat, courtesy of the long-suffering François.

"We are," Monsieur Foucault explained to Patrick some minutes later, "representatives of the court of the great sultan, Selim III."

Patrick bowed with grave courtesy. "I am most pleased to make your acquaintance," he murmured. He was well versed in the tedium of international courtesies and steeled himself for a long half-hour.

"I regret to say that my dearest companion, Bayrak Mustafa, has not yet mastered the English language," Foucault remarked. "He is a devoted acquaintance of Selim's. I wonder if you speak Turkish, my dear sir?"

"Unfortunately, I have not the pleasure," Patrick responded. He bowed toward Mole, then turned back to Foucault. "May I offer you and Mr. Mustafa some refreshments?"

Foucault turned to Bayrak Mustafa; Turkish flooded from his lips. Patrick watched with interest. For a moment, he had thought that Foucault might be an impostor, but he clearly spoke fluent Turkish. Patrick could tell that Foucault's manner was not that with which one addresses an equal. Bayrak Mustafa must be some sort of lowly satellite to the so-elegant Foucault.

Mustafa grinned and bobbed his head toward Patrick, replying in Turkish.

"My companion and I," Foucault said in his languid manner, "would be charmed to further your acquaintance."

Patrick rang the bell. "I must compliment you on your grasp of the Turkish language," he said, turning to Foucault again.

Monsieur Foucault tittered and waved his lace handkerchief. "Oh la, sir, as you noticed, I am no Turk by birth."

At Patrick's enquiring gaze, he continued. "I met my dearest Selim when he traveled to France in 1788. We found ourselves to be . . . kindred spirits." A smile curled Foucault's thin lips. It was true enough. He *had* met the absurd Selim as the Turk racketed about Paris, pinching women and generally raising mayhem.

That explanation made sense to Patrick. He too had met Selim, and this sleek Frenchman was precisely the sort of man with whom Selim surrounded himself.

"When the unfortunate events took place that necessitated Selim breaking off relations with France"—with just a wave of his white hand, Foucault dismissed Napoleon's invasion of Egypt, one of the Ottoman Empire's chief holdings—"Selim *begged* me not to abandon his friendship. In fact, I have long had a burning desire to live in the English capital, and so he was kind enough to make me his envoy. Dearest Mustafa is my devoted acolyte; between us, we await Selim's missives. Occasionally, we fulfill some small request. Selim has *such* an affection for hussar boots, for example, and everyone knows that the best boots are made by the English." Foucault paused and cast his own boots an affectionate glance.

"Selim has been made aware that you, my dear sir, will travel to the Ottoman Empire for his coronation—*such* a splendid occasion!—and so he naturally desired me to make your acquaintance." Foucault sipped delicately at his ratafia.

Patrick nodded. He was beginning to wonder what Foucault wanted from him. There was just the faintest air of tension about the man that set Patrick's nerves on alert. And his companion looked like a rabble-rouser, to Patrick's mind. Likely Foucault was some sort of procurer for Selim, and he'd be damned if the only English products Foucault sent to Turkey were made from English leather.

But there was no rushing Monsieur Foucault. After what he judged to be an appropriate number of pleasantries, he finally came to the point. "I would *adore* to attend dear Selim's coronation," he said, "but alas, my presence is required in London."

He managed to convey the impression that he was eagerly awaited in every great house. Whereas, Patrick thought rather sourly, he himself had yet to meet Monsieur Foucault in any respectable setting that he remembered.

"That being the case," Foucault continued, "I wonder whether I might impose upon you to convey a small token of my appreciation to the sultan ... or shall I say, Emperor Selim? I am loath to have my dearest Selim think for a instant that my heart is not with him on this most momentous occasion."

Patrick sighed internally. Clearly, Foucault wanted to ensure a warm welcome in Turkey, should he be forced to leave England. Because unless he missed his guess, Foucault was a sharpster, if not an out-and-out criminal.

But Patrick assured Monsieur Foucault that he would be more than happy to convey a gift to the coronation and present it personally to Emperor Selim.

At length Foucault bowed himself out of the room, leaving behind only a faint scent of ambergris and the promise of returning in two months, bearing his gift. "Selim is *so* fond of rubies," he said earnestly. "I am considering a silver inkwell set with the gems."

And the last of Patrick's doubts were assuaged, for hadn't Breksby talked of Selim's love of rubies? It was not his concern how the unsavory Foucault would acquire such an expensive item.

Patrick stared blindly at the closed door. He hadn't given Selim's coronation a thought in days. But now it took on an entirely new significance. He would have to leave Sophie. Travel to Turkey. Be gone for months. By the time he returned, she'd be living in Braddon's pocket, most likely.

That evening, as his valet carefully smoothed a coat over Patrick's broad shoulders, Patrick made up his mind. Alex was right. Bloody hell, he was acting like an adolescent girl. Wasn't his plan to make his wife fall in love with him? Deserting her bed wasn't a very sensible way to go about it.

When he walked into the drawing room, Sophie was standing on the other side of the room, looking out the window. She was dressed in a simple evening gown of pale green silk. The room was rather dimly lit, with not enough candles; rain had suddenly started to pour down at twilight, and the servants apparently hadn't had time to return and light the candelabra lining the walls.

Sophie's dress wasn't provocative. It didn't have the dipping neckline of the gold opera gown. She even had a little shawl draped around her bare arms. But Patrick was rooted to the floor by the way the soft fabric almost strained over her breasts, tucking up under their curves and then falling to the ground.

"Is Henri dining with us tonight?"

Sophie turned about, startled. "No, he—"

Patrick strode across the room and pulled Sophie into his arms.

With a startled cry she dropped her shawl. Patrick's mouth descended on hers and took her breath. She opened her lips to him as if it had been yesterday when they last kissed. Fire danced down Sophie's legs. He was back. He was back. Gratitude, triumph, love, desire: they all mixed together as she melted into Patrick's embrace.

Slowly, slowly he released her, settling her back on her feet.

He looked down at her, one finger tracing the swollen curve of her lower lip. His eyes were black as midnight, unreadable.

Sophie looked back, afraid to say a word. Now that Patrick had suddenly noticed that he had a wife, accusations were trembling on her tongue: *Where do you go at night? Why are you kissing me? Is your courtesan unavailable?* Sternly she governed her face into a smile.

Patrick didn't say anything, so Sophie half stammered, "That was very... very... pleasant, Patrick." Still he didn't reply, so Sophie took his arm and they walked silently to the dining room.

Patrick was floored. When Sophie melted so sweetly

into his arms, he felt a great upswing of joy. When she gasped against his mouth, and pressed herself fiercely to his body, it felt *right*.

But when she looked at him with that mild expression and told him his kisses were "pleasant," he felt like walking out of the room and never coming back.

He drank about three times his normal amount of wine at supper. Every time he looked at Sophie, across the table from him, his groin throbbed and he reached for his wineglass. The only thing going through his mind was exactly what he was going to do to his wife after this interminable meal was over.

She had tied up her honey curls in a careless knot on her head, and glimmering ringlets were escaping, falling in lazy spirals past her shoulders. One elusive curl was caught on the high back of the dining-room chair, clear amber against wood that had aged to near black. Patrick stared at it, mesmerized by the memory of Sophie rubbing her hair over his chest.

Clemens removed the fillet of veal and brought in a haunch of venison.

Sophie squirmed in her chair as if ants were crawling over her body. Something about Patrick's glance made her uneasy and excited at once. Chilly rain was tearing against the windows of the dining room, rattling the small diamond-shaped panes and making it difficult to talk. All of Sophie's clever conversation had deserted her. Moreover, whatever subject she brought up was ground to silence by Patrick's monosyllabic replies.

Desperately she strived to think of something to say, but Patrick cut in.

"Alex came to town yesterday."

Sophie's face lit up in a blinding smile. "How is Charlotte?"

Why doesn't she smile at me like that? "I didn't ask."

Sophie hesitated. "The children?"

"Forgot."

Sophie sighed and tried to think of another subject. Truly, being married wasn't easy. She racked her brain. Perhaps literature? They still had another course to get through before Patrick left for his evening entertainment. . . .

"Did you enjoy *The Rivals*?" They had been to the theater a few days before.

"The play is twenty-five years old and it showed."

Sophie persisted. "I thought Lydia Languish was very funny."

"Was she the heroine? The one who kept reading all those rubbishy novels?"

"Yes."

Patrick snorted. "*The Innocent Adultery! The Delicate Distress!* What a way to waste time."

"I read *The Delicate Distress*." Sophie's eyes twinkled. "It's the memoirs of Lady Woodford. She led quite a sensational life, you know."

The conversation languished once more. Sophie picked at her venison. The only thing she could think about was Patrick's kiss. Why did he do it? More important, would he do it again?

Finally she ventured to peek across the table at her husband. He was lounging back in his chair, staring at his wineglass. Dressed all in black, he looked like a devil, his silver-black hair swept into tangled curls by restless hands. A candle winked on the candelabra between them and went out, sending lurching shadows across the table that emphasized the planes of his face. How could she ever have hoped to keep a man as beautiful as this for her own?

Even looking at him made Sophie's heart start a tip-tapping dance. Maybe he wouldn't go out tonight. Perhaps her restraint had been rewarded and she *could* lure him back to her bed.

Before she could think about it and lose courage,

Sophie waved the footman out of the room and pushed back her chair. Patrick, deep in thought, didn't notice.

Softly she tiptoed around the long table, her slippers whispering against the carpet. Liquid warmth had infused itself into every inch of her body, making her bold. With a twist of her hips she inserted herself between Patrick and the table.

He looked up, startled, just as Sophie leaned forward and wantonly traced the curve of his lips with her tongue. Patrick's hands instinctively reached out and pulled her onto his knee. Sophie hardly noticed. Now that she was touching Patrick, a sensual haze, compounded by weeks of acute, wanting, desperate lust, descended on her.

Patrick savaged her mouth until she moaned. He was dimly aware that his docile, *pleasant* wife was tearing his shirt off, right in the dining room. Clemens might enter at any moment, not to mention the footmen.

Still, he waited, reluctant to break the spell. Sophie's warm body was pressed to his again; his hand had swept up her dress without a hint of reluctance and now she was uttering little broken half-shrieks against his mouth.

It was then that Patrick realized he was about to lower his own wife to the floor and drive into her right there, on the Persian carpet, probably with an audience of a butler and two footmen.

He stood up, easily pulling Sophie into his arms, and brushed by the footman standing outside the door without a word. Undoubtedly the man would be able to judge for himself that no sweets were required in the dining room.

As Patrick walked sturdily up the stairs, Sophie buried her face against his throat, as if to avoid seeing anyone. But in fact her tongue was dancing over his heated skin, and small teeth nipped him in a way that sent quaking tremors of lust down his spine.

Even as Patrick kicked the bedroom door shut behind

him, Sophie was wriggling out of his arms. And then, as he watched, Sophie pulled apart the tapes at her neck and waist, ruthlessly ignoring hooks and buttons as she pulled her gown over her head.

There she was . . . the woman he dreamed of every night.

With a deep masculine groan, Patrick lunged toward her in a surge that carried them straight onto the bed. Sophie's arms didn't wind around his neck. They went to his waist, meeting his hands in an effort to pull open the buttons on his breeches. Roughly Patrick freed himself and, without bothering to remove his garments, grabbed his wife's hips and pulled her to the edge of the bed, burying himself in her wet welcome. Sophie screamed and arched her back; Patrick groaned and drove forward again.

Later Sophie woke to find her husband's hand languorously cupping her bottom, pulling her to him. And when dawn stole into the room, it was Patrick who opened his eyes to find that a creamy white body, streaked with rosy light, was hovering just above him. He met the speculative blue eyes looking down into his with an answering smile and pulled that body down, down onto him.

Patrick's man of business arrived punctually at eleven o'clock and dawdled around the library for a half-hour before a poker-faced butler told him that the master was unavailable. Madame Carême waited in vain for Lady Sophie to appear for a second fitting of a lovely *costume parisien*.

The Foakeses did not meet for breakfast. They did not accidentally encounter each other in the hallway, nor did they attend the revival of *The Taming of the Shrew*, currently playing at the Covent Garden Theater. They did not meet because they never parted. The craving that had tormented Patrick was assuaged only by hours of wanton play and languorous touches. The despair that had plagued Sophie was soothed by a husband who gorged himself again and again on her body.

They did not speak of serious matters, but the world had righted itself again. Without words, they were back in the intimate world of the *Lark*. Sophie knew without asking that Patrick would not be going out that night. Patrick wondered at his own stupidity in ever thinking that Sophie didn't care whether he joined her in bed. He'd had his share of lustful mistresses, but none had the thirsty, joyful desire of his own wife. So he apologized silently, without words, and was accepted ecstatically in the same way.

Chapter 21

～⚖～

The next morning Patrick and Sophie went to their own chambers after one last kiss. Down in the servants' quarters, two bells chimed simultaneously.

"It's for you, Keating," bellowed Clemens in a cockney twang he never used once he passed the bronze door that separated the house from the downstairs. "And you too, Simone."

Simone rolled her eyes, pushing away her half-eaten roll. "The master must have finally let her out of that bed. I hope she can walk."

Keating gave her a slanting frown. "Don't you talk that way about the master," he growled.

Simone wrinkled her nose at his back as he dashed up the servants' stairs. "Regular hoity-toity, he is," she muttered to herself. "Just what does he think his beloved master was doing in bed all day yesterday? Playing chess?"

Sophie greeted Simone with a blissful smile. "Will you

ring for my bath, please? I shall wear the green riding costume."

Simone concealed a grin. Just what the master and mistress had been up to needed no explanation, to her mind. Just look how happy Lady Sophie was!

She did wonder whether the mistress had told him yet about the baby. Simone had guessed long ago, but the master seemed to have no idea. She looked around the room. He was sure to give Lady Sophie a piece of jewelry, or some such, when he heard the news. Diamonds, maybe. Everyone knew the master was a nabob.

For her part, Sophie was so happy that she floated into Braddon's carriage when he arrived. She and Madeleine were planning to address the intricacies of table manners.

They had included Braddon in the afternoon lesson. For the most part Braddon had to be banished from their lessons because he spent all his time staring at Madeleine or, worse, trying to angle his way around the room so that he ended up sitting next to her.

"Men," Madeleine had explained in delightful shorthand, "think only of kissing women, all the time. This I learned from my papa. He never let me meet any of the gallants who frequent the stables, because he said they would all try to steal kisses."

"Then how did you ever meet Braddon?"

"Oh, Braddon." Madeleine's little laugh erupted. "One day the stables were not yet open, and I was taking care of my favorite mare, Gracie. I remember I had made her a mixture of warm oats. She's getting a bit old," she explained, "and I like to give her a treat now and then. Well, I looked up and here was a blond giant looking down at me. It was Braddon. He had lost his cane the day before and came to find it."

She giggled. "Papa was right. Men do try to kiss you every chance they get."

In fact, Braddon was now serving as a perfect example

of why Madeleine's father had protected her from the London gentlemen who visited his stables. He constantly looked at Madeleine as if she were a truffle he longed to devour.

"Braddon," Sophie said severely. "If you cannot behave, we shall have to ask you to leave us."

Braddon's blue eyes took on a wounded innocence. "I wasn't doing anything," he said, quickly pulling his arm from around Madeleine's waist.

Sophie laughed. Today everything was delightful. "Madeleine needs her wits about her," she said with a stern look. "Now, let's be seated."

The three of them sat down at the Garniers' square dining-room table. The table was laid with a rough white cloth, but on it were three place settings of the finest china, each surrounded by some fourteen pieces of silverware. Braddon had bought them on Piccadilly Street.

"My butler keeps a stern eye on the silver," he had explained. "Couldn't have him thinking there was a thief in the house."

Sophie looked over the silverware. "Very good, Madeleine. You've laid the table perfectly."

Braddon frowned. "She doesn't need to learn such things, Sophie. For goodness' sake, I've got fourteen or fifteen footmen who don't have a thing to do all day—"

"It's not footmen who set the table," Madeleine broke in. "One of the under housemaids will lay the table, supervised by the butler."

"The mistress of the house must know everything that her servants are doing," Sophie explained to Braddon. "Otherwise how will she know if something is wrong?"

"Humph," Braddon said, clearly unconvinced. He sat down next to Madeleine, and Sophie sat opposite.

"We are in the midst of a formal dinner," Sophie dictated. "A footman is standing at your left shoulder, Madeleine, holding a plate with collared pig."

Madeleine politely gave the imaginary footman a smile and a tiny nod, indicating her willingness to taste the pork. Then she picked up the appropriate fork.

"Damme, but I've never seen so much silver in my life," Braddon complained. "Don't you think you're being a mite finical, Sophie?"

"No," Sophie said implacably. "What if Madeleine is invited to eat at St. James's?"

"That isn't all that likely," Braddon grumbled. "I'm not letting any of those randy royal dukes near Madeleine."

"If I were dining with you, Madeleine, I should be forced to give Braddon a severe set-down at this point," Sophie observed. "He's speaking to me across the table, a breach of manners. A lady speaks only to those on her right and on her left." Her eyes sharpened as she caught Braddon's movement. "And she never, *never* allows a gentleman to push his leg against hers. Pick up your fan, Madeleine."

Madeleine looked about confusedly. "I thought I gave it to the footman, along with my wrap."

"Oh no, a lady is never without her fan. Now, if the gentleman has merely offended your sensibilities, perhaps by making an objectionable jest, you can simply express your displeasure and turn to your partner on the other side."

Madeleine glared at Braddon, then snapped her head to the left.

"No, no! That's much too fierce. He's beneath your notice."

Madeleine looked down her nose at Braddon and turned the upper half of her body, with quelling indifference, to the left.

"That's it!" Sophie clapped.

Braddon's response was less moderate. He grabbed his betrothed by the shoulders and forcibly turned her toward him. "I don't like that sort of look from you," he complained.

"Think about how you'll feel if an old *roué* makes a suggestive comment to Madeleine," Sophie suggested.

Braddon's eyes brightened. "She's right, Maddie. Do it again!"

Madeleine giggled. "That's exactly how my *maman* used to look at an impertinent servant," she said.

Sophie frowned. "Servant? What servant?"

Madeleine's face looked comically surprised. "I don't know," she said slowly. "I just saw the look in my head, and copied it."

"If your father was in charge of the Flammarions' stables, your mother may have worked in the household before they married," Sophie suggested.

Madeleine nodded.

"Now let's pretend that Braddon has done something truly inexcusable," Sophie continued, "such as pressing his leg against yours."

Madeleine picked up her fan and whacked Braddon smartly on the knuckles.

"Ow!" Braddon pulled back his hand. "Maddie, you've broken my finger!"

"Don't be a wet blanket, Braddon," Sophie said. "Try again, Madeleine." She demonstrated the gesture. "Just tap his hand. The tap should not be violent, so that if anyone is looking, you could simply be flirting. You want to scold the gentleman for his presumption, but at the same time, you don't want anyone to see. If they know that he dared to put his leg against yours, they'll blame you."

"That's true," Braddon chipped in. "The old birds, like Sophie's mother and mine, always think the girl brought it on. Here goes," he said happily, pressing his leg against Madeleine's, under the table.

Madeleine pulled back her leg, gave Braddon a quelling glance, and rapped him lightly on the knuckles. "Oh, do forgive me," she crooned, her eyes hard. "Your hand must have strayed toward my plate."

"Lord," Braddon said, awed. "Damme if you don't look as cold as Sophie's mama ever did, Maddie. And she's got the nastiest eye in the *ton*."

Madeleine looked delighted.

"To pass Madeleine off as the daughter of a marquis," Sophie reminded them, "she has to be more chilly than my mother. There can't be a whisper about her manners. Now, let's say that the footman appears with an Italian cream."

⚥

A few weeks later, Patrick scowled fiercely at the tangle of papers lying on his rosewood desk. Interceding between the loading bills and letters from his managers abroad was a vision of what he had left when he slipped out of bed that morning—the soft white hand he had gently unclenched from his elbow. Sophie sighed and turned over in bed, the delicate cotton of her nightdress falling open at the neck. He had had to force himself to leave.

Suddenly the library door opened and Patrick looked up in annoyance. The staff had strict instructions not to interrupt him during the day. But it wasn't his secretary or an apologetic-looking footman. Instead, his wife slipped around the heavy door and closed it behind her.

Sophie walked soundlessly across the thick rug to Patrick's desk. He looked rather startled to see her, and she almost quailed, but kept walking. She stopped next to his chair, reaching out to put her hands on his bare arm. He had taken off his cuff links and pushed up his sleeves, to avoid ink, and her fingers irresistibly curled around his muscled arm.

"Don't you have an appointment with Braddon?" Patrick had been conscious all day that it was Thursday, and Sophie almost always spent the day with Braddon. Braddon's day, he had taken to silently labeling it.

"I canceled it," Sophie replied. "What work are you engaged in?" she asked.

"Just work," Patrick answered.

Then, as she looked at him with one eyebrow delicately raised, he cast a glance at the table. "I'm looking over the loading bills from the last Russian shipment."

"What do you do with them?" Sophie was genuinely curious. She leaned over slightly to read down the list of crabbed figures.

"What does this stand for?" A rosy-tipped finger stopped at what looked like 14.40SL.

"That's—" Patrick squinted. "Samovars. We delivered forty—no, fourteen—samovars to a merchant in the East End who requested them."

Sophie sighed. "How I would love to travel to Russia."

"You would?"

Sophie's eyes glowed. "Have you read Kotzebue's account of his travels in Siberia?"

"No," Patrick replied. He balanced his quill on its stand. Then he leaned back, looking speculatively at his young wife. In his experience, properly bred English ladies viewed a trip to Bath as a fearsome distance.

Sophie looked like the most proper of proper English ladies this morning. She was wearing a muslin morning gown, white, with a delicate key pattern along the hem. It was beautifully made, but neither startling nor outrageously sexual. It occurred to him, not for the first time, that Sophie seemed to have changed her style a bit since they married. Not that he was complaining. He felt a growing heat in his groin from the mere hint of pink leg visible through layers of white muslin.

Abruptly Patrick leaned forward, interrupting Sophie's enthusiastic description of Mr. Kotzebue's adventures. He picked up his wife and effortlessly deposited her on his lap.

Sophie giggled but showed no inclination to jump off his legs. Instead she looked up at him, her eyes darkening to a violet blue that Patrick considered a very good sign indeed. He lowered his head, ruthlessly capturing her cherry-sweet lips before she had a chance to protest.

But there was no protest. Sophie's lips opened to his as if marital intimacy was old hat to her, as if the burning flood that rushed down her limbs was something to which she had become accustomed. A strong hand pressed her head closer, ruthlessly pulling out hairpins and scattering them on the carpet, pulling until locks of honey-blond curls suddenly tumbled over Patrick's brown hand, whispering their softness against his arm.

He pulled her still closer, his mouth ravaging hers, tongue demanding the small cries which broke from her as his hand pushed down the gathered neckline of her bodice, freeing her breast. His thumb ran roughly over her nipple and Sophie's body went liquid, her hands fiercely clenched behind Patrick's neck, his mouth the center of her reality. The world dissolved into a spinning collection of senses, her body aching.

She pressed even closer, and when Patrick's hand left her head and started a seductive caress up her leg she made no protest. Her eyes stayed shut and her head fell back as he whispered something down her neck, a tongue like liquid fire pausing at the base of her throat.

And then his hand stopped. Sophie's eyes flew open. Was he horrified? Somehow she found that without even noticing, she had been moved and was now half lying on Patrick's desk, crushing a pile of papers under her. Her husband was leaning over her, his white shirt falling open in front—had she undone his collar?—showing muscles almost hidden in a mist of black curling hair. Irresistibly Sophie spread her hand flat on his chest, her fingers delicately rolling over the muscled ridges, curling in the tangles of chest hair.

Patrick looked down at his wife thoughtfully as his hand continued its caress. Where was the small ruffled band under which he normally slipped his fingers?

Sophie tipped back her head again, another small cry erupting from her as he continued his languid dance.

"No drawers?"

Sophie gulped and opened her eyes, staring at him half blinded. How could he sound so calm while he . . . he . . . Her body involuntarily twisted under his hand.

"No." Her voice quavered.

"Why not?" Patrick prided himself on his reasonable tone. Of course he knew why not. Today was Thursday; today was Braddon's day. Bloody hell, Sophie probably never wore drawers on Thursday. His hand stilled again, and something about the fierce silence which descended on the room made Sophie suddenly alert, like a fawn that hears a strange noise approaching, the unknown but dangerous sound of belling hounds. She gulped.

Patrick stared down at his wife, his beautiful wife. His! *His, his, his.* The word pounded against his ears, a drumbeat in his blood, a fire in his veins. Not *his.*

His wife sat up and wound her arms around his waist, hiding her face as her lips skimmed the hard ridges of his chest.

"When I was still in the nursery, I heard my nurse talking to one of the maids who was about to be married. I wasn't supposed to be listening, but I was. And my nurse told her that if she wanted to . . . to enchant her husband, she should sometimes neglect to put on her undergarments."

Her voice dropped even lower. "So this morning, well, you probably don't remember it, but in the middle of the night you were caressing me. You were asleep," she added hastily. "Anyway, this morning I thought I would neglect my drawers, but then of course Simone was dressing me and I *couldn't* not put them on."

Patrick was painfully aware of Sophie's soft lips moving over his chest, punctuating her breathless words with kisses, her breath tickling his hair.

"So I waited until she went downstairs," Sophie continued, "and then I took my drawers off and I folded them exactly as she does, and I replaced them in the drawer. So that she wouldn't know," Sophie added reasonably. "But during luncheon I remembered that Simone almost always undresses me at night, and what would she think if I had somehow lost my drawers?"

Patrick felt a rush of feeling wash down his spine, a glorious relaxation of tension. This was his own silly Sophie. She was French enough to wear drawers in the first place—they were still considered fast by many Englishwomen—but she was English enough to quail at her maid's reaction if she left them off.

"So," Sophie's voice was very breathless now, "so I came in to see what you were doing—"

Her voice broke off as Patrick pulled her sweet bottom up toward him, her legs instinctively going around his hips. He walked in three huge strides to the divan and put her down, going on his knees next to his startled wife. A soundless joy had grasped him, a yearning, delicious longing for possession of *his* wife's body.

"Patrick!"

Patrick didn't answer, just looked down at Sophie, his devil-black eyes laughing. Then he swooped down and pressed each eye closed with a kiss, at the same time as his hand pushed her gown up to her waist.

She was swollen, sweetly soft, softer than anything he'd ever felt before, and every touch of his was met by a gasping, pleading breath. Patrick grinned, deliberately taming the raging fire that threatened to take over his body. *His* lady wife waltzed in here without drawers . . . he'd be damned if he'd let the moment pass too quickly.

He turned the key in the door, and wrenched off his clothing. Then he eased his weight on top of Sophie, but that was all . . . he teased her, and teased her, enjoying the whimpering cries, and then the moment when her eyes snapped open and she said fiercely, "Patrick!"

He bent his head and ran a lazy tongue over Sophie's lips, enticing her mouth to open, rubbing himself against her at the same time, carefully avoiding the arching demand of her hips.

But suddenly, with a sharp twist, Sophie slipped out from under him. Small, determined hands pushed him over and down on his back on the wide divan.

His wife's eyes were shining with a mischievous gleam that matched Patrick's own. Their eyes found each other's, each bright with laughter and desire, daring the other to protest. Sophie perched herself on top of Patrick, pressing his shoulders to the velvet surface of the sofa with her palms.

"Now we'll see how you like it," she whispered against his mouth, her breath sweetly falling on his lips. She wriggled against him with a movement perhaps more inexperienced than seductive, but it was fire to Patrick. He gasped involuntarily, and Sophie grinned.

She wriggled farther down Patrick's body, enjoying the feeling of her breasts against his hair-roughed chest. Her lips found his nipples and she imitated what he did to her, blissfully tracking his rough breathing and the feeling of his racing heart under her fingertips.

Then she tipped herself off the couch, her gown falling down over her bare bottom with a silky swish. Every nerve in her body was alive, demanding. Sophie bit her lip, schooling herself to patience. She took him in her hands, giving him a butterfly kiss.

"Sophie!" Patrick's voice had an agonized roughness that she had never heard before. She grew bolder, ignoring the fact that his hands were straying over her body and had somehow yanked up her dress again, even while she knelt on the floor. Tentatively she flicked him with a small pink tongue, opened her mouth and caressed him.

A ragged moan rewarded her.

So she gave him a little nip, just the sort of small bite

he seemed to love when she kissed his nipples. But the response was not a moan, but a yelp.

"Sophie!"

Patrick rolled off the couch so fast that Sophie didn't know what was happening. In one second she was flat on her back on the thick carpet, her dress swept to her waist and her legs instinctively clenching Patrick's waist as the lovers came together in a great primal, beating dance. Sophie's broken cries drifted into the room, punctuated by Patrick's harsh breathing groans.

"Oh God, Sophie, Sophie," Patrick shouted. She strained up toward him, catching at bliss as every nerve in her body lit and burst into fire.

The silence which followed was not at all like the silence before Sophie had entered the library, Patrick thought. He rolled over, pulling Sophie onto his chest. She was still breathing in tiny pants, her body shaken by slight tremors.

"Patrick?"

"Hmm?"

"Did you dislike it when I, uh, bit you?"

"Yes," Patrick said firmly. He settled her more carefully into the crook of his arm. "We'll practice." His tone was resonant with anticipation.

"I have something to confess," Sophie whispered. "I wasn't entirely honest with you."

Patrick listened lazily to his wife's sweet voice, hardly paying attention.

"I didn't interrupt you only because I realized that I . . . I had to resolve the problem with my drawers. I wanted to enchant you. It was all I could think about this morning."

Patrick didn't answer. His arm pulled her tighter, crushing her small sweetness against his chest. Oh God, what a wonderful thing it was to have a wife, to make love to one's wife on the loading bills, and on the couch, and on the library floor. To have a wife who *thought* all morning.

It wasn't until much later that afternoon that a thought of his own strayed into Patrick's mind. Without even noticing it consciously, he was replaying the moment when he pulled Sophie's loose dress to her waist. It almost made him groan just to think about the way her breasts overflowed in his hands, their rounded plumpness begging for kisses.

They've grown, he thought. Sophie's breasts have grown. From caresses? Slowly the thought trickled into the rational part of Patrick's brain. The truth was likely a good deal less romantic.

Patrick's back suddenly grew rigid. The image of Sophie's curvaceous body entered his mind. Unconsciously he stood up, and desperately counted in his head. The night he first went to her room—Jesus, when was that? Over three months ago.

He was an idiot, an outrageously stupid idiot. He had protected women from pregnancy hither and yon . . . women he didn't give a toss about. And now, when he had found a woman whom he loved—why not admit it? He loved her, loved Sophie, with all his soul and heart. Now he had her, and he was wooing her, and it was working, he knew it was working. . . . He deliberately, stupidly, had put her in the greatest danger a woman could face.

"Idiot! Idiot!" Patrick didn't even realize that he was howling, face up to the elaborate whorls of plaster ornamenting the ceiling.

In the back of his mind, Patrick had meant to talk Sophie out of the idea of having a child. She was too small, too petite, the lovely woman he'd taken to wife. In his mind's eye he could see her slender hips, her waist, so small that he used to be able to span it with both hands. How could he be so witless? All the evidence was there.

She would never survive a birth. Look at his sister-in-law. Charlotte was much taller than Sophie, and she had almost died. Hell, compared to Sophie she was an Amazon. His mother . . . Even the Indian woman he had seen die in childbirth had been larger than Sophie.

He came bellowing into Sophie's bedchamber. "Sophie! Sophie!"

She looked up hopefully as her husband thrust open the door. After having lost her Turkish grammar to the waves, Sophie was still adhering to her self-imposed ban on languages. Unfortunately, except for when she visited Madeleine, her days were painfully dull. She talked to the housekeeper or went shopping. Given that the season wasn't in full swing, many of her friends were still in the country.

At the moment she was reading through the plays of Ben Jonson, in a rather haphazard fashion. She couldn't make head or tail of the old-fashioned dialogue. In fact, Sophie admitted to herself, I'm no scholar. I have only one skill, for languages.

Patrick crossed the room in one bound and dropped to his haunches next to her chair. "Listen to me, Sophie! I climbed the ladder to your room *three and one half months ago*! Have you—did you—bleed during that time?"

"Has it been that long?" Sophie hadn't figured out the likely dates.

Patrick's face softened. "Yes, it has," he replied. "I'm afraid, Sophie, that unless you are a very irregular sort of female, we are expecting a child."

"It's odd, isn't it?" Sophie said rather dreamily. "It doesn't seem possible. Why, we haven't been married nearly long enough."

"There's no *enough*," Patrick said. "One day is enough."

"That's not true!" Sophie retorted. "Why, my mama told me . . ." But then she fell silent, remembering the talk of maids who undoubtedly knew more of the practicalities of conception than did her poor mama.

Patrick misunderstood her silence. "Some women have trouble conceiving. Perhaps your mother is one of those sort, and that is why you are an only child. I'm sure your parents have tried to have another child, given that titles pass only to males."

He straightened up and walked restlessly to the window, looking out.

Sophie contemplated her parents' separate—extremely separate—bedrooms in silence. It felt like betrayal to blurt out the truth.

The room fell into stillness. Sophie's mind was racing. She had delayed telling Patrick about the baby. Their recent happiness seemed so fragile that she hadn't wanted to disturb it. And yet a corner of her mind blossomed with pure joy every time she thought of the babe. It *was* time that her husband knew he was expecting a child.

A tiny bit of that joy withered when she turned her head and caught a glimpse of her husband's face.

He looked about as happy as a cat thrown into puddle water. His face was rigid, his eyes angry.

"What's the matter?" Sophie steadied her voice just before it trembled.

Patrick looked at her almost as if he didn't see her. When he finally spoke, his voice was cold and distant. "I told you before, Sophie, I'm not the sort of man who howls with joy to hear that he has procreated. I've always been damn careful before this point to make sure it didn't happen!"

"But we're married!"

"What excuse is that?"

"I thought we agreed to have one child," Sophie said warily.

"We did," Patrick snapped. He knew he was behaving like an ass, but he couldn't stop himself. From the moment the knowledge sank into his mind, he had been paralyzed with fear. Why, why didn't he control the whole situation better? Why on earth had he blithely deserted the habits of a lifetime and made love in such a feckless and stupid fashion?

"Then why are you so angry?" Sophie was completely baffled.

"I'm angry at myself," he said, and then added irrationally, "Damme, Sophie, you must be as fertile as a rabbit!"

Sophie turned white. "That's a cruel thing to say," she said slowly, her eyes searching his face.

Patrick turned around and stared out the window again. "Let's just leave it, shall we? I see no reason to discuss the situation further. The die is cast."

Sophie nodded, but Patrick didn't see her. She felt as if she were speaking through a sheet of ice. "In that case," she observed, walking over and pulling the bell rope, "I shall call Simone. It's time for my bath."

Patrick looked over at his wife in bewilderment. Her face was relaxed, even pleasant. But she stood by the door looking expectantly at him, so he stamped out. It was hard to maintain rage in the face of such utter . . . pleasantness. Every step he walked down the stairs peeled off his anger, leaving cold, bitter fear at the base.

Pulses of rage and fear ran through his body like charges of lightning. He jerked open the front door, brushing past the footman who had moved to open it.

Then he stamped down the front steps and hailed a passing hackney without pausing for breath. He had to get *out*. Out of the house, away from the house.

Two hours later, the central stage in Jackson's Boxing Salon was lined with curious, cheering gentlemen, watching Patrick Foakes demolish yet another partner.

"Cool!" One of the professional boxers said to Cribb, as they stood at the corner of the ring. "He's not bad for a swell, is he?"

"Strips well," Cribb said absently, his eyes watching

Foakes's arms intently. "Lead with your right, sir," he shouted.

"He don't need any advice," the boxer said, half resentfully. Sure enough, with a final solid thunk, Foakes had knocked out yet another of Cribb's boxers.

Foakes looked over at Cribb, panting, and gestured. Cribb shook his head.

"Thank ye, Lord," the boxer next to him murmured. It was his turn in the ring next, to face whichever of the paying gentlemen wished to strip down and fight before an audience.

"Fightin' when you're angry," Cribb said to Patrick, "is not a good idea." He turned away, focusing on Reginald Petersham, who was just climbing into the ring.

Patrick stood next to the ring, letting compliments swirl around his head as he rubbed the sweat from his face and chest.

What's done was done. Sophie was pregnant. Treacherously, an image crept into his mind of a little girl with her mama's curls and beautiful smile.

He dropped the towel and headed for the dressing room. Unless he missed his guess, Sophie hadn't seen a doctor. He needed to find the best doctor in London—someone from the Royal College—and Sophie must see him tomorrow.

Patrick scrawled a note on Jackson's Boxing Salon stationery. He gave a boy a crown to deliver it to the house of his lawyer, Mr. Jennings of Jennings & Condell.

A half-hour later, Jennings looked at the message perplexedly. "Determine who is the best doctor for birthing babies in London," it said. That was it, barring Patrick's characteristically bold and scrawling signature.

Why was it delivered tonight? What on earth did Foakes think Jennings could do about a doctor that couldn't wait until tomorrow? And why had he sent it from a boxing salon rather than from his own house?

Jennings jiggled uneasily in his high-backed library chair. He would greatly dislike it if Foakes had taken to fathering children outside his own home. Messy financial transactions, those were, the ones dealing with illegitimate children. He, Jennings, should know, given that Jennings & Condell had the honor of being lawyers to the royal family.

So far, Foakes and his small household had been a joy to represent, with nothing more intricate to establish than a generous settlement on his wife. But now look: only married a few months, and already Jennings & Condell was being made party to some sort of immoral doings.

Jennings pursed his lips disapprovingly. He was a fierce Methodist, and although he unhesitatingly fought bitter lawsuits on the side of his dissolute, aristocratic clients, he saw no point in privately condoning their behavior.

It was only on the way home that Patrick remembered the unpleasant way he had parted from his wife. Lost my temper again, he thought. At least Sophie didn't get angry. Or did she?

The memory of her smiling face as she held open the bedchamber door flashed into his mind. Something about his wife's eyes. She had said he was cruel. He remembered that. And then suddenly she was smiling at him, as if they were about to go to a garden party. But her eyes weren't smiling. I should remember that in the future: Sophie's eyes speak the truth.

He climbed the steps and walked into Sophie's bedchamber cautiously. It was a wet evening, just cold enough that there was a fire lit in the fireplace. Sophie was sitting next to the fire, wearing a nightdress of thin lawn.

Patrick walked over and dropped into the other rocking chair. He stretched his legs out before him and then looked up. Sophie smiled at him, but her eyes were a dark, wary blue. Patrick felt a small pulse of triumph. He'd learned how to read his wife: that was good. An unknowing male might think she was perfectly happy, but Patrick knew better.

"I apologize," he said.

Sophie nodded. "I would have told you, Patrick, if you had asked." Her hands were twisting in her lap.

Another way to read Sophie, Patrick thought. Her face looked sweetly placid, but her hands were anxious. She said nothing, shifting her gaze to the flames trotting along the logs in the fireplace.

In fact, Sophie was stiff with rage. But what could she say? If she opened her mouth, she would scream reproaches at him for being so callous about their unborn child, so *stupid* in general. Better to say nothing. She clenched her hands together so tightly that her knuckles turned white.

"Have you consulted a doctor, Sophie?"

At that she looked up, startled. "No."

Patrick frowned. "I'll find one, then."

After a moment he stood, took one large step, picked Sophie up, and plopped into her chair. His wife's body tensed, then relaxed against his chest.

"A wife and a baby," Patrick whispered against her neck. He wound his arms around her, as if he could always keep her safe. They sat like that, together, for a long time.

Chapter 22

❦

In the beginning of May, the gentry began to flood back into London. Knockers appeared on formidable oak doors, and dust covers were pulled from damasked furniture. Housekeepers anxiously checked the number of wax candles and the state of the linen.

Butlers complained among themselves over the irresponsibility of the young, and sent desperate messages to employment agencies: "Lady Fiddlesticks *must* have four experienced footmen by next week." "Without two good upstairs maids—and we would prefer girls from the country, mind you—Baron Piddlesford's housekeeper will surely lose her mind." "Lady Brimticky searches for a matched pair of footmen, with the same hair color, weight, and height, to wear her livery and stand behind her carriage. She would prefer dark hair; redheads are not invited to apply."

The season was due to begin. Having spent the last

month poring over the pictures in *La Belle Assemblée,* ladies summoned the mantua-maker of their choice to the house, and spent uncomfortable hours being pricked by pins. Gentlemen visited their tailors, or bought new pairs of hussars, so highly polished they could adjust their intricate cravats in the shine of their boots. The more intrepid, or perhaps the more vain, tried out the newest leg and shoulder pads, acquired by their valets in circumstances of great secrecy. With calves swollen to a fashionable size, they strolled by White's or visited the House of Lords.

Within a week carriages crammed Piccadilly and the Royal Exchange. High-perch phaetons tooled around Hyde Park, only occasionally spilling their inhabitants onto the damp ground. The fruit merchants of Covent Garden grew cheerful; lavender sellers began trotting down the streets of Mayfair and around Hanover Square, hoarsely selling sweet bouquets.

Henri was packed off to begin the spring term at Harrow, sporting a new wardrobe and a sprinkling of English oaths, learned from Patrick's stableboys. He left with his dark eyes shining; with the effortless resilience of youth, Henri had put the traumas of war behind him and was ready for the excitements of a gentleman's schooling. And Sophie and Madeleine were drawing their lessons to a close. Madeleine had become far more than just "ladylike." She absorbed knowledge like a sponge. After one afternoon with *Debrett's Peerage,* Madeleine knew more about the noble families of England than Sophie had ever bothered to learn.

The most difficult aspects of ladyhood came naturally to Madeleine. She knew to an inch how to depress a presumptuous servant, and she wielded her fan like a dangerous, if delicate, weapon. She took to dancing like a duck to water. Dressed in the height of French fashion, she looked like a member of the royal family, and not in the least like a horse trainer's daughter.

So why am I not happy? Sophie asked herself. Her project was a success. In Sophie's estimation, Madeleine would make a countess *par excellence*. Tonight Sophie and Patrick were hosting a dinner at which Sophie would launch Madeleine on the *ton*.

But Patrick . . . Patrick never mentioned the baby. Not once after he delivered the name of a doctor.

"His name is Lambeth," he had said. "He will visit you tomorrow."

Sophie had looked numbly at her husband. "I thought we might use Charlotte's doctor."

"Charlotte's doctor! Are you addled? Charlotte almost died giving birth to Sarah."

Sophie jumped at Patrick's retort and said nothing. In her memory, it wasn't exactly the doctor's fault that Charlotte had trouble delivering Sarah, but what was the use of arguing? She didn't really mind which doctor she saw.

"How did you choose Dr. Lambeth?"

"I didn't. My lawyer checked maternal death rates. Lambeth is quite successful in that regard."

Sophie shivered and didn't say anything else.

After Dr. Lambeth had paid her a visit, she obediently told Patrick that the doctor saw no cause for alarm. He nodded and said nothing.

They ate dinner together, they ate breakfast together— but they never spoke of the child Sophie carried. Once or twice Sophie knew that Patrick *must* be thinking about the babe, because he abruptly spanned her growing waist with his large hands, almost as if he was measuring it. But he said nothing, and every time she brought it up, he changed the subject or left the room.

"He doesn't want our baby," Sophie whispered to herself, her eyes anxious. She crossed her hands over her stomach. There was nothing new in that, after all. Patrick had made his feelings about children clear long ago.

Perhaps he resents the fact that we can't make love, Sophie told herself hopefully. Her mother had stated that when a woman is in a delicate condition, a couple may not have marital relations. When she mentioned this idea to Patrick, he merely nodded, and from that day he had hardly touched her. Sophie didn't know how to confess that she hadn't meant to follow her mother's advice. At the very least, she thought they ought to ask Dr. Lambeth.

But she was too shy to broach the subject. Instead they slipped easily back into the limbo state in which they had lived after returning from Wales. Patrick took her arm on the way in to dinner. He guided her up the stairs. He looked at her appreciatively, but not hungrily. They said decorous farewells at the door to Sophie's room.

For her part, Sophie found herself thirsting for her husband, surreptitiously looking at his long legs, longing to touch his back. She dreamed of his kisses, of the way he used to brush her whole body with butterfly touches. Sophie was too bashful to instigate a caress. After all, she had been the one to report her mother's opinion of marital relations during pregnancy. And Patrick seemed as indifferent to her as he had when they had stopped sleeping together before. He had certainly returned to the embraces of his black-haired courtesan; once or twice each week he returned to his bedroom in the early hours of the morning.

Perhaps, Sophie thought unhappily, perhaps Patrick dislikes the fact that I am growing plump. For a moment she looked at herself and saw extra flesh everywhere ... breasts, cheeks, stomach. Disgusted, she dropped her hands and turned away from the mirror.

In the park, the carriages of high-flung courtesans mingled with the carriages of the nobility. Sophie searched the faces of those with black hair, comparing their slender elegance to her rounded form, their dark beauty to her tedious blondness.

But I am clever, Sophie told herself stoutly, in moments of desperation and shame. I am not stupid.

Resolutely, she turned her not inconsiderable intelligence to orchestrating dinners with her husband. She read *The Times* and *The Morning Post,* she read plays and the satirical ballads you could buy on the street corner. She turned the supper table into an engaging and lively encounter during which she and Patrick would fall into minibattles over the success of Napoleon's military campaigns in the East, or brisk arguments over the morality of the new labor laws protecting apprentices in factories. They discussed Patrick's imports, and at night Sophie dreamed of tall-masted ships, pushing off from the West India docks in London.

The only subjects they never discussed were children and the gossip pages of *The Morning Post.* The paper seemed obsessed with adulterous couples. Sophie read those pages only in order to find out where Patrick went at night. His name was never mentioned, which meant he was far more discreet than her own papa had been.

Sophie had no illusions about what she was doing. Her husband might be spending his nights with a courtesan. She was trying to ensure that at least he came home for dinner.

Never having left London, Sophie needed to do nothing in preparation for the new season. Madame Carême had already delivered a number of elegant maternity gowns, designed to conceal the babe growing within. But given Sophie's small stature and her rapidly expanding girth, not even one of Madame's gowns could conceal the truth at this point.

Sure enough, Charlotte knew the instant she saw Sophie. She shrieked with delight. "Sophie! Look at you! Why didn't you write me?"

Her tall, beautiful friend swept her into a hug. A minute later Alex strolled into the room to find his wife seated on a narrow settee against the wall, talking nineteen to the dozen to his sister-in-law. One look at Sophie and he swung about to face his twin.

Despite himself, Patrick's mouth quirked into a grin as he met Alex's eyes. He didn't mean to be pleased about the baby—he wouldn't let himself be pleased. But he couldn't help being just a trifle proud.

Alex gave his brother a rough hug. "Are things improved?"

"We're still not sleeping in the same room," Patrick said with a shrug. "But now it's because of Sophie's condition, so that's an improvement."

Alex looked appalled. "Sounds like an insufferable idea to me. What does your doctor say?"

"I didn't ask," Patrick replied. "After all, Sophie's pregnant. If she doesn't want to, I can't make her." Patrick's voice was so tense that Alex felt a knot form in his stomach.

"I think it's an absurd old-wives' tale," Alex said. "What's your doctor's name? I'm damn sure that other couples don't have this idea."

"David Lambeth," Patrick replied. "He's supposed to be the best in London."

"Let me get this straight," Alex said resignedly. "Last month you and Sophie weren't sharing a bedroom. Now it seems you're having a fit of the blue devils over her pregnancy. For God's sake, Patrick, I was under the impression that your marriage was about to flounder."

Alex hesitated. "Not sleeping together can draw a man and woman apart. If you ask me, that rule is rubbish."

"It is Sophie's prerogative," Patrick said shortly. "At any rate, this will be our only child. I won't allow her to go through this a second time."

"Sophie is a young, healthy woman. I am certain that she will deliver the baby with no problem."

"The way Charlotte had no problem?"

Alex's body went rigid. He knew as well as Patrick did that Charlotte's being near death while delivering their daughter had nothing to do with her size or build.

"All I'm saying," Patrick continued, "is that even a very large woman like Charlotte is in grave danger when pregnant. Sophie is a little scrap . . . like Mother."

Alex looked over at his lovely, slender wife and almost smiled to hear that she was "very large." But he picked his way carefully. He knew, better than anyone, how bitterly Patrick had taken their mother's death in childbirth.

"Sophie is not Mother," he said firmly. "Don't you remember the fragile air that Mother had? Sophie is small, perhaps, but not fragile."

Patrick opened his mouth to reply, but at that moment Clemens paused in the large doorway of the drawing room and announced the arrival of the Marquis and Marchioness of Brandenburg.

"Maman!" Sophie hurried to the door.

Eloise met her with a stream of rapid French; her father merely smiled affectionately and strolled over to the other side of the room. Although Eloise had seen her daughter only two days previously, she was full of reminders, rejoinders, suggestions.

"Oh, *Maman,*" Sophie said, half laughing, "a milk bath? Pooh!"

Eloise switched into English. "A milk bath is vital to a woman's constitution and you must keep your constitution up while *enceinte.* Think of Marie Antoinette! She had a milk bath once a week."

"I don't want to think about that poor woman," Sophie said with a shiver, dismissing the idea of King Louis XVI's wife. "And I don't want a milk bath, *Maman.* It sounds horribly sticky. Besides, I think that Marie Antoinette took those baths to improve her skin, not her health."

Clemens appeared in the doorway again. "Lady Skiffing; Lady Madeleine Corneille, daughter of the Marquis de

Flammarion, and Mrs. Trevelyan; Mr. Sylvester Bredbeck; Misters Erskine and Peter Dewland."

Sophie's heart beat a little faster. It was unfortunate that Madeleine happened to arrive at the same time as a group of guests. Sophie had hoped to introduce her to Eloise without an audience. But Sylvester Bredbeck was one of Eloise's dearest friends, and so Eloise greeted her daughter's new friend quickly and then settled into a cozy talk with Sylvester.

Madeleine, for her part, felt nothing but gratitude when the terrifying marchioness dismissed her with a kindly smile. She turned to greet the gentleman at her elbow, but her brown eyes immediately softened when she saw that Erskine—Quill—had difficulty standing.

With all her innate gentility, she instantly broke one of the rules she had learned from Sophie—a young lady never asks to be seated when her elders are standing—and announced that she was a bit tired after the carriage ride. In mere seconds, she and her chaperone were seated, with Quill relaxed in an armchair and breathing a silent sigh of relief.

"That's a pretty-behaved gal," her father said to Sophie in passing. "Saw what she did for the elder Dewland chap, the one with the ridiculous nickname—Quill, isn't it?" He snorted. "A man shouldn't be named after a writing tool, if you ask me. Pretty behaved: pretty gal, too. Too many young girls don't have any meat on their bones, these days."

Sophie looked at him sharply. Papa *couldn't* try to set Madeleine up as a flirt! But George was smiling at Madeleine with paternal approval. Sophie sent up a silent prayer of thanks. Amorous interest on her father's part would be a disaster for Sophie's plans. Then her mother would be bound to dislike poor Madeleine.

"Never heard of the Marquis de Flammarion, have you?" The Honorable Sylvester Bredbeck had finished imparting a delicate rumor about a mutual acquaintance and was scanning the room. He was a small, bustling man with a creaky corset and a fervent love of gossip.

"Certainly I have," Eloise replied firmly. She prided herself on a vast knowledge of French aristocracy. "The marquis lived a very retired life. I never met him myself." She frowned. "I can't quite place where his estates were. The Limousin, perhaps."

"Can't be too careful, these days," Sylvester commented.

Eloise bridled. Sylvester was close to suggesting that Eloise's own daughter had invited a pretender to her home. Sylvester caught her glance and quailed.

"I certainly didn't mean to suggest anything of the sort about the daughter of the marquis," he said hastily. "Seeing as she is a special friend of your family."

"Not only because of that," Eloise snapped. "Lady Madeleine is French aristocracy to the tip of her fingertips, sir. It is visible with just a glance. I, if anyone, would be able to ascertain immediately if she were an impostor, and she is *not*."

Sylvester nodded energetically. He had no wish to cross swords with Eloise (to be frank, he was terrified of her), and besides, the girl did seem to be charming.

"You misunderstand me, dear lady," he said, pouring oil on the waters. "I never meant to cast aspersions on Lady Madeleine's background. I simply made a general statement. Someone with your keen eye must have noticed that there seem to be more French aristocrats in London than there ever were in Paris, even when Louis XVI was on the throne!"

Eloise settled her ruffled plumage. "In that respect, Mr. Bredbeck, you are absolutely correct." She lowered her voice. "Did you hear that the so-called Comte de Vissale turned out to be a French nobody? In fact, Madame de Meneval told me that she suspects he was nothing more than the music instructor for the real comte's children."

Sylvester's eyes brightened. "Goodness me," he said. "Why, I had the pleasure of talking to the comte—or rather, the *not*-comte—just last week." He tittered happily.

Sophie walked up to her mother. "*Maman,* now that our party is complete, I thought we might go in to dinner."

Eloise cast a look toward the door. To be sure, Sophie had already corralled the Earl and Countess of Sheffield and Downes, Patrick's brother and sister-in-law.

But Sylvester had one more thing to ask. "And where is the former comte now? Applying for work in a music academy, perhaps?"

"Madame de Meneval told me that he has fled the country," Eloise replied. "Most likely he has gone to America. I understand that all manner of thieves and frauds live in that country."

"My goodness," Sophie said lightly. "What on earth are you two talking about?"

Sylvester turned to her. "Your mother is the best of friends with Madame de Meneval and is telling me amusing tales of false Frenchmen. Have you met Madame?"

Sophie shook her head. "Who is she?"

Eloise broke in impatiently. "Goodness me, Sophie. I told you about dear Madame last week. You must not have been listening. She was a valued member of the court of Louis XVI, and she personally knew every single member of the French aristocracy. Now she is in London, and one of her more unpleasant tasks has been unmasking the large number of pretenders who are thronging our streets, pretending to be French nobility!"

Sophie's eyes widened. Madame de Meneval was clearly someone whom Madeleine must avoid at all costs. But Eloise was already turning away, going to join her husband at the door.

Sophie had placed Madeleine between Quill and Lord

Reginald Petersham. Quill would never do anything to overset a lady's composure, and while Reginald was practically guaranteed to bore Madeleine's ear off with some lengthy bits of gallantry, he too was harmless.

Braddon was *not* invited. Sophie judged him too likely to forget himself and smile intimately at Madeleine. Although she had to admit that Braddon was taking this particular scheme with deadly seriousness. It was he who had insisted that Madeleine have a chaperone who herself came from the highest ranks of English society. Mrs. Trevelyan was a highly respected widow, formerly married to a bishop who had been, as it happened, the younger son of a duke.

Living now in reduced circumstances, she had happily agreed to chaperone a motherless young Frenchwoman, the dear friend of Lady Sophie Foakes's. Sophie could see that Mrs. Trevelyan lent Madeleine a great air of respectability. Braddon had been right to choose a well-bred English-woman rather than one of the many Frenchwomen scattered around London.

When everyone was finally seated, Sophie found that she was too nervous to touch the lobster. She looked past the four candelabra that separated her from Patrick, at the far end of the table. He was leaning slightly to his left, talking to Lady Skiffing.

Sophie had invited as many dedicated gossips as she could without making her intent obvious. The idea was that if they met Madeleine in Sophie's house, under the eagle eye of the Marchioness of Brandenburg, at least these particular gossips would not question Madeleine's ancestry.

And it seemed to be working. Lady Skiffing was smiling happily at whatever Patrick was telling her. Lady Prestlefield was holding forth in a shrill undertone, detailing the latest disgraceful expenditure of the Prince of Wales, who was rumored to be over seventy thousand pounds in debt. None of the three appeared to have had a qualm when they met Madeleine.

Madeleine herself was playing the part of a maiden born to the highest ranks of French society, without turning a hair. In fact, she wasn't terribly afraid. She was too busy remembering all the rules Sophie had drilled into her head. At the moment she was counting silently. Nine minutes, ten minutes . . . It was time to smile politely at Lord Petersham, turn her head to the left, and talk to Erskine Dewland.

Wonder of wonders, Mr. Dewland had just ended his conversation with Chloe Holland, who was sitting to *his* left. We must look like a dance troupe, Madeleine thought with a giggle. All of us are turning our heads to and fro at exactly the same moment.

"If I may enquire," Quill asked, "what on earth are you thinking about, Lady Madeleine? I should tell you that English dinners are very serious affairs, and one rarely, if ever, laughs."

Madeleine smiled at him. "I was thinking that we must all resemble a choreographed ballet. I saw one once, as a young girl in France. All the dancers balanced on their toes and turned their heads just so, and then back, just so. Here we all are, sitting about a table, and turning our heads at precisely the same moment."

Quill's dark green eyes filled with laughter. "It sounds more like a bankside interlude, as you describe it."

Madeleine looked curious.

"A puppet show," Quill explained.

Madeleine gave him a tiny smile. "I, sir, would never be so impolite as to describe the crème of English society as puppets."

At that Quill laughed out loud, instantly drawing the attention of Lady Skiffing, Lady Prestlefield, and the Honorable Sylvester Bredbeck.

Lady Skiffing frowned slightly. "Lady Madeleine could

do much better than Erskine Dewland," she remarked to Patrick. "True, he will be a viscount someday, but one must ask: Is he capable? Although he *appears* to have almost recovered from the accident, I hear that his father has arranged for the younger boy to marry an Indian heiress, so the family must know something we don't."

Patrick resisted the impulse to give his dinner partner a sharp set-down. Sophie had been so worried about the success of her dinner that he didn't want to cause further anxiety by snapping at her guests, although Lady Skiffing was a petulant old witch.

So he looked down at her benignly, his face smooth and friendly. "Quill is a particular friend of mine; I can assure you that Lady Madeleine could not do better than to accept his hand in marriage, were he to offer it."

Lady Skiffing sniffed disapprovingly. As someone who spent her days spicing gossip with an intonation, giving faint blame and even fainter praise, she thoroughly understood the language of the undertone.

Smiling graciously, she inclined her head. "You put me to shame, dear sir," she crooned. "One should remember, of course, that when your brother was abroad for such a long period of time, many people believed that you would inherit his title, and yet here you both are." She smiled happily at Patrick and turned to the Marquis of Brandenburg, seated on her left.

Touché! Patrick thought appreciatively. She managed to remind me that I am a younger son and untitled.

And he wondered for the fortieth time why Sophie had assembled such an odd group for their first dinner as a married couple. True, Quill seemed happy talking to Sophie's friend Madeleine, and that was splendid, given that Quill rarely left his house. It was a pleasure to see Will Holland and his lovely wife, Chloe. And at least Braddon hadn't been invited.

But why on earth had Sophie invited that dried-up old

prune, Lady Skiffing? And why, in God's name, had she invited Lady Sarah Prestlefield, the woman who had walked into the salon at the Cumberland ball and caught them kissing?

With a sigh he turned to Sophie's mother. Eloise was picking at her stuffed capon in an unsatisfied sort of way.

Patrick bent toward her. "May I summon a footman to dispatch with your capon?"

Eloise jumped, just slightly. A true lady, of course, is never startled because she is never lost in thought. All her attention is directed to her dinner partners.

"I was thinking about Sophie's babe," Eloise said forthrightly.

It was Patrick's turn to be startled. He and Sophie had achieved a sort of calm equilibrium. They did not discuss the subject, and there were days when he forgot that his wife was with child. Certainly he hadn't thought about it tonight. Sophie sat at the bottom of the table glowing like the fairy on top of a Christmas tree. She didn't look pregnant. She looked as delectable as spun sugar.

Eloise continued. "I am not convinced that Sophie is adhering to a correct diet."

"She seems to be eating regularly," Patrick said lamely.

"I believe that bathing in milk would strengthen her constitution." Eloise looked at Patrick, her eyes shadowed with worry. "She refuses to do so. And when I recommended that she add oranges to her diet—oranges soothe the stomach, you understand—she refused to do that either."

"But her stomach has not been indisposed, has it?" Patrick asked cautiously. It was a bit shameful to find that he did not know if his own wife had been ill.

"I believe not," Eloise replied. "But I still could wish that she would eat an orange a day, and perhaps a glass of bitters once a week."

"Bitters!"

Eloise nodded. "Drinking bitters is extremely salutary for the health. It strengthens the blood, you know."

"I didn't know that," Patrick replied gravely.

There was a moment's pause broken by the clamor of sixteen well-bred voices chattering of this and that. The marchioness launched into an explanation of her recommendation that Sophie should eat partridges on a regular basis. Patrick looked down the table at his wife.

Tonight Sophie looked very much the grande dame, a far cry from the sensual little sprite who had frequented his bed on the *Lark*. She was wearing diamonds at her ears and around her throat; their chilly brilliance perfectly suited the creamy luster of her gown.

Suspended from the dining room's arched ceiling was a chandelier that Patrick had shipped from Italy, long before that country had been swept into Napoleon's net. Its crystal shards hung, sparkling, far above their heads. A draft caused by footmen moving silently in and out of the dining room caused the crystals to turn and gleam. They caught the reflection of Sophie's diamonds as they twinkled in the candlelight.

But the diamonds didn't turn her into an icy reflection of themselves. If anything, they made the rosy, creamy tint of her bosom look even warmer, softer, more delectable.

Patrick swallowed. If there is one thing a gentleman must *never* do, at his own dinner party in particular, it is to stare at his wife until his breeches are uncomfortably tight.

Patrick tried to look at his wife objectively. Why had he never enquired whether Sophie's stomach was upset by her condition? Apparently it was a common occurrence. Why had they never talked about the child she carried?

For an instant he listened again to Eloise's monologue. She seemed to have returned to the beneficial qualities of milk baths.

"I shall recommend it to Sophie," Patrick said with perfect gravity, then stopped listening again.

He was very conscious of the distance growing between himself and his wife. He was caught in a web of his own making. Strangled by fear, he didn't want to think about the baby because that meant thinking about its birth. Strangled by jealousy, he didn't want to think about what Sophie did with Braddon on their long afternoon excursions, and yet he couldn't help thinking about Braddon some twenty, thirty times a day. So he ended up walking the streets for hours at night, fighting against dual foes: his fear and his jealousy.

He knew, rationally knew, that Sophie and Braddon were not indulging in an affair, although sometimes he persuaded himself otherwise. It was just that his wife greeted Braddon with an affectionate smile whenever they met him, and they seemed to meet that blighter everywhere. If they went to the theater, there he was. If they attended the opera, the Earl of Slaslow was certain to attend. The only explanation Patrick could find was that Sophie informed him of their plans.

Why? So that she could greet her ex-betrothed with an insufferably intimate smile? So that Braddon could linger next to them, his hand on Sophie's arm, until Patrick was ready to burst with rage? Red heat rose in his ears, and he forced himself to calm down. If gentlemen don't stare lustfully at their wives at dinner parties, they also don't work themselves into fevers over unanswerable questions.

He turned to Eloise, only to find that their ten minutes had passed and she was briskly talking to Peter Dewland. Apologetically, he turned back to Lady Skiffing, who was kind enough to forgive him for his inattention.

"Your wife is looking particularly radiant, given her condition," Lady Skiffing observed.

Patrick silently groaned.

"I expect she will go into confinement in the near future," Lady Skiffing continued. "I must say, it is quite unusual for a lady to give a dinner party when she is in an interesting condition. In my day, we remained on a couch for a good six months. But nowadays it seems that young women gallivant around the streets as long as they wish."

Patrick nodded. In fact, he'd completely forgotten that women stopped going into society in the last few months of their pregnancy. Again he looked at his wife. Sophie happened to look up at the same moment.

Color raced delicately up her cheeks as her clear blue eyes met his black ones, down the length of the starched linen tablecloth. Silently Patrick raised his wineglass in a salute. She was his wife; she was carrying his child; she was unbearably beautiful.

A tiny smile hovered on Sophie's lips and she raised her wineglass in return. Patrick was gazing at her with the same suggestive look he used to have, before her mother announced that sex was forbidden.

They would sit together at dinner, talking innocently of the state of the war with France, and all the time Patrick's eyes would lazily slide over her face and down her shoulders, lingering on her breasts until she felt like fireworks about to explode. Every pulse in her body would be pounding by the time Patrick rose from his chair and held out his arm so that they could leave the dining room.

Thinking of it, Sophie put her wineglass down with a soft thump and wrenched her eyes from Patrick's. This was no time for seductive games. She turned decisively to Patrick's brother, Alex, to her right, only to find that he was grinning at her. Sophie blushed again. I suppose he caught Patrick's look, she thought to herself.

"Do you know," Alex said conversationally, leaning close to her ear, "I am very glad that you married my brother, Lady Sophie."

"Thank you," she said hesitantly.

Much later that night, Patrick and Sophie were finally left alone in the drawing room. Sophie dropped into a chair, with an exhausted sigh.

Patrick stood looking down at her for a second. "It was a great success, Sophie my wife," he said quietly.

She looked up and smiled. "Thank you. I thought Madeleine did very well, didn't you?"

Patrick looked a bit surprised. "Naturally. She is a lovely young woman."

Sophie couldn't explain that she was proud of Madeleine because she carried herself to perfection. Not a soul at the party, Sophie would be bound, even considered the possibility that Madeleine was not born into the French aristocracy.

"Has your stomach been indisposed, Sophie?"

It was Sophie's turn to look startled. "No, not at all." Then she grinned. "I placed you next to my mother, didn't I? Did she mention milk baths, by any chance?" And, at Patrick's answering grin, "Bitters?" Sophie gave a melodramatic shiver. "I *hate* bitters."

Patrick laughed and put out a hand, helping her to her feet. "It was Lady Skiffing who said that you ought to be resting."

Sophie paused and looked up at him sympathetically. "It sounds as if they talked your ears off, and just on a subject you dislike. I am sorry."

Patrick looked down at his wife, then took her arm and led her toward the stairs. "Time for bed."

His voice was resonant, almost seductive, Sophie thought. But when she looked up, Patrick's face was impossible to read.

She paused in the doorway of her bedchamber and turned around, saying rather uncertainly, "Good night, Patrick."

Out of the blue, Patrick smiled at her, a suggestive, sweet smile.

Sophie almost jumped, she was so surprised.

"Why don't I act as your lady's maid tonight?"

Sophie opened her mouth but couldn't think of anything to say. Patrick walked toward her, stopping so close to her that she could feel the heat of his body.

"But Mama . . ." Sophie whispered.

"Didn't say we couldn't *kiss*," Patrick said. He lowered his head, opening her lips with fierce hunger. He backed her into her bedroom before he broke the kiss, gently pushing Sophie onto the stool before her dressing table, and dismissing Simone with a nod.

Sophie's hair was pinned up in a simple, smooth twist. Patrick found the end, carefully tucked under by Simone, and pulled it free. Then he shook it briskly. Gold-tipped hairpins flew in all directions, tinkling against the glass of Sophie's dressing-table mirror, plunging into the thick rug, falling into her lap.

She laughed. "I feel like a pony—and you're shaking my tail!"

Patrick's eyes darkened as he met Sophie's in the mirror. He lowered one hand and stroked her neck in a whisper-soft caress. She shivered uncontrollably. "If you were my pony," he said, his voice a velvet whisper, "I would take you for a ride."

Sophie blushed, rosy pink stealing up from the low bodice of her gown. Patrick's eyes drifted down and he almost groaned out loud.

"Oh God, Sophie, I don't know if I can make it!" One of his hands stole, willy-nilly, to her bodice and cupped the soft curves of a breast.

Sophie couldn't help grinning. It was so wonderful to discover that Patrick hadn't been indifferent the last few weeks.

"Then you don't mind the fact I am getting plump?" she said, just a trifle anxiously.

"Plump! You have put on flesh in all the places designed to drive a man mad, Sophie." Patrick's other hand now possessed her other breast.

Sophie looked at herself and her husband in the mirror for a moment, then threw her head back, like a true wanton.

"Kiss me, please, Patrick." Her voice came from her throat in a husky murmur.

He dropped to his knees next to the stool and drew her face to his, capturing her lips. She wreathed her arms around his neck.

After a long time, Patrick drew back, pushing Sophie back onto the stool. Somehow she had ended up on his knee. His eyes were sooty, wild, full of desire. His heart pounded in his throat.

For a moment, husband and wife just stared at each other.

"I'll probably die before this is over," Patrick said conversationally, recovering himself.

Sophie worried her lower lip, with her small white teeth, eyes anxious. "I'm sorry, Patrick. Mama was quite insistent about it." There was a moment's silence. "Perhaps we could simply think of this particular idea as akin to milk baths and bitters?"

For a moment his heart beat a surprised *Yes*! "We'd better not," he said heavily. "After all, it's only once. I can survive."

Sophie bit her lip before she admitted that *she* couldn't survive.

"Well," Patrick said with a sigh, "I'll be off to my lonely bed."

Sophie stood up so quickly that she almost knocked over her stool.

"Would you—perhaps you could sleep here," she said in a rush. "We could just sleep together." When Patrick didn't answer immediately, hot embarrassment flooded up her face.

He moved a step closer. "Sophie," he said, "you don't understand, do you?"

She shook her head.

"Sophie, my love, look at the front of my breeches for a moment."

Obediently, Sophie looked. He was wearing the skintight breeches demanded by fashion. Instantly her eyes dropped and her flush deepened.

"I can't sleep next to you, Sophie, because I wouldn't sleep a wink. Instead I will lie over there"—he nodded toward the door that connected their two rooms—"and wrestle with an urge to break down the door. If I were sleeping with you I would probably ravish you in my sleep, I want you so much."

Sophie grinned. Never mind the fact that Patrick sometimes spent an evening with his mistress. It seemed he wasn't altogether bored with her body yet.

"God!" Patrick half whispered, looking at the honey silk of his wife's disheveled hair, the sultry smile in her eyes, the rosy beauty of her fading blush. "I'd better leave now." He snapped around and slammed the door behind him.

Left standing alone in the bedchamber, Sophie broke into a fit of giggles. She hugged her rounded tummy, swinging in a lopsided circle. He wanted her! He still wanted her!

As a lady's maid Patrick left a good deal to be desired. He may have uncoiled her hair, but he had left intact the hooks running down her back. Giddy with delight, Sophie rang the bell for Simone.

Down in the kitchen Simone registered the ringing bell with a disgruntled frown. Danged if she'd ever understand the ways of the gentry. In the bed, out of the bed. It was a new story every week. With a sigh, she began trudging up the back stairs.

Chapter 23

❧

Y ou may not stop," Braddon insisted, with a note of panic in his voice.

"Why on earth not, Braddon? Madeleine was an undoubted success last night, and I can't think of anything else that I might teach her." Sophie unfurled her parasol. Braddon had picked her up in his phaeton, and the sun was entering the carriage at a slant.

"We won't know which invitations to choose without you."

"Nonsense!" Sophie said a bit sharply. "We already discussed this. In the next few weeks Madeleine will attend eight or nine public events, and you will pay your addresses to her at each one, and then you will announce your engagement at Lady Greenleaf's ball."

Braddon looked at her desperately. "*Why* don't you want to?"

"Well," Sophie said irritably, "if you must know, I

would like to stay home from now on. I would like to see my husband." Patrick invariably absented himself in the evening when Sophie spent the afternoon with Braddon, and she had made up her mind to see whether she could lure Patrick away from his black-haired strumpet.

"I told you Patrick wouldn't like it," Braddon retorted. "Got his back up about all these carriage rides with me, hasn't he? Now I think of it, he's been devilish sharp-set with me in the last few months."

"He hasn't said a word about them. Frankly, I don't think he's noticed." Sophie's voice was quiet but resolved.

"In that case," Braddon said, remembering the more important agenda, "you don't have any reason not to see Madeleine."

Sophie pulled down her parasol and turned squarely to face Braddon. They were tooling their way down Water Street making, she thought with some irritation, straight for Vincent's Horse Emporium, although she had clearly said no. "Lord Slaslow, pull the carriage over, please."

Braddon hunched his shoulders and thought about how glad he was that he hadn't married Sophie.

"Braddon!" The word had all the icy force of her mother's commands.

He pulled over and hooked up the reins.

"Why do you want me to continue seeing Madeleine every week?" Sophie asked.

"She won't see me unless you're there, Sophie. Damme, she never even gives me a kiss anymore!"

"You will see Madeleine in the evenings. If you wish, after this week, you could invite her to go for a ride in the park with you, or to attend an afternoon entertainment. Suitably chaperoned, of course," she added.

Braddon looked mutinous.

"Don't be foolish, Braddon. I should like to go home now." Sophie picked up her parasol again.

"I'm afraid, Sophie."

She turned her head. Had she heard correctly? It seemed she had. Braddon's sad beagle eyes were miserable, and fixed pleadingly on her face.

"We need you to help us, Sophie, right to the end. It's only three weeks," Braddon urged. "All this doesn't come easily to me, you know. I'm afraid I'm going to make an ass of myself, and everyone will know that Madeleine is who she is, and—oh God, Sophie, when I thought up this scheme, I was thinking only of myself and Madeleine. I didn't realize until a few days ago what it will do to m'mother if the truth gets out."

Sophie sat silently for a moment. "I still don't know what else I could teach Madeleine," she said.

"You can give her a top-up on the manners front," Braddon replied. "My mother is a nasty old battle-ax. You know that. But she doesn't deserve a dunderhead like me for a son, either. And if I try to pull the wool over the eyes of the *ton,* and it doesn't work out, she'll never be able to show her face again."

Sophie had to acknowledge the truth of Braddon's summary. "Perhaps you should have thought of that before," she pointed out.

"I know it," Braddon said wretchedly, "but I never was the best at thinking out schemes afore time."

"Oh, all right," Sophie finally said with a sigh.

The next morning she woke with a sense of happy satisfaction. Madeleine had appeared with Mrs. Trevelyan at a champagne musicale the previous evening, and no one could have missed the fact that the Earl of Slaslow was greatly taken with her. He sat next to Madeleine during the second half of the program and assiduously plied her with champagne. Given that the *ton* had been privileged to see Braddon single-mindedly pursue a suitable wife for some three years, no one had any difficulty in surmising that the pretty young Frenchwoman, Lady Madeleine Corneille, was now the target of Slaslow's marital ambitions.

Bets were immediately laid in the betting book at White's as to whether Madeleine would take him, and (for larger amounts of money) whether she would jilt him at the last moment and marry another, as Lady Sophie Foakes had done. Braddon read through the bets with a frown, but with secret relief. He hadn't heard a shard of gossip suggesting that Madeleine Corneille was not exactly what she seemed to be, the daughter of a French marquis.

In fact—although the *ton* didn't know this yet, of course—Madeleine and Braddon were planning to cause an even greater sensation tonight. They were going to a ball being held by Lady Eleanor Commonweal, in honor of her daughter Sissy's engagement, and Madeleine was going to allow Braddon to take her in to supper.

By nine o'clock Patrick had not appeared to escort Sophie to the Commonweal ball, so she drifted around the house by herself until she finally summoned the carriage and went alone, head held high.

It happened just as she entered the ballroom. The Duke of Cumberland happened to be at the door. He looked at her with his usual lustful kindness. He was very much the royal duke this evening, wearing a large swath of royal blue wrapped around his shoulders and held in place by a medal of honor granted by the king some years ago.

"Hear you're a duchess now, m'dear," he said, plastering his wet lips against the back of her hand.

"Excuse me, Your Grace?"

"You're a duchess, aren't you? Let me see, Duchess of Gisle, that's it! They don't tell me much," he said, stepping as close as he possibly could to the beautiful new duchess, "but they couldn't keep it from me. Heard it passed the Parliament this afternoon."

Seeing her look of complete bewilderment, the duke smiled. Obviously the rumors did not underestimate the discord between the lovely Lady Sophie and her husband. As soon as she dropped the brat she was carrying, he would make his move, the duke thought.

"Parliament has granted your husband a title," he explained slowly. "They've made him the Duke of Gisle. That makes you the Duchess of Gisle."

Sophie instinctively stepped backward, away from the royal duke's hot breath on her neck.

"Oh, of course," she murmured, dropping into a deep curtsy. "For a moment I had forgotten. Thank you for reminding me, Your Grace."

She read in Cumberland's eyes the humiliation she felt deep in her bones. He'd never be able to keep it to himself—the delectable news that the Duke of Gisle hadn't even bothered to tell his wife that he was being made a duke. A duchess who didn't even know her own title!

Patrick never appeared at the ball. After an hour or so Sophie went home. Cumberland's gossip had spread like wildfire. She couldn't bear any more people addressing her as "Your Grace," their carrion eyes bright with curiosity. ("Where *is* the duke tonight, Your Grace? Such an honor he received! One might think he wasn't interested in his new title.")

At the house she had a word with Clemens and then walked into the library.

Patrick was seated comfortably in front of the fire, reading a book.

Sophie flushed a deep, furious red. "How dare you not arrive home in time to escort me to the Commonweal ball?"

Patrick looked up and politely rose to his feet. "As it happens," he said nonchalantly, "you didn't tell me where we were going, m'dear, or that we had accepted an invitation. Had you informed me that you wished my company, I naturally would have accompanied you."

Surely she had told him about the ball. Although she *was* forgetting all sorts of details these days. She might have forgotten after all.

"You should have assumed that I needed your escort," Sophie retorted.

Patrick's eyes were shadowed, black with reserve. "In that case, I apologize."

"Well," Sophie said impatiently, suddenly remembering why she was furious, "that doesn't matter. You—you didn't tell me that you're a duke!"

"Oh, did Breksby push it through so soon?"

Sophie looked at her husband as if he were a visitor from a foreign land. Patrick seemed mildly interested, as if he'd heard that his favorite horse had won the Ascot.

"Are you entirely deranged? What are you talking about?" Her voice rose nearly to a shriek.

"I'm talking about the title," Patrick said with a touch of hauteur. "I hadn't realized that Lord Breksby managed to get it through Parliament."

"And it didn't occur to you to *tell me*?" Sophie was in a fine rage now. "Do you know how embarrassing it was to have the Duke of Cumberland inform me that I am now a duchess? Do you have any idea how dreadful it felt to have no idea why one has suddenly been made into a duchess, and to find a roomful of people tittering because my husband had obviously not bothered to tell me about it?"

Patrick's face took on a wry, unreadable look. He moved over to his wife and took her arm, leading her to a chair. "I can see that it upset you very much," he said soothingly. "To be frank, it slipped my mind."

"It slipped your mind!" Sophie stared up at her husband as he stood before her. Then she erupted back out of her chair. "It slipped your mind that you were becoming a Duke of the Realm! It slipped your mind that you might want to tell your *wife* that she was becoming a duchess!"

"I don't see why you are so irritated about it," Patrick

retorted, starting to lose his temper now. "You always wanted to marry a title, as I recall. Well, now I outrank your precious Braddon!"

There were a few fiery moments of silence. Sophie tried to think of ways to answer Patrick's attack, but it was so outrageous that she couldn't think of a response.

"What makes you think that I wanted to marry a title?" she asked, finally.

Patrick shrugged. "I always knew you did." He certainly wasn't going to sound like a pompous ass by declaring that Braddon was plump and foolish. Besides, he suspected more and more that Sophie actually had had a true affection—if not love—for that blunderhead. Truth be told, Braddon was rather lovable in his own way.

Sophie felt a huge, desolate emptiness pressing on her heart. Her husband's reasoning processes were utterly incomprehensible to her. "Would you care to inform me," she said, her tone dangerously gentle as she sat down again, "why the Parliament made you a duke? The Duke of Gisle, I believe?"

"I'm off to the Ottoman Empire as an ambassador in the fall," Patrick said with a shrug. Now he really felt like a muckworm.

"You are going to the Ottoman Empire . . . something to do with Selim III?" Patrick registered his wife's unusual knowledge without surprise. Sophie was a remarkably intelligent woman. At least he'd learned that about her during their marriage. "In the fall?"

Sophie looked at him. In the candlelight, her eyes were as black as his. "Well, you needn't worry about *us*," she said, her tone dripping with sarcasm. "I shall move back with my mother." Her hands compulsively caressed her stomach.

"Of course you won't move back with your mother," Patrick retorted irritably.

"Why on earth not? I will be giving birth to my child in early autumn, as I believe you have forgotten."

Patrick registered with a pang that Sophie talked of *her* child. "You won't move back with your mother because it wouldn't look right," he said dismissively.

Sophie narrowed her eyes. "It wouldn't look right." Her tone was glacial. "I gather you spend a good deal of time worrying about how our marriage looks to outside eyes, *Your Grace*." She punctuated the title with an awful irony.

Patrick flushed. "I apologize for not informing you about the title, Sophie." But he couldn't see the point of going into further explanations. What was he supposed to say? Admit that he had entirely forgotten about the useless title? His wife didn't think titles were useless! Look at all the fuss she was making because she had been made a duchess.

"You're a duchess now. Can't you just be pleased about it?"

Sophie stared at her husband's back as he looked down into the fire. Pleased? Her marriage was a disaster, worse than she had ever pictured in her youth.

"Perhaps it would be better if you did stay with your mother," Patrick said now, kicking the logs with his foot. "I shall likely be gone for several months."

This is the end, Sophie acknowledged to herself. Even her own mother had never been sent home by her husband. Patrick cared so little about her that it seemed he'd forgotten she existed. How else could he have neglected to tell her that he was becoming a duke? And he certainly had ignored the forthcoming birth of their child. It appeared he wouldn't even be in the country at the time.

Tears prickled so hard at the back of her eyes that Sophie had to swallow, so she rose and quietly walked out of the room. There was, literally, no point in talking further.

Only innate, fierce pride kept Sophie's head high during the next few weeks. She registered Madeleine's social triumphs with some pleasure. But Patrick came home late every night now. Twice she sent a message to Charlotte and joined their party for the evening, since her husband was no longer accompanying her to social events.

Alex looked at her with his black eyes that were so like and unlike Patrick's, but neither he nor Charlotte ever asked her why Patrick had seemingly disappeared from London society. Sophie drew strength from Charlotte's silent support.

Only Eloise demanded an explanation. Sophie was taking tea with her mother and rather absentmindedly fending off the suggestion that she eat at least one partridge a week in order to sustain the growing babe.

Then her mother folded her hands in her lap and looked at her. As always, Eloise's back was as straight as a poker.

"Was it the languages, Sophie, *chérie?*"

For a moment Sophie didn't understand the question.

"Languages?"

"Was it the languages that pulled you and Patrick apart?"

Sophie flushed. "Oh no, *Maman*. At least, I don't think so."

Eloise's eyes sharpened. "You don't think so?"

"When he found out—in Wales—he did seem—"

"It's my fault," Eloise cried, anguish in her tone. "I should never, *never* have allowed your father to have his way! All that education has given him a dislike of you, hasn't it?"

Sophie shook her head. "I don't think so, *Maman*. Patrick simply doesn't care very much for me either way. He forgets that I exist."

"He couldn't do that," Eloise said simply.

Sophie smiled at her. Whatever her mother's faults, she was fiercely loyal. "It's not so bad, *Maman,* really. I don't mind very much. And Patrick ... he has his own amusements." She shrugged. "He does not appear to notice whether I'm around or not. In fact, he suggested that I come back here and stay with you and Papa in the fall. He will be traveling to the Ottoman Empire as an ambassador."

Eloise's face was as sharp as an eagle's. "Your father will see about that! So Foakes thinks he can toss his bride out like a piece of laundry, does he! And what about the babe?"

Sophie's hands twisted in her lap. Somehow it all sounded so much worse when her mother formulated it. Her eyes filled with tears. Sophie cried at the drop of a hat these days.

"Please, *Maman*," she said, her tone half stifled. "Can't we just let it be? There's nothing anyone can do—*please* don't tell Papa."

Eloise sat down next to her daughter on the couch and wrapped a loving arm around her. "Don't worry, *mignonne*," she said soothingly. "You think about yourself and the babe. We would love to have you make us a long visit in the fall."

Tears dripped onto Sophie's hands. "I don't want to talk about it." But she continued anyway. "I never made a fuss about Patrick's mistress. But it made no difference. He stopped coming home in the evenings. And then . . . and then he . . . We don't talk. So I didn't know that he was a duke, and I didn't know he was going to Turkey—just when the baby is to be born. . . ."

"We won't mention it again," Eloise said soothingly.

After a moment they collected themselves and the Marchioness of Brandenburg reseated herself. Eloise looked over at her lovely daughter, now the Duchess of Gisle.

"Have I ever told you how proud I am of you, darling?"

Sophie laughed. She didn't see anything Eloise should be proud of. Her daughter had managed to make a disastrous marriage.

"I am proud of you because you show true breeding these days," Eloise said fiercely. "I know how cruel one's so-called friends can be when a marriage is faltering. But you have behaved with absolute grace on every occasion. I am truly proud of you, Sophie."

Sophie swallowed, tears rising to her eyes again. It was an odd legacy to hand from mother to daughter: the ability to stand proud among the ruins of one's marriage.

"Thank you, *Maman*," she said finally, swallowing the terrible lump in her throat.

Chapter 24

⁓

The following morning, Sophie had barely made her toilette when Clemens announced that Lady Madeleine Corneille had come to call.

Sophie entered the drawing room a trifle anxiously. She had seen Madeleine the preceding evening, and she had said nothing of making a morning call.

With her usual charm, Madeleine made sure that Sophie was comfortably seated—not an easy thing, given her increasing girth—before she spoke of the reason for her call.

"I have decided to stop the masquerade." Madeleine's voice rang clear, calm, and unshakable in the quiet chamber.

Sophie gasped. "Why?"

"It is not honest. I cannot have a marriage based on this . . . this foundation of lies. Can you imagine pretending to be a false person, for the rest of your life, Sophie? I cannot do it."

"But you won't have to," Sophie pointed out. "Once you are married to Braddon, you will be the Countess of Slaslow, and no one will care a fig for your background."

"I will," Madeleine replied simply. "Braddon and I will have children . . . and what will we tell them? *When* will I tell my son that I am a liar, a pretender from the lower classes? How old will he be when I tell him that I grew up over a stable, and that he will have to worry his whole life that people might find out about his mother's past?

"And what of my children's grandfather? Will I make my father into Braddon's stable master? I would not do such a thing to my father! This is not possible, Sophie. We were fools to think it so."

Tears came to Sophie's eyes. "I'm sorry," she said. "I never meant to . . ."

Madeleine looked equally teary. "Oh, Sophie, in no way is it your fault! I am so grateful to you for your friendship, as well as for what you taught me. But Braddon and I were living in a fool's paradise. We would never have a happy marriage on this basis."

"You can't know that," Sophie protested. "Braddon loves you so much, Madeleine."

"We cannot have a good marriage when our life is based on falsehoods," Madeleine replied, French practicality resonating in her voice. "Love is not enough."

"Yes," Sophie murmured. She loved Patrick, after all. But somehow her marriage was falling to shards and tatters . . . love or no. "What will you do now?"

"Braddon and I discussed it last night. We may go to America. Braddon says he will not stay in England without me, and Braddon is very determined."

"He will never let you out of his sight," Sophie confirmed. "But what of his family, Madeleine?" She hesitated, remembering Braddon's anguished fear that his mother would be humiliated.

Madeleine nodded. "It is a problem, that. So we have

come up with a new plan, Sophie. I will continue the masquerade until next week. At Lady Greenleaf's ball, our engagement will be announced. The following day, we will let it be known that I have suddenly fallen ill. Then," she said briskly, "when I am dead of a fever, Braddon will make a trip to America to recover his spirits."

"And you will go with him? Oh, this is a true Braddon scheme!" Sophie said. She felt a smile pulling at the corners of her mouth.

Madeleine wrinkled her nose. "I—I do not care for it. But I can see that I have woven my lies, and now I must play to the finish. I shall go to America and be a plain horse trainer's daughter, and if the Earl of Slaslow is foolish enough to marry an American horse trainer's daughter, well, so be it. Our children may return to England someday. I shall not."

"I shall miss you," Sophie said. And she meant it.

"I am so grateful to you, Sophie, for teaching me to be a lady," Madeleine said. "I too shall miss you." She hesitated, then rushed on. "Your Patrick . . . he does love you, you know."

Sophie started. A glow of humiliation heated the back of her neck.

Madeleine's brown eyes were earnest and passionately sympathetic. "He *loves* you," she repeated. "I see him—watching you. Whenever you are not looking, he watches you. And his heart is in his eyes, Sophie."

Sophie smiled, a pinched little smile. She and Madeleine hugged a long good-bye.

A few minutes after Madeleine left, Clemens appeared in the doorway of Sophie's sitting room, holding a salver with a card on it. "Mr. Foucault and Mr. Mustafa are calling," he said.

His tone was resonant with hostility, and Sophie knew instantly that Clemens, who was a ruthless judge of character, did not approve of these particular callers.

"Do I know them?" Sophie asked.

"Certainly not, Your Grace," Clemens replied. "They are acquaintances—distant acquaintances—of His Grace."

"I don't understand, Clemens. Did they ask for me?"

"They asked for His Grace," Clemens said, "and when I informed them that he was not at home, they requested to speak with you." He let it be known by the curve of his lower lip just what he thought of such a gross lack of propriety. Requesting a call with the mistress when the master was out of the house! Absurd. "I shall inform them that you are not at home."

Sophie nodded, and Clemens backed out of the room. He returned a few minutes later. Now there was a miniature silver castle on his salver, a willowy, fantastic castle whose turrets were crowned with glowing rubies.

Sophie's eyebrows rose.

"A gift for the sultan, Selim III," Clemens pronounced. His tone was still rancorous but he was clearly appeased by the obvious worth of the castle. "Mr. Foucault claims that His Grace is expecting the inkwell and has agreed to present it to the sultan on Mr. Foucault's behalf."

"Oh, dear," Sophie said, rising from her chair. "I had better greet him, hadn't I? Why, what a lovely piece!" She approached and reached out toward the castle roof. "This must cover the well."

But Clemens shook his head. "Mr. Foucault desired most earnestly that the inkwell remain untouched at this juncture, as it is temporarily sealed for the trip to the Ottoman Empire. Apparently the well is filled with the sultan's favorite color ink—green." Clemens's lower lip conveyed his opinion of green ink.

"Of course," Sophie said, withdrawing her hand. "Why don't you set the castle over there, Clemens?" She waved toward a small parquet table in the corner. "Where are they?"

"In the drawing room," Clemens replied.

"If you would ask Simone to join me, we shall greet the gentlemen in fifteen minutes."

Clemens bowed and retreated backward. Ever since Patrick had acceded to the title of duke, Clemens's self-esteem—and his worth among London butlers—had gone through the roof. The extra consequence had translated into a formality unmatched except in the halls of St. James's itself.

By the time Simone had been located, and fussed with Sophie's hair, rather more than fifteen minutes had passed. But Monsieur Foucault pooh-poohed Sophie's apology.

"It is a pleasure merely to be in the same room with such elegance," he said, brushing the back of her hand with his mouth. "So many Englishwomen are so—so *quaint* in their attire!"

Sophie barely averted a shudder at the touch of Foucault's silky lips. When Foucault introduced his companion, Bayrak Mustafa, Sophie wondered for a moment whether to greet him in Turkish. She certainly had mastered enough of the language to conduct a simple conversation. But pregnancy had had a terrible effect on her memory, and she might make a total dunce of herself. So she merely nodded and said a polite greeting in English, trusting Monsieur Foucault to translate.

She had no trouble understanding Monsieur Foucault's translation of her greeting. But Mr. Mustafa's response was rather more interesting. In fact, it made absolutely no sense, as far as Sophie could tell. His sentence—delivered with a deep bow—appeared to be a line from a nursery rhyme or a children's song. She *must* have misunderstood! After all, Foucault showed no signs of surprise. He translated the nonsense line as a most conventional greeting and compliment.

Sophie sank into a chair, feeling even more confused. But her curiosity was piqued. Monsieur Foucault seemed eager to speak of French fashions versus English; after a bit, Sophie managed to steer the conversation back to Bayrak Mustafa.

"I am so sorry that Mr. Mustafa is neglected in our conversation," she said sweetly to Monsieur Foucault. "Will you please ask him, for me, how our English cities compare to the great city of Constantinople?"

A flash of annoyance passed Foucault's face, but a beatific smile quickly replaced it. "How very kind of Your Grace," he cooed, "to think of my companion, Mustafa. As it happens, he and I have overstayed our welcome in your beautiful house, and must be on our way—"

"Please," Sophie said, her tone as charming and as determined as his. "Do allow me to keep you for a moment. I am *so* curious about Constantinople!"

Foucault nodded politely and turned to Mustafa. Sophie listened closely, trying to keep her face brightly polite.

Sure enough, Foucault relayed her question. But Mustafa's reply was a nonsensical jingle-jangle of words. And unless she was greatly mistaken, Mr. Mustafa spoke only nouns, no verbs.

What's more, Foucault's translation did not represent what she had heard, even given her imperfect knowledge of the Turkish language. In Monsieur Foucault's words, Mustafa had found the capital of England to be far superior to the great city of Constantinople.

Foucault smoothly moved from his translation to a grandiose apology. "Do forgive me, Your Grace, but we must be on our way. I am"—he swept forward and kissed Sophie's hand yet again—"your most obedient servant. I trust His Grace will find the inkwell amusing." He paused for a moment. "I must beg you, Your Grace, to convey the fact that the inkwell is sealed. It *must* remain so until after it makes its long journey to the Ottoman Empire."

Sophie smiled, rising to her feet as well. "Naturally, we will not disturb the inkwell in any way," she said. "May

I compliment you on your thoughtful and most beautiful gift, sir?"

Foucault bowed once again, then ushered Bayrak Mustafa out of the room, leaving in a babble of English words. Mr. Mustafa bowed silently and did not venture again into Turkish.

After they left, Sophie frowned and walked up the stairs to her sitting room. She walked over to the inkwell, touching its delicate, jeweled turrets with one finger. There was something wrong, deeply wrong, about Monsieur Foucault and Mr. Mustafa.

And yet she had scarcely even seen Patrick since the whole debacle of the Commonweal ball. How could she bring up the subject of Monsieur Foucault? As she thought about it, Clemens appeared at her door with more cards on his silver salver. The Duchess of Gisle was much in demand, and Sophie dismissed her concerns for the moment.

❦

Later that week, Patrick ran into his brother on a crowded street, and they stopped for a moment, nonplussed.

"You're giving me a damned bellyache, man," Alex finally said.

"Your stomach is not my problem," Patrick retorted. His temper was worn to a thread by nights of sleepless walking.

Alex scowled. "You might at least instruct a footman to help your wife," he said acidly. "I found Sophie clambering out of her carriage yesterday by herself. She almost fell to the pavement."

Fury raced down Patrick's spine. He bowed his head politely. "I will of course instruct the footmen to be more assiduous." He ignored the unspoken criticism—that he should be shepherding his wife around town now that she was almost seven months pregnant.

Alex swore. He had come to love his petite sister-in-law dearly, and something about the wounded bewilderment deep in her eyes told him that she had no idea why her husband was behaving so irrationally.

"Have you talked to Sophie about your fear of the birth?" he demanded abruptly.

Patrick's body became even more rigid, if possible. His eyes were smoldering. "My 'fear,' as you put it, is an entirely reasonable reaction to the fact that one in five women die in childbirth. Unlike you, I hoped not to put my wife in danger for the witless pleasure of reproducing myself."

The look in both men's eyes was barbarous now, unsuited to the polite environs of Oxford Street.

"If you weren't my brother," Alex said with icy politeness, "I would call you out for that. As it is, I'll tell you, *brother,* that you have gone stark raving insane. You are making yourself and your wife miserable for no good reason other than senseless, childish terror."

Patrick's teeth ground together as he stopped himself from slugging Alex on the spot.

"You tell me," he finally said, "you tell me what is senseless about thinking that the odds of one in five are not good."

"Those odds include women giving birth without doctors, without midwives, when they are ill or dying. How many gentlewomen can you think of who have died in childbirth?"

"Plenty," Patrick said with quiet force. "And so should you, given that your wife almost joined their ranks."

For a moment neither man spoke. Then Alex's voice emerged raw, half strangled. "Charlotte was having no problem with the birth until I appeared, Patrick. You know that. You know it was my fault. Are you trying to break my heart?"

The silence was broken only by the rattle of carriages passing.

"Oh God," Patrick said quietly. "I should just shoot myself, shouldn't I?"

At that, Alex smiled a little. "Not without giving me a chance first."

The two men came together in an improvised, unfamiliar hug. Patrick swallowed hard. Alex roughly patted him on the back. He didn't know what to say.

"There's only what—two or three months left?"

Patrick looked at his brother helplessly. "I don't know. Sophie and I do not discuss the child."

"The whole town is chattering about the fact that you didn't tell Sophie that she was being made a duchess. What in the bloody hell were you thinking, Patrick?"

"I forgot. I just forgot." He shrugged. "You know how little titles mean to me. I thought Sophie would be happy to be a duchess, but she's furious because I didn't inform her. We don't really talk much anymore."

Alex nodded, accepting silently what he had already sensed. His brother's marriage was in a dangerously fragile state.

"I believe Sophie is beginning her seventh month," Alex said, no trace of judgment in his tone. "She told Charlotte that she was going to stop attending public events after Lady Greenleaf's ball tomorrow night."

Patrick had had no idea that Sophie was giving up the rest of the season. "I'll accompany her," he said quietly. He knew that Sophie often joined Charlotte and Alex in the evening.

Alex nodded. "I don't suppose it will do any good to say that you might have a conversation with your wife?"

Patrick winced. "I shall try, Alex."

That night Clemens scratched on Sophie's bedchamber door and informed Simone that the duke had announced his intention to eat supper at home. The master hadn't eaten in the house for two or three weeks, and Clemens thought, rightly, that the duchess ought to know that she would be eating with her husband rather than alone.

Sophie stopped short in the middle of fastening a bracelet on her wrist. Simone's eyes flashed to her mistress's face, then dropped to the floor. The whole household knew, of course, that the master and mistress were estranged.

In fact, Simone and Patrick's man, Keating, were engaged in a flaming battle over the master's whereabouts at night. Keating maintained that the master was not up to hanky-panky; Simone scoffed and said the duke was spending time with a fancy lady somewhere and that Keating ought to be ashamed. The battle had grown so heated that Keating actually brought one of Patrick's coats down to the servants' quarters, the better to demonstrate its utter lack of female perfume or face powder.

Sophie finished fastening the bracelet, quite as if Clemens's message hadn't arrived. She was wearing a loose sea-green evening gown, constructed with an extra panel in the front to accommodate her growing belly.

For a moment she hesitated in front of the mirror. She felt ugly these days, an ugly, unwanted wife. *Pregnant* wife, she thought savagely. Perhaps I should just take a tray in my room.

Then she steadied her courage and walked down the stairs. She walked slowly, concentrating on balancing the extra weight that jutted out before her. Patrick met her at the bottom of the stairs.

Sophie smiled at him politely and took his arm as they walked into the dining room.

Automatically Sophie forked pheasant into her mouth.

"Isn't this the second time this week that Floret has served pheasant?" Patrick asked.

"Yes, it is. I'm afraid that my mother managed to bribe him." Sophie suffered through two more bites, wondering how Patrick knew that Floret had also served pheasant on Tuesday. That evening he hadn't come in until long after she fell asleep. These days she had stopped waiting for his return. She needed sleep more than she needed the confirmation that her husband rarely arrived home before dawn.

Sophie ate another bite. The pheasant tasted like sawdust.

"I will accompany you to Lady Greenleaf's ball tomorrow night, if I may," Patrick said. "I believe that it promises to be a great crush."

Sophie nodded. Her husband had come home for supper, and now he was going to take her to a ball?

In the face of Sophie's silence, Patrick kept talking. "You might be amused to hear that there are bets at White's on whether Braddon will announce his engagement to your friend Madeleine in the next week or so."

Sophie said nothing. Patrick cursed silently. What was he doing? Sophie was unlikely to be thrilled to hear that Braddon was getting married to someone else, given her feelings for the man.

"Perhaps we might take a picnic to the countryside, if the weather stays fine this weekend," he said, suddenly inspired. Surely it would be a good deal easier to talk to Sophie if they were alone, rather than sitting at the table flanked by two footmen.

Suddenly Sophie's head swung up, and Patrick saw to his astonishment that her eyes were narrowed, blazing.

"I'll be *damned* if you can just waltz into this dining room as if nothing happened in the last month and ask me on a picnic," she said furiously.

Patrick looked up and nodded to Clemens, who directed the footmen out of the room with a wave, then quickly followed them.

"Why not?" Patrick looked at his wife with stupefaction. This was a new Sophie. There was no difficulty reading the fury in her eyes.

Sophie stood up and threw her napkin on the table. "I never complained when you went off with your mistress. I didn't reproach you—*once*. If you want to go, go! But don't come back to me as if I were a fish that you could reel in when you pleased. I suppose you think I will smile gratefully and go on a picnic with you, now that you've decided to grant your wife a bit of your time?"

Patrick stared at his wife, his face imperturbable.

"I'm going to my chambers," she said abruptly. "I will accept your escort tomorrow to the ball, but I must decline your kind invitation for a picnic. I don't feel like a wanton trollop today, and I don't expect to feel like one tomorrow either. Therefore," she said with savage irony, "I'm sure you wouldn't be comfortable in my company!"

And with that she walked out of the room and up the stairs, as quickly as she could manage in her state.

The Duke and Duchess of Gisle lay in their separate bedrooms that night, both staring at the ceiling. If an angel had happened to look through the roof of the mansion on Upper Brook Street, he would have seen separate, sleepless figures. Patrick was, perhaps, the more despairing; Sophie, having rediscovered anger, was finding it a not unpleasant emotion.

Had the same angel bothered to peer through the elegant silk roof of the Gisle carriage as it inched its way to a halt before the entrance to Lady Greenleaf's mansion in Hanover Square the following night, he would again have seen two separate, silent figures, but with one difference: Sophie was staring at the wall, and Patrick was staring at her.

Sophie was dressed in a ball gown that deliberately emphasized her newly lush figure. Gossamer silk in a pale, pale blue, more lucid than a robin's egg, wound its way around her bodice, playing hide-and-seek with the curves of her breasts.

Oblivious to Patrick's gaze, Sophie adjusted her cashmere wrap as the carriage drew to a halt, an action that unconsciously caused her breasts nearly to topple from their frail cover.

I am not lustful, Patrick thought to himself. I am not jealous. The small hope that reiterating those statements would make them a fact died a quick death. All right, he thought, I am lustful. He jumped down from the carriage and automatically held out a hand to help Sophie from the carriage. And I *am* jealous, he thought fiercely, seeing the widened eyes of the London populace that had gathered to watch the swells go to a party.

If only . . . if only Sophie would throw him a laughing glance and accidentally brush against his arm. If only she had toppled from the carriage into his arms, rather than dropping his hand the moment her feet were safely on the pavement. But she was obviously merely tolerating his presence. For a moment, agony clutched Patrick's heart. He was better off walking the streets of London than being in the presence of his so-beautiful, so-desirable, so-uncaring wife.

The minute they passed Lady Greenleaf's receiving line, a flock of gentlemen descended, arguing over the privilege of dancing with the beautiful young duchess. Patrick stood there silently for a moment, then rudely interrupted an impudent young whelp and claimed the supper dance.

Sophie looked at him, briefly, but said nothing. As Patrick well knew, she would never cause a scene in a ballroom. He bowed and sauntered off.

Sophie watched him go, ignoring the prattling crowd around her for an instant. Somehow all her righteous anger was starting to fade away, just when she needed it. She took a deep breath. Tonight was the last of these agonizing public appearances. After that, she would retire for the season. A pregnant woman's "confinement" was sounding better every moment. And, in fact, it was just as well that she dance with Patrick. She was getting tired of thinly veiled, solicitous comments about her husband's frequent absences.

The supper dance started, and Patrick appeared at her side. But just as he began to bow before her Sophie shook her head, nodding at the other end of the ballroom. Patrick turned around. Braddon was standing at the top of the room, holding Madeleine's hand.

Lord Greenleaf cleared his throat importantly, and said loudly, "I have the honor to announce that Lady Madeleine Corneille has agreed to marry the Earl of Slaslow."

Braddon's mother stood beside them, smiling happily. As the strains of a minuet fell into the quieted room, Braddon turned and thanked Lord Greenleaf. Then he took his new betrothed in his arms and swept into the clear space. The newly engaged couple remained a demure three inches apart. Braddon Chatwin did not allow his legs to brush Lady Madeleine's gown, nor did he touch her in an overfamiliar fashion.

But when Braddon smiled so sweetly at his Maddie that she lost her fear of dancing in front of the *ton* and returned his smile, Sophie wasn't the only woman in the room who got a lump in her throat and a shine in her eye.

The tightness in Patrick's chest had nothing to do with Braddon. That bounder had obviously played fast and loose with Sophie's emotions. There she was, almost crying in public because Braddon was engaged again.

But it couldn't be called Braddon's fault, could it? Patrick's conscience was uncomfortably awake. Sophie would be married to Braddon right now, he thought with dogged self-hatred, if I hadn't slept with her first.

He swept his wife into the dance. If nothing else, I can protect her from curious eyes, Patrick reasoned. Sophie would be ridiculed for crying over a man she had jilted.

They danced silently. Sophie kept her head turned away, afraid that Patrick would be able to read in her eyes that she had lost her anger. She was too humiliated to face the fact that she would probably always welcome back the rake she had married, no matter how far he strayed. She loved him too much.

They were swept in to dinner in a wave of babbling dancers and found seats around a large round table. Halfway through the meal Sophie excused herself from the table, not coincidentally when Patrick had gone to fetch another cup of syllabub.

"Please, Sissy, do tell my husband that I will be in the ladies' retiring room," she said to her friend.

Sissy Commonweal looked at her with the sympathetic eyes that seemed to greet her everywhere in the *ton* these days. I'm sure she knows where Patrick spends his nights, Sophie thought tiredly. It's a wonder that no one has told me the black-haired woman's name. She walked away from the table without looking back, not even seeing Patrick weaving his way back to the table with her syllabub.

She couldn't stay in the retiring room forever, however, and Patrick found her later and claimed a second dance. Thankfully, it was a country dance, which meant there would be little intimacy. Sophie was mechanically going through the figures when suddenly, through a gap in the crowded room, she saw something that made her heart thump sharply in her throat. Her mother, Eloise, was smiling sweetly and drawing Madeleine over to speak to an elderly Frenchwoman—undoubtedly Madame de Meneval, famed for her ability to expose fraudulent French aristocrats. Without a second's hesitation, Sophie snapped out of the steps, dropped her husband's hand, and set out across the dance floor.

Patrick looked after her in stupefaction. Daughters trained by the formidable Marchioness of Brandenburg did not abandon their partners on the dance floor. Mentally shaking himself, he hurried after his wife.

But Sophie got there too late. Even as she dodged around a last cluster of people, she saw Madeleine sinking into a dulcet curtsy before Madame de Meneval.

"Merde!" Sophie whispered, and stopped running. Eloise looked up and held out a welcoming hand.

"My dearest, do come meet Madame de Meneval. I have just introduced her to dear Madeleine."

With a sinking heart, Sophie walked to her mama's side. In another second, Madame would declare that Madeleine was an impostor, bringing Braddon's whole scheme crashing down around their ears.

Patrick appeared at her side and touched her arm. Sophie cast him a frantic glance.

He frowned in confusion. What in thunder was going on? Here was Sophie, apparently quaking with fear to meet an old Frenchwoman dressed in rusty black silk. True, the woman had a beak that could grace an eagle, but there was nothing intrinsically terrifying about her. In fact, she looked to be a bit of a soft touch to Patrick. Wasn't she crying?

Definitely, Madame de Meneval was crying, just a trifle, only a single tear. She dropped her cane and stretched her hands out to Madeleine.

"Madeleine, dear Madeleine! I thought you were dead. I have missed your mother so much, and here you are . . . You are the very image of her. I remember you as a young girl, my dear, when you were only five years old. Your mama brought you all the way to Paris just to see the ballet. Your mother loved the ballet. Oh, how she loved to dance."

Sophie didn't say a word. Neither did Madeleine. They both stared at Madame de Meneval as if she had suddenly grown a horn on her forehead. But Madame didn't notice. She was pulling a handkerchief of the finest lace out of her reticule, and gently patting her eyes.

"Just so your mother used to look when she was out-shining every lady of the court. It's as if I see my dear Hélène before me again. You have her eyes, and her hair . . . your figure is exactly like hers. Why, I remember dear King Louis ogling Hélène's bosom, as if it were yesterday. How Marie Antoinette used to bridle at your mother! But there was nothing she could say. Your mother was perfectly behaved, a truly modest lady who never put herself forward. It wasn't Hélène's fault that Louis always found her *très désirable*."

Then Madame suddenly noticed the look of stunned surprise on Madeleine's face. "Did you not know that you are the image of your mother, my dear?"

"My father always said so, ma'am," Madeleine said slowly, "but I could hardly believe it."

Just then Braddon came up behind Madeleine and touched her elbow. "I believe this is my dance," he said, bowing.

"Braddon!" she cried, ignoring the rule that she address him formally in public. "Madame de Meneval says that I look exactly like my mother!"

Braddon's mouth fell open and for a moment Sophie tensed. He's going to say something idiotic, she thought. Her fingers tightened painfully on Patrick's sleeve.

Patrick glanced down at his wife's white fingers. He hadn't the faintest idea why Sophie was so agitated.

Luckily, Madame de Meneval broke in before Braddon could expose Madeleine's true identity.

"You must be the Earl of Slaslow," she said, looking over Braddon critically. She didn't care for the overly English sort herself: all that hearty blond hair and blue eyes. "I have heard that you are to have the honor of marrying the daughter of my dear friend, the Marquise de Flammarion."

"That's right," Braddon said uncertainly. He bowed again.

Madame snorted. Stupid as they come, she thought to herself. Still, at least he's not as odd as Hélène's husband was.

"Your father, the marquis, must have survived as well, then," she said curiously, turning back to Madeleine. The girl was still standing there, white faced, as if she'd been turned to stone.

"My father brought me to England in 1793," she replied.

"Oh, 1793." Madame shivered. "That was a dreadful year, a dreadful year. Yes, that was when your dear mother was denounced. In April, it was. A dreadful year."

If possible, Madeleine turned even paler. "My father always told me that my mother died of a fever," she said carefully.

"Oh no," said the Frenchwoman. "She was arrested. Fouquier, that butcher, didn't need a reason. She rarely came to Paris, you know, since your father was such a recluse. But she was there, perhaps to buy something... new clothing. I am not sure."

Madeleine knew. In her head resounded her father's frequent and fierce condemnation of fashion and female love of fashion in particular.

"She was caught," Madame continued. "I know that your father came to Paris and pleaded for her life before the Tribunal. The only reason he wasn't imprisoned himself was that he was such an odd sort. Always messing about in the stables, always covered with dirt. There were rumors that he even learned how to shoe horses."

"Yes, he did," Madeleine said numbly.

"Well, it saved his life," Madame replied. "The Tribunal judged him to be better than a useless aristocrat—those canaille! Degenerate pieces of rabble, judging the lives of their betters!" Her eyes glowed fiercely at Madeleine. "You're better off here, girl. Even married to an Englishman. Even without your father's estates. Did he manage to bring anything to England?"

"Yes," Madeleine answered, thinking of the huge sum of money her father had suddenly, and most surprisingly, produced when it was time to buy her clothing and to hire Mrs. Trevelyan. "Yes, he did."

"Well," Madame de Meneval said with grudging respect, "I never cared for Vincent Garnier overmuch. He was an odd sort, even as a young man. But Hélène loved him. She was absurdly in love with him. Wouldn't hear a word against him. And then after she married him, he took her off to his estates in the Limousin, and hardly let her come to court at all. I don't know how she got permission to come to Paris in '93." She fell silent.

Madeleine turned to Braddon, her eyes bright with unshed tears. He responded promptly. "I am afraid that I must claim my future bride," he said, bowing deeply in the general direction of Madame de Meneval. "Madame, your servant."

Madame inclined her chin an inch as if she, rather than Louis XVI, had been king. But her eyes softened as she turned to Madeleine.

"Dear child, I can see that I unwittingly gave you some unpleasant news. You must forgive me."

"No, no," Madeleine said softly. "It is lovely to meet someone who knew my mother. I am afraid I have very few memories of her."

"Perhaps you will come and take tea with me someday. I knew your mother from the day she was born. I would be happy to tell Hélène's daughter about her. How proud she would have been of you, my dear!"

At that, Madeleine's tears threatened to overflow. As she made a hasty curtsy, Braddon drew her gently out of the ballroom. Braddon may not have been overbright, but he knew his Maddie. Without a word he pulled her into an adjacent salon, shut the door, and wrapped his arms around her.

"Braddon, Braddon," Madeleine sobbed. "It is Mama, Hélène is Mama."

"What?"

"Madame . . . she was talking about *my* mama!"

"Impossible," Braddon said kindly. "Your mama married a horse trainer, m'dear. She couldn't possibly have been friends with a member of the French court."

"Don't you see, Braddon?" Madeleine looked up at him, brown eyes shining with tears. "My father is the marquis who was so strange that he learned how to shoe horses. When Papa brought me to England, he opened a horse stable. That's why he suggested that I pretend to be the daughter of the Marquis de Flammarion. I thought it strange that he agreed to a scheme of this sort so quickly."

"You mean, you really *are* that woman's daughter?"

Madeleine looked at her beloved. His blue eyes were still confused. "My papa is the Marquis de Flammarion," she explained patiently. "When my mother was condemned, he must have taken me and fled to England. When he arrived, he opened a stable."

Braddon gaped. "You *are* a French aristo!"

Madeleine nodded. Tears were still rolling down her cheeks.

"But my mama, Braddon!"

He rubbed her hair awkwardly. "You knew she was dead, Maddie."

"Yes, but in such a way, the guillotine . . ."

"I'll tell you what, Maddie, that old woman is right. Your mother would be proud of you now. You learned all the things that she would have liked to have taught you, and you've turned into the most beautiful, most proper lady I've ever seen."

Madeleine buried her face in Braddon's shoulder. "Oh, Braddon," she said, half muffled. "I love you."

"You do? You do? Do you, Maddie? Really?"

At that Madeleine laughed, a watery little laugh. "I do."

"Oh, Maddie."

And, when he raised his head again: "Marry me, Maddie, please."

"I already said I would," she whispered, with just a trace of her normal impish humor.

"No, I mean marry me now. Let's get married tomorrow."

"Do you mean elope?"

"For you, I will even climb a ladder," Braddon said seriously.

Maddie's endearing laugh erupted. "I sleep on the ground floor, Braddon." Then she grew more serious. "No, I can't elope. My father wouldn't like it. But perhaps we could marry quite soon."

"Tomorrow."

"Not tomorrow."

"Day after."

"No!"

"Next week?"

Braddon's kisses were so sweet. Maddie's heart flip-flopped madly in her chest. "Next week," she conceded.

Chapter 25

The following morning Sophie walked into her sitting room with a renewed sense of energy. To this date, Sophie had simply inhabited the room; now she planned to make it her own. True, the room had been wallpapered by its last occupant in a dizzying series of trellises crammed with roses so fat that they looked like pink clouds, but that she didn't mind. Although she did object to the figurehead of a naked woman that incongruously decorated one wall.

The first thing Sophie did was ring the bell for a footman. Then she began pulling books from the low shelf under the window. The books had spilled out of Patrick's library downstairs. She pulled them out at random, created spiraling stacks on the polished wood floor. They were an odd mixture. Sophie dumped *The Care and History of Husbandry* on top of *God's Exhortation Against Witchcraft,* followed by a series of dusty bound pamphlets explicating the miracle of the steam engine.

As the door opened, Sophie said "Good morning," briskly, but didn't turn around. "I'd like all these books taken up to the attic, please, as well as that . . . that woman." She waved at the figurehead gracing the south wall.

"Sophie! You should be more careful." Patrick loomed behind her, frowning. "You are not lifting heavy books, are you?"

Sophie dusted her hands on her dress, not even thinking of Simone's reaction to the brown streaks she left on her lemon-yellow morning gown. She looked up at her husband, trying to keep all traces of sarcasm from her voice. After all, she might have been hoisting boxes of books in the last month, without his knowledge.

Then she pointed at the slim volumes strewn about the floor. "These are not very heavy; in fact, most of them seem to be pamphlets."

"Why did you want my figurehead in the attic? She's supposed to be Galatea, the sea nymph."

"I don't want a half-naked woman jumping out of the wall of my sitting room."

"She's not half naked," Patrick said, strolling over to look at Galatea more closely. "Look: she has a bit of drapery on her left breast. Quite tasteful, really."

Sophie dumped two more dusty pamphlets on the stack at her feet without replying.

"All right," he said. "I'll have it removed to the attic." There was a pause. "Alex pointed out that I have been remiss in allowing you to go about without escort," Patrick said stiffly. "From now on, I would like you to inform me when you wish to use the carriage, and I will accompany you."

Sophie's mouth tightened. There was the explanation for her husband's unexpected appearance: Alex!

"I have decided to begin my confinement," she replied, "so I doubt I will have to bother you overmuch." In fact, she decided at that moment never to leave the house again.

Patrick stared down at his wife's small figure in despair. He couldn't think of anything to say to her. Talk, Alex had instructed. Talk about what? Sophie had just stiffened up, all over her body, so already he'd said something wrong.

He hesitated, then bowed and turned, pulling open the door just as a footman raised his hand to knock on the panel. Patrick stood aside, then looked back for an instant.

"Sophie, would you like this wallpaper changed?" To him the roses looked like rosy mushrooms.

Sophie looked up, a ghost of a smile on her lips. "No, I rather like it. It's very cheerful. I do intend to buy some new furniture for this room, however. Unless you have an objection."

"Shall we go shopping this afternoon?"

"Perhaps later in the week."

But Patrick wanted to do something for her now. "Are you sure you wouldn't like to take a carriage ride in the park?"

"Quite sure, thank you."

"Would you like me to send a message to Charlotte or your mother and ask them to visit you?"

"No, thank you, Patrick." She was clearly waiting for him to leave.

So he did. What else could he do? He went downstairs and wondered about what made pregnant women happy. He sent a footman up to remove Galatea to her new home in the attic. Then he sent another footman out to buy three huge bouquets of roses, "the fat, floppy kind." If roses made her cheerful, why not fill the house with them?

Sophie finally arranged all the bookshelves to her liking. Given the chance, she preferred strict organization. So her Dutch grammar was followed, in alphabetical order, by

French, German, Italian, Portuguese, and Welsh books. Between Portuguese and Welsh she left a little space. *That's for Turkish,* Sophie promised herself. *As soon as I get a chance, I shall buy another Turkish grammar.*

At lunch Patrick again asked Sophie if she would like him to accompany her anywhere in the afternoon, and again she refused. She was feeling tired, with a dragging ache in her back.

"I met Monsieur Foucault and his companion, Bayrak Mustafa, when they brought the inkwell to the house," Sophie said abruptly, breaking the strained silence that ruled over luncheon. "I cannot like him, Patrick."

Patrick looked up, surprised, from the peach he was delicately peeling. He had been lost in a daydream in which Sophie smiled at him the way she used to do.

"Monsieur Foucault? No, he isn't a terribly likable sort," he agreed.

"It isn't a question of likableness," Sophie said. She really was tired to death. "I understand some Turkish, and his companion was not speaking properly. Monsieur Foucault spoke Turkish, but twice Mr. Mustafa responded in gibberish."

"Gibberish?" All the uneasy feelings Patrick had had about Monsieur Foucault on their first meeting returned in force—so much so that he didn't mark the fact that Sophie's comment revealed a knowledge of Turkish. "I knew there was something odd about that fellow," Patrick said. "Damme, but I should have been in touch with Lord Breksby from the start!"

Sophie wasn't certain what he was referring to, but she was too tired to care. After lunch, she slowly plodded upstairs, not realizing that Patrick was standing at the bottom of the stairs, looking after her with a worried expression.

She took a nap, but by dinner she felt even more sluggish. Finally, she decided to have a tray in her room. It was exhausting enough just being out of bed, without facing

Patrick as well. Patrick ate alone (pheasant again—he must have a word with Floret), wondering whether Sophie was avoiding him or truly not feeling well.

All evening he fought the impulse to go upstairs and see how she was. When he finally gave in, she was lying in bed fast asleep. Patrick looked at her for a moment. Sophie looked exhausted, her face papery white with dark circles beneath her eyes.

Patrick gently laid a hand on her stomach as it rose into the air. Sophie didn't stir.

"Hello," he whispered. Then he snatched his hand away, feeling more embarrassed than he had in years. He left the house, his feet leading him on the now-familiar streets nearby.

The next morning Sophie didn't feel any better. In fact, the sluggish feeling had spread throughout her body. She managed to get out of bed, but only as far as a chair. Perhaps she would feel like this for the next two months. The very idea gave her a headache.

Slowly, slowly, a niggling worry was growing in her mind. She felt lethargic, hot, and headachy. But why was the baby so listless? Anxiously she clutched her stomach but she couldn't feel any fluttering movements.

A minute later Sophie snapped out of her hazy languor and yanked on the bell cord. When Simone appeared, she said, "Send a message to Dr. Lambeth, please. I need to see him immediately. The messenger can wait and bring him back in our carriage."

Simone curtsied. Sophie heard her running down the corridor toward the stairs. Then she sat, hand on her stomach, willing a movement, a ripple, something... There was nothing. Her stomach arched before her, heavy, inert. *The baby is sleeping,* Sophie told herself. *I am becoming ill, and so he feels tired.*

When Dr. Lambeth entered her room, half an hour later, she looked up at him with terrified eyes.

"I apologize for insisting that you come immediately, Doctor."

"Nonsense," Lambeth snapped, walking over to her chair. He reached down and spread his wide, clean hands on her stomach. After a second he straightened.

"I have to ask you to unbutton your nightdress, Your Grace," he said gently.

Simone was hovering behind the doctor, and as he discreetly walked to the window and looked out, Simone helped Sophie unbutton her nightdress and pull it forward so that her stomach was free.

Sophie watched the rusty red hair on the doctor's head as he bent over her body.

As the hands kept moving and pressing, and the doctor said nothing, a heavy truth settled in Sophie's heart.

"Why don't you get dressed, Your Grace?" In Lambeth's experience, people were a good deal calmer when they were fully clothed.

Sophie looked at the doctor mutely, then nodded to Simone. Dr. Lambeth retired and stood in the hallway. He stared at the wall. Remembering the stern face of Foakes's lawyer as he questioned his medical record, Dr. Lambeth had no doubt but that the husband would make a good deal of fuss about his child's death. He sighed. Sometimes he wondered why he spent so much time with aristocratic patients. Money, he reminded himself.

Simone opened the door and summoned him back into the master bedroom. Sophie was seated on the chair again. When Dr. Lambeth met his patient's eyes, he saw no fear. Terror had been replaced by despair.

"I am indeed sorry," he said gently. "I think it is likely that your babe has not survived, for some reason. All we can say in these cases is that it is the will of God."

"He's dead," she said dully.

"We'll have to see," Dr. Lambeth replied. "I dislike

making absolute statements but I cannot find any indication of life. Sometimes children do not live through the gestation period . . . no one can say why. Do you feel any pain here?" He delicately touched Sophie's stomach.

"No."

"If the baby has ceased to live, your labor will likely begin today or tomorrow."

"Labor."

"The baby will have to be delivered, Your Grace."

Sophie couldn't find any words to say.

"Would you like me to inform your husband?"

Sophie just looked at him and shook her head.

Dr. Lambeth persisted. "I'll ring the bell and see if the duke is in the house, shall I?"

"No!" Sophie's face was dead white. "I need to think. I . . ."

"Are you sure that you wouldn't like me to inform your husband?" Dr. Lambeth started to turn toward Simone.

"No," Sophie said drearily. "I'll tell him myself, later. Please, Dr. Lambeth."

The doctor nodded and turned to Simone, giving her a muttered series of instructions. Then he turned back to Sophie.

"I have told your maid what symptoms to expect," he said, picking up her wrist and taking her pulse. "Please, send a messenger as soon as there is any sign of labor or birth. I suggest that you retire to bed. I will attend you first thing in the morning."

Birth seemed an odd word to Sophie. Birth was for babies who were living.

"I can't do that," Sophie replied. Go to bed and *wait*? A horrible notion. Innate politeness and her mother's training got her out of the chair.

"Tomorrow, you said?" she asked, quite as if she were talking about a garden party.

Dr. Lambeth nodded, his eyes shrewdly assessing Sophie's near-sleepwalking state. In shock, he thought. Well, probably just as well.

"Keep her warm," he said, turning to Simone.

The maid nodded, her eyes full of tears.

Dr. Lambeth bowed politely. "I shall visit you tomorrow, if I may, Your Grace."

"I shall walk with you downstairs," Sophie replied.

Dr. Lambeth said nothing. It certainly wasn't normal for his aristocratic patients to accompany him to the door. He doubted very much that this patient was thinking clearly.

He tried once more. "Madame, are you quite certain that you don't wish me to speak to your husband?"

"Quite certain, thank you," she replied with dull civility.

They walked down the wide steps of the great marble stairs side by side, Dr. Lambeth an odd, dignified figure with his red hair and tired eyes, and Sophie looking blazingly beautiful. Her face was no longer stark white; her cheeks had taken on flaming circles of red that would have given Dr. Lambeth pause, had he registered them.

But his mind was already racing ahead to the rest of his day. He'd better go see the viscountess next—a mother of four whom he rather thought would give birth today. The birth was going to be easy, as she'd had no problems with the last four girls, but if the babe was another female, he was likely to have a hysterical mother on his hands, not to mention the viscount himself. The viscount had not taken the arrival of his fourth daughter well. If there was a fifth . . .

So Dr. Lambeth nimbly bowed again in the foyer and took his leave, promising again to visit in the morning. He hopped into his carriage and directed his driver to the viscount's residence, thinking intently of soothing phrases.

Chapter 26

❦

Sophie showed the doctor out, quite as if she weren't shaking inside. As she walked up the stairs, Patrick stepped out of the library.

"Weren't you planning to tell me what the doctor said?"

"Yes, later."

"No." Patrick's denial came through clenched teeth. "Join me, please. I should like to know why you summoned the doctor to the house."

Sophie took a quick look about. No footmen happened to be assigned to the hallway at that moment.

"I don't think I shall, at the moment. I am going to my room."

"Sophie!"

They probably heard that bellow all the way to the servants' quarters, Sophie thought. She walked back down the stairs to within three steps of the bottom and paused.

"He said . . . he said . . ." She could not say what he had said. "He said that he will return tomorrow morning." That was half the truth, less than half. Sophie's heart twisted in unbearable anguish. Oh God, she had to get upstairs, away from Patrick's hard, questioning face. Her head was throbbing in heavy, unending waves of pain.

"You didn't want the baby," she heard herself say, hearing her own words dully, as if from under water.

The savage look on Patrick's face made her grasp the railing in alarm. What *was* happening to her head? Patrick was speaking, but she didn't hear. Her heart was thudding, heavier than her head, two claustrophobic rhythms going on at once. Sophie clutched the railing tightly, the sensation of clenched fingers pulling her out of the maelstrom of pain for a moment.

Patrick was shouting at her. And behind him, down the hallway, Clemens paused, his face startled and horrified. Sophie forced her mind to clear, to concentrate on what Patrick was saying to her. She looked down at him. His black eyes were flashing at her . . . with disgust, probably, she thought dully.

"What in bloody hell are you saying?" Patrick's voice was thick with rage. "How can you say such a thing to me? I *do* want the child!"

Sophie gave him a little smile. Quite suddenly she felt as if her head were about to float off her shoulders. At least the terrible throbbing was lessening. "I know you don't want children," she said to him, almost chidingly, as if *he* were a child.

"Oh God, Sophie, what are you talking about?"

"You were glad you married me, don't you remember? Because I'm probably just like my mother, and so you won't have to deal with brats underfoot. But I'm not like my mother—" The thought made her head even more unsteady.

Patrick finally realized that Clemens was in the hallway and dealt the butler a glare that sent him whisking back through the door to the servants' quarters. He tried to calm the surges of rage pressuring his chest. Sophie didn't know what she was saying. She was pregnant. Pregnant women were always irrational.

"What are you talking about?" He spaced his words very carefully, as if he were speaking to a child.

Sophie looked at him in surprise. How she wished that this silly conversation were over so that she could lie down and be still. "You told Braddon," she reminded him. "You told Braddon, and I heard you, that you were just as glad to be marrying me if you had to be leg-shackled, because likely I would be as incapable as my mother, and then you wouldn't have a lot of brats underfoot."

There was a moment of pounding silence.

"May I go to bed now?" Sophie began to back up the stairs. Now she felt certain that her head was floating above her, and her heart was beating so fast that she felt dizzy. She cautiously felt backward for the next stair, holding tightly to the railing. She was afraid to turn about and walk away while Patrick's face was so black with rage. She shivered.

When Patrick spoke, his voice was grating, splintered. "I didn't mean it, Sophie."

Sophie just looked at him. His voice had started to have that otherworldly quality again, as if she were hearing through piles of cotton batting.

She nodded helpfully. "I'm sure you're right," she murmured.

Patrick looked at his wife hopelessly. She was backing away from him, a smile fixed on her lips. A pit of black, bottomless despair opened at his feet. Sophie believed the horrible words she had heard him say. No wonder she'd never fallen in love with him. No wonder she was looking at him as if he were the devil incarnate.

"Sophie!" He bellowed it, with all the force of pent-up frustration and raw pain swelling his heart. "Oh God, Sophie, I want the baby!"

But Sophie didn't grasp his statement. She heard his rough voice as another bellow of rage, and it was one too many; she gasped almost thankfully as a sweet darkness flowed through her head, numbing the painful beat of blood in her ears, relaxing her clenched, throbbing fingers.

As Patrick leaped toward her in horror, Sophie swayed slightly and plummeted forward. It all seemed to happen so slowly. Her body fell forward like a rag doll, knees striking the next-to-bottom step, pregnant stomach slamming against the marble floor. The only thing Patrick caught as he desperately threw himself toward her was her head. With both his hands outstretched, he managed to stop Sophie's head from striking the marble.

Carefully, carefully he turned her over and drew her into his arms. His wife's face was dead white except for high-arching circles of red. Oh my God, that was no rouge. Her face was burning with fever, her body totally inert. The only thing Patrick could hear was blood pounding in his ears, a horrible rhythm that sorted itself into "please, please, please, please, please."

Help. He needed help. Sophie's eyes were closed, the eyelids pure blue.

"Clemens!"

Clemens appeared in fifteen seconds, a sure sign that he had retreated no farther than the opposite side of the servants' door.

"Summon the doctor," Patrick snapped.

Clemens looked stupefied, staring at the duchess lying on the floor. Then he looked up at his master and the expression of horror in his eyes turned to one of reproach.

"Dr. Lambeth, man! Now." The blame in his butler's eyes only confirmed the blame in Patrick's heart. He turned back to Sophie, gently kissing her eyelids. She didn't move.

Swiftly he felt his wife's limbs to see if anything was

broken, but they seemed intact. He whispered, "Sophie, I'm going to carry you upstairs now." No response.

He gathered her up in his arms. Sophie's head fell back against his left arm. Between the rise of her shoulders and the rise of her knees, where he held her, her stomach rose even higher.

Patrick swallowed hard. Oh God, if anything had happened to the babe. The drumbeat in his ears increased: *please, please, please, please.*

When Sophie's maid arrived, running, Patrick had already stripped off Sophie's morning gown and was pulling a nightdress over her head. Simone helped him silently, for which he was grateful. When Sophie was arranged in bed, the sheets drawn up to her neck, Patrick looked at Simone helplessly.

"What do we do now?"

"She hasn't moved or spoken?"

Patrick just stared at her.

"She hasn't woken up since falling down the stairs?"

"No." His voice was husky with dread.

"We need to cool her down," Simone said practically. "She's burning up with fever, poor lamb."

Patrick stepped outside the room and snapped at the footman hovering at the end of the hallway. Then he watched as Simone tenderly bathed Sophie's face. Sophie twisted and moaned, trying to get away from the icy cloth. Finally he couldn't bear to stand there helplessly, and took the cloth from Simone's hands, pushing her away. He sat on the side of the bed.

"Wake up, Sophie," he commanded softly, rubbing the cloth over his wife's forehead. After a few minutes she opened her eyes.

"It hurts." She fixed her eyes on his.

"Sophie, I'm sorry, I didn't mean to shout. . . ." He was almost babbling with relief.

Sophie frowned at him. "It hurts," she repeated.

Patrick cupped her little face in his hands, giving her a quick kiss on her forehead. She was alarmingly hot under his lips.

"You have a fever, love. Fevers always hurt. Don't worry. Dr. Lambeth will be here soon."

"No! No, don't let him come! He'll make it happen."

"Nothing is going to happen, darling." Patrick began to rub the cloth over her face again. "I won't let anything happen."

"I don't think you can stop it," Sophie whispered. Her eyes were a dark midnight blue, still fastened on his. "You'll hate me now." Tears welled up in her beautiful eyes and spilled over.

Patrick's heart jolted. She must be delirious, he thought as he bent over, kissing away the tears.

"Nothing could make me hate you, Sophie. Don't you know that? Don't you know how much I love you?"

But Sophie's eyes had shifted away from his face. "It hurts!" she cried suddenly.

It was only when Simone handed him another cloth that Patrick realized that the one he was rubbing over her neck and face was now hot.

And so it continued. Occasionally Sophie opened her eyes and said incomprehensible things about how much he hated her, and meanwhile Patrick kept washing her face until the little rivulets of water trickling off her face had soaked through the sheets beneath her. He didn't know what else to do, and he had to do something besides sending out more and more footmen with infuriated messages for Dr. Lambeth.

When the door finally opened, Patrick leveled a glare on the good doctor that would have shaken a less toughened practitioner. But Dr. Lambeth had dealt with many an angry relative, most recently a viscount who had just welcomed his fifth daughter into the world, and he judged husbands to be on the lesser side of rationality at the best of times. He bustled in importantly, standing at the head of the bed with two fingers delicately poised on Sophie's forehead.

"A fever," he said meditatively. Then he turned to Patrick. "Has it started yet?"

"What started yet?"

"The miscarriage, of course!" the doctor snapped. Really, he had no time for this sort of nonsense.

"Miscarriage . . . You're quite sure that she will lose the baby?" Patrick's heart felt as if someone had thrust a dagger into it.

"Yes." The doctor didn't bother to say anything further, and when Patrick opened his mouth to ask a question he just raised a finger condescendingly. Patrick realized that he was holding Sophie's limp wrist and counting her pulse. Finally the doctor raised Sophie's head and poured a hefty dose of laudanum down her throat.

Then he shot Patrick a glance. "I must request that you leave the room now, Your Grace."

Patrick just looked back at him. Privately, Lambeth thought that although most husbands acted like the very devil when this sort of thing happened—an unfortunate business, losing the heir—this husband really looked like the devil. And he didn't like the story of the young duchess falling down the stairs. Not that it would have made any difference.

When Patrick stood up, towering over him, his black eyes burning furiously into his, Lambeth thought again, Foakes looks like the devil *and* acts like him too.

Patrick's voice was measured but the fury about to erupt in it was clear.

"I will stay here." He backed up one step.

The doctor shrugged. Briskly he pulled down Sophie's sheets and hauled up her nightdress, ignoring the barely suppressed movement of the husband. What did he think doctors did when they examined their female patients? Looked at them from across the room? He did a brief examination. Good: It looked as if her waters had already broken. Shouldn't be long now.

He turned around, girding himself to deal with the husband, whose face had gone dead white, Lambeth noted dispassionately. Really, men didn't belong in a birthing room. And he couldn't think why this one was refusing to leave. The man looked as if he might faint, although there was only a small show of blood. Lambeth turned about and pulled up his patient's sheet.

"I must insist that you leave," Dr. Lambeth said as firmly as he could, instilling his voice with every drop of authority he had in his body.

Patrick shifted burning eyes to the doctor's face.

"Why?"

"Your presence makes me uneasy," Lambeth said bluntly. "I need all my wits about me to deliver a stillborn child when his mother is in a raging fever and half unconscious. I can't have you standing about and almost giving me a facer every time I conduct a routine examination."

Patrick met the doctor's unsympathetic eyes. "Couldn't the babe live? It's . . . he's seven months old."

"No." The doctor's tone was final. "The child is not alive."

"I won't do anything. I will remain here." Patrick pointed to the wall.

"No."

Patrick looked at him and knew that he couldn't intimidate Lambeth. The doctor had far too much sense of his own consequence.

"Is my wife in any danger?"

"I doubt it," Lambeth said calmly, not even looking back at his patient, who was sleeping restlessly. "It's probably better that Her Grace does not fully experience the birth. Not that it will be very painful, given that the child is not yet full-grown."

Patrick swallowed, hard. He started to walk to the door. He stopped, wheeled about.

"I want to see the baby. When it's born." His voice grated, hardly disguising the blunt agony raging in his heart.

Oh for God's sake, Lambeth thought to himself.

"I can inform you whether you would have had an heir," he said, his voice rigidly disapproving.

Patrick's eyes blazed from a bone-white face. "What the devil does the sex matter? I want to see the baby, Doctor. In case Sophie doesn't wake up in time, she would want to know what her baby looked like."

Dr. Lambeth allowed his patient's husband a small smile. Now that was the kind of response he was pleased to hear.

"I shall call you at the appropriate moment, Your Grace," he said primly, ushering Patrick to the door. "I would prefer that you went downstairs, perhaps to your library, and I shall ring the bell when I wish to have you summoned."

Patrick numbly allowed himself to be pushed out into the hallway. He walked down the stairs like a ghost, his hand trailing over the places where Sophie's hand had been, a short two hours ago. He walked down the stairs and stood at the bottom as if he'd been turned to salt, moving to the side only when a nurse gowned in white was ushered in the front door and started up the stairs accompanied by Clemens.

If only he hadn't shouted at her. If only he had realized that she had a fever and wasn't feeling well. Why, why did he shout at her and make her fall down the stairs? Not knowing what to do, Patrick walked into the library and poured himself a brandy, but set it down, untouched, twenty minutes later.

For an hour, two hours, he walked up and down the same strip of rug, beginning just in front of the oak bookcases and walking precisely to his father's book stand, then wheeling about and walking back. And the only things he could think of came from that burning hole in his heart, the same questions rising again and again. Why didn't he control his temper? Why didn't he realize his wife had a fever? He *knew* she never wore rouge!

By the time there was a quiet knock on the door, Patrick felt twenty years older, drained of life, awash in a sea of self-hatred. The nurse stood on the threshold, looking at him with some trepidation. She'd had a tea break about an hour ago and heard all about the duke terrifying his wife into falling down the stairs. He didn't sound like the sort of man one would want to cross.

"Your Grace—" She stopped. She'd never had a father want to see a *dead* baby before. She'd brought fathers their sons and announced them as "heirs"; she'd brought fathers their daughters and announced them as "wee beautiful creatures." But her experience failed her this time. "It's a girl," she finally said.

Patrick moved over to her silently and took the tiny bundle from her arm. The nurse's mouth dropped open.

"Go," he said brusquely.

Nurse Mathers fled, clattering her way back up the stairs to tell the doctor that he'd better be the one to take that poor dead child from the father, because she didn't want anything else to do with a man as devilish looking as that. Those eyebrows! She shivered deliciously, thinking of how she would describe him to her mother.

Alone in the study, Patrick sat on his favorite armchair. They'd wrapped a sheet over her face. He pulled the cloth away from his daughter's little face and tucked it around her neck. Then for a second he just leaned back, holding a scrap of humanity, so light that it felt as if she might float off his arm. She was so pale, her skin as white as first snowfall.

Finally he got up and climbed the stairs, slowly, as if he had ninety years rather than thirty.

When Sophie really woke up, woke up clearly, four days later, she knew instantly what had happened. A fountain of dread poured out from her heart, and her hand fluttered willy-nilly to her midriff . . . but it no longer held her baby. It was gone, gone as if the baby had never rested there, kicking and floating in its little house.

She didn't say anything, but the quality of the silence in the room had changed. Patrick was sitting in a chair next to her bed, and he saw her looking at the wall before her with an awful knowledge in her eyes. The moment he had dreaded for days had arrived. She seemed not to have seen him and was just staring ahead as tears slowly slipped over her cheeks.

Patrick lurched forward, out of his chair, and half fell to his knees on the wide step leading to the bed. He reached out and pulled Sophie's small, fragile hands into his large brown ones, burying his face in them.

Sophie looked at him silently. Her tears felt oddly cool, sliding down her cheeks one after another.

"I'm sorry, Sophie." The words wrenched from the deepest wells of Patrick's soul. "I know I can never make it up to you, but oh God, I'm so sorry!"

Sophie frowned. "Did you want the babe, then?"

He raised his head and she realized with shock that his cheeks were wet with tears. "I wanted the babe. I don't know why I said such a cruel thing to Braddon. I lied. I used to think all the time about the baby."

Sophie swallowed. "I'm sorry, Patrick. I don't know what I did wrong."

Patrick's voice emerged half strangled, rough. "What are you talking about?"

"The baby, the baby. I don't know what I did wrong. I don't know what I did to make my baby die." Sophie's hands had twisted out of Patrick's grip and were restlessly clutching and reclutching her sheet. Miserably she met Patrick's eyes.

The pure shock she saw there startled her. "How could you do anything?" He whispered it. "*I* frightened you. *I* made you fall down the stairs."

Sophie shook her head. She had only a jangled, jumbled

memory of the past few days, and nothing to do with stairs. "Stairs?"

"You fell down the stairs," Patrick said slowly. "You fell down the stairs, and then you miscarried, Sophie." He repeated, "I'm so sorry."

"No." Sophie was shaking her head. "I don't know about the stairs, but the baby stopped living, that was what Dr. Lambeth said. I felt so ill that I couldn't think clearly." She paused and drew a long, shuddering voice. "But I knew before the doctor told me, because he stopped moving—"

"She," Patrick automatically amended.

"She?"

"We had a little girl, Sophie, a lovely little girl. Do you mean that the fall didn't cause the baby to be born early, Sophie?" His voice was so hoarse that it was almost a gasp.

She nodded, then murmured something.

Patrick dropped his head on the cover as harsh, wrenching sobs forced their way up his chest. He felt two slim arms curve around his shoulders.

"Ah, love, don't, don't! It wasn't either of our faults," Sophie whispered with new wisdom in her heart. "She just wasn't ready for this world yet, that's all."

Patrick stayed still, savoring the sweetness of having Sophie's arms around him again. The sense of sharp joy in his heart mingled with grief—but it was a healthy grief, a looking-forward grief.

"Lie back." Gently he pushed her back against the pillows.

"Did you see her?" Sophie's voice was so small it floated on the air.

"She was a beautiful baby, Sophie. She looked just like you." Tenderly he wiped away her tears. "I told her how much you loved her."

Tears poured down Sophie's cheeks. Patrick sat on the edge of the bed and ran his hand along Sophie's hair.

"She looked cold in the sheet they put her in. So I

brought her up here and I wrapped her in one of my winter cravats, a cashmere one." He looked down at his wife, who was still crying.

Sophie lifted a trembling hand and tugged at Patrick's shoulder until he carefully bent forward, swinging up his legs so that he was lying by her side. With a sigh she buried her face against his shoulder.

"Where is she?"

"She's buried in the family plot," Patrick said quietly. "I didn't want to leave you, so Alex and Charlotte took her to Downes. She's next to my mother . . . my mother loved babies." He rubbed his cheek against his wife's soft hair.

Sophie buried her face deeper in his shoulder. When she finally spoke, it was so softly that he could barely hear her voice.

"Did you give her a name?"

Patrick shook his head, then realized that she couldn't see him. "I thought we could do that together."

He didn't want to explain that priests couldn't baptize children who had died before being born. Or that their family priest wasn't the family priest anymore because he had refused to bury their child in consecrated ground. Alex had dismissed him on the spot and ridden all the way back up to London to fetch David Marlowe.

"Alex sent a letter, and there's also a letter from Charlotte to you. They're coming to London tomorrow. David said a service for the baby—you remember David, don't you?"

Sophie nodded. Of course she remembered David, the sweet, brown-eyed curate who been friends with Braddon and Patrick since their school days.

Then Sophie started crying so hard that her whole body shook, and Patrick couldn't do anything other than hold her and murmur tender, loving words.

Chapter 27

For the next few days Sophie lay in bed, listlessly eating a bite or two of Floret's lovingly prepared invalid food. Patrick sat with her for long hours, reading aloud her favorite novels, the gossip sheets from *The Morning Post,* and the international news from *The Times.* Sophie didn't really listen. She would follow a story for a few minutes, then her mind would drift back to the present. Sometimes tears would start silently running down her face, and Patrick would put down his book and wipe her cheeks and pull her against his shoulder, and sometimes she just stared at the wall, feeling a roaring emptiness descend on her mind.

Her mother visited every day, making bracing pronouncements about future pregnancies. Once, her father tiptoed in and stood silently by her bed.

"I wish we'd had another child," he finally said. "Then you might have a sister to help you through this."

Sophie just looked at him, her eyes bone dry. "It wouldn't matter, Papa."

"We made a lot of mistakes, your mama and I. I was a fool." Sophie just looked at him. Perhaps her father was finally giving up all those other women? But after wishing for it her whole life, she found she didn't care at all.

"That's nice, Papa," she whispered.

George hesitated, his eyes strained. Then he left the room.

Finally, after several weeks of lying in bed, she stopped bleeding and Dr. Lambeth pronounced her well enough to get up. Sophie wearily got up and sat in the steaming bath Simone had prepared. She couldn't look at her body now without hating it for its failures, for its inability to provide a good home for her daughter.

So she sat in the rapidly cooling water, rigidly staring at the wall until finally Simone took the soap from her mistress's limp hand and rubbed a washcloth over her body.

Patrick walked in just as Simone was drawing Sophie to her feet and bundling her in a warm towel. Sophie moved like a sleepwalker, not even registering that her husband had entered the room.

With a nod he dismissed Simone and drew his wife over to the velvet stool before the fireplace. He helped her sit, then started toweling her long, wet hair. It was beginning to worry him, this listlessness. Dr. Lambeth said it was natural. But what did the doctor know? It wasn't natural for his vital, laughing Sophie. A shadow of fear touched Patrick's heart every time he saw her still face and shadowed eyes.

But he spoke of this and that until Sophie's quiet voice cut through his talk.

"I want to go to Charlotte's house . . . to see the grave."

Patrick paused, then rubbed her hair even harder.

"We'll leave for Downes tomorrow morning," he promised.

"I want to go now," Sophie replied. "And I want to go by myself." There was something implacable in her voice.

Patrick's heart lurched and he dropped the towel, coming around in front of Sophie and dropping to his knees before her as she sat on the low stool.

"Don't shut me out, Sophie," he whispered. "Don't." The grinding tightness in the back of his throat made it impossible to say anything more.

Sophie looked at him calmly. The bouts of tears had receded in the last two days. She felt as if she were looking at the world through a thick, cottony pile of clouds.

"Of course I'm not shutting you out, Patrick," she replied. "I simply would like to visit the grave for the first time by myself."

Patrick stared at her, his eyes black holes in his exhausted face. "Why?"

"I'm her mother." Then she amended her statement: "I was her mother."

"I'm her father," Patrick replied.

"I carried her in my body for months," Sophie cried, "and I have to say I'm sorry."

"For what?"

"I . . ." She began to tremble. "It was *my* body, don't you understand?"

"No," Patrick said definitively. "What are you talking about?"

Now the tears returned to Sophie's eyes. He was cracking her hard-won control by making her talk about it. "I failed her . . . I failed her."

"You didn't fail her." Patrick's voice was tender, consoling, as he drew his hand lovingly over the curve of Sophie's cheek.

Sophie looked away. "I want to go by myself," she said stubbornly. "I need to—"

"You *didn't fail her*!" Patrick reached out, giving Sophie's shoulders a little shake. "She wasn't ready to live yet, remember, Sophie? *You* said that to me. It wasn't your body. She was too fragile."

Patrick drew Sophie into his arms, carrying her to the armchair. He sat down, snuggling her as if she were a child who had fallen and scraped her knee.

"It was because she knew I didn't want her," Sophie said, her voice breaking.

"How can you even say that? You wanted her so much that you wouldn't let me touch you for months!"

There was a moment of silence in the room. "I was afraid," Sophie said finally. "I was afraid that I would lose the baby."

"Then how can you say that you didn't want her?"

"You were with your mistress and you weren't coming to my room. I knew we would never have another baby. I wanted this baby so much, but still, sometimes, I thought that if I hadn't gotten pregnant you would have still come to my bedroom—" A burning wave of sobs clawed its way up her throat. "I shouldn't have thought that," she said brokenly. "I should have just accepted it and been thankful for the baby."

Patrick sat, stunned, clutching his wife in his arms. "I was not with another woman, Sophie."

"I could tell," Sophie said, not even listening to his response, "that you were bored by making love to me."

"I *wasn't*— Why wouldn't we have another baby?" Patrick's strained voice punctuated Sophie's sobs as she fought to control herself. She had lost all wish to hide anything.

"Because," she said with devastating honesty, "you are tired of being married, and so we won't have any more children since you don't care whether you have an heir. When I got pregnant, part of me resented the child because it meant the end. . . ." Her voice trailed off exhaustedly.

"Sophie." Patrick's voice was rough, strangled. "What

are you saying? Don't you know that I lay in my room, night after night, in agony because I couldn't come to you? You're not making sense! If I was going mad wanting to make love to you while you were carrying a child, what on earth would make me stop longing for you after the child was born?"

Sophie blinked. It had all made perfect sense, before. "But . . . but in the last month you weren't home five nights out of seven." She gulped, remembering all the tears she had shed at home alone. "I know about your mistress," Sophie said painfully. "The black-haired woman.

"I'm not blaming you," she added hastily. "I knew what it would be like when I married you. I just didn't understand how much it would hurt."

Patrick's arms tightened so roughly that she gasped and was silent. "That's not true," he said fiercely, tipping up her chin and looking into her eyes. "As God is my witness, I haven't wanted to be with another woman since I kissed you at the Cumberland ball." Sophie stared at him, stunned. "I haven't slept with any woman other than you since that night. There is no black-haired woman in my life. I haven't even *looked* at another woman, for Christ's sake! All I've thought about is you, and your body. Oh, Sophie, you've ruined me for a rake's life, don't you see that?"

Sophie didn't say a word. She was too emotionally exhausted to take in the enormity of what he was saying. But she grabbed at one strand.

"Does this mean that you'll still, that you still want to—"

"God yes!" Patrick's voice was harsh with suppressed emotion. His grasp tightened convulsively.

Sophie didn't say anything. She just put her head against his shoulder. She was still confused, but one idea was clear in her mind: Patrick still desired her. That was what he had just said. And that meant that when her body was completely mended he would come to her bed again and they could make love and perhaps, perhaps have another baby. Her body involuntarily relaxed, melting against his body as nerves and muscles which had been strung as tightly as violin strings began to ease.

"You really mean it?" Her voice was muffled against Patrick's shirt. "You really want to make love to me? You're not bored?"

"Bored! In God's name, Sophie, where did you get that idea?"

"I thought you had a mistress. You stayed out night after night, Patrick." His eyes dropped before her clear gaze.

"I was torturing myself," he admitted shortly. Patrick couldn't bring himself to raise the issue of Sophie's Thursday jaunts. Even as his stomach twisted with jealousy, he fought the idea of hearing her talk about her feelings for Braddon. He couldn't bear it, and he was almost certain that she had never betrayed him sexually. What was the point of making his wife admit she cared for another man? Sophie was honorable, and she hadn't betrayed him—so what right had he to demand her love as well? Especially given the way he'd seduced her into marriage.

Sophie was still waiting for a longer answer. "Why would you torture yourself? I was here—" Her gaze dropped to her hands. "I was waiting for you," she finally whispered.

Patrick felt as if he were strangling. What was he to say? *I didn't want to see you, to eat supper with you, to speak to you—because I know you don't love me?* His wife would laugh out loud.

"I don't know what I was doing," he finally admitted, his voice a bleak thread of sound. "But I wasn't sleeping with other women, Sophie, I swear it. Mostly I walked the streets; sometimes I went to my offices in the warehouse."

Sophie's ear caught the unmistakable sincerity in her husband's tone.

"I'm . . . I'm very glad," she whispered. "Even if— I know it won't be like this forever, but—"

"God *damn* it, Sophie!" Patrick's voice was harsh. "What makes you think I'm such a despicable character? What did you hear about me?"

Suddenly Sophie woke up to the fact that she had insulted her husband. "I didn't mean anything in particular about you, Patrick," she said anxiously. "But I know what men and women are like, or what men are like anyway," she said with some confusion. There was no point in pretending that she would ever lose interest in Patrick's body. "I know that you won't be satisfied with just one woman forever, but I will not be a troublesome sort of wife. I wasn't, was I? I never complained when you stayed out."

"That's certainly true," Patrick said through clenched teeth. "I thought you didn't give a damn whether I was around or not."

"Oh." Sophie gasped. "But I didn't want to make you feel trapped—"

"Because I might never come to your bed again, am I right?" Patrick was beginning to see a pattern here. A family pattern, as it were.

When Sophie nodded, he said gently, "I'm not your father, sweetheart. And you are not at all like your mother. I have complete confidence that I will still be coming to your bed every night when I am eighty-four years old. In fact, I think I'm going to burn your bed in your room, and then we'll just have one bed. What do you think?"

Sophie looked at him, dazed. "Why?"

"Because I want to sleep with you every night," he said fiercely. "We haven't talked enough, Sophie. We should have been talking, all those hours when I was walking the streets, sweating at every pore with longing to come back and climb into your bed."

Again Patrick shied away from talking about Sophie's feelings for Braddon. Yes, they had to talk—but time enough when she was well and when he himself felt less battered. Then he could bear to hear her tell him about

Braddon. The important thing was that Sophie wanted him, Patrick, in her bed.

Patrick bent his head, pressing butterfly kisses all along the line of Sophie's jaw. "I was an idiot," he admitted, achingly. "Will you forgive me? Will you let me sleep with you for the next sixty years or so, Sophie mine?"

Sophie's small hand slipped up Patrick's cheek. "Yes. Oh yes." She turned her head a fraction of an inch and his mouth hovered above hers, just hovered until she gave a little lurch forward and brought her soft lips up to his. It was a kiss not without passion, but more about love.

Finally Patrick drew back, looking down at her drenched eyes. "There's one thing I have to tell you, Sophie."

She swallowed and nodded, small teeth clamping down on her bottom lip.

"I do want children. I wanted this baby more than I can say."

There was a heartbeat's silence.

"Then why were you so cruel? Why did you say those things?"

"My mother." Patrick paused and cleared his throat. "After my mother died, I didn't ever want to make someone—my wife—go through that pain, perhaps not even survive. I know it's not rational, but after she died, Alex and I were alone. We had no home to go to. During school breaks we went to whoever would take us. It was better than going back to that empty huge house. I swore never to have children. And I never wanted them until I met you."

Sophie wound her arms around Patrick's neck and gave him a silent hug. "Alex and I were alone" spoke eloquently of the life of children brought up by servants.

"But I would love to have children with you," Patrick whispered, his voice roughly tender. "We'll have another babe, Sophie. I'm not saying that I will stop fearing for you, but we can have as many as you want—three or four, even ten." His voice took on a teasing lilt, remembering Sophie's vow to Braddon that she wanted ten children.

Sophie pressed silent kisses into his neck. She was afraid to speak, afraid that she'd blurt out hysterical vows of love. Patrick had said he lusted for her, and he didn't want to sleep with other women. He'd said that he wanted to have children. That was enough; that was *enough*.

"I love you," she whispered, unable to stop herself from saying the words. "I love you."

Patrick drew back a little and raised her chin. "You don't have to say that, Sophie. I know how you feel. We'll have more babies."

Startled and ashamed, Sophie's eyes slipped from his. He knew how she felt? After all the pretending and masquerading, he'd known all along that she was in love with him? She felt a sickening pulse of humiliation, but then she bit her bottom lip and sank back against his shoulder. What else could she do? She did love him. She was frantically, hopelessly in love with her husband.

For his part, Patrick felt as if daggers were piercing his heart. After all the time he had thought he wanted to hear those words, he found he didn't want to hear them after all. He didn't want love that was really gratitude, based on his promise to father another child. He didn't want the tenderness that had blossomed between them since the babe was lost—or at least, he didn't want that labeled "love." He wanted her to feel the same fierce burning love as he felt, the raging certitude that he would go mad if anything ever happened to her.

"Sophie," he said into her hair, his throat suddenly tight again. Sophie waited, but Patrick didn't say anything else, just kept kissing her hair and her ear. When he finally spoke, it was on an entirely different subject.

"Do you still want to leave for Downes today?"

Sophie glanced at the window. Miraculously, even

though she felt as if they'd been talking for hours and hours, the sun was still shining. She took a deep breath.

"Yes, please."

"I'll make arrangements," Patrick said quietly. There was a moment's pause. "May I come in a few days, Sophie?" Patrick's voice was humble.

Sophie buried her face in his neck. "Come now, Patrick." Her voice trembled. "Come with me."

Patrick couldn't stop himself from capturing her soft lips again. "I'll come with you. I'll always come, anywhere you ask me to."

When Sophie woke up a few days later, tucked in a large bed at Downes Manor, she felt as if a breath of grace had poured healing balm over her heart. Her baby—their baby—was gone, but there *would* be other babies. And there was her husband, sprawled next to her on top of the covers. He was wearing a silly lace-trimmed nightshirt that his brother insisted he wear, for some unknown reason. Patrick's face looked lean and exhausted, and stubble darkened his chin. She thought he'd never looked more beautiful in his life.

Chapter 28

～

S omeone was tickling her nose. With a flower, Sophie
found as she opened her eyes. Then she smiled
drowsily.

"How long did I sleep?"

"Around an hour," her husband said, leaning over her,
his smoky eyes caressing her face.

Sophie stretched, feeling the prickling grass under her
shoulder blades. Patrick's eyes dropped to her breasts as
they strained against the soft cotton of her gown. The
daisy left her cheek and stroked its way down her throat
and paused at her breasts.

"This dress needs ornamentation," Patrick said, his
voice slightly hoarse. Nimble brown fingers turned the
daisy into a shower of silky white petals that drifted over
her bodice.

Sophie shivered instinctively and looked up at her husband.

Patrick's hair was standing in wild disorder. He must have napped as well. They had eaten a light picnic . . . elegant trifles and a bottle of lightly sparkling wine.

It had been two long months since Patrick and Sophie arrived from London, sick at heart.

They found their child's grave and chose a simple white tombstone for her. They had her name, Frances, and one other word engraved on it: "Beloved." One day Charlotte and Sophie went to the family cemetery and planted dozens and dozens of snowdrops on the grave while Charlotte's gardener hovered, scandalized at the idea of ladies getting their hands dirty. But still Patrick and Sophie didn't go back to London.

The thought of their town house, with its memories of speechless days and chilly nights, was not a happy one. They settled into one of Downes Manor's huge bedrooms like two slightly wounded birds.

It was a healing time. Charlotte and Alex were a comforting, laughing presence. Indeed, Downes Manor was no longer the empty cavernous place that Patrick had hated as a child. The summer term at Harrow ended and Henri arrived, to Pippa's delight. Now the manor's hallways rang with children's laughter and grown-ups' chuckles.

But, more important, wherever Sophie turned, Patrick was there. He helped her out of chairs. He wouldn't let her carry anything larger than an embroidery hoop. In the evening he delighted in dismissing Simone and brushing Sophie's hair with slow, seductive strokes.

At night they slept in a sweet heap together, Patrick's face buried in Sophie's neck. If she rolled away in the night, she would wake to find his arms pulling her back. Even in his dreams, Patrick wouldn't let her go.

That evening, guests were due to arrive at the manor for a small house party. Seeing the confusion generated by the preparation of some ten or twelve bedchambers,

Patrick had seized Sophie and almost flung her and a picnic basket into the carriage.

"Where's the coachman?" Sophie said lazily. Looking about, she could see the blanket Patrick had spread on the grass, and the assorted remains of their lunch, but she didn't see the carriage.

Patrick didn't look up. He was intent on his daisy caresses. "I sent him home," he said absently.

"Home? How will we get home ourselves?" Sophie asked. It was so beautiful by the river, basking in the idle, warm sunshine, that she didn't feel much interest in the response.

Patrick didn't answer. He had discovered a new game. Their rosy blanket lay in the shade of a honeysuckle hedge, and Patrick was pulling small tendrils of honeysuckle off the hedge and tucking them into his wife's bright curls.

"Patrick?" Sophie smiled lazily and stretched again, enjoying the way her husband's eyes turned coal black.

"Yes?"

"My nurse used to pull the petals off daisies, the way you do," she teased.

"Why?"

"You can tell whether someone is in love with you," she said. Feeling suddenly a bit shy, she sat up. Curls and honeysuckle blossoms hid her face. But a strong hand silently presented her with a perfectly formed daisy.

"He loves me," she said slowly, pulling off a petal. Tender fingers pushed away the curtain of tawny curls that sheltered Sophie's face.

"He loves me not," she said. Teeth nipped her ear. Sophie trembled as she chose another petal.

"He loves me." In a sudden movement, Patrick slipped behind her, pulling her onto his lap.

"He loves me not."

"He loves me." Strong arms encircled her, and Sophie

relaxed back against Patrick's chest. Whisper-smooth lips caressed her forehead. Petals fell gently from her fingers.

"He loves me not."

And: "He loves me." The last petal drifted to the ground.

"He loves you," Patrick said, his deep voice unquestioning, strong, there for her life and beyond.

"Do you know how much *I* love you, Patrick Foakes? I'm in love with you."

Sophie's soft words sank slowly into Patrick's brain. There was a moment's pause, as if the whole warm lazy afternoon held its breath. For a second Patrick didn't hear the chirping burr of crickets and the singing hum of bees. The world narrowed to his wife's vivid blue eyes.

He didn't want to speak, to disturb the moment.

"You do?" His voice came out hoarse, disjointed. "You are?"

Sophie's face had turned a rosy pink, color stealing up from the creamy bodice of her dress.

She twisted about, placing her hands on his face. "Of course I do." And then: "Why do you look so surprised? I thought you knew. You said you knew."

"I thought . . ." Patrick's voice was still a little hoarse. "I thought you were in love with Braddon."

"Braddon!" Sophie's eyes were sharp, *shocked,* Patrick thought dizzily. "How could I be in love with Braddon? He's in love with Madeleine!"

"It doesn't follow that you couldn't be in love with him," Patrick insisted. It was time they straightened all this out.

Sophie's hands fell from his face. "How on earth did you get such an odd idea?"

"Odd idea?" her husband said, an ironic note in his voice. "Braddon said you were madly in love with him, and you seemed to be. You insisted on eloping with him, for God's sake. And then when he announced his engagement to Madeleine, you cried."

"I cried?"

Sophie tried desperately to remember. "Well, I can't have been crying over Braddon's engagement," she said practically, "because to be honest I don't give a hang whom Braddon marries, and I never have."

There was a second's pause. "Braddon told you that I was *madly in love with him*?"

Patrick nodded.

Sophie's eyes turned a fierce, midnight blue. "That pompous, egotistical worm! Me! In love with *him*!"

Patrick pulled her back onto his lap. Happiness was beginning to sing in his chest. "Let me see," he said teasingly, "if I've got this right, he said that you adored him madly."

"I'll have his skin," Sophie shrieked. Then she laughed. "I'll tell Maddie to take revenge on him. As soon as they return from their wedding trip."

"I like Madeleine," Patrick said. "Where did you say you first met her?"

"Oh," Sophie said weakly, "I think it must have been at the Cumberland ball."

Patrick shook his head. "It can't have been. She told me that her first ball was the one Lady Commonweal gave in honor of Sissy's engagement, and you had Madeleine to dinner long before that."

He looked at Sophie but she had turned her head. Her mind was in a jumble. It was hateful, lying to Patrick.

Finally she settled for a half-lie. "I think Braddon must have introduced me to her, but I can't quite remember where."

"Braddon!" Patrick was silent for an instant.

He had an unerring memory, which he'd found useful in negotiating the intricacies of international shipping. At that moment a sentence dropped like a netted herring into his mind, a sentence of Braddon's. "Madeleine is different: she's going to be mine forever." Braddon's new mistress— the mistress who replaced Arabella. He wanted her to live in Mayfair, Patrick thought; he wanted to be near her at all times. . . .

Then, like a lightning flash: Oh Lord, Braddon involved Sophie in one of his schemes. And *this* was a dangerous one, socially, at least.

And finally, like a benediction: Sophie was with Braddon's mistress on Thursdays. Madeleine. Madeleine was Braddon's mistress.

"You taught that girl how to wear gloves and when to curtsy, didn't you?"

Sophie giggled, a guilty giggle. "Madeleine didn't need much instruction."

Patrick took a deep breath. "I thought you were with Braddon on those long drives."

"Well, I was," Sophie said, half absently. She was still thinking about Madeleine. "But most of the time we couldn't let him stay with us because Braddon was like a puppy dog. He couldn't stay away from Maddie."

Patrick's arms tightened around his wife. What an infernal ass he was.

"You didn't . . . You did! You were jealous," Sophie accused, looking up and meeting his eyes.

For a wild moment Patrick wanted to deny it. But they had promised to be honest with each other from now on.

"I was savagely jealous," he admitted, lowering his lips so that they just touched Sophie's. "I used to writhe with jealousy."

"But you—I thought *you* had a mistress!"

"I mean to ask you about that," Patrick said, with some curiosity. "Who was that black-haired woman you fancied I was spending my time with?"

Sophie was still giggling over Patrick's irrational jealousy. "Charlotte suggested you were jealous of Braddon, but I couldn't credit it." Then her eyes widened. "Charlotte! Oh, Patrick, your mistress must have been Charlotte!"

Patrick laughed. "Not that I noticed." He pulled his wife's delicious self back onto his lap.

"You see, Henri saw you with a beautiful black-haired woman—"

"And Henri never had a chance to meet Alex before he went off to school, so he didn't know that I have a twin brother," Patrick finished. "That will teach you to mistrust your husband!"

He took a deep breath and leaned his forehead against hers. "We're a pair of idiots, Sophie. Why didn't we talk?"

Sophie sweetly rubbed her nose against his. "I couldn't," she said simply. "I thought you were behaving like my father, and so what was the point of discussing it? I was grateful that you didn't flaunt the woman in the ballroom, in front of me. So what right did I have to complain?"

"What right to complain!" Patrick was aghast. "You had every right to complain! You're my wife, for God's sake."

"You didn't complain about my excursions with Braddon," Sophie reminded him softly. "Braddon worried that you would get angry, but I thought you hadn't noticed."

"I couldn't," Patrick said. "How could I complain if you wanted to see Braddon? If it hadn't been for my insufferable behavior, you would have been happily married to Braddon!"

Even the thought of it wrenched his heart. "Sophie," he said suddenly, "are you sure that you love me? Alex says that Braddon is very lovable."

"Braddon *is* lovable," Sophie replied. She cupped his face in her hands, brushing her lips across his. "You, sir, are not lovable. You are argumentative and you come to ridiculous conclusions. You ignore me and then insist that you were actually thinking about me." Her voice dropped. "You make me want you in my bed, and then you leave me, without telling me why. You are made into a Duke of the Realm, and forget to tell me about it. I can't understand the way you think. And I certainly don't know why I love you so much."

To his horror, Patrick felt his eyes fill with tears. Ruthlessly he toppled his wife backward, his mouth taking hers with a savage ferocity. As always, passion flared between them, melting Sophie's bones, turning her legs to water. Patrick gentled his mouth.

"It's not hard to know why I love you, Sophie. You *are* lovable."

"Mmmm," his wife replied. She ran her hands through his wild curls and then arched up to kiss him again.

Their eyes met with a silent promise. "I'm sorry, Sophie," Patrick said, his voice husky. "I was jealous . . . and then when you became pregnant, I was so afraid— and I'm not used to being afraid. I was furious at you, and terrified for you. All I could think of was to stay away from you."

Sophie kissed him, her lips a silent pardon. For a moment they just stayed there, Patrick's large hands cupping his wife's delicate face as he stared down at her.

"I'll never stay away from you again, Sophie." The most important vow of Patrick's life arose from the deepest part of his heart. "Not in my body—or spirit."

Sophie's lips were whisper soft on his. "If you do I'll scream at you like a fishwife. How's that for a bargain?"

Patrick nipped her lip. "I'll risk it," he said. "Although I happen to know that you are entirely too intelligent to make a comfortable wife."

Sophie grinned up at him. "Jealous of my success with Madeleine, are you? My next project," she whispered against his lips, "is to make the Duke of Gisle into a proper duke."

"Oh yes?" Patrick kissed her again. "What's the matter with the Duke of Gisle?"

"He has no sense of his own countenance," Sophie said decisively. "His carriage is lined with simple blue silk, without a blazon to be seen. He is rarely rude to his underlings, and he doesn't even have a personal snuff mixture."

"I hate snuff, Sophie!"

"It doesn't matter." She laughed. "All proper dukes have a mixture prominently displayed in the shops, which no one else is allowed to buy."

"I think the problem is really with the duchess," Patrick said, running his hand down Sophie's body. She shivered.

"I've heard that the duchess is a master at etiquette," Sophie whispered. "I heard she made a horse trainer's daughter into a countess."

"The problem is that the duchess has been fibbing to the duke," Patrick said.

There was just a hint of seriousness in his eyes, enough to make Sophie suddenly alert. She shook her head. "I couldn't tell you about Madeleine, Patrick."

"It's not that," he said, sitting up and running a hand through his hair until it stood straight up. "Do you remember telling me about Kotzebue's travels in Siberia, Sophie?"

Her eyes remained puzzled as she propped herself up on both elbows.

"That afternoon in my study," he prompted her.

Sophie blushed. "Oh yes."

"I went to Water's Bookstore and asked for a copy of Kotzebue's travels."

Sophie's eyes grew instantly wary.

"That's right, oh my wife," Patrick said, nodding. "The only book they could offer me was *Merkwürdigste Jahr Meines Lebens.*"

Sophie turned a bit pink. "I think a man named Reverend Beresford is working on a translation," she said in a small, guilty voice.

"You can give it to me for Christmas," Patrick said. He

was smiling, although he tried to keep his voice stern. "And I received a letter from Lord Breksby yesterday, Sophie. Bayrak Mustafa was no Turk, although it seems his mother might have been Turkish. But to all intents and purposes, Mustafa was an illiterate Englishman more commonly known as Mole."

Sophie's eyes grew wide. "Why did they bring us that inkwell?"

"Monsieur Foucault and Mr. Mole were in the pay of Emperor Napoleon," Patrick said comfortably. "In fact, they planned to blow Selim III sky high."

"The inkwell!" Sophie gasped.

"Exactly so, my dear wife." Patrick ran his finger down Sophie's uptilted nose. "Exactly so. Apparently, Napoleon reasoned that an explosion would cause Selim—if he survived—to declare war on England. Except that his henchmen were foiled by the intelligence of my wife."

Patrick leaned over Sophie, looking straight into her eyes. "Why didn't you tell me, Sophie?"

"My mother," Sophie said in a stifled voice. "My mother said you would take a dislike of me if you knew I was a bluestocking. She said that no man wants to think that his wife knows more languages than he does."

"A bluestocking!" For a moment Patrick was silent, looking down at his petite, gorgeous wife. Even having taken a nap, and picnicked in the open, she looked like a plate from *La Belle Assemblée*.

"I was so proud when I realized you were able to read German," Patrick said. "I doubt any other man in London has a wife who is able to speak French, Welsh, Turkish, and German!"

There was a moment's silence, like the hushed pause before a stone, dropped into a well, hits the water far below.

"Oh Lord," Patrick said. "I'm a nodcock, aren't I? How many languages can the Duchess of Gisle speak?"

Sophie turned even pinker. "Well, Italian doesn't even count, really, because it's so close to French."

"I should have guessed that," Patrick said in a resigned tone, a smile gleaming in his eye. "I should have nobbled it the moment you knew the proper word for Leghorn, shouldn't I?"

Sophie grinned at him.

"Any more?" Patrick gave his voice a mock-grim tone.

"I know a little Portuguese and a little Dutch," she said in a rush.

"A little?" He bent down and planted a hard kiss on her lips. "Does that mean you are a fluent speaker?"

"No," Sophie said hastily. "We couldn't find an appropriate woman with whom I could practice my Dutch. . . ."

"Is *that* the end?"

"Are you angry?" Her eyes searched her husband's anxiously.

He looked genuinely surprised. "Why should I be angry, Sophie my love? I love to travel; you are brilliant at speaking foreign languages. You are a marvel and I consider myself damned lucky. I'm particularly glad you speak Turkish!"

Sophie looked at him, her eyes huge with an unspoken question.

"Didn't you know that I would take you with me?"

She shook her head.

"I'm not happy away from you," Patrick said, his eyes truly serious now. "I don't want to ever sleep alone again. And that means that we are traveling to the Ottoman Empire next month . . . together."

"Oh, Patrick," Sophie said "That will be wonderful."

"Good," he replied, rather absentmindedly. His hands were wandering up and down her body in a very disturbing fashion.

Sophie grabbed his wrists. "You don't mind that I . . . I speak all these languages and you don't?"

Patrick's eyes were making sinful promises. He bent over and licked the corner of her mouth with tantalizing slowness.

"You have the sweetest lips," he said huskily. And then: "I don't care what language you speak to me, Sophie mine. As long—"

"As long?" she said teasingly.

"As long as you let me have my way with you morning, noon, and night."

"That's all?"

"And you have to love me forever."

"I suppose so." She laughed.

"And you have to forgive me for not explaining my silences."

She propped herself up on one elbow. "I didn't speak to you either. I was afraid. I thought it was worth anything to avoid the kind of bitter fights my parents had. But perhaps a civilized silence is just as bad."

Patrick nodded. "The minute you start tearing off on one of those weekly jaunts with Braddon, you will find just how noisy I can be."

Sophie's eyes were half solemn, half merry. "And if you don't come home until four in the morning, I shall turn into a termagant and throw the chamber pot at you."

"I have one more requirement," Patrick whispered. "You have to give me at least five children."

For an instant she couldn't speak. Her eyes filled with tears. "Do you really mean it, Patrick?"

"I'm going to be terrified," Patrick said frankly. "I shall probably behave like a regular hellion, Sophie. But I . . . I loved little Frances the moment I saw her. I think we should have another child.

"Silly wife," he muttered as Sophie's tears spilled over and ran down her cheeks. His eyes took on a wicked glint. "I suppose I should try to take your mind off your troubles." Gently he kissed away her tears, but his hand took

an altogether less innocent path, running up the softness
of her inner leg.

Far above, the sky was azure blue, marked only by a
few clouds drifting on a lazy breeze. Somewhere close to
them bees were building a hive, their warm buzz adding to
the afternoon's small sounds of crickets and birdsong.
After a minute she closed her eyes and simply let her
hands do the looking: wandering their way over the
smooth muscled expanses of Patrick's bare skin, feeling
the little shivers that followed in the wake of her hands,
the gravelly roughness of the hair on his chest.

Afterword

S ophie woke with a start and propped herself up on one elbow. It was the middle of the night, and the only light in the room was the glow cast by firelight. For a moment Sophie drowsily watched the dancing shadows cast on her bedroom walls. The room was warm, even though it was an unusually chilly December.

Then she heard it again: a low, rippling gurgle, followed by a deep chuckle. Sleepily, Sophie narrowed her eyes and squinted at the back of the high rocking chair next to the fire. Sure enough, it was tipping cozily forward and back.

"Patrick?"

"We're here."

Sophie smiled and propped her pillows up against the high mahogany back of the master bed. She and Patrick had seen the bed in the royal suite of a Turkish palace, and Patrick had bargained fiercely, finally buying it from the pasha who owned it. When they returned home, he kept to his promise and had the bed in Sophie's chamber removed.

"This is the *only* bed that the Duchess of Gisle and her devoted husband have to sleep in," he had said, winding his arms around Sophie and pulling her backward on the silk counterpane. "If you are angry enough to banish me, you will have to contemplate my sleeping outside the door on the bare boards."

Sophie had laughed, and since then the duke and duchess had shared a bed that was, in truth, built for a king.

Another trill of chortling syllables rang out from the rocking chair.

"Oh, Patrick, you shouldn't," Sophie said. It was hard to be severe when a baby's laughter filled the room. "She'll never go to sleep after playing with you."

"Yes, she will," Patrick said lovingly. "You'll go to sleep, won't you, sweetheart? Won't you sleep for your mama? Yes, you will."

The baby gave a little squawk in return, and then a trilling, laughing string of syllables.

"Time to eat?" Patrick said thoughtfully. "Well, I suppose we might."

He rose and turned toward the bed, carrying a snugly wrapped bundle. All Sophie could see was one happily waving fist.

Patrick walked slowly, rubbing noses with his daughter as he came. "Ouch!" The fist had closed on his hair.

"Katherine?"

" 'Tis a wise mother who knows her own child," Patrick said with mock severity, as he settled the baby into the crook of her mother's arm. "This little jester is Ella, of course."

Ella lost her happy look and took on a more serious expression, turning her face expectantly toward her mother.

"Here, sweetheart..." Sophie rearranged her night-clothing.

Her husband plopped down on the bed and was watching with frank enjoyment. "Katherine is sleeping the sleep of the righteous. When Nanny brought Ella, she said she was hoping that Katherine would sleep until the morning."

"She's an optimist."

"A good thing in a nanny," Patrick observed. "But you notice that even our optimistic nanny doesn't think that Ella will be sleeping through the night anytime soon."

Sophie looked down at little Ella, rapturously drinking milk. "She's a piglet," she said affectionately. "She wouldn't want to sleep too much in case she missed a meal."

"Or a laugh," her father said loyally. "She always likes to play, even when she's hungry."

"I think she eats more frequently because she was smaller than Katherine at first," Sophie said.

"Well, she's spent the past three months catching up," her husband replied. "Look at this stomach!" He gently poked Ella's round tummy with one finger.

"We had a message, after you retired to bed," Patrick said teasingly.

Sophie's eyes shone. "Is it Mama?"

"That's it. Your mama's a mama again. Mother and baby are doing well. And George's message said the birth took all of four hours, so I gather your mother takes after you, sweetheart."

Patrick's eyes twinkled lovingly at his wife. After all his fears, which had become acute as Sophie grew as unwieldy as a ship, the twins had been born so fast that Dr. Lambeth barely got there in time, and he hadn't had time to order Patrick from the room. So Patrick was holding Katherine when Lambeth broke into a surprised laugh and caught the head of Ella as she rushed into the world to join her sister.

Patrick's heart thudded with happiness even to think of that moment.

"Do I have a sister or a brother?"

"They had a little boy, so I imagine your father is in seventh heaven."

"He never cared overmuch about the title." It was Sophie's turn to be loyal.

"Well, now he has a male heir. Alexander George is the future marquis."

Sophie looked at Patrick curiously. "Does hearing about Alexander cause you to want a male heir?"

"No," Patrick replied. "Although I have to admit that since giving birth to the girls was so easy for you, sometimes I think about a son. Not an heir, just a son."

Sophie laughed for pure happiness. In truth, the only tense moment during the birth of the twins had been when Dr. Lambeth observed that the duchess had the hips of a peasant, to which comment Patrick took violent exception.

But she shook her head teasingly. "I don't know, Patrick. Now that Charlotte has a third daughter, and we had Frances and the twins, you and your brother have produced six girls. Perhaps girls are your lot in life."

Patrick only laughed and kissed his wife lightly. "Practice makes perfect," he whispered against her lips.

Ella gave a little grunt, and when her parents looked down at her, she was fast asleep.

"I'll take her back to the nursery." Patrick reached out and deftly took his little daughter in his arms.

"I could ring for Betsy," Sophie said, smiling up at her husband as he tucked Ella's blanket around her chubby form.

"I like to fetch and carry my daughters. When I was little I told my father I wanted to be a footman. I liked their livery."

Sophie grinned. "What did he say?"

"I can't remember. Most likely he was outraged. He had a great sense of his own consequence, which didn't include footmen for sons."

Just as Sophie was drifting back to sleep again, the door to the master bedroom opened and Patrick walked back in.

"Oh Lord," Sophie moaned. Now he had *two* flannel-wrapped bundles, one on each arm.

"This one's for you," her husband said with obscene cheerfulness. He handed over a squirming, red-cheeked baby.

"Katherine, I presume?" Sophie murmured, reaching out her arms.

"Katherine it is," Patrick agreed. He kicked off his slippers and lay down on the bed next to Sophie, Ella still sleeping in the crook of his arm. When Katherine had settled in for a midnight snack, Sophie looked at Patrick enquiringly, nodding toward Ella.

Patrick smiled a bit guiltily. "Nanny was asleep in the chair when I got to the nursery, and Betsy was asleep on the cot. In fact, Katherine was the only one awake. She was kicking about and just starting to think about howling. So I scooped her up and brought them both back here."

"Ella should be in her bed," Sophie said with mock severity.

Patrick didn't bother to answer. He was looking down at Ella's little face.

"She's going to be a great beauty, Sophie. I'll have to beat off gentlemen with a stick."

Thoughtfully, Sophie looked at the little girl she was holding. The twins were as alike as peas in a pod; both had inherited a dizzying combination of arching eyebrows (from their papa) and silky, golden reddish curls (from their mama).

Just for a second, Sophie wondered whether their first daughter, little Frances, would have been as beautiful, had she lived.

Patrick's shoulder bumped hers, and a kiss landed on her ear. "She was very beautiful, sweetheart, but in a different way. She had your eyebrows."

Sophie's eyes got a little sheen of tears. She leaned her head on her husband's shoulder as he wound his free arm about her.

"Don't cry, Sophie," he whispered tenderly.

Sophie looked up, and their eyes met, both touched with sorrow for the daughter they would never stop loving. In the space of a heartbeat, it was all there between them: their grief and the healing balm of love, those small threads of life that meshed them together closer than the weave of a wedding dress.

"I am very lucky to have a husband who always knows what I'm thinking." Sophie rubbed her head against Patrick's shoulder like a grateful cat.

Patrick grinned a bit smugly. In the three years since they married, he had learned to judge the darkening of Sophie's eyes to an inch. Now she even frowned at him occasionally, having found that she couldn't hide her feelings anyway.

Patrick dropped a kiss on his wife's eyebrow. "A good wife always knows what her husband is thinking. Do you?"

"Are you thinking about breakfast?"

"No."

Katherine burped loudly and her body relaxed back on Sophie's arm. Rosebud lips puckered and a tiny snore sounded in the room.

Patrick sighed. "I'd better take them both back to the nursery, I suppose." He was gone for a few moments and returned to find Sophie still awake.

He stopped for a moment and looked at his delectable wife, propped against the pillows, looking tired but beautiful.

"Have you decided what I'm thinking about?"

"Perhaps . . ." she said teasingly. "I know! You're thinking about the *Sophie*!" Patrick's newest ship was named after his wife.

Patrick propped himself up on one side, facing her. "The *Sophie* is due to dock tomorrow after her trip to China," he said, his eyes wicked. "I am looking forward to boarding her."

The neckline of Sophie's lacy white night rail was still disarranged from nursing the girls. Patrick tugged it gently, exposing one of his wife's pink-tipped breasts. She shivered as he ran his hand around the bottom of her breast and then left it there, dark strength against creamy whiteness.

"So tell me, O my love, what am I thinking?" One eyebrow sent her a seductive message.

Sophie searched his beloved face, the strong planes of his cheeks, shadowed now from waking up every night, the fierce desire in his face, the fierce love there too.

"If you are thinking about boarding the *Sophie*," she said a bit shakily, moving closer to him and curling an arm around his neck, "I think she just docked."

The master of the *Sophie* rolled over and captured his wife's mouth with hungry force.

Behind them the last log in the fireplace succumbed and fell into two, sending a tiny blizzard of sparks up the chimney. Dying firelight danced a final minuet on the ceiling above the matrimonial bed, but no one noticed. The log crackled and squeaked as it burned down, but no one added another log from the basket next to the fireplace.

The only sounds from the bed were inarticulate ones: sounds of desire, sounds of pleasure, finally of ecstasy. Gasped, at the moment of greatest bliss, words of love.

The great master bed fell into silence again. Even the fire was silent now, reduced to a sultry heap of embers, glowing a deep carmine red in the depths of the fireplace.

The silence was broken only by a deep voice. "*Être avec toi, c'est toujours comme retourner à la maison,* Sophie. Being with you is always like coming home."

Sophie reached up and caressed her husband's cheek, love shining in her eyes. "You are my home, Patrick." And again, as he buried his face in her hair, holding her so close that his large body seemed imprinted on hers: "With you, I am home."

A Note about Scepters, Sultans, and the Pleasures of Eloping with Strangers

‑‑‑‑‑‑‑

In 1613 Robert Tailor's play, *The Hog Hath Lost His Pearl*, was performed in London. In the first act, a young gentleman, Carracus, stands below the window of his beloved Maria, waiting for her to climb down a ladder and elope with him. But alas! His best friend, Albert, descends from that window, where he has pretended to be Carracus and has (in his words) "robbed Carracus of what's more precious than his blood"—Maria's virginity.

The Hog Hath Lost His Pearl grows a bit tedious after this climactic scene, since all three lovers end up wandering about the woods in disguise. And from a romantic point of view, the last act is rather disappointing: Carracus and Albert swear eternal union—"nothing now but death / Shall cause a separation"—and the three people return to London together. Clearly, male bonding was alive and well in the 17th century!

The liberties I have taken with Tailor's plot are naught compared to my endowment of Napoleon with an exploding scepter. In fact, Selim III (the Ottoman sultan from 1789–1807) did recognize Napoleon as emperor in 1804, and he did declare war on England in 1806. But the idea that Selim might have discarded the noble title of sultan for that of emperor is purely my own invention. And Emperor Napoleon was likely far too busy with his unrealistic and hazardous plans to invade Great Britain to pay attention to a ruby scepter, unless it would grace his own coronation ceremony in December.

About the Author

❦

Eloisa James is also the author of the acclaimed novel *Potent Pleasures*. She is a professor of English literature who lives with her family in New Jersey.

Eloisa loves to receive mail from readers, and can be reached through her publisher, Bantam Dell, at 1540 Broadway, New York, NY 10036, or directly through her website at eloisajames.com.

Visit our website at www.bantamdell.com.

Look for the next exciting novel
from Eloisa James

Enchanting Pleasures

Available from Dell

Chapter 1

F ate had just dealt Viscount Dewland a blow that
would have felled a weaker—or more sympathetic—man. He gaped silently at his eldest son for
a moment, ignoring his wife's twittering commentary. But
a happy thought revived him. That same wife had, after
all, provided him with *two* male offspring.

Without further ado he spun on his heel and barked at his
younger son, "If your brother can't do his duty in bed, then
you'll do it. You can act like a man for once in your life."

Peter Dewland was caught unawares by his father's sudden
attack. He had risen to adjust his neckcloth in the drawing-
room mirror, thereby avoiding his brother's eyes. Really, what
does a man say to that sort of confession? But like his father,
Peter recovered quickly from unpredictable assaults.

He walked around the end of the divan and sat down. "I
gather you are suggesting that I marry Jerningham's
daughter?"

"Of course I am!" the viscount snapped. "Someone has to marry her, and your brother has just declared himself ineligible."

"I beg to differ," Peter remarked with a look of cool distaste. "I have no plans to marry at your whim."

"What in the bloody hell do you mean? Of course you'll marry the girl if I instruct you to do so!"

"I do not plan to marry, Father. Not at your instigation nor at anyone else's."

"Rubbish! Every man marries."

Peter sighed. "Not true."

"You've squired about every beautiful gal that came on the market in the last six years. If you had formed a true attachment, I would not stand in your way. But since you haven't made a move to attach yourself, you *will* marry Jerningham's girl.

"You will do as I say, boy," the viscount bellowed. "Your brother can't take on the job, and so you have to do it. I've been lenient with you. You might be in the Seventh Foot at this very moment. Have you thought of that?"

"I'd rather take a pair of colors than a wife," Peter retorted.

"Absolutely not," his father said, reversing himself. "Your brother's been at the point of death for years."

Inside the drawing room, the silence swelled ominously. Peter grimaced at his elder brother, whose muscled body proclaimed his general fitness to the world at large.

Erskine Dewland, who had been staring meditatively at the polished surface of his Hessians, raised his heavy-lidded eyes from his boots to his father's face. "If Peter is determined not to marry, I could take her on." His deep voice fell into the silent room.

"And what's the point of that? You can't do the job properly, and I'm not wedding Jerningham's daughter to . . . to . . . in that case. I've got principles. The girl's got a right to expect a sound husband, for God's sake."

Quill, as Erskine was known to his intimates, opened his mouth again. And then thought better of it. He could certainly consummate the marriage, but it wouldn't be a very pleasant experience. Any woman deserved more from marriage than he could offer. While he had come to terms with his injuries, especially now that they had ceased to bother his movement, the three-day migraines that followed repetitive motion made his likelihood for marital bliss very slight.

"Can't argue with that, can you?" The viscount looked triumphantly at his eldest son. "I'm not some sort of a caper merchant, passing you off as whole goods when you're not. Mind you, we could. The girl wouldn't know a thing, of course, until it was too late. And her father's turned into such a loose screw that he's not even accompanying her out here.

"Point is," Dewland went on, turning back to his youngest son, "the girl's expecting to marry someone. And if it can't be Quill, it's got to be you. I'll send your picture over on the next boat."

Peter replied through his teeth, each word spaced. "I do not wish to marry, Father."

The viscount's cheeks reddened again. "It's time you stopped gadding about. By God, you will do as I say!"

Peter avoided his father's gaze, seemingly absorbed in flicking the smallest piece of lint from the black velvet collar of his morning coat. Satisfied, he returned to the subject at hand. "You seem to have misunderstood me. I *refuse* to marry Jerningham's daughter." Only the smallest tremor in his voice betrayed his agitation.

The viscountess broke in before her husband could bellow whatever response he had in mind. "Thurlow, I don't like your color. Perhaps we might continue this conversation at a later time? You know what the doctor said about getting overtaxed!"

"Balderdash!" the viscount protested, although he allowed his wife to pull him back onto a couch. "By George, you had better obey me, Mister Peter Dewland, or you will find yourself out the door." The veins of his forehead were alarmingly swollen.

His wife sent a beseeching glance to her youngest son.

His jaw was set in a manner that his father would have recognized, had there been a mirror in the near vicinity.

But before Peter could say a word, his father erupted out of his seat once again. "And just what am I supposed to say to this young girl who's coming all the way over from India? Tell her that you 'prefer not to marry her'? You planning on telling my old friend Jerningham that you decline to marry his gal?"

"That is precisely what I suggest," Peter replied.

"And what about the money Jerningham's lent me over the years, eh? Given it to me without a word of advice—just sent me over the blunt to do with as I like! If your brother Quill hadn't pulled down a fortune speculating on the East India Company, Jerningham might still be lending me money. As it is, we agreed to consider it a dowry. You *will* marry the gal, or I'll ... I'll ..."

The viscount's face was purple all over now, and he was unconsciously rubbing his chest.

"Quill could pay back the money," Peter suggested.

"Bloody hell! I've already allowed your brother to turn himself into a merchant, playing around on the Exchange—I'll be damned if I'll allow him to pay off my debts!"

"I don't see why not," Peter retorted. "He's paid for everything else."

"That's enough! The only reason your brother—the only reason I allowed Erskine to take on the smell of the market was because—well, because he's a cripple. But at least he acts his age. You're naught but a fribble, a sprig of fashion!"

As the viscount drew a breath, Quill raised his head and met his younger brother's eyes. In the depths of Quill's silent apology, Peter saw the manacles of marriage looming.

His father was glaring at him with all the frustration of a ruddy, boisterous Englishman whose younger son has proved to be nothing like himself. Peter cast a desperate look at his mother, but there was no help to be found.

He quailed. His stomach churned. He opened his mouth to protest but could think of nothing to say. And finally the habits of a lifetime's submission took hold.

"Very well." His voice was hollow.

Kitty Dewland rose and came to give him a grateful kiss on the cheek. "Dear Peter," she said. "You were always my comforting one, my good child. And in truth, darling, you have escorted so many women without making an offer. I'm certain that Jerningham's daughter will be a perfect match for you. His wife was French, you know."

In her son's eyes there was a bleak desolation that Kitty hated to see. "Is there someone else? Is there a woman whom you were hoping to marry, darling?"

Peter shook his head.

"Well, then," Kitty said gaily. "We will be right and tight when this girl—what's her name, Thurlow? Thurlow!"

When Kitty turned around she'd found her husband leaning back and looking rather white. "M'chest doesn't feel so good, Kitty," he mumbled.

And when Kitty flew out of the drawing room, she was far too discomposed to note how odd it was that her beloved butler, Codswallop, was hovering just on the other side of the door.

"Send for Doctor Priscian," she shrieked, and trotted back into the room.

The plump and precise Codswallop couldn't resist taking a curious look at Quill before he rang for a footman. It was that hard to believe. Quill had a physique Codswallop had secretly admired: a body remarkably suited to tight pantaloons and fitted coats, the kind of body housemaids giggled about behind stairs. Must be some sort of injury to his private parts. Codswallop shuddered sympathetically.

Just then Quill turned about and looked Codswallop in the face. His eyes were a curious greeny-gray, set in a face stamped with lines of pain and deeply tanned. Without moving a muscle, he cast Codswallop a look that scathed him to his bones.

Codswallop scuttled back into the hall and rang for a footman. The viscount was supported off to his bedchamber, followed by his clucking wife. Young Peter bounded out the door looking like murder, followed rather more slowly by Quill, and Codswallop pulled the drawing-room doors closed with a snap.

∽⊷∾

Some three months later, the whole affair was tied up. Miss Jerningham was due to arrive on the *Plassey,* a frigate sailing from Calcutta, within the week. There was one last explosion of rage on the part of the viscount when Peter announced, on the day before Miss Jerningham was due to arrive, that he was taking a long sojourn in the country. But by supper on the fifth of September, the sullen bridegroom had taken himself off to his club, rather than to Herefordshire, and Viscount Dewland repeated over stewed pigeon that the marriage would be an excellent solution to all their problems. There was an unspoken acknowledgment between Thurlow and his wife that Peter, if left to his own devices, might indeed never marry.

"He'll settle down once the girl arrives," Thurlow declared.

"They will have beautiful children," added Kitty.

Only Quill seemed to have a growing sense of unease about the forthcoming marriage. After his parents left the salon, he walked restlessly to the windows overlooking the gardens. He leaned forward, resting his forehead against the hard curve of his forearm, shifting his weight slightly from his protesting right leg. He was accustomed to the blustery explosion of his father's rage. He had tolerated it for years by listening in silence and then following his own inclination. Peter had ever bent with the wind, and so it was no surprise that ultimately he gave in to the viscount's plans. Surely Peter could not have really thought to escape marriage, once it became clear that he or his son would inherit the title someday.

But an uneasy chill sat on Quill's heart. He remembered the girl's name, even if no one else did: Gabrielle Jerningham. And what would Gabrielle's life be like with Peter as her husband? It would be an urbane life, a sophisticated life. Likely the young couple would share the kind of marriage Quill saw frequently in the *ton:* cool and friendly.

He straightened, moving into a great arching stretch. His body was outlined by light thrown against the dark glass, every muscle caressed by his clothing. It was a body honed by denial, exercise, and pain: a body whose master knew its every strength and its every weakness. It was not the body of an average gentleman of the London *ton* in 1806.

Quill shrugged back his hair. Damned if it wasn't getting unfashionably long again. For a moment he froze, struck by a memory of the wind screaming past his face, wrenching his hair back from his scalp as he rode a galloping stallion.

But horses, like sex, had become a delight whose payment was greater than the offered pleasure. The rhythmic motion of horseback riding invariably instigated three days of agony in a darkened room, covered in sweat and gripped by nausea, his head clenched in a steel band of pain. And the only advice doctors had offered was that his head injury of six years ago had led to an inability to endure rhythm. Any kind of rhythm.

Quill's jaw hardened and he mentally shrugged off the image of a galloping horse. To his mind there was nothing worse than lamenting over what could not be. Women and horses were simply part of his past, and no part of his future.

Then he grinned. The very sports he was mourning—a hard riding session and a woman's nightly companionship—were delights that held absolutely no interest for Peter. Lord, but he and his brother were as alike as chalk and cheese.

At any rate, he was likely worrying about Gabrielle and Peter for naught. Peter might not like the idea of marriage, but he did love female companionship. A decorous French miss, with whom Peter could gossip, discuss fashion, and attend balls, might well become his closest friend. And Gabrielle was an elegant name, one that brought to mind a woman versed in the ways of the world. Peter had a great admiration—nay, a passion—for beauty. Surely an exquisite young Frenchwoman would be able to coax him into compliance with an unwanted marriage.

Unfortunately, Quill would have abandoned that hope could he have seen the aforementioned exquisite Frenchwoman.

Peter's fiancée was kneeling on the floor of her cabin, looking into the eager face of a young girl who sat before her on a small tuffet. Gabrielle's hair was tumbling about her ears, and her old-fashioned dress was crumpled. The last thing she resembled was a sophisticated French miss from *La Belle Assemblée*.

"The tiger crept through the tangled jungle." Gabby's voice was a thrilling whisper. "He put one paw softly before the next, barely disturbing the song of the magpies far above. His long tongue licked his chops at the thought of the delicious meal that trotted before him."

Phoebe Pensington, a five-year-old orphan being sent back to live with English relatives, shivered as Gabby, whose soft brown eyes had taken on a tigerish glare, continued.

"But when the tiger reached the edge of the forest, he stopped short. The goat was walking along the shore, his white hooves prancing at the very edge of the tumbling azure waves of the Indian Ocean. And the tiger was afraid of water. His stomach urged him to follow, but his heart pounded with fear. He stopped in the speckled shade of a bongo-bongo tree—"

"But Miss Gabby," Phoebe broke in anxiously, "what did the tiger have for supper that night if he didn't eat the goat? Wouldn't he be hungry?"

Gabby's brown eyes lit with amusement. "Perhaps the tiger was so mortified by his own lack of courage that he went to a far-off mountaintop and lived on nothing but fruits and vegetables."

"I don't think so." Phoebe was a very practical little girl. "I think it's more likely that the tiger would have gone after that goat and eaten him up."

"The tiger had a cat's natural abhorrence of water,"

Gabby said. "He didn't see the beauty of the waves as they danced into shore. To him the curling waves looked like the claws of tiny crabs, reaching out to nibble his bones!"

Phoebe gave a thrilled little shriek just as the door to the cabin swung open, breaking the spell of Gabby's voice.

The black-gowned figure of Eudora Sibbald stared at the scene before her. Miss Gabrielle Jerningham was unaccountably positioned on the floor. As always, her hair was tumbling out of its knot and her dress was rumpled. It wasn't for Mrs. Sibbald to recognize the beauty of Gabby's shining golden-brown hair as it worked loose from pins and combs and assumed its normal position: halfway up and halfway down. No—what Phoebe's governess saw was a proper hoyden, a young lady whose hair echoed her general demeanor.

"Phoebe." Her voice rasped like a rusty gate.

Phoebe scrambled to her feet and bobbed a curtsy.

"Miss Jerningham," Mrs. Sibbald continued, rather as if she were addressing a recalcitrant scullery maid.

Gabby was already on her feet and greeting Mrs. Sibbald with a charming smile. "Do forgive us—" she began.

But Mrs. Sibbald interrupted. "Miss Jerningham, I might have misunderstood you." Her bearing indicated that she never misunderstood anything. "I trust that I did not hear you mention *nibbled bones*?"

Really, Gabby thought to herself, Sibbald couldn't have entered at a worse moment.

"Oh, no," Gabby said, her voice soothing. "I was merely telling Phoebe an improving tale from the Bible."

Mrs. Sibbald's jaw lengthened. She'd heard what she'd heard, and it didn't sound like any Bible tale to her.

"The story of Jonah and the whale," Gabby added hastily. "You know, Mrs. Sibbald, since my father is a missionary, I find it quite natural to relate stories from the Bible wherever I go."

Mrs. Sibbald's mouth relaxed slightly. "Well, in that case, Miss Jerningham," she allowed. "However, I must beg you not to overexcite the child. Excitement is injurious to the digestion. And where is Master Kasi Rao Holkar?"

"I believe Kasi is taking a nap at the present, Mrs. Sibbald. He mentioned a wish to retire."

"If you'll forgive me for saying so, Miss Jerningham, you coddle that boy. Prince or not, a deserving tale from the Bible would do him some good. After all, he's a native. Lord only knows what sort of influences he had as a child."

"Kasi grew up in my house," Gabby said. "I assure you that he is as Christian as little Phoebe."

"An unfeasible comparison," Mrs. Sibbald announced. "No Indian could be as Christian as an Englishman.

"It is teatime," she continued. "Miss Jerningham, your hair has fallen again. I advise that your coiffure receive immediate attention." And on that lowering note, Mrs. Sibbald left the cabin.

Gabby sighed and sank into a chair, realizing that there did seem to be a large number of wispy curls hanging about her face. Then she felt a tug on her gown.

"Miss Gabby, she forgot me. Do you think I ought to remind her?" Round blue eyes stared worshipfully at Gabby.

Gabby pulled Phoebe's leggy little body up onto her lap. "I swear you have grown half a head in this trip," she said.

"I know," Phoebe replied, looking with disapproval at the hem of her gown. She stuck out a booted leg. "My dress has become so short that my pantaloons are beginning to show!" Her eyes were round with horror at that idea.

"When you reach England, I'm sure that you will have a new dress."

"Do you think she'll like me?" Phoebe whispered into Gabby's shoulder.

"Will who like you?"

"My new mother."

"How could she not like you? You are the sweetest five-year-old girl aboard this whole ship," Gabby said, rubbing her cheek against Phoebe's soft hair. "In fact, you may well be the sweetest five-year-old who ever sailed from India."

Phoebe pressed closer. "Because when I had to say good-bye to my ayah"—a farewell that seemed to have traumatized her far more than the untimely deaths of two parents she scarcely recognized—"my ayah said that I must be very, very good or my new mama will not like me, since I don't have any money to bring her."

Gabby silently cursed Phoebe's ayah—and not for the first time. "Phoebe," she said as firmly as she could, "money has nothing to do with whether a mother loves her babies or not. Your new mother would love you even if you arrived in your nightdress!"

And she devoutly hoped it was true. From what the captain had told her, there had been no answer to the letter sent to Phoebe's only living relative, her maternal aunt.

"Miss Gabby," Phoebe said, her tone hesitant. "Why did you tell Mrs. Sibbald that your story was of Jonah and the whale? My ayah told me never to tell an untruth—and especially never to a hired person. And Mrs. Sibbald is a hired person, isn't she? She was hired to accompany us to England."

Gabby gave Phoebe another little hug. "Your ayah was right in the main. But sometimes a fib is permissible if you can make someone feel happy. Mrs. Sibbald would very much like to think that you are learning stories from the Bible. And when I told her you were, she felt happy."

"I don't think Mrs. Sibbald ever feels happy," Phoebe observed, after thinking about it for a time.

"You could be right," Gabby replied. "But in that case, Phoebe, it is even more important not to overset her."

"Do you think that if I told my new mama that I had some money it would make her happy? Would it make her like me?"

Gabby swallowed. "Oh, sweet pea, I am only talking about little fibs. You couldn't say such a thing to your new mother! That's a *big* untruth, as opposed to a small one. And it is very important not to tell even small untruths to important people like your new mother."

There was an unconvinced silence.

Gabby thought desperately. Really, for all her eagerness

to have children, she was beginning to see that it was far more difficult than she had imagined.

"Are you bringing any money to your new husband?" Phoebe's voice was muffled because she had her face pressed to Gabby's shoulder.

"Yes," Gabby said reluctantly. "But that money will not make Peter love me."

Phoebe's face popped up like an inquisitive robin from its nest. "Why not?"

"Peter will love me for myself," Gabby said with quiet conviction. "Just as your mother will love you for yourself."

The little girl hopped onto her feet. "Well, then, why did you tell Mrs. Sibbald that Kasi was in his chamber having a nap? That wasn't true, and it didn't make her happy."

"A different kind of rule," Gabby explained. "My sweet Kasi is frightened to death of Mrs. Sibbald."

"What kind of rule?" Phoebe inquired.

"You have to protect the weak from the strong," Gabby said, and then amended herself. "That's not exactly right, Phoebe. You know what Kasi is like. Handing him to Mrs. Sibbald would be like feeding the goat to the tiger."

There was a slight noise behind the screen protecting the tub from plain sight. The little girl peered around the screen. "Kasi Rao, it's time to get out of there." She put her small hands on her hips. "What would Mrs. Sibbald say if she could see you in the tub with all your clothes on?"

"Let him stay there if he prefers," Gabby called across the room.

But Phoebe shook her head firmly and stated, with a force that Mrs. Sibbald would have admired, "It is time to have tea, Kasi. You needn't worry. I won't let Gabby talk about the tiger again."

A very slender boy with innocent eyes that took up half his face peeked around the corner of the screen and then checked, unwilling to emerge from the safety of the corner.

Phoebe took his hand and tugged. "There is no one here but us, Kasi."

Soft brown eyes darted back and forth between Gabby's smiling face and the hand she held out to him. Kasi wanted to come out, obviously, but it was so far across the room, and the room was so very open.

Phoebe pulled at him impatiently. "Mrs. Sibbald thinks you're napping, so you're quite safe."

"We'll have tea together," Gabby said reassuringly, as Kasi gathered his courage and hurtled himself to her chair, sheltering under her arm like a chick that had strayed from its nest. "Are you hungry, little brother?"

"Kasi isn't your little brother," Phoebe said. "He's a prince!"

"Well, that's true. But his mother was related to my father's first wife. And he grew up with me, so I feel as if he is my brother." Kasi had stopped trembling and was playing with the locket Gabby wore around her neck, humming a tuneless, happy song as he tried to open the catch.

Phoebe came around to the other side of the chair and leaned against Gabby's leg. "May I see the picture of your husband again?"

"Of course you may." Just before they set sail for England, a miniature of her future bridegroom had arrived. Gabby gently took the locket from Kasi's fumbling hands and opened it.

"Is he waiting for you in London, Miss Gabby?"

"Yes," Gabby said firmly. "We shall all be met at the dock, Phoebe love. Your new mother will meet you, and Mrs. Malabright will meet Kasi, won't she, sweetheart?" She looked down into Kasi's pointed little face.

To her satisfaction, he nodded. She had been reminding Kasi every day that Mrs. Malabright was coming to see him when the vessel landed.

"And then what will happen, Kasi?" she prompted.

"Live with Mrs. Malabright," he replied with approval. "I *like* Mrs. Malabright." A shadow crossed his eyes and he added, "I don't like Mrs. Sibbald."

"Mrs. Malabright will take you to her house, and you needn't ever see Mrs. Sibbald again," Phoebe said, rather bossily. "I will come visit you though, won't I, Miss Gabby? I will visit you secretly, and I won't tell anyone where you are."

"Yes," Kasi said with a contented lilt in his voice. And he returned to playing with Gabby's locket.

"Do you like your new husband, Miss Gabby?" Phoebe asked.

Even looking at the miniature portrait of Peter, of his soft brown eyes and wavy hair, made Gabby's heart beat faster.

"Yes, I do," Gabby said softly.

Phoebe, who was a true romantic, even at age five, sighed. "I'm sure he already loves you, Miss Gabby. Did you send him a picture of yourself?"

"There wasn't time," Gabby replied. And even if there had been, she would not have sent one. The only portrait her father had ever commissioned made her look horribly round in the face.

She tucked the locket away again.

But even as she, Phoebe, and Kasi munched on dry toast, which was the only treat offered now that they had been at sea for months, Gabby couldn't help daydreaming about her betrothed and his gentle eyes. Somehow, by the grace of God, Gabby had been given a husband who was everything she had dreamed of: a man who looked perfectly capable of carrying on a quiet conversation. He seemed as unlike her cold, ranting father as possible.

Gabby's heart glowed. Peter would obviously be a devoted and loving father. Already Gabby could picture four or five small babes, all with her husband's eyes.

Every day the ship drew farther and farther from India and thus farther and farther from her father's frenzied reproaches: *Gabrielle, why can't you put a bridle on your tongue! Once again, Gabrielle, you have embarrassed me with your graceless behavior!* And the worst of all: *Oh, God above, why have you cursed me with this disgraceful chit, this prattling excuse for a daughter!*

Gabrielle's happiness grew with each ocean league that passed.

Her sense of confidence grew as well. Peter would love

her, as her father never did. She felt as if Peter's sweet eyes were already looking into her soul and seeing the Gabby inside: the Gabby who was worth loving, the Gabby who was not merely impetuous and clumsy. The real Gabby.

❧

Yes, a glimpse of Gabrielle Jerningham, along with insight into her dreams, would have shaken Quill to the backbone.

But since Quill was not overly given to imagination, nor had he ever demonstrated the gift of precognition, he convinced himself that Miss Gabrielle Jerningham would make his younger brother a very good wife indeed. And when he encountered Peter at his club later that evening, he told him so.

Peter was in a tetchy mood, and well on the way to being drunk as a lord. "I don't follow your reasoning."

"Money," his brother replied shortly.

"Money? What money?"

"Her money." Quill had a flash of guilt, talking about Gabrielle as if she were a commodity, although in a sense she was. "With Jerningham's money, you can afford those clothes you love so much."

"I wear the very best clothes now," Peter said loftily, with the smug understanding that he stood at the very pinnacle of London fashion.

"You wear clothes that I pay for," Quill replied.

Peter chewed on his lip. It went against the grain—and against his fundamentally kindly nature—to point out that his elder brother's money would all be his someday, unless a miracle cured Quill's migraines.

Yet it would be pleasant to have his own money, no doubt about that.

Quill saw the telltale interest in Peter's eyes and laughed, his heart lighter. He slapped his brother on the back and left the club.